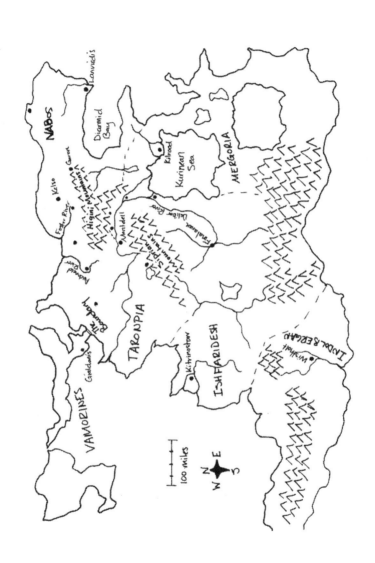

SHATTER

THE CHILDREN OF MAN
BOOK ONE

ELIZABETH C. MOCK

Shatter: The Children Of Man: Book One

This is a work of fiction. All the characters and events portrayed in this novel are either fictitious or used fictitiously.

To Michelle Witmer Nelson,
because this all started in a basement in Richmond eating bad fast food while discussing psychics and philosophy. Without you this never would have seen the light of day, meldnossier.

SHATTER

PROLOGUE

Near the top of the embankment, Mireya paused and pushed her sweaty mane of curly brown hair back from her brow. Unbuttoning the top of her high-necked, blue dress, she parted the muslin fabric. The breeze flowing up from the surface of the bay below cooled her overheated caramel skin. She shivered. With her weight rocking forward onto her foot that perched on a granite outcropping, she put her hands on her hips trying to recoup the energy stolen by the last few yards of the climb. Determined, she tilted her head back and pinched her eyes shut to summon the motivation to summit the hill.

Convincing herself that she did have her third wind, Mireya kept moving despite the burning in her thighs. It was close now. She could see the tips of the yellow flowers peeking over the rise where one of her favorite patches of Klamath weed carpeted the hillside. Mireya cursed again for letting her stockpile run low just when Camille needed the tea the most.

After a few agonizing minutes, she reached her destination. When she plopped to the ground, the thump was audible and so was her breathing as she sucked in the air with greedy gulps. Her gaze skimmed across the ridge until it settled on the sturdy back of a raven-haired man waiting on a boulder that overlooked the water. She narrowed her eyes in annoyance. Thumb and index finger between her lips, she whistled like a shrieking bird shattering the stillness that surrounded him. It got his attention. At his approach, she thrust her hand above her head palm up. With her fingers, she waved for him to give her something. Light glinted off the well-oiled metal as the man pulled out a dagger from his wrist guard.

"Thanks, Dathien," she said with an absent, sweet smile, her irritation evaporating as swiftly as it had come. Knife in hand, she bobbed it at him with mock menace. "No fair running ahead and leaving me behind though." Tilting her head up, she widened her eyes exaggerating her imagined peril. "I could have died alone and out of breath. I must be getting flabby in my old age."

Dropping to a crouch, Dathien draped an arm across a knee as he examined her. He lifted her chin, moved her face side to side, up and down, then seeming satisfied, he leaned forward and kissed her full lips.

"I won't abandon you to the clutches of death again, love," he promised. Though he wore a sober expression, his deep blue eyes glittered. "I better stick close. You might keel over any second at your advanced age."

Scrunching her nose, her pale blue eyes fought between indignation and amusement. The amusement won, but it did nothing to stop her from jabbing him in the ribs in retribution.

"You weren't supposed to agree with me!" Mireya pouted, sticking out her lower lip. "I'm only nineteen. If anyone's ancient here, it's you ser."

With her tool in hand, she crawled on all fours to the edge of the yellow brush. As she swept away the dirt and debris with her palm, Dathien stretched to his full imposing height and wandered back to the edge of the cliff. Beneath it, rocks filled the bay, choking the water with them. To the line of the horizon, the rocks impeded the tide causing waves to crest and crash in a constant, unpredictable rhythm. Though the pounding abuse of the water had eroded the obstacles over the years, it had failed to mask the odd uniformity of the rows and intersections the stones formed. Even after several millennia of erosion, the watery streets still divided the destroyed buildings of the submerged city.

Saddened by the skeletal decomposition of the city poking through the waves, Dathien looked away and back to Mireya who had grasped a handful of stems together. Pulling the weeds taut, she made her cut with a surprising proficiency. With a quick tug, she wrapped string around the ends, bundling the starred flowers. Dirt covered her hands, so she wiped them across the gathered ruffles that flanked the dress' buttons without a single thought for the preservation of the cornflower blue fabric. Clean enough in her own estimation, she held her hand out to Dathien. He steadied her as she rose with her herbs. Intertwined their hands were a weaving of contrasts, hers dark and smooth like sepia-stained satin, his callused and ruddy like a redwood's bark.

Waving the herbs like a baton, she considered their flowers. "It will take about three weeks for these to dry properly. So here's hoping that my stash lasts that long. Given what happened yesterday, I don't want to see how bad Camille could get without it."

Tickling her dark, but freckled face, Mireya tugged her wild hair behind an ear. In the process, she managed to smear pollen from the Klamath weeds on her cheek. Dathien chuckled and wiped off the yellow smudge with his thumb.

Annoyed at her unmanageable locks, she blew air into her cheeks, but she couldn't help giggling at herself. As they began the descent home, the air around them seemed to charge, raising the small hairs on the backs of their necks. Before they could even tense in response, Mireya's hand slid out of Dathien's and she crumpled to the ground as if someone had cut the strings that held her bones together. Not a breath had passed before she rose again with her back rigid but her head lifeless. Penetrating yet unfocused, her eyes crackled and swirled with blue smoke. Chin resting against her chest, one voice rose from within her, a seamless harmony of bass and soprano, alto and tenor. It seemed to move through her.

"Seven shall come to undo what was done.

From shadow revealed, three destinies sealed.

Daughter of night shall succumb to dark sight.

He who walks time out of fire must climb.

Son of the earth shall steal from its birth.

Speaker of truth, guide you must be, trust in that which only you see.

Keeper of truth, watch and protect, never dismiss all you suspect.

Twin branches extend, a choice here resolved,

Either shall end betrayed or absolved.

From death shall be life; a world formed anew."

The blue light veiling her eyes cascaded out and enveloped her body. Her hair flowed back in a wind that seemed to touch her alone. Her head snapped up. Her eyes locked on the sky.

"A promise was made; redemption pursue."

The light flared once in a sudden flash, as it seemed to recede into her eyes, but her hands still glimmered, shining like cobalt. Blood trickled from between her knuckles as she lowered her head and unclenched her fists. The pressure around them dissipated in a blast of cold air off the bay, which brought the return of the crashing waves and chattering gulls. Mireya stood staring at the backs of her hands, tattoos glowing like sapphire embers sinking back into her skin until only faint lines remained.

She flexed her fingers, wincing at the lacerations. Strong, but deliberate hands turned her wrists so that Dathien could examine the cuts. A soft glow of red light flowed from his hand and the pink lines of newly healed flesh replaced the scratches on her palms. Only the smears of blood bore witness to her injury.

On the ground, the broken bundle of yellow, star-shaped herbs lay scattered. They had been crushed by her fall. Mireya huffed at the loss. Short lived, her frustration transformed into excitement as her cheek dimpled with a grin.

"It's time to leave."

CHAPTER ONE

One Year Later

Leaning over the high rail of the steamboat as the *River Rat* pulled into the bustling Davenford dockyards, flakes of rust scraped against the woman's palms. A canvas rancher's hat sat low on her brow and a mud-spattered brown overcoat, clearly made for someone taller and broader, reached past her knees. After they bumped against the pier, swaying slightly with the passing current, the captain walked up to her and leaned against the rail.

"This is as far as we go. You'll have to find other passage if you want to keep heading north toward the border." Though a stocky man, the captain still stood half a head taller than the woman. He tried to position himself to get a better look at her under the hat, but she used her shorter stature to her advantage and rarely looked up enough for him to get a clear view. Peeking out from under its brim, her snub nose had a crooked hump along its bridge that only came from a break that had healed wrong. What he could see revealed her rounded cheeks and chin, but the constant tension in her jaw removed any appearance of softness that those curves should have created. Despite his obstructed view, one thing was clear, she had changed.

"You sure you want to be heading for the border? Nabos ain't no place for a lady."

"Rest assured, Aaron," the woman smirked, "that isn't a concern."

Aaron folded his muscled arms across his chest straining the knit of his thick gray sweater. "I still don't think your father'd be too happy with me, Faela, may he rest in peace."

"I haven't been my father's problem since I was four," Faela responded trying to keep her tone light, "and twenty-two years later, I have managed to travel all over the world in the service of my Order without dying or getting kidnapped by slavers. Now tell me, who would dare attack a healer from the Tereskan temple? Don't worry yourself over me. We don't want you to mar that rugged face with wrinkles, yeah?"

"I just don't trust them Virds," Aaron said spitting over the rail superstitiously. "If they'd kill lawmen like the Daniyelans, ain't no one safe."

"That was almost nineteen years ago, Aaron," Faela said readjusting her pack's buckles strapped across her chest and waist. "It's been ten years since the war ended."

"But I heard from other river runners that things ain't been the same up north in Nabos since the war. The land ain't right and people get mighty desperate when their younglings are hungry. It's why I stick to the Taronpian and Mergorian river ways. Ain't no profit if you're dead. Something's brewing up there, mark my word, miss. If I can't convince you to go back to Kilrood or go home to Finalaran, you promise me you'll watch yourself, yeah?"

"I promise, Aaron. You just keep this old girl running." Faela turned and hugged the captain around the neck shocking him by the uncharacteristic display of affection. He squeezed her once before letting go. "And remember, if anyone asks–"

"You were heading west for Kitrinostow," he repeated. "I know where my loyalty lies, Faela. Your father was always fair with us."

She hopped off the weather-bleached deck of the steamboat onto the narrow plank that bowed as she bounced down its short length. Reaching its end, she looked up at the sun's position before jumping onto the water-slick pier. The wide brim of her hat shaded her deep-set silver eyes from the worst of its piercing mid-morning brightness. She turned and waved at Aaron, who just shook his head muttering to himself as he strode toward the helm.

Faela shoved her hands into the pockets of her overcoat as she headed down the pier to find a boat sailing up the Bramm River. Though she had dismissed Aaron's concerns, she had heard more than stories about the current state of Nabos since leaving Kilrood and none of it comforted her. But right now her biggest concern was finding a boat willing to risk sailing upriver and she had the sinking feeling that this search was going to cost her time. Something she could little afford.

Situated between the Siprian and the Higini mountain ranges, few would call Davenford a large town, but it sat on a jut of land where a river split into two making it a natural center for trade. Flowing to the Kurinean Sea to the southeast, the Yaniv River brought traffic to the coastal country of Mergoria. While the Dalibor River traveled to the southwest through Taronpia's jungles to its central plains and finally Finalaran, the urban seat of the Merchant Houses. Where these two rivers began, the Bramm River stopped. Flowing out of the Siprian mountains, it passed the hub of the railways, Montdell, which straddled the border of Taronpia and Nabos.

Standing on the major thoroughfare of the Dalibor wharf, Faela craned her neck looking for any signs pointing the way to the Bramm's docks. It was late enough in the morning that most of the boats that transported cargo had already left, but boats that had recently arrived from nearby towns like Wickcester were still in the process of unloading their goods. A whip cracked in the air nearby as a drover prodded the oxen pulling his cart to start moving. The squeak of its wheels grated against her ears as the wagon laden with crates swayed into motion. It rolled up the hill at a slow, but steady pace toward the rows of storehouses kept by competing Merchant Houses.

She tugged at the brim of her hat habitually when she looked at the large storage area that blocked her view of the town and decided to continue following the bank of the river. Hopefully it would lead her to the northern docks. She picked her way past kids mending nets, sailors sauntering as they enjoyed their brief leave, and men lifting and hauling cargo while voices shouted from shore to boat and across the wharf to one another. After the relative silence of the *River Rat*, the dissonant clamor made her shoulders pinch together.

Before several minutes had past, Faela found the sounds of industry fading behind her. Most dockyards, especially river dockyards, tended to follow the same basic layout and finding her way to the Bramm's wharf proved easier than she had suspected. Only a handful of vessels were scattered across its long pier, a few older wherries and one steamer. Built to handle four or fives times the number of vessels that used it now, the pier looked like the leftover bones of a carrion's scavenging. Unhooking the brass buttons of her coat with one hand, her other drifted to the knife sheathed in her belt. Her fingers brushed its smooth, ivory hilt and settled there as she examined her options.

The steamer appeared empty and the smell of rotten fish rolling off it forced her to hold back her gag reflex by willpower alone. She wasn't desperate enough to try her chances on that boat — at least not yet. The closest wherry's sails were furled as though docked for an extended stay, so she continued down the boardwalk. A young man lounged on the roof of the long cabin that ran the length of a wherry's deck clearly asleep. Faela grinned.

As she got closer to the wherry, she saw scrawled on its side *Light's Lady* in worn gold lettering. She hoped the name would prove a good omen. Leaning against its prow, she said, "Oi! Aboard the *Light's Lady*, you awake, mate?"

He opened one eye and glared openly at her. "I am now, darkness take you," the man growled and coughed to clear his lungs. "What's so important that you got to shout at people minding their own business?"

"You heading up the Bramm's today?" she asked with a wide grin, which was all he could see of Faela's face due to the long shadows cast by her hat.

The man barked with laughter. "Not today, not tomorrow, not any time soon, my fine wench. I like my skin to stay on my back and my money in my purse, thank you."

Faela kept her smile from faltering. "Then why're you docked at the Bramm's, if you don't mind me asking?"

"I do mind, but it's cheap and people don't bother me none," he said stringing out the last phrase pointedly.

"You know if any of these boats are planning on heading that way?" Faela allowed some of her impatience to bleed through.

"There are a couple nutters who still make the run. Try Roderick, that's his girl down there, the *Sun Winger*. He's right mad, that one. But you flash him enough coin, or something else," the sailor's knowing laugh was harsh and gritty like sand, "and he'll take you."

"Thanks. Wind be with your lady," she said in way of a farewell as she sauntered toward the weathered, rust-brown wherry the sailor had pointed to. The paint that declared it the *Sun Winger* had chipped so it looked more like the *Sui Winge* now. Its sails drooped unfurled from its mast at the prow of the boat, but fell slack. Either this Roderick was preparing to leave very soon or his sloppiness would give any sailor she'd ever met an apoplexy. She silently hoped for the former.

Knowing better than to board an unknown boat, she projected so her voice would carry and yelled, "Any aboard the *Sun Winger?* I'm looking for Roderick."

A head peeked out from the cabin looking confused. When he saw Faela waving from the pier, the tall, shaggy redhead exited. "You yell wherever you go, lady?"

"Depends on whether I need to be heard or not," she replied shifting her weight to the side as she leaned her hand onto the knife hilt. "So, you him?"

"Aye," he said with a shake of his head. His hair seemed compelled to fall in front of his eyes. "But I don't take passengers, sorry."

Roderick had said his piece and needed to get back to work, so he made no farewell before returning to his preparations. Faela swept her gaze around the wharf. Her options were narrowing quickly and she thought about that smell on the steamer.

"Why not?" she asked Roderick's back.

"I don't like people on my girl who couldn't tell their aft from their prow."

Faela chuckled at the clumsy wordplay. "What makes you think I don't?"

That made Roderick stop, but not turn to face her as he gripped the edge of the cabin's roof. "I can see that vial 'round your neck clear as day, lady. You're one of them healers. Magic users don't know boats."

"Well, that's a bit of a generalization, yeah?" Faela said as she tucked the telltale glass vial under her shirt.

Swinging up onto the cabin, Roderick balanced an elbow over the long boom that reached back over nearly the entire length of the boat. He pulled at some of the rope. "What's this?"

"Line that's rigged to the sail is the sheet," she answered with a bored tone of voice, "and that is specifically part of the mainsheet, because it's attached to the boom."

"What kind of rigging is this?" He fired at her without acknowledging whether her answer had been correct.

"All wherries have gaff rigs. And before you ask, I can tell because it's a fore-and-aft rigging system running along the line of the keel," she said with knowledgeable efficiency as she pointed up to the four-cornered sail, "which is controlled at its peak by the throat and peak halyards."

Roderick grunted in surprise and hopped off the cabin. "You from sailing stock before you went to the temples?"

"I just know my way around a wherry. Looks like you could use an extra hand," she said looking at the two other sailors working at the aft to get ready to sail, "and I can pay."

After a few moments of examining the woman on shore, Roderick said, "You're lucky that Jack broke his leg." He liked her direct approach and she didn't seem like one to waste time yammering.

"You'll take me?" she asked waiting for confirmation before she boarded.

Digging into his jacket, he removed a dented brass pocket watch to check the time. "We're running behind," he said with a begrudging shake of his head as he clicked it shut. "Just don't breaking nothing, yeah?

Hands splayed on the side of the wherry, the wind misted Faela's burnished and freckled face as it carried the sweet smell of wet and rotting plants onto the deck. Roderick had gone inside the cabin after they had launched well before midday. One of the other hands, a quiet man that Roderick called Beau, walked behind her with some line slung across his chest. He nodded to her, but otherwise ignored her presence. As her weight readjusted, she felt the reassuring outline of the dagger in her boot press against her leg.

On the far bank, sheep dotted the gently sloping hillside as they did their best to keep the vegetation under control. After her initial help with the halyards, they hadn't needed her assistance. With nothing to keep her hands busy her mind began to wander. Beau swung up onto of the top of the long cabin and began raising the throat halyard to keep from losing the wind to the bend of the river.

With the prow to herself, the tension in her back eased. As the sails caught the wind again, the animals receded into a mass of clumped white fluff. Faela wondered if sheep ever longed for freedom, to break away from the herd. More than likely, they never thought beyond the grass in front of them and the occasional delight of finding a tasty bit of clover. Sailor and sheep alike disappeared from her field of vision as the riverboat corrected course and veered away from the bank. Sailing on her family's trading wherries had taught her how to tie an anchor's bend before she was five as well as the routines of their crews. Beau would have plenty to keep him busy at the stern, Faela estimated. It should be long enough.

As the sun dipped below the horizon, the water shimmered pink and orange like swirled ribbon candy as the boat sent waves rolling toward the banks. Considering the sunset, Faela looked down at her interlaced fingers and thought, *He should be going to bed soon. And I should be there.*

She pulled them apart and her right hand found its way to the vial that hung at her throat from a leather cord. As her fingers curled around it, she hummed the simplistic melody of a lullaby. A red mist covered her eyes. The notes of the melody continued and matching golden designs wove into her temples. Her mind skimmed over the riverbank, past the sheep, past Davenford, down the Yaniv, and across the northern edge of the Kurinean Sea as blood called to blood.

She felt the mind of her infant son gurgle happily as she brushed it with a kiss. She projected to him images of cradling him in her lap fast asleep, just as she had after his birth a few months ago. No almost half a year now, she correct, but pulled back her guilt and instead said to him, *Time to sleep, lamb.*

Her humming changed key as she began to sing the lullaby her older brother had sung to her when her nightmares would come. Unlike most children, Faela's nightmares had not come at night, but during the day when she was awake. Back then, only her brother could calm her hysterics. Now, she finished singing the final line of that same song to her son hundreds of miles away.

Shine, shine like the sun. Light will come and night be done.

She could sense his thoughts of feeling full and warm as his eyes fluttered and closed as though they were her own. Sending him the ghost of a caress, she withdrew. *Mama loves you, Sammi.*

Faela felt her throat thicken as she let the contact slip away. Inhaling the cold, moist air of the incoming night, she chewed on her thumb and the now familiar void settled back into her chest. The horizon had finally swallowed the sun and she wiped away the wetness from her cheeks. "I'll come back for you when I know it's safe, love."

Feeling a touch on her shoulder, Faela woke instantly tipping her hat back off her head. Her dagger flashed between herself and what had woken her, while her other hand captured what had touched her. There was a metallic clatter and a muffled curse in the dark. Blinking, she saw the sputtering light of the lantern that she had knocked out of her assailant's hand. In the jumping shadows, she saw red hair.

"Darkness, if this is the greeting you give anyone who wakes you," Roderick muttered, "no wonder you're traveling alone."

"Are we there?" Faela asked without apologizing. She pulled her hat back down on her forehead, then twirled her dagger and returned it to its boot sheath.

"Aye, we're at the Ravenscliffe ferry dock." Roderick munched on a pear noisily as he retrieved the lantern.

Moving her pack from where she had been using it as a pillow, Faela unlatched one of its outer pockets and removed a pouch. She opened it, retrieving a handful of coins. Counting out five silver, she returned the rest. She braced her feet against the deck and pushed against it to stand. When she handed the money to Roderick, his eyes widened. He lifted one of the coins to inspect the stamp.

"Lady, this is too much," he shook his head causing his hair to settle back into his eyes again. He pocketed two, but tried to give three of the coins back to her.

Threading her arm through the strap of her pack, she held up her free hand. "You didn't have to take me on, but you did."

Faela laced the pouch back onto her belt. Cinching the leather tight, she refastened the belt and let it fall onto her hips. After she clasped her pack into place, she closed his hand around the payment. "Let's just call the rest gratitude, yeah?"

He led her to the side of the boat where they had tied off. It lacked a plank, but the drop down to the dock seemed manageable. "You be safe out there, lady."

Faela offered the young captain her hand. "My thanks, Roderick. May the winds always be at your back."

He shook her hand with a fast and firm squeeze. "You as well, lady."

Vaulting over the side of the wherry, Faela staggered as she hit the deck hard, but kept her feet. Roderick didn't seem one for prolonged farewells, so she didn't bother to turn around as she jogged toward the road. It would still be a few hours until dawn and the closer she could get to crossing the border before it broke the better off she would be.

At this early hour, the bluish light did little to warm the forest as the chill moisture of the night before still clung to the morning, promising colder nights ahead. Faela unhooked the last buckle and shrugged off her pack as she stopped in a cluster of evergreens. Their branches intertwined creating a thick screen between her and the road. Shivering, she pulled her hat off while she unknotted her copper-gold hair out of its messy pile on her head. It fell around her shoulders in waves providing her with a bit more warmth. Filling her lungs with the crisp, fresh air that left the aftertaste of damp earth in her throat, she turned to face the rising sun. As she relaxed her stance, she rotated her shoulders before closing her eyes.

Though shut, her eyes seemed to glow with a red light that had nothing to do with the sunrise and the vial that hung from her neck shone with the same scarlet. Her breathing slid into the rhythm of the blood pumping through her veins and she hummed a low note. As the note resonated with the foundational rhythm of her heart, intricate lines of gold light thickened on each of her temples. Her senses raced across the forest searching for a different cadence. Pain shot through her fingers and up her arms as she stretched further for that other pulse past the mountains, but habit born of long practice forced her breathing to remain steady. Then faintly, she felt the pulse she sought far to the north on the moors of Nabos and a pressure descended on her chest that threatened to crush her lungs. Gasping for breath, she broke the contact and stumbled, falling to her knees. Her breath came in ragged gulps as if she had stayed underwater for too long.

Shoving back her thick hair that had fallen into her face, she rested her hands against her thighs while she waited for the tremors to pass. She felt for her pack and slung it across her back, while numb fingers latched the buckles into place. Once secure, she scooped her hat from the needle-strewn carpet and pulled it back on.

"Well, north it is," she said to a finch hopping along a nearby stone searching for his breakfast.

Pushing through the dense branches, one slipped past Faela whipping across the bottom of her cheek. Her fingers brushed the stinging welt to see if it had drawn blood as she turned away from the road and further into the woods. The twig just barely broke the skin leaving a tiny stain of red on her fingers. She rubbed it off on the sturdy fabric of her overcoat.

As a gentle breeze rustled the leaves, it left a lazy peacefulness in its wake. It conjured images of her little sister's cat, Lusi, stretching after a sun-soaked nap on the cracked, slate terrace behind her parents' kitchens.

Such a wickedly slothful, hedonistic beast, she thought as she ducked under some low-lying branches. Just as quickly as the memory tugged her lips into a smile, the pain that crept into her eyes removed it. Her fingers laced through the silver chain also around her neck and her thumb circled the medallion as if seeking some solace in the contact.

Time seemed to freeze along with Faela as the morning's quiet shattered as something crashed through the brush like a hunted animal. Dropping the necklace, she yanked the brim of her hat forward. Her face hidden, she clasped the vial that hung at her chest. Her fingers tightened as the light surrounding it bled into crimson.

Before she could turn to face the source of the noise, a man appeared blocking her path. No sound had alerted her of his swift approach. Halting, he inclined his head, his thin, sloping nose in the air, as if to catch a scent he had momentarily lost. The movement caused the water in his sable hair to glint in the increasing morning light as it stuck to his shoulders. His appearance bore a strong resemblance to a wet terrier. When she noticed his light brown eyes, Faela stepped back increasing the space between them as she recognized the telltale sign of a magic user capable of wielding several colors.

"Your first mistake was taking it," he growled low in his throat, "but your last was making me chase you, you son of a flea-ridden whore."

Faela's mind went blank at this man's sudden appearance and in that moment all she seemed able to focus on were the spots of dust and pollen drifting in the light behind him. Transfixed by the floating motes, her panic began receding. With a steady resolve replacing the shock, her expressionless face transformed as the corner of her mouth jumped into a half smirk.

"Well now, this is just awkward," Faela said with a shake of her head. "You have me at a definite disadvantage by having such intimate knowledge of my mum, when I don't recall ever having met you before. But given your current choice in attire," she said indicating his bare chest and feet, "you seem well acquainted with that particular profession. And I know that this coat is a bit bulky, but does it really make me look like a boy?"

"What?" the man demanded his brow furrowing clearly confused by her response.

"My gender," she said enunciating each syllable. "You seem confused. 'Cause I'm a girl, not a boy."

Though adrenaline still rushed through her from the shock, as she awaited his response, her artist's eye could not help pausing to appreciate the lean musculature of his lithe build marred only by a network of thick, raised scars. Yet, the Lusicans at Kitrinostow had taught her that beauty was often found in imperfection.

Annoyance soon replaced his astonishment, as the man leveled his unfaltering gaze at her obscured face. Her chest constricted under the predatory menace in his amber eyes before he looked past her. "I wasn't talking to you."

It was Faela's turn to look confused as she remembered the forgotten commotion that had come from behind her. Turning to find its source, she discovered that her coat was caught on an unseen object. She twisted her head and saw a man crouched behind her in an attempt to hide his gangly form. He looked up at her with emerald green eyes from under the bottom of her overcoat's stained hem, which he had used to cover his nose.

"Howdy." His voice cracked as he spoke.

Repressing a scream, Faela snatched her coat out of his hands and stumbled backward until she ran into a tree, her hand clutched at the vial. Only her shallow breathing gave any outward indication of her alarm. She had allowed the silent man to distract her attention. Though an innocent enough mistake, it had been sloppy of her. Her only consolation was that the boy could hardly be a magic user of any strength, if one at all, with eyes as green as his.

The man who had used her as a human shield unbent himself to his full height, placing him easily a foot taller than Faela. He shook out his worn barn jacket whose too-short arms left his tops of his wrists exposed, making his limbs appear even longer than they were. He smiled a warm, affable smile at Faela.

Before he could say anything beyond his greeting, the terrier, as Faela had begun to think of him, asked, "Where are they?"

"Well, it's quite an amusing story actually. You see I was—"

The quivering throwing knife embedded in the tree behind the lanky man's left ear cut off his explanation. No one had seen either of the terrier's hands move and Faela could not imagine where he had hidden the weapon. The terrier stood with a coiled stillness as he watched the lanky man shuffle his weight uncomfortably.

After stretching out the silence, the terrier said, "If I wanted a story, I'd find a Lusican to tell me one. So, let's try again and this is the final time I ask nicely, mate. Where are they?"

Pushing his unkempt nut-brown hair out of his eyes, he

rubbed his flattened nose. "Well now, for some reason they seem to have decided that this was the right time to take a trip to the Kurinean Sea. You know, eat some fish, visit the great Tereskan temple, take one last holiday before the harvest."

The terrier's hands flexed, but he reached for nothing. Instead, he drew out each word. "Heading for the Kurinean Sea?"

"Indeed," the lanky man said with an exaggerated sigh. "Because during our merry little chase, we — your boots and me — tragically parted ways. You see, our lives were heading in very different directions and I'm just not a very good swimmer. Never found the time to learn really. But I can't blame anyone but myself for that, can I?" He directed his last statement to Faela with a shrug and that infectious smile.

Without intending to, Faela found herself returning it. "Wait, so you dropped them in the Bramm?" Faela asked, suddenly connecting the details of their situation. With these men fixated on each other, her fear had dissolved, leaving only her curiosity regarding these two.

"Technically," the boy said with a bob of his head, "in a stream that feeds into the Bramm. But one could interpret the events that way."

Faela had to repress her laughter now at the absurdity of this situation as the terrier stomped past her, crunching the stray twigs and pine needles underfoot. At the sound, Faela winced a little thinking about the lacerations that had to be ripping up his feet. The boy took Faela by the shoulders and kept her positioned between the terrier and himself. They circled each other for a few moments before the terrier grabbed a fistful of the lanky boy's shirt collar and yanked him away from Faela. He drew the boy's face close to his own. "Do you know the punishment for theft, you—"

She cleared her throat interrupting him. While amused by the lanky boy's demeanor, given the anger in the other man's brown eyes, Faela recognized that this situation had the potential to deteriorate into something much more serious. "Gentlemen, I'm so sorry, but I don't have time for this."

"You again?" Much like his tone, the terrier's mouth had stretched thin. "This has nothing to do with you."

"You very well may be the rudest man I've ever had the

misfortune to meet." Faela placed her hands on her hips. "Look, I've got somewhere to be, but I'm not leaving unless I know this won't devolve into you boys calling each other names and wrestling in the mud." She paused suddenly as if something she hadn't previously considered had just occurred to her. "Actually, that could be fun to watch. I think I have just enough time." She gazed up at the columns of light streaming through the leafy roof of the forest. "Yeah, never mind me. Please, by all means, continue."

The terrier felt the nagging tug of a half-formed memory at this brash woman's mannerisms. Something about her demeanor and address danced just outside his recollection. While his mind tried to place why she seemed so familiar, he only managed to verbalize a single thought.

"What are you?"

With a martyred sigh, Faela spoke with deliberate care as she hooked her thumbs into her loose belt, parting the opening of her coat with her arms. "I thought we'd covered this bit already? I'm a girl."

"Since I can't get a single straight answer out of you that goes without saying."

As if smelling something unpleasant, she wrinkled her nose, which only served to highlight its crookedness. "If that's how you're going to be, then fine. So be it. My name is Faela. My brother is sick and I'm traveling southwest to visit him."

Still hunched over, the captive boy said, "It was a pleasure to cower under you, mistress Faela. Some call me Jair the Destroyer, but you can call me, Jair. But to you," he point down at his captor with a maniacal gleam in his grass-green eyes, "you will call me the Destroyer, Lord of Destruction—"

The boy's command was cut off as he squealed in a higher pitch than Faela could have ever managed.

The terrier had pulled Jair down into a headlock. "If you stop talking, you get to keep breathing, mate."

"Yeah, I'm convinced now. You are the rudest man I've ever met," Faela interjected as she cocked her head to the side observing the tangle of limbs in front of her. "Because typically after someone introduces himself to you, it's customary to introduce yourself, not put them into a headlock. So, if you don't mind releasing the Lord of Destruction's seemingly fragile and thin neck-"

"Jair, Faela," he quipped from under the terrier's arm with that same unruffled smile, "call me, Jair."

Given his current state of imprisonment, Faela could hardly believe that this boy's unquenchable good humor could be real. Yet all evidence pointed to his sincerity.

"Thank you, Jair. If you could release Jair's neck, we could have a constructive conversation like adults, that includes more problem solving and less violence."

"Kade."

"Pardon?" Faela asked confused.

"My name, it's Kade." Now that Faela had attracted his attention, Kade's brown eyes tracked her, seeming to search for something. Under that scrutiny, Faela felt a chill of fear between her shoulder blades, like she was being hunted. She tried to push the feeling aside.

"Well met, Kade. May you always walk in the brightness of the Light." Holding onto the brim of her hat with a finger and thumb, Faela bowed low to the ground with a flourish of her coat. As she straightened back up, she smiled. "Since it seems no one taught you how to play with other children, let's see if we can't work this out so everyone's happy and quickly, if you please. I've already traveled a long way and I'd like to get to my brother's before he no longer needs my help. Otherwise, it's going to make this entire trip pointless."

Releasing Jair, Kade walked over to the tree to recover his throwing knife. He grasped the hilt and levered it clear of the rough bark. To test its edge, he ran his thumb along the length of its blade. His gaze followed Faela as she crouched down, her arms encircling her knees. Now that the tension had broken and the adrenaline was dispersing, she felt drained with as much strength as wet parchment.

"It's very simple really. I was washing up in the stream when he stole my clothes. More importantly, he stole my boots. I just want them back."

She looked over at Jair. "That seems fairly reasonable to me."

"Ah yes, well," Jair stared over their heads as if searching for a solution in the tree branches, "that's where we come to an impasse. As I already pointed out, the boots should be enjoying the relaxation of the Kurinean beaches soon. They're gone and they don't plan on returning."

Knife still in hand, Kade advanced in Jair. "Talking really is a poor replacement for thinking, mate. There aren't any towns for leagues, which means I have to walk barefoot for leagues to replace them. I'm thinking that even if your boots are too big for me, they'd be better than nothing. And you've managed to really annoy me; so killing you to get your boots just seems like an added bonus. What do you think, Jair? What would you do?"

"Well," Jair stopped as if thinking through the possible scenarios, "clearly, I'm against the killing me option."

"But that's the fun part." His dark tawny eyes sparkling with glee, Kade grinned.

Faela assessed Kade. From all she had seen, she believed he was capable of exactly what he suggested, but something about his eyes told her that he took more pleasure in making Jair uncomfortable than anything else. Betting on that likelihood, she stood and interposed herself between the men and faced Kade.

She placed a hand on his chest stopping him. "You can always kill him later." Addressing the boy, she asked, "Jair, can you compensate him for the boots or not?"

"Obviously he can't. Otherwise, he wouldn't have taken them in the first place," Kade concluded, twirling his knife in a habitual gesture causing it to flash in the increasingly golden daylight.

Faela turned back to Jair who surveyed a nearby knobby tree branch as he whistled absently. She sighed in resignation. For a morning that had started off so well, this day seemed destined to bring her trouble. Then again, no matter where she traveled trouble seemed to have become her one constant companion.

"Fine then." Unlatching the pouch at her belt, she removed several iron and bronze coins. They bore the stamp of a crescent moon and a harp. She grabbed Kade's free hand and dropped six bronze and five iron into it. "Look, I can't change the fact that you'll have to walk barefoot, but this should more than cover his debt."

Standing only a little more than a head taller than Faela, Kade tried to get a better look at her shadowed face around her hat. While he had enjoyed playing with the boy, it had not been his intention to involve this stranger that seemed so familiar, yet was completely unknown to him. But he still wanted to see the boy squirm just a bit more.

"That covers the cost of replacing the boots, but does nothing to compensate my time and the inconvenience he's cost me."

"Interesting, you didn't strike me as a bandit," Faela said reaching back into her money pouch. "How much more will satisfy you?"

"Oh, it's not money that will give me satisfaction." Kade stopped spinning the knife and settled his grin on Jair.

Faela pursed her lips unhappily at that grin and also at how bright the forest had become. She had lost too much time already.

"I have a feeling I'm going to regret this," she said more to herself than the two men. "Jair, I hope you didn't have any pressing engagements."

"No," Jair answered automatically before pausing. "Why?"

"Because you're in my debt now and this wasn't charity. You're going to pay that off."

Jair swallowed and licked his lips. "How?"

"You're coming with me. I could use the company, because I always know how conversations with myself end and it couldn't hurt to have a strong, strapping young buck like yourself along for protection. Travel as my companion and we'll call it even."

Jair glanced at Kade then back to Faela as if weighing his options. "How could I ever refuse a lady desiring my company? It would be my honor and a pleasure to escort you, Faela."

"Then it's settled." Faela grabbed the front of Jair's jacket as she dragged him down the game trail after her.

As they disappeared marching to the northwest, she raised her voice so Kade could hear her. "Ravenscliffe is over that ridge to the northeast. You should be able to replace your boots there. Ask for Marvin and show him those coins. Don't think me as rude as you, but I would live a happy life if I never saw you again."

As her voice drifted bodiless through the forest and back to the clearing, Kade called after her. "I thought your sick brother lived to the southwest?"

CHAPTER TWO

Faela bit into a yellowish-green apple with a juicy crunch. Startled by the noise, Jair stopped and spun looking in all directions for its source. When he finally saw Faela chewing loudly with an amused smile, he sighed at his own stupidity.

"My, aren't you wound tight," she said after swallowing the tart fruit.

"It would seem so," he said eyeing her snack with obvious lust.

Faela produced another apple from her coat pocket and tossed it to him before she started walking again. It bounced off the side of his hand, but he caught it with the other before it dropped to the dirt. With a cry of success, he took a huge bite, which dripped juices down his chin.

"He's not following us," she reassured him addressing the unspoken question raised by his earlier jumpiness. "He headed east a couple hours back. He can't catch us before we reach Aberley and once we're there he'll lose our trail. I don't care how good he thinks he is, he shouldn't be able to track us once we leave town."

Jair nodded skeptically, licking the sticky liquid on his fingers. "Yeah, I guess so."

He was holding something back, but Faela didn't pry. If he had secrets he would rather keep, she of all people had no business forcing him to divulge them.

"We should make it to Aberley around dusk," she said as she enjoyed the heavy smell of resin in the air. She had always liked forests. "Once we get there, you don't need to stay with me, you know."

"Why part ways in Aberley?" he asked around the piece of fruit he chewed.

"You can catch a ride with a river runner back down to Davenford or up to Montdell, if you want. From either place you can go just about anywhere."

"No, I get why Aberley," he said with a wave of his hand. "But I was under the impression that the price of my freedom was sticking with you?"

Faela looked down at her feet with a smile. "I just didn't want to see that pretty face get mashed up. I like being on my own."

"Yeah, but this close to the border isn't the safest place for anyone to be traveling alone. I heard back in Ravenscliffe that some bandits have taken up in one of the caves along the pass. People are afraid to even go down to the ferry dock."

"You were alone," she pointed out as she hopped through a network of exposed roots.

"I didn't have a choice." Finished with the fruit, he tossed his apple core toward the sound of chattering squirrels in the bushes.

"And neither did I."

"Maybe before," he countered shoving his hands into the pockets of his jacket, "but you have a choice now."

"Look, don't take it personally, but I never intended for you to go with me any further than Aberley." She twirled her apple core by its stem. "My good deed for the month is done."

"He might not have realized how much coin you gave him, but I do." Jair grabbed her arm to make her stop. "That wasn't a small sum to throw around."

Faela pulled herself out of his grasp and fought back the urge to hit him. This change in his demeanor surprised her as much as his flippancy had before. While he had been in danger, he acted as if it were game, but now his levity had gone entirely.

"It's my business how I choose to spend my money," she said examining this boy trying to make this sudden change fit with his earlier affability.

"And I repay my debts," he said with earnest sincerity. "And your price was a traveling companion, not mine."

No matter how hard she tried, Faela couldn't stop the laughter that bubbled up. She covered her mouth with a hand. "This from the thief?"

His earlier smile crept into his face as he rubbed the back of his neck. "Yeah, I know how that sounds. But I mean it. I mean to stay with you until it's paid."

Faela popped off the stem of her apple and flicked it at him. It hit him in the chest. "I'm heading for the border and I wouldn't ask anyone to follow me there. I don't care how much they think they owe me."

"You're heading for Nabos?" he asked somewhat surprised. He took a closer look at the woman standing across from him again. Her gear was well used, but of good quality and in good repair. It showed signs of recent wear that told of someone who had been traveling for months, not someone on their way to visit kin.

She nodded as she started eating the core, seeds and all. "That's right."

"Then I definitely ain't leaving you in Aberley," he said betraying a hint of an accent he had managed to mask before. "You're stuck with me, fairest Faela."

*   *   *

Long, creeping shadows stretched out from the trees that stood as wall behind Kade as he left the forest. The sun had already begun its nightly descent when a small town nestled beneath a series of cliffs at the foot of the mountains came into view. It had been early in the day when he stopped following Faela and Jair to turn east to Ravenscliffe. This side journey had given him time to think about the meeting in the clearing. Everything had happened so fast after he spotted Jair stealing his clothes and Faela's meddling failed to slow anything down. They had only interacted for ten minutes at most, but he couldn't shake the feeling that he knew her. Kade remembered individuals, their faces, their names, and that skill had saved him more than once, but despite searching his memory for hours, he kept running into dead ends. As far as he could tell, he had never seen her before this morning.

Throwing the coins she had given him in the air, he looked around at the approaching town. Its southern edge opened to a checkerboard of brown and olive-colored fields. In the slight breeze, the crops looked wilted. All the vibrancy seemed leeched out of them. His brow furrowed. Kade knew from first-hand experience that the rainy season had started just a few weeks ago in these mountains, but these crops looked like victims of a drought.

Though the sun still blazed in the sky, the fields lay empty. Most farmers that Kade knew worked well past sunset this close to the harvest, but no one tended these crops. The meadows to the west of the cliffs offered rolling grazing pastures, yet no sheep, no goats, no alpaca fed there. Only a tepid breeze that stirred enough to taunt, but not to cool, rolled over the meadow. Everything was too still. Kade shrugged off a shudder as the road gave way to the main thoroughfare of the town.

Passing the smaller stone and tile-roofed buildings on the outskirts, he could feel eyes watching him from behind curtains and shutters. Their silence seemed to condemn his intrusion. Kade became uncomfortably aware of his near nakedness as the buildings appeared more frequently and closer together. Rubbing his chin and mouth, he smirked. His shoulders squared, he walked toward the village's center with a sauntering confidence that belied his state of undress.

A few stragglers moved on the streets that fed into the town square dominated by empty, wooden market stalls. None stopped; none spoke a greeting to their neighbors. It seemed to him that necessity alone drove them from the illusory safety of their homes. Some acknowledged him by gawking at his scandalous appearance before hurrying on their way, but none risked speaking to him. Kade sighed and leaned against a stall waiting for an opportunity. He didn't have to wait for long as a young boy shuffled by him on an errand he seemed bent on prolonging or avoiding as long as possible.

"Evening," Kade said conversationally, "feels like this might be one of the last warm nights before fall hits hard."

The boy jumped at the voice. Spotting the man wearing only pants, his eyes widened as he saw the lacing of scars on his chest and arms. An impertinent sneer settled on his lips. "What d'you want?"

Well, that tells me quite a bit about where things stand here, Kade thought. Addressing the boy, he said, "I'm looking for someone named Marvin. Do you know him?"

"Might be I do. Might be I don't." Indicating Kade's

questionable apparel with his hand, he asked, "Who you be to ask?"

Kade tossed an iron coin to him. He caught it easily. "Does that improve your memory at all?"

The boy pocketed the currency and wiped his nose. "This way."

Kade followed the opportunist further under the shelter of the cliffs to a building facing the square with a painted sign that had a picture of an open palm. Underneath the symbol was the single word, Ravenscliffe.

Direct and to the point, Kade thought as he turned to the boy. "My thanks," he said in dismissal.

The boy shrugged feigning indifference as he walked away. Once Kade had turned his back, however, the boy glanced over his shoulder to watch him enter the building before he returned to his errand, his face filled with curiosity.

The fading light made it difficult to see within the shop. An elderly man, with skin like the leather boots he sat polishing, pushed his foot against the high wooden counter. Brown polish streaked his brow and jaw line.

At Kade's entrance, he frowned and put down the boot with a thud. "Ain't none too many travelers come through here, ser. State your business."

"That's quite a greeting from a trader," Kade observed to no one in particular. "Aren't you required to be polite?"

"Being friendly hasn't paid much in years this close to the border. Not since before the war," the trader replied. "And, if you please, your appearance don't exactly scream respectability."

Kade liked the man's blunt approach and responded in kind. "I was told to ask for Marvin and to show him these." He threw the coins Faela had given him on the counter, except for the iron piece that he slipped into the leg sheath of his dagger.

The coins clattered on the wood worn smooth and shiny with age and use. One spun off the counter and the man caught it without looking down, raising it between his thumb and forefinger. The stamp of the crescent moon and the harp winked in a streak of sunlight.

"You must be a mite more respectable than you look to have

these," the man remarked gesturing at Kade with the coin. "I be Marvin. What can I do you for?"

Kade motioned to his chest and feet. "As you can see, I'm missing a few essentials. I need a solid pair of boots that can take some abuse and a shirt that won't tear easily. I wouldn't mind getting more than that, but I don't have any extra coins beyond those."

"Ser, you know how much these coins be worth?" Marvin asked with a half smile.

Kade shook his head. "I'd never seen the stamp before."

Marvin grunted his surprise at Kade's ignorance. "You got enough there for three pair of boots with some left to kick around."

Kade raised an eyebrow. "I didn't recognize the stamp, where's it from?"

"Where'd you get them?"

Kade saw no reason to hide their origin. "A woman named Faela."

Marvin quickly turned his back to Kade. "What's your foot measure?"

"You know her?" Kade leaned onto his arms on the counter.

"Can't say I do." Marvin rummaged through the shelves that lined the back of the shop. "You about ten, eleven inches?"

"Eleven. Who is she?"

"Ser, like I told you," Marvin said as he came back with two pairs of boots and dropped them on the counter, "I don't know no one named, what was it, Kayla?"

"Faela." Kade lifted the pair the color of freshly turned soil and flexed the ankles of the boots before putting them back down.

"Right. Like I said, can't say I know the girl. How many shirts you be needing? And you want a pack to put this all in? You'll be needing a cloak or a jacket, and a blanket, definitely a woolen blanket with fall coming fast. We got some good wool from our alpacas last summer and the weaving here is some of the finest in the Taronpia, if I do say so myself."

Marvin looked between the rows of goods giving Kade a measuring glance. "Since it don't seem like you got nothing with you, you want an extra pair of trousers too?"

"You seem quite generous, Marvin," Kade felt compelled to point out. "I've never heard of a trader that'd part with so many goods without discussing prices first."

Marvin reemerged from the back with his arms full. "I told you, you got the coins for it."

Despite Marvin's refusal to discuss Faela, he seemed honest enough and Kade sensed he wouldn't try to cheat him. "Fine. I'll take that brown duster, the vest hanging back there, three shirts, a pair of canvas work trousers, five pairs of woolen socks, a oiled traveling pack, and you sold me on the alpaca blanket."

Marvin nodded curtly and began gathering the additions. When he returned, he also carried a cloth bundle and a water skin. "This," he referred to the bundle, "has tack bread, deer jerky, yellow cheese, and summer pears."

"Darkness, how much did she give me?" Kade muttered under his breath.

"You've the Light itself looking out for you, ser." Marvin captured Kade's gaze as he slid four of the bronze coins back across the counter. "Should you ever find that there girl again, I'd show her some right proper gratitude."

Kade recalled the parting image of Faela as she marched out of the clearing revealing her wavy, strawberry blonde hair trailing from under her hat. Her parting words echoed in his mind.

"That doesn't seem too likely," Kade said as he pawed through the goods piled on the counter. "Do you have somewhere I could change?"

"Back there," Marvin said pointing to a pine, tri-fold screen to the left of the counter.

Kade grabbed a couple items and disappeared behind it. He shrugged into a rough-spun cotton shirt and flipped his hair out from under the collar.

"If you don't mind me asking," he began, his fingers moving deftly as he fastened its buttons, "how's the harvest going to be this year?"

"You got to have seen on your way into town. The crops be half dead already and ain't no one minding them proper. Can't blame them none though. Not after those bandits killed young Rufus and his woman, not to mention their livestock they run off with."

"Bandits?" Kade kicked his pants against the wall and slid into the thick but pliable canvas trousers and tucked in the shirt before fastening them shut. Looping his belt on, he tightened it and sank to the floor, socks in hand.

"Worst scum I seen, since the gangs during the war, bunch of cowards." Marvin shook his head. "People say they be holed up in the caves, but there be so many caves in these mountains, ain't no one found them. The magistrate sent an appeal to the Daniyelan temple right quick, but nothing been done yet."

Kade slipped on a boot and extended his leg as he pulled the laces taut. "Not even a messenger from the temple?"

"I been hearing, as a trader do sometimes, that the Daniyelans be stretched real thin. Ain't enough born with the gift to replace those what were lost in the war, they say."

Kade grunted his agreement. "How long has it been since these bandits last struck?"

"None too long, couldn't be more than a week or so. Most people still scared they be back. Gustav, an alpaca herder, said he seen a pack of riders heading north a day or so ago. I'm inclined to think it be them."

"How many of these bandits were there?"

"Couldn't say, but Gustav said he seen five riders."

Kade made a noncommittal noise in the back of his throat as he rocked forward onto his toes and rose to his feet in a single fluid movement. He shrugged into the vest but left it open. Retrieving his discarded pants, he turned and approached the counter. His other purchases were already in the bag. Kade folded the pants and stuffed them on top before drawing it closed and latching its buckles. Swinging the satchel around, its weight settled across his back.

Marvin surveyed the now dressed Kade and nodded curtly. "You look mighty fine, if I do say so myself, ser. Don't think no one would mistake you for a ruffian now."

Kade offered his hand to the trader who clasped his forearm. "My thanks, Marvin."

"None needed," he replied. "I'm but a simple businessman."

Kade grinned at the likelihood of that last statement as he

turned and stepped into the soft purple twilight. Despite his grin, his mind was troubled by Marvin's report. If some bandits had decided to take advantage of Ravenscliffe's remote location, they could cripple the town and be gone before the Daniyelans managed to dispatch any help. Even if Kade could find the bandits, he would be outnumbered at least five to one and that would be a conservative estimate.

As he crossed the square again, seeing all of the vacant and unused market stalls and remembering the abandoned fields, he kicked at a stone in frustration. It created puffs of dust as it skipped across the square until it hit the well in the center. Ravenscliffe would just have to cope until other help could arrive.

*   *   *

"There's no fresh beef?" Jair tried to peer around the plump woman at the counter. "None at all?"

The woman with gray hair placed her hands on her ample hips and said, "Look, son, I already been telling you. All we got is venison jerky. Might not be fresh, but it sure be better than nothing. With the animals so skinny and sickly, we're lucky we got any. So stop your bellyaching and take what we got or leave."

With a lopsided grin, Jair rubbed the back of his neck. "How can I say no, after such kind words from a proprietress as lovely as yourself?"

The elderly woman snorted and walked back behind a curtain, muttering. "Sweet talking, ain't going to get you nothing. I known too many boys like you, with sweet faces and sweeter words." She returned with a cloth bundle and dumped it on the table. "Ain't none of them sweet — ever."

"Well, m'lady, I'll just have to prove your experience wrong." Jair winked. He swung his bag around to the front and rummaged through its contents. He removed a pouch and pulled out an orange token made of stiff leather. He handed the token to the woman, who snorted as she accepted it.

"Guess the Daniyelans'll take anyone since the war." She bent over and pulled out a ledger from under the counter. She wrote in two of the columns and then spun the book to face Jair and handed him the stylus. Jair signed and picked up his package.

He grabbed the woman's hand and kissed it. "I thank you for all your compassion and advice."

Pulling her hand out of Jair's grasp, she waved him away, but her wrinkles deepened as she smiled. "Be off with you, you scoundrel. Save your words for someone it'll work on and watch yourself. The roads ain't safe these days, not even for a lawman."

Jair swept into a low bow with a grin then left the tavern. The air outside held a wet chill that made him pull his coat in tighter around him. The breeze coming off the river was colder than the forest had been. Looking around, he could see little in the deepening darkness of the evening. Lights had just begun to spill into the damp streets from the buildings that lined the river.

Someone whistled from the alley next to the tavern. In a few strides, Jair's long legs brought him into the alley. The smell of decomposing produce seemed to linger in the air along with the rhythmic sound of dripping water that echoed between the walls. Faela leaned against its brick facade in the shadows. With her foot propped against the surface behind her, she looked down absently at a medallion resting between her fingers as her thumb traced its raised design. Woven within its stylistic harp and crescent emblem was the word "Ella."

She put the silver chain back under her shirt. "Find enough to satiate that beast within?"

Jair shook his bundle at her. "Of course, fairest Faela. I will never be thwarted when it comes to food. What's that?" He indicated the necklace.

"It's nice to know where your priorities lie." Pushing her shoulders off the wall, Faela walked past Jair, leaving the alley. "It was a present from my brother."

Jair nodded and turned to respond, but Faela was already three shops down the street. He kicked up mud as he trotted to close the distance. "So, why can't we stay here in Aberley tonight? Camping near the pass doesn't seem like the best plan to me."

"Shall I explain again?" They walked parallel with the rushing river as they headed toward the forest line. "Saving your skin cost me time, my darling lad, therefore, we need to keep moving."

"But it's already dark."

"And the more distance we put behind us, the better." Faela picked up her pace as they passed a grizzled dog that looked more wolf than pet. The dog dug in his back heels and sank low to the ground, his hackles raised. He snarled in the back of his throat. Faela locked eyes with him and he lowered his head and sat back on his hunches.

"Why is it so important to keep moving?" Jair looked from the dog and back to Faela. "Better alive and late if you ask me."

"Well, I didn't," she pointed out. "You're the one who decided not to shove off here at Aberley. You still can, you know." Faela watched his reaction out of the corner of her eyes.

"We've already been over this," he said ignoring her hint. "So keeping moving? Why?"

Faela hid her smile by wiping her cold nose. "I need to find someone and he has a considerable head start."

"A friend?"

"In a manner," Faela said, as she begun humming unconsciously. "He's a friend of someone-" Faela's voice shook for a moment, then she cleared her throat. "He has some information that's important to me."

"So where does this mysterious man of," Jair broke off grasping in vain for an adjective, "mystery, live?"

"He's a retired Tereskan who still travels to heal," Faela answered as the glow of the town faded from sight behind them, "so that depends."

"Wait." Jair stopped. "Didn't you tell that Kade guy that you were going to visit your sick brother?"

"Hmm, yes, there is that." Faela swerved to avoid a branch, which she pushed out of her way. "I lied."

"You did?" Jair sounded shocked. As he stopped, the branch Faela had avoided thwapped him in the stomach. "Son of a mother!" he croaked barely audible. All the breath had been knocked from his lungs with the strike.

Faela turned at the noise and her hand went to her mouth with a laugh. "That takes some talent, Jair. Try to watch where you're going next time. And since when did you claw your way up to the moral high ground? I just saved you from getting beaten bloody for thieving."

Doubled over, Jair said, "No, no really, I'm fine.   Your concern is overwhelming." Once he regained his breath, he stood with a worried look in his eyes. "You just sounded so convincing."

"That was the idea," she said in a distracted tone. "Well, my lad, if you think you're going to pull through, let's see if we can't push a bit further before we make camp. You just keep an eye out for those attack trees."

Though the tall ceiling of the forest blocked her view of the sky, Faela could smell the rain. It might not fall while they slept, but she didn't plan on taking that chance. Retrieving her pack, she removed the oiled canvas cloth strapped underneath. Once it was free, she unhooked the straps that held it in place and slung them over her shoulder. With the tarp under her arm, she rose, her knees popping as she stood.

Tapping a four-beat rhythm with her foot, she scouted for some low-lying branches that looked sturdy. While the straps and rings on the canvas made erecting the shelter by herself an easy enough task, it would go faster with a second pair of hands and she was beginning to feel the demanding pace she had maintained all day. Though they had made good time, she could already feel she would pay for it tonight.

With a short, sharp whistle, Faela got Jair's attention as he built up a fire. He looked around the close huddle of evergreens and hemlocks that penned them in against the cliff face and grinned at her.

Wiping the dirt from his hands, he asked, "Yeah?"

"Give me a hand, will you?" She unfurled the tarp. "Grab an edge."

Jayr complied and they used the natural tenting of the evergreens to secure the rain shelter. The boughs of the trees would shield them from most of the rainfall and the tarp would deflect the rest as long as the wind stayed calm. But if it turned into a storm, the shelter would do little to keep them dry. They worked in silence and by the time they had finished, the fire burned nicely and they had created a small, but protected nook.

"Hope you're not shy," Faela warned him trying to gauge how

much of the space his length would occupy.

"You'd be surprised at the small spaces I can squeeze into," he told her with his ever-present grin. "But with as many siblings as I have, you get used to sharing. Truly, I have no sense of personal space."

"I noticed," she said with a wry smile remembering their meeting earlier that day. She had a hard time believing that introduction had occurred this morning. It had been a long day. Though she couldn't remember a day in recent months that had felt any different.

"Really?" he asked seeming genuinely surprised.

"Mmm, yes," she said sinking into a cross-legged position in front of the fire. "I noticed this morning, when you were practically hanging on me like a cloak."

"Ahh, yes, that," he said as though he had already blocked the memory. "I would be good at being a cloak." The smile on his face faded.

"What?" Faela asked sensing the change in his mood.

He held a finger to his lips as he gave the tented fire a quick shove and kicked nearby earth over top of it with his feet. Muffling a curse at the sparks that flew up his pant leg, he disappeared as their hollow fell into darkness. Blind, Faela crawled as silently as she could across the ground. She could feel the rocks and twigs and needles tearing her palms, but she ignored the stinging until she reached the rock face. Groping along its edge, she pressed her back against the cliff. Though the granite jabbed into her spine and ribs, its solid bulk reassured her. Her breath felt wet and hot condensing in the cold as she tried to quiet it, straining to hear what had alerted Jair.

That's when she heard it, the crunch of hooves, the snorting, the low murmuring voices and they were getting closer. Faela slid her hand down to her ankle and loosened her dagger from its sheath. At the sound of the slight click, she felt Jair's large hand close over hers without any fumbling. Turning her eyes to where she imagined him to be, she could barely make out shapes. Her eyes were unaccustomed to the sudden shift from light to darkness. She was amazed that he could see enough to know where she was; yet his grip hadn't hesitated when he reached for her.

Whoever was out there rode close to where they flattened themselves against the cliff. Biting down on her lip, she thanked the Light that the trees stood close enough together to keep the horses from wandering into the hollow unintentionally. The voices that had merged together in the forest a few moments ago, had separated into distinct voices, but their volume remained hushed.

Closing her useless eyes, Faela focused on only the voices. They were male and there were several of them, at least four that she could distinguish. She still couldn't make out what they discussed but she felt its underlying agitation and malice like a stab in her stomach.

A horse snorted. It was so close and she had been so focused on sorting out the voices that she flinched at the noise. Jair squeezed her hand to steady her. They stayed immobile for what seemed like hours. The tip of her nose felt cold and numb and her knees felt like someone was trying to pry her joints apart by the time the clopping crunch of the horses faded completely. Her vision had finally adjusted to the minuscule amount of ambient light coming from the cloud-covered sky and she looked over at Jair who had slumped against the cliff in relief.

Still not wanting to break the silence, she pointed over to the wreckage of their fire as she got to her feet. Her limbs protested at staying in one position without moving in the cold night air and she limped to the circle and began digging out the charred wood. Jair blocked out what light the night provided when he knelt beside her and began digging the pit again.

They still needed to eat, but Faela wanted nothing more than to crawl under the shelter and sleep, but she had traveled long enough to know that she had to replace the energy she had spent that day.

Once they had the fire going again, they sat side-by-side munching on strips of jerky and hard white cheese in silence. Faela had emptied her water skin into a cook pot to heat it up for tea, one of the few luxuries she had allowed herself to carry. She stared into the small fire as something occurred to her.

Gnawing on the dried salty meat, Faela finally voiced her realization. "You know, I have good hearing."

"Yeah?" Jair cut off some of the cheese and popped it into his mouth.

"I have very good hearing and I'm paranoid, but I didn't hear anything before you put out the fire. I didn't hear anything until a little while after the fire was out." Faela poked at the cook pot snuggled into the embers with a stick. "How did you know they were there?"

"You didn't hear the horses?" he asked surprised as he ripped off a hunk of jerky with his teeth. "They weren't exactly stealthy."

Faela leaned into her knees and hovered her palm over top of the water. The steam curled around her fingers and she held them suspended, letting her joints soak in the warmth. When she finally pulled them back, her fingertips felt singed. Sucking on her middle finger to cool the burning sensation, she considered Jair's explanation.

As she watched the boy, who was barely a man, next to her, she wiped her hand off on her coat before measuring some loose tea into her scraped-up palm. The incongruity still nagged at her, a single cracking twig would have alerted her to their approach. She had traveled alone and off the roads for long enough to know when someone approached her camps, but there had been nothing. As Jair smiled benignly into the fire chewing on his jerky, she decided for now to just be thankful that he had noticed.

She nudged the cook pot out of the embers with her stick and sprinkled in the leaves to steep. Brushing off her hands, she said, "Well after the innkeeper's warning and those riders, I'll take first watch."

"You're exhausted," Jair objected as the first misting of rain began dripping through the leaves and needles.

One fat drop dangled off the brim of her hat and sparkled in the firelight before plopping onto her hand. "I'd rather be tired then dead."

*   *   *

The forest slumbered in darkness as the unseen rustling of nocturnal life whispered through the night. Kade strode in isolated silence through the trees. He stopped and dropped to a knee. His hand hovered over the debris-strewn ground. Pushing aside a dry, crinkled leaf, he lightly traced the surface of the soil and rubbed the dirt between his fingers. He stood and continued forward.

The wind blew through the forest cold and damp, causing him to shudder and shove his hands under his armpits. Even at the end of summer, the nights in the foothills of the Higini would rob a soul of any warmth. Whistling through the leaves, the breeze carried the scent of wet clay to his nose and he could hear the clear tinkle of water breaking over rocks. The brush grew denser here, but Kade navigated a nigh invisible path through the brambles. Pushing the springy branches of a sapling aside, he stepped into the clearing at the bank of a creek.

The moonlight shone, illuminating the world in a soft silver light that the trees had previously hidden. With a break in the clouds, he was exposed beneath the stars. Closing his eyes, he tilted back his head. Solitude surrounded him and he smiled.

Snapping his eyes open, he found a grouping of three misshapen rocks, worn smooth by seasonal flooding, a dozen feet from the bank. He passed the rocks and headed straight for a cluster of evergreens to his left. Their lowest branches wove a thick veil of needles that hid the ground beneath from sight.

Kade crouched and parted them. A solitary, orange, leather circle lay amongst the discarded needles. There was nothing else. Heavy clouds pushed by unseen winds blotted out the bright light of the stars and the moon. Kade grimaced. Those clouds held rain.

He dropped the branches. Looking over his shoulder to the north, the direction he had last seen Faela and Jair heading, he rested his elbows on his knees and put his forehead in his hands. "Fantastic. That lying blighter took it."

Focusing his rising anger, Kade calmed his nerves. He pushed aside the branches again and grabbed the leather medallion. Lying in his hand, he saw the stamp of a sword consumed by fire. Just as he felt a drop of rain hit his ear, he closed his eyes and reached for the fire within himself. Heat licked his body as the flames inside him grew. Within his mind, a light whipped like a crack of lightning, shooting away from him and out of sight. An orange glow pulsed along the forest floor. Kade had a trail.

CHAPTER THREE

The night had passed without further incident and Faela kicked Jair awake before dawn, not that she could tell when the sun rose with the clouds socking in the mountains around them. While searching for water as they waited for the fire to burn down, Jair had found some berries to eat with their porridge. With the damp chill having seeped into their skin, they welcomed the hot breakfast.   Unfortunately, Jair had only managed to find enough water to fill their skins and make their meal, so they couldn't even clean up before they started out and Faela felt like she had grown a second skin of dried sweat and dirt.

Once they did finish packing up the camp, the day entered the odd half-light of dawn and they left the safety of their hollow.

Not long after the sun had risen behind the clouds, Faela said, "We'll be crossing the border in another league or two.   Last chance to turn back."

Jair hitched the straps of his pack up higher on his shoulders. "No such luck, my fair one. You're stuck with me."

Though Faela would never admit it aloud, she had hoped he would choose stay. His unsinkable good humor helped to keep away her darker thoughts, but she had felt obligated to give him the opportunity to go before leaving behind the relative safety of Taronpia.   Turning, she favored him with a smile and they continued their hike through the forest that was turning steeper and rockier with every step they took.

It was late morning before they reached the border. Though she could see no discernible difference between where they stood now in Taronpia and that invisible line that meant they had crossed into the territory of the northernmost kingdom, Nabos, she could feel the border like a high-pitched ringing in her ears, a fading remnant of the war. Before the war, the border had been nothing but a division of the countries' lands, but several years into the conflict the Virds had pressed the Phaidrians of Lanvirdis into military service. They erected a barrier along the border that knit the life of the forest itself into a tight net of energy. Faela had only been a young girl when it happened, but the stories of men turning to ash still made her shudder even now.

The barrier had been dissolved in the years following the ceasefire and the treaty, but she could still feel the tingle of the energy on her skin as they approached. As she prepared to continue the climb, she realized that Jair no longer waked beside her. Looking down the incline, she saw Jair standing still as though his flesh had turned to marble; even his lips had lost their color.

"It gives me the shivers too," she reassured him. "Everyone one can feel it, even the ungifted. Everyone can sense that something unnatural happened here." When he didn't move, she trotted down the slope and skidded to a halt next to him causing a tiny avalanche of stones and pebbles. "I promise, nothing's left of the barrier. We'll be fine."

Jair tore his gaze away and even though Faela stood above him, he still looked down on her. Scratching his scalp with both hands, his light brown hair stuck out from the tousling and he said, "Right. Yeah, let's go."

"Good man," she said with a slap on his arm before she scrambled back up the hill.

They made their way through the barrier without incident, but it felt like standing too close to a lightning strike as they passed through and the ringing turned into a shrieking. When Faela was sure she could bear no more, it faded back to the soft ringing. They made it through.

Faela clambered sideways up the incline as she reached where it plateaued. Turning around, she placed her hands on her hips and bent over to catch her breath. "See, nothing. I told you we'd be fine."

Jair took her outstretched arm as he hopped onto the level ground with her. His color had returned and so had his smile. "I shall never doubt you again."

"As it should be, my lad," she said with a jab at his side. "Well, no lollygagging now. Off we go."

They continued along the level, but rocky path for half a

league before it turned to the right and hugged the cliffs. Jair began whistling to himself having regained his wind after the extended climb. "So, Faela," he began.

"Yeah?" she asked trying to get a look around the bend when she felt that same stab of malice she had felt last night and dropped to a crouch. "Jair, get down," she hissed grabbing for him, but she was too late.

A wide, muscular man came around the bend leading with his fist. It caught Jair in the chest, knocking his legs and his breath from him. He hit the ground hard and Faela could hear his head bounce off the rocks. She prayed the fall had only knocked him unconscious. Red mist flashed in her eyes as she checked to see if his skull and neck had fractured. They were intact. He was fine, unconscious, but fine for now. Though if they survived this, she didn't envy the headache that awaited him.

Her attention focused on Jair, she missed that the man had closed on her until it was too late.

"None of that now, little miss," he said capturing her hand that had gone for her boot as he held onto her other arm. "We don't want no trouble. We just want whatever valuable baubles and coins you and your man got. That be all. Like this," he said releasing her arm to hook the silver medallion around her neck with a swollen, knuckled finger.

Faela looked past him and saw that he had friends, several friends. But even immobile, Faela was far from helpless.

"No," she said in a steady voice as she clamped down on her fear. "Anything else, just not that."

"Anything?" he said licking his bottom lip. He looped the chain around his fingers drawing her closer, when he noticed the vial. "Shit." He let go of her and backed away putting his sword between them. "She's a Tereskan," he called back to his fellows.

"Darkness," one of the men with pinched, close set eyes and greasy blonde hair swore, "kill her quick. I don't want my guts on the outside."

Faela balanced on the balls of her feet, waiting. Without warning, the man advanced with an efficient thrust of the blade and had Faela not gained so many bruises from sparring with her brother, he would have killed her with that strike. As it was when she dropped to her side, he still managed to catch her above her hip. Her hat fell, bouncing to the ground. The thick fabric of her coat and the direction of her fall alone had kept it from slicing open her torso. Biting down on her lip until it too bled, she muffled her cry. The wound felt like it was on fire, but she knew she that if she stopped moving she was dead.

She didn't stay down for long. Before the man could prepare for another strike, she rose bringing her knee up between his legs with as much force as she could throw behind it. The man cursed and backhanded her. Chips of loose rock fell down her collar as she slammed into the cliff her head ringing and dazed.

"This bitch is mine." The man wheezed doubled over in pain. "No witnesses; kill the boy."

The greasy blonde loosed his sword and kicked Jair over onto his back. He raised the sword.

"Stop!" Faela commanded using all the strength of her voice. Her eyes sparked with a deep scarlet and she reached out her hand. Angry red lines swirled on her palm and she gazed at the blonde. He froze paralyzed and the sword clattered from his hand and a drop of blood fell from his nose. Faela closed her palm into a fist and the man fell to his knees, his back beginning to buck with tremors that threw him to the ground.

*   *   *

Kade sniffed the stagnate air. The break in the rain he had enjoyed for the last few leagues wouldn't last much longer. Though the sun had risen hours before, the day seemed trapped in a gray twilight. The world felt penned in by bluish-black clouds that pressed in close, while indigo slashes of light seeped through the blanket of those swollen clouds. The air seemed to hold back a restrained violence. Glancing at the sky, Kade increased his gait as he jogged up the rocky hill.

He wanted this business concluded before that rain let loose again. Thoughts of a soft, warm, and, more importantly, dry bed kept him moving. Though this was hardly the first time he'd sacrificed sleep by tracking through the night, it didn't mean that he liked repeating the practice. Early that morning, he had run across a camp abandoned with its fire still smoldering, but it showed signs of six or seven inhabitants with horses, not a man and a woman traveling on foot. Though the trail he had followed all night did cross with those from the camp and continued in the same direction toward the border. He had passed the border not long ago and even after all these years it still made his skin crawl.

The tracking spell blazed like the setting sun. He was close. As Kade reached the top of the hill when he heard a noise that caused his stomach to convulse. A woman's voice cried out for someone to stop. That one word seemed to drive out all other sound in the woods, leaving behind a tense silence.

Reacting instinctively, he ran toward the scream, knife already drawn. He slowed as he approached the bend created by the cliff rising above him. Crouching low, he saw a long-limbed man crumpled on the ground and another lay thrashing, afflicted by some unseen force. Several more men stood, weapons in hand.

A stocky man with a thick neck held a sword loosely, blood fell from its tip. He addressed his prey, a woman who slumped against the cliff. "Now that were mighty stupid, you little bitch. You should've been a good girl. Don't make me hurt you no more." A wicked delight sparked in his eyes at the thought of causing her pain.

The woman's wavy hair tumbled into her face, but could not hide the blood oozing from the jagged gash on her cheek, nor could it hide the blood that stained her mouth. She stared at the man standing over her with a calm hate. Her eyes flashed a dark scarlet and the man who thrashed on the ground made a strangled gurgling noise, then his back arched and his body went limp.

"You Tereskan bitch!" the man yelled and raised his sword to strike. She remained motionless, staring at the bandit with serene resolution. Though she made no outward move to defend herself, the air around her crackled.

Flipping the knife in his hand, Kade found the balance and let it fly. Before the man could utter a sound, he pitched forward with the dagger buried in his back. The woman rolled away in time to avoid being trapped beneath the falling corpse. Her face contorted in pain and her hand went to her side smeared with blood.

The other bandits stared, frozen, unable to process the sudden change in their situation. Unarmed, Kade rushed the man nearest to him whose braid fell past the small of his back. The braided man swung clumsily with his sword. Kade evaded its wide arch easily as he dropped to the ground and kicked behind the man's knees. His foe hit the ground, gasping as the breath was forced out of him. Kade brought down his heel onto the jaw of the inert man with a wet crunch.

A black blur moved in Kade's peripheral vision. Grabbing the hilt of the fallen sword, he rolled to his feet in time to divert the strike of his next opponent down his blade as his body moved out of its arch, but the impact knocked the blade from his grasp.

"Kade, behind you!" the woman yelled her voice hoarse with pain. She lifted herself off the ground with her elbows.

Whirling, Kade dodged, avoiding the swing of the advancing steel, but was left off balance. Ignoring the opening, the man in black left Kade to his companion and approached the woman. Kade swung his pack from off his back and threw it at the remaining man using the momentum to spin and bring around the back of his fist to strike him in the temple. As the man fell, Kade looked at the woman for the first time.

"Faela?" he asked, his brain processing sluggishly in the midst of fighting. Shaking his head, he recovered. "Get up, blast it!"

As if compensating for its earlier absence, the wind returned with a howling blast. Leaves ripped off the trees and the debris on the floor of the forest swirled in a violent dance. Faela did not hesitate, her hand slipped around the vial at her chest. The bandit was closing the gap. Kade would not reach them in time.

Seeing no other alternative, Kade hefted the sword reversing his grip, tested its balance, and threw the blade at the man's back, willing it to hit. It shimmered orange like a hot ember and connected with a cracking thunk and the man fell.

Kade's triumph, however, was short lived. A searing pain exploded in his chest. He looked down and the glint of metal caught his eye. The tip of a sword peeked through his vest. A drop of rain landed on the back of his neck and slid down his shirt. The first of the rain had fallen.

The man behind Kade laughed coarsely and whispered in his

ear, "Guess you should've left the girl to us and minded your own business, friend."

Kade coughed causing blood to trickle from the side of his mouth and laughed, a bubbling laugh. He reached behind him, gripped the man's head, and twisted with one swift motion. The body slumped to the ground like a sack of grain.

Kade looked down at the blood welling around the ripped fabric. "And I just got this shirt," he said in an oddly high voice.

His legs shook and he sank to his knees. Faela pushed herself off the ground and half-caught him as he pitched forward and they both fell. His head resting against her shoulder, she grasped the blade behind him and wrenched it clear of his body. She threw it away from them. It hit the rock face with a metallic clang. Her hands were sticky with blood.

Kade's weight sank further into her shoulder. Cradling his head, she began lowering him to the uneven ground until he lay horizontal and she stood straddled over him. The jagged stones scraped against her knees. He began to tremble with increasing force. Faela searched his face. It had faded to the color of exposed bone.

"Don't you even think of dying." Faela tried to keep her tone light. "You're going to be just fine, Kade. I've seen men sleep off worse than this. I see Marvin took care of you. Good man, yeah?"

At the sound of her voice, Kade's eyes fluttered and he looked at her face for the first time. Silver eyes, the color of moonlight, stared back at him. She fumbled for the vial under her shirt and her eyes disappeared beneath a red haze as her lips began moving in a regular rhythm. Golden light flared at her temples, pulsing in time with the soundless movement of her lips.

Kade blinked and coughed. He looked at Faela like a confused little boy. His fingers brushed her wet temples. "You're a Gray," he said with a painful wheeze before his eyes rolled back in his head and he sucked in a breath that would not come. His fingers dug into the dirt as he tried to breathe.

The rain came down in sheets now, soaking everything in a matter of moments. Though it was slick with blood and water, the leather thong, laced tightly through her fingers, held the vial close to her palm. Pulling out the dagger from her boot, she sliced his shirt open, not bothering to even rip off the buttons. Ignoring his heaving, she placed her hands above the wound and a bright scarlet light pooled around them.

Faela closed her eyes and saw the darkness flaring in his chest as it seeped through his lung. The sword had punctured his right lung and it had begun collapsing as it filled with blood.

Faela moved to draw out the darkness around the wound, but a pliable barrier impeded her progress. "No," Faela whispered in panic, "not now."

Water running into her eyes and down her jaw, she shook her head. "Darkness take him, not this time."

Pulling a hand away from Kade, she brought it to the ragged wound at her side and pressed against it causing her blood to cover her palm. She flinched in pain and brought her hand back and began to audibly hum a clear and low note. Placing her palm over the wound, she allowed her blood to mix with the blood welling from Kade's chest. As the two energies mixed, the barrier hardened, then shattered.

"Kade," she said attempting to keep her balance as Kade tried again unsuccessfully to bring air into his starving lung, "I know this is going to be hard, but try to be still. I know how frightening it is, but you have to be still."

He stopped moving. She wasn't sure if he had heeded her advice or if he had lost consciousness. Right now she didn't care which as she followed the flows deep into the wound. A ravenous and flaming darkness spread through his lung like fire. It headed for his heart. Faela began siphoning the darkness away from the lung. It surged against the healthy red that she had begun to weave back into the wound.

He gulped again, unable to suppress the reflex any longer, taking gasping breaths that tore his throat, but brought no air into his suffocating lung. She continued knitting the energies into a springy lattice that would close the wound. The melody she sang matched and shaped the weaving of the energies that mended the rupture.

Sweat mixed with rain fell into the cut on Faela's face. It burned. Despite the sweat, she could feel the warmth leaving her the longer she worked. Her skin grew cold and wet like a dead fish. Her humming rose into a low musical chant.

"Faela?" a groggy voice asked from the ground. Jair levered himself up onto his elbows, his hair, dripping wet, was plastered to the side of his face. Seeing Faela covered in blood, Jair scampered to her side like a newborn foal. He slid in the mud. "What happened? You're white as the dead, Faela, and you're shaking. What's he doing here? What happened to him? What happened to you? Are you singing? Faela?"

Faela ignored Jair's questions and focused solely on reinforcing her net. Kade's tremors stopped. He drew in a strangled breath as his lung inflated and he closed his eyes gratefully. Her patches would have to hold for now. Faela released the energies and the crimson and golden light surrounding them dissipated.

Kneeling, her legs straddling Kade's torso, Faela stared ahead of her with a strange, yet satisfied smile, then collapsed to the side.

Jair caught her. "Faela?" he asked, fear in his eyes.

Faela patted his cheek with a blood-streaked hand. "Watch my body for a few days, Jair."

Her head lolled back unsupported and her body fell limp. Her breathing was shallow, but steady. She had fallen into the peaceful oblivion of sleep.

*   *   *

"Over by the bar," the elderly herder said, in a low voice to his companions, "that man be wearing all black." He turned his head and spit on the floor superstitiously.

"Ain't no one dressed like that up to nothing good." The man with a full beard glared openly at the man. "Aberley ain't need his kind around."

"I mean, look," said the young man with a hooked nose who kept tapping his foot as he fidgeted, "he got that halberd there strapped to his back, plus those big old knives. Looks like a merc from the war."

The group made no secret of their glares or their topic of conversation. Knowing this, the man at the counter turned his hips slightly exposing the holster sitting low on his belt. This wasn't his first experience with those living along the border. Let them talk.

He heard the hook-nosed boy squeak as his voice cracked. "You see that? He got one of them revolvers. I ain't want to know what he done for Evensong to get one from those cutthroats."

"Keep it down, Andy," the herder said beginning to look nervous, "we ain't need no more trouble."

The voices of both the young and old men at the tables drifted to the ears of the man in black. He grinned, but the scar running from his mouth up to his temple pulled his lips into a leer. His legs crossed at the ankles, he rested his elbow against the counter, waiting. His dark auburn hair stuck out in a short ponytail from under a black kerchief. He fingered the grip of the revolver in an unconscious gesture.

Finally, an aged woman came out from the back to the bar. Though she appeared plump, she moved with a swiftness and more energy than a woman half her size and age. Looking at the man, she sniffed. "The boy told me you be needing something?"

"I was told you seen a young man in his early twenties who was tall and lanky. Would've been a few days back," the man said, leaning forward, "and I heard you talked with him. He would've seemed a real charmer."

The woman pulled a rag out of her apron and started wiping down the counter. "Oh, I remember that one. You mean the Daniyelan boy. Oh, he laid it on thick, that one did."

The man's eyebrow rose in surprised amusement. "One of the Daniyelans?"

The woman looked the man over again before she responded. "Of course, he used a Daniyelan temple token, signed for it and everything. What innkeeper would turn away a token? We all use the Orders' services."

"Can I see the ledger?" His hand reached into the pouch at his side. When his hand left the countertop, a few coins remained behind.

The woman smiled and swept the coins into her hand where they disappeared into the pocket of her apron. She reached under the counter. "Don't see the harm." She placed the ledger on the bar and opened it. Spinning the book, she pointed to a row near the bottom of the page. "That'd be him."

The man read the script and laughed. "He say where he was headed when he left?"

"He came through pretty late, but he ain't get a room, just some supplies then he was gone. If you ask me, I'm a mind to think he gone up into the hills. But Daniyelan or no, leaving when he did, he's good as dead now."

"Why'd you say that?" the man asked with interest as the tavernkeeper's tongue loosened as she began to warm up to him. He had no illusions regarding what warmed her up and it wasn't his winning smile.

"We're a border town, ser. And I don't care none that he's a Daniyelan, ain't no one survive long on the border alone."

"My thanks for the information, mistress. You been real helpful."

She waved at him with her rag. "Thanks be all well and good, but it ain't pay my bills."

Placing another coin on the bar, he nodded. "Good day, mistress."

Leaving the tavern, he saw the wide, swift running river in front of him and looked to the left where a woman in tight, black leathers stood balanced up on the toes of one leg. She smiled at him and her entire face sparkled, then she flipped backward onto her hands and sprang back onto her feet. Her short black curly hair bounced with the movement.

"Imp." The man stood observing the woman's figure with appreciation. "Always showing off."

The woman planted her hand on her hips and walked suggestively toward him as she pouted. "Oh, come now, Caleb. Can't I have a little fun?"

"See." Caleb caught her around the waist and pulled her close to him. "I was thinking more of the kind of fun where I get to play too."

"Lecher," the woman whispered, as she laced her arms around his neck and kissed him soundly, then pulled back smiling. Her fingers played with the silver chain that hung around his neck. At the end of the chain was a medallion with the emblem of a harp and a crescent. "Well, was the information reliable?"

"Talise, you are a horrible tease." He laughed with regret. "But yes, it was. He seems to have finally gotten desperate. He's trying to pass himself off as a Daniyelan and seems to have succeeded here. Somehow, he got a hold of some temple tokens. Though darkness knows how he pulled that off."

"He didn't sign for them using his proper name?" Talise asked with a musical laugh. "Did he?"

"Oh, yes, he did. Looks like our luck is finally changing."

"You're still irritated, aren't you?" Talise said with entertained surprise.

"It took four days to regain his trail," Caleb said defensively as the preface to his rant. "Everything was going so good, beautiful scenery, even more beautiful company. Tracking him was like following a child who had just run through a puddle of paint. This was supposed to be a quick and easy retrieval and his trail just up and vanished at that creek. I had to pay for information to find him again and you better believe we're getting that money back. So yeah, I'm a little put out."

Talise let her amusement at his annoyance shine through her dancing blue eyes. "Which way are we heading?"

"Eventually, into the foothills toward the border."

"He's going back into Nabos?" Talise drew her eyebrows together in concern. Despite Aberley being a river town, she didn't question the direction Caleb had chosen. She had never met anyone to equal him as a tracker. "That's seems counterproductive."

"You're surprised? When has this boy done anything that made good sense, since we started tracking him?"

"Why 'eventually'?" she asked suspicious of his earlier choice of words.

He slid his arm around her waist and steered her toward their horses. "If I'm any judge, there's a right proper storm building in those hills and they're not paying us enough for me to try to pick up his trail in the rain. We'll stay here tonight."

"You're still grumpy," she said in a teasing voice. "But it has been awhile since I got to sleep in a proper bed."

"Who said anything about sleep?" he asked as he tilted her chin to kiss her.

CHAPTER FOUR

Before leaving the llama in the stable, Sheridan scratched Ossi behind his tall, soft ears. In gratitude, Ossi licked her hand with his rough tongue. She smiled at the gentle-eyed creature and left the enclosure. As she walked down the cobblestone street, the sun shone high in the sky over Wickcester, a seaside town caught between the rolling green wall of the Higini Mountains and the endless blue-green expanse of the Kurinean Sea.

Despite the chill in the air coming off the inland sea, she felt stuffy and hot in the wool of her uniform's amber-colored jacket in the direct sunlight. She pulled at its stiff, high collar, but kept it fastened shut. She still had one more task that required her attention before she was off duty. As she skipped up the steps of the local Daniyelan temple, her brown riding boots, that reached up to her knees, glinted in the light from habitual polishing.

Sweeping her deep brown hair back with her fingers, it fell in a silky cascade down to the small of her back. Sheridan stopped and scanned the red and tan brick buildings across from the marble temple, but catching no sign of her partner she entered the building. The gas lamps lining the walls sent a pleasant glow to the high ceiling of the temple's entrance, but her goal was far less grand than the sweeping arcs of the ceiling and the columns of the entry. As she took long strides toward a small wooden doorway at the end of the room, her boots clicked on the mosaic of a enflamed sword inlaid with glass and ceramic chips of every shade of orange imaginable.

Pushing open the door, Sheridan found a young man with a low black ponytail wearing a similar uniform to her own standing behind a counter with rows of books and stacks of parchment lining every flat surface imaginable. The man was by no means small, but he still stood slightly shorter than the tall, willowy woman in front of him. She opened a leather pack, slung across her body, with the same emblem of the flaming sword and removed a stack of papers held together with twine and sealed with orange wax. She set them on the counter.

"Where's my sweetheart, Noah?" she asked peering around the room as though she expected the elderly man to unearth himself from under one of the stacks.

"That leg of his was acting up again, which of course got him on about his glory days," the young clerk said taking her papers as he imitated the old man's grating voice, "which of course got him telling the tale of that riot down in Gallow's Way in Kilrood back forty years ago, when my mum were still playing with her rag dolls, back when there were Daniyelans in every town and city of the world with none of this circuit riding nonsense."

Sheridan grinned at the imitation. "That's spot on. Really, well done."

The boy shook his head in amusement. "I'll tell you what, for someone who claims to never have trained with the Lusicans, he can sure spin a tale like one. I'm Tanner, by the way."

"Sheridan," she answered in turn. "Those reports are judgments from the Dalibor jungle circuit to be forwarded on to the archives in Finalaran."

"Sheridan?" he said with an excited glint in his brown eyes. "You're not Sheridan Reid by any chance, are you?"

"Last time I looked in the mirror," she answered leaning her elbows on the high counter. The movement caused her slippery hair to slide over her shoulders.

"Oh, that's brilliant," he said throwing his hands wide in excitement. "Oh, that makes things so much simpler."

"What does?" she asked with a tolerant amusement at his reaction.

"We're very low on the Amserian post priority. We only get our packages and letters popped in once a week, but Oscar needs a letter delivered to Finalaran to the main temple as soon as possible and our post was delivered yesterday. Do you think you could help us?"

"I think I could manage that," Sheridan said with a nod. "My partner should be here any moment if she's done spoiling that mare of hers. You'd think it was a child the way she fawns over it. Can you tell her where I've gone?"

"Surely, how will I recognize her?" he asked.

"That shouldn't be too difficult," Sheridan said with a small smirk. "Imagine someone around my height, my build, same angular bone structure, similar almond eyes, except she'll have cropped hair. Actually, just imagine me looking really annoyed. Where are your deliveries?"

Tanner gave her with a blank expression of confusion at her description, but handed her a bundle of letters and packages. Without further explanation, she gave him a conspiratorial wink before she wandered out the door adjacent to the counter and down a hall that led further into the temple. It didn't take her long to make her way to the winding staircase that led to the tower. Her long legs took the stairs two at a time and brought her to the empty room at the top that only held several woven baskets of various sizes ringing the walls.

Standing in place, she spun in a circle taking in the visual aspects of the room, the joints of the walls, the flaking of the mortar, the slick shine of worn stone. Once she was sure that she had a good lock on the room, her eyes glowed with a purple light and with a cracking pop the light flared around her and she disappeared. When the light dissipated from her vision, she stood in a different room fashioned out of orange-veined marble. A teenage girl in the lilac robes and trousers of an Amserian sat on a cushion on the floor.

"Sheridan!" she said when she saw the tall woman. Scrambling to her feet the redheaded girl threw her arms around Sheridan.

Knocking the breath from her lungs, Sheridan laughed and returned the hug. "Well met, Gwen. How's the big city life treating you here in Finalaran? You enjoying being amongst us rowdy Daniyelans?"

"Oh, they're not all loud and obnoxious. But, I miss snow," she said with a dramatic sigh before she lowered her voice, "but I cheat. I've been popping back to my rooms in Wistholt. I know we're not supposed to during our post rotations, but I get homesick."

"Naughty girl," Sheridan admonished, "wherever did you pick up such bad habits like that? I'll not have your good character warped by such ne're-do-wells."

Gwen giggled before releasing Sheridan. "Too late, Sheridan. I learned that trick from you long ago."

"Hush, don't let the whole Order hear my secrets," she said pulling the girl in close by the shoulder. "I am a pillar of virtue and personal sacrifice. Unless of course it means sacrificing my glorious featherbed in Wistholt."

"What are you doing here?" Gwen finally asked. "I thought you were riding circuit near the Kurinean?"

"What's a couple hundred leagues to Finalaran, when I go to Wistholt on the other side of the continent, because I have a craving for one of Martha's snow plum tarts?" Sheridan said dismissively with a wave of her hand. "See, there I go corrupting the youth again." Sheridan gave a martyred sigh before returning to the task at hand. "Any way, I'm here because Oscar from the Wickcester temple needed these delivered immediately."

"Oh, Wickcester, that's right," Gwen said her ivory-colored hand covering her mouth. "I was supposed to deliver a letter to Wickcester with yesterday's post. Could you take it back with you?"

"That's sloppy, Gwen," Sheridan said narrowing one eye. "Don't you tarnish the Amserian Order's good name now."

"Sorry," Gwen replied her ears turning red as she blushed.

"Just don't make a habit of it, lovey," Sheridan said with a quick hug. "I need to get back before Eve notices I'm gone. Take care, Gwen."

"Bye, Sheridan!" Gwen waved as she returned to her flowered cushion.

The indigo haze flared in her eyes engulfing her and with a pop she disappeared and reappeared in the same tower room hundreds of leagues away an instant later. Rolling her shoulders, they cracked and resettled as she descended the staircase. Her hand trailed along the wall of the winding corridor before she hopped off the last step. Walking back to the clerk's office, she flipped over the envelope Gwen had given her and saw the name Reid scrawled across the front.

She pulled up the latch of the door and entered the clerk's office to see an irritated looking woman who could have been her mirrored reflection except that her brown hair was cut short, close to her scalp. Ignoring the expression on her face, Sheridan turned the envelope back over and saw the dark orange wax seal of an enflamed sword.

"Sheridan, why did you leave me to carry all of our gear in by myself?" the woman asked with her arms crossed.

"Our dear Scion sent us this from Finalaran yesterday, Eve," Sheridan said waving the letter as she ignored her twin sister's comment.

"He did?" Eve asked as she sidled up against Sheridan her curiosity dispelling her annoyance. "What would be so important for Tomas to contact us directly?"

"Who knows," Sheridan shrugged breaking the seal. Registering movement in her peripheral vision, she glanced up from under her thick lashes and saw the shocked expression on Tanner's face at their casual reference to the head of the Daniyelan Order. She worried out the parchment and once it was free Eve grabbed it and started to read.

"Thanks for that," Sheridan said with a grimace and a dry tone as she mimed grabbing the paper in the empty air.

Eve stuck her tongue out at her sister as she read the letter. "Well, it appears that our particular talents have been requested for a murder investigation in Montdell."

"What caustic wit and stunning good looks?" Sheridan asked as she snatched the letter back with a cry of dismay from her sister.

"Well that's a given," Eve began as she ran her hand through the short tufts of her hair.

"Why would we be needed in Montdell?" Sheridan asked her brows drawn low. "That's the city where Kaedman's the Daniyelan representative on the council. Why wouldn't he have contacted me himself if something were wrong?"

"Who knows? It's not as though Tomas gave us much with which to work," Eve said rereading the note over Sheridan's shoulder.

"You're not joking. I've seen limericks longer than this. Telling us that the suspects have fled isn't exactly enlightening. Why would he bring us into this in the first place?"

"Well, being in Wickcester, we're probably the closest circuit riders if there's reason to mistrust the objectivity of the Daniyelans stationed there," Eve suggested with a frown. "It would make sense to bring in circuit riders, if they've been compromised."

Sheridan waved her hand as she reread the letter as if hoping it would divulge new information this time. "I trust Kaedman with my life."

Eve flattened her lips into a thin line of disapproval. "You give him too much credit."

"I don't like this," Sheridan said tapping the letter against her open palm.

"Of course you don't."

"What's that supposed to mean?" Sheridan said her tone dropping for the first time.

Opening her mouth to say something, she thought better of it. "Look, Sheridan, you don't like picking somewhere to stay for the night without a detailed explanation of my rationale in making the decision. So, Tomas was a bit terse in giving us details. He is the Scion after all. He's got more important duties to attend to then making sure you feel prepared walking into an investigation. It's an investigation; a little bit of mystery is necessary. Otherwise it wouldn't be an investigation, it'd be a trial."

"I don't know. Something about this doesn't smell right to me," Sheridan said glaring at the letter as if it had been intended to personally offend her. "Even if he knew nothing regarding the circumstances of the crime, why wouldn't he have told us the victim's name? Instead all he gave us is a vague order to report to the magistrate without any mention of Kaedman or any other Daniyelans in the city. That doesn't strike you as odd?"

"I'm not saying it's sitting well with me," Eve argued, "but try to see the good in this. We get to go to Montdell. It's been ages since we were able to travel up north. You'll get to see Kaedman and we haven't seen Nessa or Uncle Rahn in so long."

"It has been quite awhile and he does owe me a drink," Sheridan admitted grudgingly. "Well, I guess we'll have to find passage going up the Dalibor in the morning."

"That's the spirit," Eve said with a bright smile as she hooked arms with her sister. "Oh, and by the way, the part that doesn't smell right about this is you. You stink. You smell like Ossi after it rains."

Eve pulled down on the hem of her wool jacket to readjust the structured garment. Smoothing it against her torso, she drew her orange-dyed leather pack over her head and let it settle across her body. The insignia of the Daniyelan Order, a flaming sword, was embossed on its flap. Pulling it open, she checked one the pockets sewn on the inside to see how many temple tokens she had left. Only three of the orange leather disks remained. They would have to requisition more before they left Wickcester.

Letting the flap fall closed, she rested her hand on the curved, long knife sitting on her hip and skipped down the temple's steps. Though she and Sheridan had arrived just after midday, the shadows had lengthened as the afternoon wore on and Tomas' orders had stressed the necessity for speed. After Eve had point out her sister's pungent aroma, Sheridan had insisted on bathing and changing her uniform, which left her the responsibility of booking their passage to Montdell. While the ride from last stop on their circuit, Cottonwood Bog, had tired Eve, she would gladly make the sacrifice of trekking down to the river docks if it meant that she could escape that smell.

The wheels of carts and the stepping of beasts of burden on the cobblestone streets of Wickcester created an odd, offbeat syncopation that caused Eve to slow down or speed up her gait in response. It took her three blocks to even notice that she was doing it. When she did notice, she pursed her lips irritated at herself and felt the familiar pang of grief before she started a quick march down the street away from the seaside wharf toward the riverside docks.

The peaks of the mountains rose like the spine of a great, moss covered, sleeping beast in front of her. Unlike Sheridan, Eve had never liked the mountains. Though they had been born in the mountainous southern land of Indolbergan, they had left home to train in the temples when they were five. Ever since, Eve had hated the sight of mountains, even these forested mountains filled her with a cold knot of dissatisfaction.

Her mind preoccupied with the mountain pass they would

have to travel through, Eve had fallen back into the odd dance-like gait created by the street's rhythm. Turning at the next alley, Eve felt the rhythm recede in the height of the corridor. Her boots splashing in the runoff from nearby roofs, she found herself on the riverside commercial district.

Bolstering herself from the discordant racket of the docks and the assault on her sense of smell, she read the signs of the businesses lining the boardwalk until she found the one she was looking for: House Evensong Trading & Supply.

Pushing the door open, a high bell tinkled at her entrance. The storefront's wide window let in plenty of the afternoon light and illuminated the tiled counter. A woman with mouse brown hair that silvered in streaks sat behind the counter meticulously filling out ledgers. At Eve's entrance, the woman looked up revealing scars from a burn that went from her temple down to her left ear.

Like Eve, she wore trousers, but instead of the military style jacket, this woman wore a red vest laced tightly over a collarless stripped shirt. Hanging loosely around her neck was a brown-and-red stripped kerchief. She set down her stylus and grinned.

"G'day, Sister. The name's Gladys. You'll need to speak into my good ear." She tapped her right, unscarred ear. "Got caught in a fire during the war and hasn't been the same since. Now, what brings you down to our fine docks today? Picking up cargo? Shipping it? Needing passage down to Finalaran or across the Sea to Kilrood?"

Eve smiled at the woman's good natured and fast-talking greeting and got straight to the point. "Well met, Gladys. I'm Evelyn Reid. My partner and I require passage to Montdell on the next boat heading that way."

"Up the Dalibor, eh?" Gladys said with a furrow of her weathered brow. Pulling her hand along her jaw, she got up and yanked another book off of a shelf and flipped it open. She leafed through its pages. Tapping her thumb on the counter, she skipped back and forth between two different pages nodding. "That's going to be tricky, Sister Reid. We just had a ship head up that way last week, the *River Rat*. We don't have anything else going that way for another three days. I'm sorry, I wish we could be of better service to the temples."

Eve pursed her lips, but forced herself to smile brightly. "You've been of great service, Gladys. It's just a shame you were unable to accommodate us.   And I assume none of your competitors have any boats heading to Montdell?"

"None, Sister," Gladys said shutting the book and sliding it back into its place on the shelf. "Very few captains are willing to make the run along that much of the border. The only reason our captains will go is because we can't afford to be cut off from our rail yards in Montdell. If you're able to wait a few days, we'd be more than happy to take you as far as you needed to go."

Eve traced the stylized design of a songbird on one of the tiles with her fingertip.   "I wish we could, but our orders are fairly urgent. We do have an alternative means of transport available to us, but my partner would be much happier if we didn't have to utilize that option."

"I know it's none of my business," Gladys said perching back on her stool as she leaned forward with an eager expression crinkling the skin around her eyes, "but what might it be?   If speed's what you're needing, going overland won't be any faster than waiting the three days for our next boat."

Being of a curious nature herself, Eve loved to see it in others. She smiled widely. "No intrusion at all, Gladys. My partner also trained with the Amserians."

Slapping her hand on the tile, Gladys made a noise of affirmative low in her throat. "Just as I figured, your partner's a popper. Well, why'd you even come looking for passage in the first place?"

Eve stopped tracing the design and brought her hand back to her wide belt. "Well, to tell you the truth, Gladys, I'd rather lose the three or four days of travel time than listen to my partner complain endlessly about having to pop my mare, Kimiko. I'll have to listen to her bellyaching about it for longer than the trip would last. For the sake of my peace and quiet, I'd rather take the boat. But orders are orders, so I'll just have to endure it."

Eve gave Gladys a martyred expression that made the older woman chuckle.

"I think we've all got someone like that in our lives, Sister

Reid. But should you decide it's too big a burden to bear, the offer still stands. We'll save room for you, should you need it."

Eve took Gladys' outstretched hand and shook it firmly. "My thanks, Gladys. May the Light brighten your days."

"Yours as well, Sister Reid. You stay safe," Gladys commanded as she picked up her stylus and returned to balancing her ledger as Eve left the storefront.

Slapping her open palm against the side of her thigh, Eve turned back the way she had come. She hadn't exaggerated about how much Sheridan disliked popping Kimiko, but they had no other choice. They couldn't afford to wait three days for another boat to depart. The longer they waited the colder the evidence would become.

It didn't take Eve long to reach the temple again and she headed straight for the personal quarters. They were much smaller than most of the local temples she was accustomed to, because Wickcester was just large enough to warrant a local installation of the Daniyelan Order. Entering the room where she had deposited their gear earlier, she saw Sheridan doubled over as she toweled her hair. When Sheridan heard Eve enter, she whipped her head back up splattering Eve with water droplets.

Eve cried in dismay and wiped off the water with her sleeves. "Ugh, Sheridan, don't do that!"

Sheridan combed her hair back with her fingers and made no attempt to disguise her amusement. "Sorry, Eve, didn't see you there."

"Lies," Eve said pointing at her sister in accusation, "you aimed for me. I saw you."

Sheridan shrugged her shoulders in mock ignorance. "Would I ever do that?"

"Would you like me to remind you of all the times when you have done exactly that?" Eve said with an arch of an eyebrow.

In response, Sheridan became very interested in rummaging through her gear, which she had spread out on her bed in meticulous rows. "Lies, slander, and vicious rumors," she said in her own defense. "By the way, when are we leaving? Please tell me in the morning, because I'm more than a little annoyed that Tomas is cutting into our leave. We just finished riding circuit and this was supposed to be our last stop before we got to rest for a few days."

Eve just folded her arms and leaned against the doorway. "We won't be leaving by boat any time soon."

"Really?" Sheridan said drawing out the word as she peeked under her arm at her sister.

"That's right. The only Merchant House running boats up to Montdell is Evensong and their last boat left last week and they don't have another charted for another three days."

Making room on the mattress for herself, Sheridan flopped down in a huff. She stared up at the stonework arch over the doorway following the seams of the masonry with her eyes. "So that means that I have to haul that beast of yours all the way to Montdell. Fantastic. Well, I demand that you bring me tea while I'm in bed recovering from moving that much mass at once and those delicious boysenberry scones from the baker at Montdell keep. That's my price."

"It's not like we have a choice about it, Sheridan," Eve said shaking her head at the predictability of her twin. "We have to get to Montdell as quickly as we can. This is the only way."

"I'm not disagreeing," Sheridan pointed out as she grabbed her brush and waved it at her sister before she started brushing her hair over her shoulder. "I'm merely pointing out that I'm going to have a headache as big as that beast of yours when we get there, which means I expect the proper accommodations to aid in my recuperation."

"I would expect nothing less, sister dear," Eve said with tolerant amusement. "But we don't have to leave tonight, we can wait until morning."

"Deal," Sheridan agreed tossing her brush on the mattress. "But first, I want to enjoy being in a civilized town, while we can. First order of business is checking out the market, then find somewhere that has good seafood, because I'm starving."

"You're always hungry, so that hardly counts, dear," Eve said reminding her sister of her stomach's absolute rule over her. "But I do request somewhere that has more than just seafood please."

"How can you hate seafood, when it's so very tasty? I just can't understand. I really can't, Eve." Sheridan shook her head with saddened pity at Eve as she stood and sighed at her uniform's jacket. "What I really wish is that I had another coat with me. It'd be nice to not have to watch what I say while we're in town."

"At least in uniform, I know I won't have to worry about fishing you out of the sea because you had too much wine." Eve watched her sister pick through the items on the bed and shove her finds into her leather side satchel. "Besides, it's not as if we're heading into the wilderness never to see civilization again. Montdell's twice the size of Wickcester, not to mention being the hub of the northern rail system."

Sheridan shrugged into the jacket and began hooking its brass buttons. "Okay, so I just want to see if I can find some new gloves. Mine were ruined by that toddler in Culgarth when he vomited all over them." Sheridan shuddered at the memory. "Children are just so dirty."

"Oh, come now, Sheridan. They aren't all that bad," Eve said with an affectionate smile as she pictured the round little boy. "He was a cute child."

"You say cute. I say plague-carrying, sticky-fingered dirt monsters," Sheridan said slapping Eve on the shoulder as she passed her to leave the room.

The market district of Wickcester sat on the eastern edge of the town providing a clear view of the Kurinean harbor. But the market sat far enough away that the telltale smells of its docks remained down wind. The goods and wares of competing shops spilled out in the street and those sellers who lacked the revenue to rent a storefront had carts set up against bare brick walls and blocked alleyways. The particular street that Sheridan sauntered down was too narrow for any carts to pass through, but a single rider could manage to squeeze through the crowd.

Though she did hope to find a pair of gloves to replace her ruined pair, she felt no need to hurry and enjoyed the beautiful craftsmanship of the clothes and shoes and weapons and trinkets on display throughout the market.

Stopping in front of the display window of one shop named "Bernard's Cogworks," she saw engraved fob watches in every metal imaginable with their covers open so customers could see the watches' dials. Some of the lids boasted intricate floral designs and some bold geometric patterns, while the dials varied from precisely inlaid shell to simple metal plates. Sheridan loved watches, their precision, their artistry, and, especially, their design. Everything about a watch was both artistic and functional.

Regardless of her desire, she had a watch still in good working order and she could not justify purchasing a new one no matter how exquisite its movements were. Pulling herself away from the temptation, she began searching the signs for a leatherworker's shop. She only managed to pass two more shops before an elderly woman at a cart called to her.

Though the woman's braided hair resembled highly polished silver, she stood straight without any assistance. Her skin was dusky and weathered as if scoured by the winds of the Rainier plains in Taronpia. Behind the cart covered in garish, clashing shawls, and jewelry of every kind imaginable, a young boy clung to her full, multicolored skirt. The woman captured Sheridan's gaze with her sparkling blue eyes.

"Good afternoon, Sister. May Ashalioris guide your way," she said with a throaty, musical voice. She swept her hand above the cart causing the rows of silver bracelets that ran halfway to her elbow to fall toward her wrist with a series of tinkling clinks. "Do you see anything you like?"

Shocked by the woman's eyes, Sheridan stepped closer to the cart and inspected its contents. "Well met, mistress, and may Tallior guard your tribe," she responded with the traditional Deoraghan greeting. Though Sheridan did not share their odd faith in a three-fold deity, she felt no need to disrespect their beliefs by greeting her in the name of the Light. "And which tribe might that be?"

"You know the ways of Lior's children," the woman said with a surprised smile as she put her hand to her forehead, then brought it to her lips. "That is rare amongst the Daniyelans and rarer still is one who would greet us in his name. I thank you, Sister. We are of the Eaststar tribe."

"The Eaststars," Sheridan said searching her memory, "your elder is Lennox Eaststar, isn't it?"

"My, you are full of surprises," the woman said with a laugh. "Lennox is indeed our elder."

Sheridan grinned pleased with herself at successfully remembering that detail as she continued to admire the jewelry on the cart. Her eyes kept returning to a silver ring. Thin lines of metal interwove like liquid in a complicated knot-work that stretched across the top of the band. The delicate complexity of the ring fascinated her. Picking it up, she traced its lines lightly with her pinky. As she followed its endless flow, the woman watched Sheridan and her eyes sparked with bright blue light for the briefest of moments. Her expression saddened.

Sheridan put the ring down and dug around the inside of her bag. "How much for the ring, mistress?"

The woman had already retrieved a tiny, carved sandalwood box from behind the cart and was nestling the ring inside. "I merely ask that you accept it, Sister. It is a gift."

Sheridan shook her head. "I couldn't possibly. You must let me pay you something."

She shut its lid with a soft click and put the box in Sheridan's hand. "You made an old woman feel less alone amongst the followers of the Light. This is my way of thanking you for your courtesy and kindness, young lady."

"It's too much," Sheridan protested trying to return her hand to her bag.

The woman caught it before it reached its destination and captured Sheridan's gaze again. "Though you don't seem the superstitious type, you wouldn't refuse a gift from the Deoraghan, would you?"

"You won't curse me if I refuse, will you?" Sheridan said half-joking, but something in the intensity of the woman's gaze made her feel like something was crawling across her skin.

"The stories are right in one sense," the woman said her voice turning serious. "When the Deoraghan offer a gift, it is for a reason. The only misfortune that falls on those who refuse the gift is that they lack the gift when they have need of it. Please, Sister, the ring is yours. I can give or sell it to no other. It is meant for you."

Sheridan nodded. When she withdrew her hand cradling the

box, the noises of the street flooded back. Bringing with it the voices of traders and customers engaged in commercial sparring as they circled one another each searching for the upper hand. With a start, she realized that she hadn't noticed the absence of the sound until it returned.

CHAPTER FIVE

Eve sat on the bench outside The Fattened Trout waiting for Sheridan. They had agreed to meet back here for dinner after six, but Sheridan was late – again. The bouncing rise and fall of someone playing a mandolin floated from a tavern further down the street. With her arms folded, her thumb tapped out a counter-rhythm to the music. As her mind wandered with the music, her senses extended and she traced the flows of the green glimmers of life that flared around her, from the smaller sparks of rodents and tabby cats to the larger flares of horses and people. But no matter how small or how large, they all contained that connecting green life.

When the music stopped, so did her thumb and she let the second sight fade away with a blink. Swiveling her head, she saw Sheridan weaving around a carriage that had stopped in the middle of the street to unload its occupants. Eve waved at her sister and Sheridan increased her gait, but never moved faster than a quick walk.

Finally reaching Eve, Sheridan collapsed onto the bench. "Sorry, it took me forever to find a pair that fit." As it to emphasize her point, she wiggled her long, thin fingers in front of Eve's face. Eve batted them away, which caused Sheridan to retaliate by poking her in the side.

"Stop it," Eve said with a hiss as she trapped her sister's hand. "Do try to have some sense of decorum."

"You started it," Sheridan told her with an innocent expression.

"Oh, I surely did not," Eve said standing up as she pulled Sheridan up with her, "but I will most definitely finish it tonight if you try anything else."

Sheridan's eyes flashed as she leaned in close to her sister. "I accept your challenge," she said then kissed her sister on the nose with a quick peck.

Eve couldn't stop herself from laughing at her audacious twin and linked her arm through Sheridan's as they entered the tavern. "You are impossible, you know that?"

"Why thank you, sister dear." Sheridan steered them toward the back of the open room where a set of wide windows overlooked the Kurinean harbor. They each took a seat at the end of a long table that ran the length of the windows where they could enjoy the view of the boats skimming across the water. They had only just sat down when a server came to take their orders and left as unobtrusively as he had appeared.

When they were alone again, Eve said, "So let me see these gloves that usurped our dinner plans. They better be marvelous."

Sheridan picked her bag up off the floor and removed a pair of caramel-colored lambskin gloves that she set on the table with a flourish. "They're like a buttery-soft second skin. Try them on."

Eve had already slid one on her hand and flexed her fingers and found her mobility only marginally restricted. "Oh, Sheridan, these are exquisite. I retract my earlier complaints. These are definitely worth delaying dinner, if not missing it entirely."

"Hey, now," Sheridan said raising her hand, "let's not talk like we're mad. Not even these pretties warrant missing a meal."

"Speaking of missing meals, did you notice how many of the cases we heard dealt with theft and more often than not stealing food?"

"It's been getting worse," Sheridan said losing all of her frivolity. "The number of cases has been increasing with every circuit we ride and not just regarding theft. Think about that smithy in the last town, Boris. I remember him from a couple circuits backs. He's a good man."

"I can't understand what could have driven a hard working, honest man like that to helping slavers," Eve said tracing the grain of the table with the tip of a finger.

"You saw the fear in his eyes, just like I did, Eve," Sheridan said as she wove some strands of her long hair into a tiny braid. "He didn't know what else to do. Barely anyone in town's been requiring his services and they're too isolated for him to travel to sell his good. His got that whole brood of seven kids. Keeping them fed has to be a fulltime occupation in and of itself."

"But that doesn't justify what he did," Eve said her voice holding a serious tone. "Nothing can justify helping slavers. I wouldn't even call them animals. Their kind shouldn't be allowed to exist."

"I'm not saying I think what he did was right," Sheridan said in a slow voice, "I'm just pointing out that his circumstances are tragic and are becoming disturbingly common. At this rate, half the towns are going to be under judgment."

At that moment, their server returned with white wine for Sheridan and cider for Eve as well as their dinners, which Sheridan descended on with a voracious appetite.

Flakes of halibut melted on Sheridan's tongue, leaving behind a smoky flavor. Only a few hours ago, the fish had been swimming in the Kurinean Sea blissfully unaware of the culinary fate that awaited him. She speared another mouthful and savored the taste.

"You know," she said, sucking on the tines of her fork, "it isn't decent to enjoy food this much."

"Well, not all of us are as fortunate as you in our ability to consume anything and everything that is placed before us, dear one." Eve took a small bite of her couscous and roasted vegetables. The slight searing of the vegetables gave a nice charcoaling, but kept them crisp.

"Eve, how can you be my twin," Sheridan asked in exasperation, "when you can't eat meat?"

"I was just wondering the opposite about you, you carnivore."

"This barely counts," Sheridan argued punctuating her statement with a stab of her fork in the air.

"Fish are animals too, Sheridan," Eve reminded her. "I'll stick to my grains and vegetables and fruits, I'll thank you."

"It's truly tragic, Eve, truly tragic," Sheridan said around the rim of her cup as she took a drink of her wine.

"Let's talk about something other than my inability to consume animal flesh. Have you confirmed that there's any truth to the rumor that Kaedman made Nessa an offer?"

"Well, I haven't made it that far north since he was installed as the Daniyelan representative on the council, but he's known Nessa as long as he's known us. He's always been fond of her, but I don't know."

"What do you mean?" Eve swirled the contents of her plate with her fork.

"I don't know. Kaedman just never seemed like the marrying type to me. You know how he is."

"Yeah, he's a bit single-minded in his service to the Orders."

"He wasn't always like that," Sheridan said with a resigned sigh. "That last year in the war changed him. But wouldn't Nessa have told you if he did? You two were always closer than we were."

Eve shrugged. "It seems that as she's gotten older, her cousins rank a bit lower on her priorities. I haven't received a letter in over a year."

"Well, I wouldn't mind having him in the family officially and I'm sure his mother's family will be thrilled."

"Which would be evidence against the rumor, if you ask me," Eve said raising her mug as she redirected the conversation away from the possibility of Kaedman joining their family.

"Too true. I think he would marry Ossi if he thought it would irritate his aunts and uncles," Sheridan suggested with a laugh.

After they finished dinner, the sisters strolled through the market together and Sheridan took Eve to the leatherworker who had made her gloves and to Bernard's Cogworks to show her a brass watch with tiny floral enameled embellishments. As the sun began to set, they returned to the Daniyelan temple to resupply and repack. After they had everything ready, the two women gladly sought their beds. Their day had begun before dawn that morning and this day should have ended their circuit. Instead of a fortnight of leave, their orders sent them back into the field with only this one night to rest.

Eve stared at the wall next to her bed, following the lines of the mortar's intersecting patterns and thought about their imminent departure for Montdell. Several years had passed since the last time she had seen Kaedman and this arrangement suited her just fine. She didn't dislike him; she even respected him. Few Daniyelans possessed his gifts and dedication. Despite this, she preferred to keep her distance from Kaedman Hawthorn and knots of anxiety clenched her shoulder muscles at the prospect of working with him.

Gentle snoring drifted from Sheridan's bed. Her twin was fast asleep. Eve had always envied Sheridan's talent for falling asleep regardless of the circumstances. Even when physically exhausted, Eve could never get her mind to slow down enough to fall asleep immediately. Tonight simply proved the rule.

Rolling onto her back, Eve tucked a hand under her head and closed her eyes. She knew that Sheridan shared none of her hesitance where it concerned Kaedman and instead of easing her worry, it increased it. The only reason for their summons to Montdell, that she could see, would be if the local Daniyelan representatives had been compromised, which meant Kaedman had been compromised. Sheridan would refuse to accept this conclusion and that could make everything more complicated.

Pushing aside her troublesome thoughts, Eve began counting her inhalations and exhalations until she lost track around three and sixty.

The next morning Eve woke to the sound of morning doves quarreling outside the window just as the sky glowed with the gentle rosiness of dawn. Untangling herself from the covers, she swung her feet over the edge of the bed and heard metal resonating against metal amidst the hooting of the doves on the windowsill.

"Morning, Eve," Sheridan said as she drew the top of her pack closed. "Your things are already packed except for your uniform, which I laid out over the chair for you. I'm taking my load down to Ossi before grabbing breakfast. So, if you get dressed now, I can take yours down with me."

With her long hair braided down her back, Sheridan looked impeccable in her clean and pressed uniform as she stood waiting for her sister's answer. Eve hated to think how long Sheridan had been awake to look so put together.

Rubbing the sleep from her eyes, Eve nodded, but said nothing as she stumbled over to her clothes. In only a few moments, she had changed. Still barefoot she stuffed her nightclothes into her pack and hefted it up for Sheridan to take.

Her own gear already in place, Sheridan looped her arms through the pack's straps and left the room.

"I'll be in the kitchens," she called from down the hall. With no other Daniyelans in the temporary quarters, they didn't have to worry about waking anyone who wished to sleep past the sunrise.

After pulling on her socks, Eve shoved her feet into her shiny boots and wiggled them up to her knees. Still feeling groggy, she shuffled her way to the bathing room with an odd sliding click of her boots on the stone floor. Washing her face with warm water, she felt the last vestiges of sleep melt away and thanked the Light for whichever engineer invented the piping that brought the water into the temple.

When she found her way to the kitchens, she discovered Sheridan perched on a counter with an apricot pastry in hand while she sipped something hot from a mug.

"There's a plate over there," Sheridan said licking off the liquid on her lips. She pointed with the mug to a heaping plate of steaming pastries on a thick wooden chopping block.

Eve grabbed a strawberry one and bit into it as she stole her sister's mug and took a swig off the dark, bitter liquid and made an unpleasant face. "Darkness, Sheridan, why didn't you warn me you hadn't cut it with milk?"

"Maybe because you took it before I could?" Sheridan said as she reclaimed her drink and drained it before Eve could take it back. "It's not my fault you're so impulsive, m'love."

Sticking out her tongue at her sister, Eve poured herself some cider. "So where do you plan on popping us in?"

"The local temple," Sheridan said around bits of pastry. "I know its courtyard the best. Because there is no way I'm going to be able to fit that beast of yours into the Amserian receiving room. Not to mention the fact that it's on the third floor. I can't imagine that horse being happy about going down the stairs."

"She has a name and it's not 'that beast,' Sheridan," Eve said annoyed. "You know that Kimiko isn't just a horse."

"So you keep telling me," Sheridan said wiping the crumbs from her hands as she held them away from herself.

"She's quite intelligent and she knows that you dislike her," Eve said after finishing the last of her cider. "She's just as much my partner as you are, you know."

"Great, I've hurt the beast's feelings." Sheridan hopped off the counter. "You know just because I'm popping us to Montdell does not mean you can equate me with a beast of burden."

"Why do I even bother?" Eve asked no one taking both of their mugs to the sinks where she left them to be cleaned later. "You don't even try to understand."

"Oh, c'mon, Eve," Sheridan said hugging her sister from behind, "you know, I'm just playing around with you. I know you're bonded to Kimiko."

"I think you're just jealous of my affection," Eve suggested with a smile.

Sheridan kissed Eve on the cheek with a loud smack. "Of course I am. Now let's get going. I'd like to get the heavy lifting done sooner rather than later."

Sheridan offered Eve her arm, which she took and they walked side by side to the stables where Ossi and Kimiko waited for them. Each animal had an array of packs and bags slung across their backs. Disengaging her arm, Eve stroked Kimiko's forehead and the horse whuffled blowing warm air onto her neck. At their approach Ossi sauntered toward Sheridan and started sniffing at her pockets.

Pushing back the llama's head, Sheridan scratched behind his ears in way of apology. "Sorry, boy, I bring you no offerings." Eve had her head resting against Kimiko's with her eyes closed, when Sheridan said, "We'll start light with Ossi first."

"Did you just imply that I'm fatter than your smelly pack animal?" Eve asked without opening her eyes.

"Absolutely," Sheridan agreed with a laugh as she stepped to Ossi's side and placed her hands on his neck and back. Her eyes glowed indigo and the light enveloped both her and the animal. With a pop that felt like the release of intense pressure, they disappeared.

Kimiko sidestepped shying away from the spot where Sheridan had stood. Smoothing down her mane, Eve whispered encouragements into her ear. Kimiko's large brown eyes looked at her in accusation as if she knew what was about to happen. With another pop, Sheridan returned.

"One down," Sheridan said her face already glistening with a sheen of sweat. "No chance that Kimiko will go without you this time?" Sheridan looked hopeful.

As if she had understood Sheridan's question, Kimiko bucked with a sharp whinny and bumped her head into Eve's shoulder.

"Stubborn, co-dependent beast," Sheridan said with an exasperated sigh. "You know, one day I might just pop you to the ice-filled tundra in the south and leave you."

"And you wonder why she doesn't trust you," Eve said turning her face that pressed against Kimiko's.

"I wouldn't actually do it," Sheridan said with a slight whine. "If I pass out, you better catch me. I do not want this uniform getting dirty. I just had Tanner press it last night."

"You know my reflexes are faster than yours, Sheridan," Eve said with a little smirk. "You won't even scuff your boots."

"I better not," Sheridan grumbled as she placed her palm on Kimiko's flank and Eve's shoulders.

With a descending pressure and a pop of purple light, a red brick courtyard replaced the carved stone stables of Wickcester. Kimiko danced in place shaking her mane in protest and just as Sheridan predicted she wobbled losing her balance. Eve slid her arm under her sister's shoulder just as she slumped sideways lacking the strength to hold her own weight.

Spotting several adolescents standing in the courtyard staring at them, Eve said her voice straining, "I could use a hand here. In your own time, gentlemen."

One of the taller boys in a seeker's orange tunic ran over and supported Sheridan's other side. "Apologies, Sister. We didn't expect Sister Sheridan back so quickly. She said she was hauling a lot from Wickcester, so we thought she'd pace herself."

"Sheridan's never been one to pace herself," she said with a laugh as they stepped sideways through the door that led into the temple. "What's your name, seeker?"

"Wiley, Sister," he said with a sheepish grin. "We've been expecting your arrival. We received word from Finalaran day before yesterday."

"It seems you knew we were coming before we did, Wiley." Eve repositioned her hold on Sheridan as they entered the personal quarters of the temple.

Unlike Wickcester, Montdell had seekers in their last years of training with the Daniyelans before their journeyman year, which both increased the number of rooms as well as their occupancy. A few heads peeked out from doorways at their arrival and Wiley steered her into an empty room.

Furnished in a similar fashion to the room they had just vacated in Wickcester, they deposited Sheridan into the bed closest to the door. With some effort, Eve pulled her boots off and covered her with the quilt folded at the foot of the bed to keep her from losing any more body heat.

"Could you get a cup of peppermint willowbark tea from the kitchens please, Wiley?" Eve asked as she sat on the edge of the bed. "And a couple grain-and-berry honey bars if they have some."

"Right away, Sister." Wiley left the room and she heard hushed and hurried voices as the other seekers questioned him about the newest arrivals as he walked down the hall, even amongst the Daniyelans someone gifted with purple magic was rare.

Her face shiny and pale, Sheridan's eyes fluttered open and she winced in pain. "So, we all made it in one piece?"

"We did," Eve said keeping her voice low, but it still wasn't low enough.

Sheridan pressed the palms of her hands into her eyes. "Is there any tea?"

"Not yet. I just sent Wiley to get some, but I think his fellows waylaid him as soon as he left the room. I don't know how long it'll be before he gets back. How much time do you need to rest before we can seek out the magistrate?"

"A week?" Sheridan suggested with a thin, but hopeful voice.

"Well, it's good to know that you're feeling good enough to jest," Eve said as she brushed Sheridan's hair back from her forehead. "Do you want me to check in with the magistrate while you recover?"

"No, I just need to eat something and get my head to stop pounding and we can go together."

Eve squeezed Sheridan's arm and stood. "I'll go rescue Wiley from his interrogators."

Sheridan murmured something unintelligible and pulled the quilt over her head. Poking her head out into the hallway, Eve saw Wiley balancing a nearly overflowing plate and two ceramic mugs as he walked as quickly as possible without spilling any of their contents. Eve met him part way and took the mugs. Thanking her, Wiley stabilized the plate and they reentered the room.

Setting down her mugs on the side table, Eve took the plate from the boy. "Could you let Silvia know that we've arrived, Wiley?" Eve prodded Sheridan with a finger and pulled off the quilt as she handed her sister one of the mugs. Sheridan sat up and scooted back against the headboard.

"I sent a seeker to notify her when I fetched the tea, Sister. But I'll go check on her progress," Wiley answered, but before he left he addressed Sheridan who sipped her tea. "Feeling better?"

"Thanks to you," Sheridan said with a little smile as she lifted the mug. The color had started to slowly return to her lips. "Now, go tell Silvia to get her creaky old bones down here already."

Wiley raised an eyebrow at Sheridan's familiar manner of address, bordering on disrespect, in her references to the chief Daniyelan representative in Montdell. "Not in so many words, Sister, but I'll deliver your request."

"Oh, you use my exact words, Wiley," Sheridan said in a cranky tone after she rested the mug against her leg. "If only for the chance to beat me bloody, she'll get here faster, the old bat."

Looking at Eve for either an explanation or a means of escape, Wiley stood unsure of what to do. Before Eve could explain her sister's demented sense of humor, a raspy voice interrupted. "You are a spoiled, insolent, child, Sheridan. Don't think these bones are too creaky to knock you silly."

"Sister Silvia," Wiley said his adolescent voice cracking as he jumped as if caught sneaking back in after curfew. "I was just coming to see you."

"Silvia, m'love," Sheridan said with a wide and infectious grin, "I missed you. You look ravishing as always. Is that new leg cherry? The carving is lovely."

"Oh, don't you try to sweet talk me, you viper," Silvia said leaning her weight on her walking cane. "You may have completed your journeyman circuit six years ago, but that doesn't mean I won't have you back out there mucking the stalls with the rest of the seekers."

"You know how I hate to disappoint you," Sheridan said with a resigned sigh, "but Tomas was fairly insistent on us getting to work as soon as possible."

At the mention of Tomas and their assignment, Silvia's brown eyes dropped and lost their hard edge. When she looked back up, she addressed the boy. "Wiley, go and see that Eve's horse is being taken care of properly. She always needs to be calmed down after being popped and I won't be calling in a Tereskan to take care of those wool brained compatriots of yours if they get their skulls kicked in."

Sheridan and Eve shared a quick look at Silvia's unspoken reaction and her dismissal of the seeker, but said nothing. With a nod to each woman, Wiley excused himself and left the room to attend to his tasks. Silvia hobbled over to the door and shut it before turning back to the twins.

Though in her sixties, Silvia's auburn hair had only recently begun to gray within the last few years. She had a strong, square jaw and had retained her athletic build despite her handicap. The loss of her right leg wasn't the only testament to a lifetime of service as a Daniyelan Sister that she bore. She carried the weight of experiences in her unyielding brown eyes.

Leaning against the door for support for a moment, Silvia turned back to the other women with a momentary look of regret and pain. "I missed you, girls," she said with a genuine smile as she pulled a chair next to the bed and sat down. "But, I can't let the seekers think anyone can get away with back talking me. Not even you, Sheridan. I have a reputation to protect and I worked hard to convince everyone I'm a heartless, old battle axe."

"But you are, Silvia," Sheridan said widening her eyes innocently. "At least that's what I keep telling everyone."

"You're lucky you just popped or I'd cuff your ears, you guttersnipe," Silvia said waving her cane within inches of Sheridan's face.

"I know." Sheridan smiled wickedly as she drained the last of her tea. "You'll just have to take comfort in the fact that I already feel like my head's trying to break apart without your help."

Eve had sat on the edge of Sheridan's bed when Silvia had shut the door. As she watched the older woman joking with her sister, the tension Silvia masked with the banter was clear. "Silvia, what's the matter?"

Silvia twisted her grip on the smooth, polished wood of her cane as she laid it across her lap. When she raised her gaze, the sympathy laid bare in her eyes startled Eve.

"Darkness," Sheridan breathed, seeing the same thing she grabbed Silvia's wrist, "Silvia, what happened?"

"Girls, when we all took our vows to the Orders, we knew that we may be called upon to do difficult, sometimes impossible things, to sacrifice ourselves a hundred different ways in the service of the Orders. But I cannot fathom why Tomas would ask this of you. I can't understand why he didn't send someone else — darkness, anyone else."

"By all that walks in the Light, Silvia, tell us what happened," Sheridan pleaded as Eve sat motionless barely breathing.

"By order of our Scion," Silvia said her voice harsher than normal, "you have been sent here to investigate the murder of Nessa Reid of House Fireglen and to bring her murderer to justice."

Though several hours had past since Silvia had left, Sheridan still sat curled up in the corner of her bed, her cheeks still moist with tears. Her fingers moved along the ridges and creases the quilt made, concentrating on the erratic patterns. Eve paced in front of the door, her back rigid. Her brown eyes simmered with a murderous gleam.

"You know, you're going to have to talk about it sometime," Sheridan said without looking up from the quilt.

"I'm fine."

"Right. So that's why you haven't stood still since Silvia told us that Nessa-"

"We have a job to do, Sheridan," Eve interrupted. "I shouldn't have to remind you of that. You heard Silvia, we knew we'd have to make sacrifices when we took our vows. We have a job to do."

Sheridan nodded as she watched her sister's endless pacing.

"What we know so far is that neither Daniyelan has been seen since the victim's body-"

"Nessa's," Sheridan stated firmly, but without anger.

"-was discovered, but some of the border guards confirmed that Brother Hawthorn left the night before the body was found and no one has seen him since. Additionally, no one knows why he left. Why would a Daniyelan on the council leave the city without informing someone? I don't like this. His departure the same night the victim was killed does not speak well for his innocence."

"His fiancé, Evelyn," Sheridan said with steel in her voice. "You heard what Silvia said. He made her an offer last month. She was our cousin and we've known him since we entered the Orders. He's the closest thing we have to a brother. Stop treating this like they're strangers."

Sheridan was cut off by the sound of someone knocking on their door.

"Enter," Eve called without turning to face her twin.

The wooden door creaked open and Silvia entered. "The arrangements have been made. Are you ready to see her body? It can always wait until tomorrow, if you would like to visit your aunt and uncle tonight."

Eve strode to Silvia's side. Easily half a head taller than the older woman, she met her gaze without any emotion. "Like you said, we have a job to do."

Sunlight spilled through the high, glazed window and pooled around the wheat-colored hair on the pillow. The young woman's face looked pale like a porcelain doll and her delicate hands lay folded on her chest. The absolute stillness of that chest was the only indication that she would never wake.

"She looks like she's sleeping," Sheridan said under her breath.

"We had the city's Tereskan, Martel, put the body in stasis, to keep it from deteriorating before we transported it to the temple," Silvia explained as she examined the two women standing with her. Sheridan's red-rimmed eyes clearly showed her grief, but Eve stood with her joints locked and a blank expression.

Sheridan walked over to the bed holding the woman and knelt beside her. Standing back, Eve crossed her arms and loosely gripped the sides of her torso, saying nothing. As Sheridan's eyes closed, a red mist covered them. Resting the palm of her hand on Nessa's forehead, Sheridan crouched motionless for several minutes. Her statuesque pose broke as she raised her hand a fraction above the woman's skin and began moving down her face. Her hand stopped its downward descent over her chest, and she flinched, jerking her hand away as if she had been scalded.

"Where was she originally found, Silvia?" The red lines faded from Sheridan's palm.

"The reports from her family said that her maid found her in her bed when she came to wake Nessa. But the odd thing was that there was barely any blood in her bed at all. After his examination, Martel determined she had been killed the night before."

Sheridan nodded and stood. "So she was killed elsewhere and the body brought back to her rooms. That's troubling."

"It means that her murderer had access to and familiarity with her family's townhouse," Eve said her fingernails digging into the fleshy sides of her stomach to keep herself from shouting who she thought the guilty party was. Sheridan needed to concentrate and Eve's accusations would destroy any hope she had of focusing on the task at hand.

Cracking her neck, Sheridan inhaled and rubbed her hands together, as the red tattoo reappeared on her palm and her eyes disappeared beneath a red haze. Placing both hands back over the spot that had caused her to recoil, she peeled back Nessa's blouse. Though the decomposition of the flesh had been arrested, the charred wound swirled with violent, warped energies.

At the shock of the contact, Sheridan reeled back and wretched on the stone floor. Although the sight had been hideous, she had seen and treated far worse as a young battlefield healer during the war. What had disoriented her though were the malevolent, twisted energies writhing within the wound, grasping at her, trying to consume her, as it had her cousin.

Eve rushed to her twin's side and, in an absent-minded gesture, brushed away some stray hairs that clung to her face with bits of vomit. "What did you see?"

Sheridan shook her head, her braids swinging. Eve put her arms around her sister's shoulders and helped her stand. Leaning on Eve for support, she took hold of a red vial from under her shirt. She plunged her free hand back into the angry, tangled energy of the charred gash.

The desire to empty her stomach rose within her again. Restraining the reaction, she clenched her teeth and reached through the barrier toward her goal. As she pressed against this unseen wall, the energies that Sheridan touched flared and dissipated.

After what seemed like hours, and yet only a few heartbeats, Sheridan reached it – Nessa's blood. Her fingers grazed the tepid liquid. Flashes of images assaulted Sheridan's mind, moving too fast for her to process. Yet, one final image seared itself into Sheridan's heart.

The world was tilted on its side and she could taste blood and smell burnt flesh. Moving away from her was a thin-faced man in Daniyelan battle dress. His dark amber eyes were empty, save for a sociopathic rage as he turned and ran up the cellar stairs.

Dragging her twin to the floor with her, Sheridan collapsed unable to support her own weight. Tears streamed down her cheeks and she whispered a name, "Kaedman."

Eve's fingers dug into Sheridan's shoulders at the name. "Did he?"

Sheridan interrupted by shaking her head, unable to speak. The cost of the information had nearly robbed her of consciousness. After a few moments, she answered. "I don't think so. But, he was the last," Sheridan breathed in slowly, "the last thing that Nessa saw."

Eve's eyes went flat and cold. "He had unrestricted access to the townhouse. He fled the night she was murdered. He was the last thing she saw. What other proof do you need?"

Sheridan closed her eyes and inhaled with a deliberate calm. "Find him. We can't know for certain what happened here unless we find him. You need to leave as soon as possible. He was last seen four days ago. He's got a significant lead on you and he knows how to stay lost if he doesn't want to be found. I'll stay and see what else I can uncover. The other missing Daniyelan, Gareth Burke, is still unaccounted for. Finding him may answer a lot of questions. Just don't jump to any conclusions. There are several possibilities to explain this evidence. I don't think Kaedman did this, Eve."

Eve ignored her sister's final statement and smiled with a restrained savagery. "The murderer will be brought to justice. Our cousin's death will not go unpunished."

Sheridan bit her lip. "I'll find you when I'm done here. He's a good man, Eve. Just remember that. I don't want to lose them both unless I have to."

CHAPTER SIX

Darkness surrounded Faela, no sound, no sight, just nothingness. She floated until a single noise vibrated through the emptiness. The splashing of running water broke through the darkness that trapped her. She could not suppress the now rushing water; it remained. Invited by the sound's incursion, more invaders crept into the vacant expanse.

A moist chill caressed her skin. She felt herself shivering. The featureless void began to waver and dissipate as light rose and fell filling the emptiness. She groaned. Her eyes fluttered and she squinted in the dim light.

A fire burned near the mouth of a cave, providing only a fickle glow. The rain hid anything beyond its entrance, which Faela had mistaken for a waterfall. Flexing her back muscles, pain shot through her head and side.

"Bad idea," she mumbled to herself as she slumped back, examining the damp ceiling of the cave.

"Faela, you're awake." The voice chirped at her from the direction of the fire.

"Noise bad." Faela slurred her words. "Noise, definitely bad."

Jair crouched at her side and pulled her coat up around her shoulders to lessen her shivering. "How're you feeling?"

"Everything hurts." She blinked, her eyes struggling to focus. "Jair? What time is it?"

"Late evening." Jair's eyes looked sunken and his skin sallow. "You've been out for a while."

"How many days?" Faela rubbed her temples in a vain attempt to alleviate the pressure that threatened to squish her head like an overripe fruit.

"Days? It's still the same day, Faela. You were out for a long time, but it's still the same day."

"That can't be right." She pushed herself into a sitting

position. Her head spun and she rocked forward into her knees. Jair put his hand at the small of her back to steady her. She rested a hand on his arm. "I'm all right. I'll be fine, but that can't be right."

"But it's true."

"No." She shook her head. Her hair cascaded over her knees veiling her face. "Healing something that severe should've put me out for days. It's not possible."

Jair shrugged. "Well, you weren't, but you do look awful."

Glaring through her fingers up at Jair, she grimaced. "You know just what to say to make a girl feel special."

"I do try." Jair smiled his cheeks dimpling. "But you seem to be feeling better."

"I'll feel better once I eat; I'm ravenous. Hand me my bag."

Jair leaned over, grabbed her pack, and passed it to Faela who drew it into her lap. Groping inside, she pulled out another green apple and a fresh shirt. She bit into the apple and held it in her mouth.

Shirt in hand and apple in mouth, she pointed. "Jair, turn around so I change," she commanded though the clarity of her speech was greatly impeded by the apple gripped between her teeth.

Sighing, Jair walked over to the fire and sat down, his long legs stretched out before him. "You take the fun out of everything."

Faela swallowed a bite of apple and set it on top of her bag. Sliding off her torn and muddied shirt, she winced. The fabric stuck as it pulled away from the wound at her side reopening the gash.

She sat for a moment, her forehead resting on her knees, while she slowed her breathing down to control the pain. Purple bruises discolored her shoulder and collarbones where the bandit had kicked her. They ached and throbbed with every breath. She blinked away the tears that had formed in her eyes. That had been a little too close.

Wiping the tears off her cheeks, Faela used the ruined shirt to staunch the bleeding and placed her palm over the wound. Her hand flashed red and the blood clotted forming a thin scab. Feeling woozy from even that minor amount of healing, she drew on the clean shirt.   To keep from reopening her injured side further, she held her right arm bent.

Picking up her apple, she took another bite. Some of the juice dribbled down her fingers. Her hair caught underneath the shirt, she pushed against the cool, lichen-encrusted wall so she could stand. On unsteady legs, she teetered to Kade's inert body.

"I'm decent, Jair," she informed the lanky man. She sank to the floor with an awkward half fall and knelt over Kade. She pulled back the blanket that covered him to examine the wound. Her fingertips pressed lightly on the skin around the puncture. It was hot to the touch and moist. The wound itself burned an angry red. Pushing back his dark, sweat-soaked hair, Faela rested her palm on his forehead. He felt like hot coals.

"He's been like this since I moved him," Jair said from the entrance. "What's wrong with him? I mean besides having a gaping hole in his chest."

"The wound's poisoned," she answered, "and he's running a high fever."

She chewed on her lip, thinking. The fever meant his body was doing most of the work for his recovery, which was good, but the poison concerned her. She had diluted its effect when she repaired his lung, but it would continue to feed the fever and the cold and musty conditions of a cave were not ideal surroundings for successful healing.

Examining the wound again, she prodded the area gently with her fingertips. At her touch, Kade sucked in too much air and coughed, his body seizing. Grabbing Faela's hand, his eyes opened and he rolled onto his side, spitting out blood.

"What'd you think you're doing?" His voice sounded raw. He tried to catch her gaze, but she looked away.

"Treating your wound," she replied with a snap. "What does it look like? Painting?"

Kade's face went from confusion to anger in a matter of seconds. "Where is he?"

"Where's who?" Faela asked returning to a steady and soothing tone, her hand still captured in his.

He grasped her hand, crushing her fingers together. "Where's the book?"

"I don't know what you mean. What book?" Her expression never registered the pain though her lips paled.

Kade's glazed eyes roamed until he located Jair who had crept toward the entrance of the cave. "You." His voice carried over the rain low and dangerous. "Where's my bag?"

Kade released Faela's hand and pushed himself off the gritty floor and advanced on Jair. Jair stood still, but his eyes darted around the cave as if searching for escape, but he found no relief, only jagged rocks and water and darkness stretching down behind them.

"Kade, sit down." Her voice commanded calmly, yet firmly.

Stumbling, Kade wheezed, but he pulled himself back onto his feet. Faela saw a line of blood trickle down his back.

"You're ripping your wound wide open, you idiot. You need to sit."

"The bag, mate. The one I hid under the pine, it had the temple tokens in it. It's gone and I know you took it." Kade collapsed against the side of the cave panting. His face was flushed and his eyes stared, unable to focus.

"Jair, do you know what he's raving about?" Faela hovered near the delirious man without touching him for fear of injuring him further. "If you do, by the blessed Light, please tell him. He's going to kill himself, if he doesn't sit back down."

"The logbook." Kade's speech slurred and he shook his head fighting to remain conscious. "The logbook in the bag, do you have it?"

Jair looked from Kade and back to Faela. Without a word, he walked over to his pack and removed a smaller satchel. On the flap was the emblem of a sword in flames. Approaching Kade, he offered him the orange leather bag.

"Jair," Faela asked her voice slow and even despite her rising panic, "why do you have an Daniyelan circuit kit?"

Jair studied his boots, his eyes avoiding Faela. He opened his mouth then closed it, as if reconsidering his answer. Rubbing the back of his neck, his shoulders slumped. He grabbed his coat before he walked out of the cave into the rain-filled night without an explanation.

Kade ripped open the clasp and pulled out a tattered leather book. He flipped through the pages and the frenzied alarm left his face. Closing his eyes, he allowed himself to sink down the wall of the cave.

"For the love of the Light," Faela whispered, terror overtaking her flat gray eyes, "I had to save a Daniyelan, didn't I?"

Lowering her head so that her hair veiled her face, she crawled back to her possessions and considered her options. Regardless of who this man was, she needed to treat his wounds and her own. By now, Jair probably had a raging headache, but nothing that required her immediate attention. He would be fine. At least she tried to convince herself that he would be fine. She pulled out her dagger from its boot sheath and started cutting her ruined shirt into strips for makeshift bandages. Distracted by her own anxiety, she abandoned the cloth after making only three and removed from her gear a cook pot and a small, blue-and-white-checkered, cloth packet.

Still drained and unable to move freely, she propped her shoulder against the wall and shambled her way to the mouth of the cave. Curtains of water poured down the sides of the entrance. Thrusting the pot under the water, it overflowed in a matter of moments and drenched her hand in the process. Before she could use any of the strips, she needed to boil and treat the dirty fabric.

Taking slow, methodical steps toward the fire, Faela flopped to the floor without any grace. She edged a flat rock half into the fire with her foot and set the pot on the rock. Untying the packet, she dumped the contents into the water her hands trembling. Exhausted from the effort, she breathed shallowly, but she forced herself to keep moving.

Returning to the tatters of her shirt, she picked up the dagger once more. With an aggressive cut, she sliced through the fabric with a tearing sound. When she set the strip on her overcoat, she noticed the rip where the bandit's sword had slashed through its thick fabric. One more thing to fix. This was going to be a long night.

His vision blurry with sleep, Kade blinked and rubbed his eye with the base of his palm. He breathed in deeply through his nose, which triggered a new coughing fit. It felt like someone sat on the right side of his chest. To relieve the rasping within his lungs, he tried to keep his breaths shallow.

His arms curled around himself, to lessen the pain, he brushed strips of cloth wrapped around his ribcage. Hints of lavender and a musky spice he had not smelled in years scented the bandages.

He heard scuffling noises and the aroma of crushed cinnamon drifted around him. Sitting cross-legged next to the fire, a familiar silhouette of a woman wearing a rancher's hat poked at the contents of a pot as the late morning sunlight streamed into the interior of the cave. His hand fumbled along the ground until he felt the corner of a leather book. He sighed in relief; it was safe.

To test his injuries, Kade moved slightly. When he failed to incur any immediate repercussions, he used his forearms to lift himself into a sitting position with a painful wheeze. As he picked up the book, a slip of parchment fell from its pages and into his lap.

Scrawled hastily on the paper was a note: *Finally got that hunting cabin. You know where to find me. — CDM*

He placed the scrap in a pocket sewn into the book's cover and set it down.

"Is that ready?" Kade croaked, his throat parched.

The person by the fire did not answer, just dished some porridge into a bowl and grabbed some tack bread. The figure stood and walked toward Kade with the food. Wavy reddish-gold hair flowed out from under her hat. Without a word, Faela handed the bowl and the bread to Kade, then sank to his side and began checking the entry wound at his back with a light touch. He felt tingling warmth on his skin. The wound seemed to itch.

Shoveling the porridge into his mouth with the bread, Kade's mind mulled over the events of the past few days. No matter how hard he tried to avoid it, his thoughts kept returning to the image of her silver eyes. He began to wonder if it had merely been a feverish delusion from the shock. He studied her in his peripheral vision, but the combination of her hair and hat effectively hid her eyes.

Faela circled from behind him. "Move your arms."

Kade raised an eyebrow, but complied. Faela loosened the bandages and laid her fingertips on the already closed gash. Red light flared from the vial hanging from her neck and pulsed from her palm up to her fingertips. Kade felt another tickling rush of heat.

Faela's body moved closer to his as she examined the injury. He could feel warmth radiating from her. Her proximity caused Kade's curiosity to seize control of him. He had to know if he had imagined it. Staring down at her, he made a decision.

"You seem to be over the worst of it." She replaced the bandages with the deft touch of competence, but its gentleness surprised him. "It's healing nicely. As soon as I'm sure the risk of infection has passed, you're on your own."

As she rocked forward onto her toes to leave, Kade seized her wrist stopping her. His gaze intent, he drew off her hat. Feral with terror, Faela's silver eyes stared back at him.

She pulled against his grip. "Let go."

"It wasn't a fever dream." His voice echoed in the cave as if lost in thought. "Darkness, you really are Gray." His hand dropped her wrist and slipped to his side.

Faela jerked her hat out of his grasp and yanked it back on, her heart drumming in her ears. "Figure that out all by yourself, did you?" Her voice was cold, but her body trembled. "And here I was under the impression that independent thinking was discouraged within the Daniyelans."

"You have a strange way of showing gratitude." Her biting words jolted Kade back into the present.

"Typical, self-righteous Daniyelan," Faela said almost to herself. "Did I ever ask for your help?"

"You would have died," he said with a definitive starkness. "That's not arrogance, sweetheart – that's fact."

"I had it under control." Faela's eyes bore a deep pain as she rose to her feet to leave. As she stood, the ground seemed to move beneath her. A rush of heat washed over her, leaving behind an icy chill in its wake. Her stomach tightened and she gagged, just barely holding back her breakfast. Her vision narrowed as she watched the ceiling move further away. Knees buckling, she collapsed into a heap.

Kade shoved himself off the ground and hobbled to Faela's crumpled body. Stooping, he swept back her hair that had fallen sprawled across her pallid face. She had livid bruises along her jaw and collarbones and her skin burned to the touch and left his hand wet. Her limbs twitched as she shivered.

Looking around, he noticed a nest of blankets and lifted Faela off the ground. He cradled her against his chest. She was lighter than he expected and small in his arms like a child. Careful not to jar her, he set her down. His breath wheezed with an odd hiss from the effort.

Her eyes flickered and she writhed against the blankets. Her shirt scrunched up revealing the bruised, untreated gash in her side. The edges of the wound burned red with the same poison his had.

Kade searched the cave and located his water skin. Fumbling for the container, he grasped the strap and dragged it toward him. He picked up the tatters of his shirt and balled up an edge. Pouring water into the fabric, he began to dab the wound.

Faela gasped in pain regaining consciousness. She knocked his hand away. "Don't touch me," she commanded her eyes rolling back as she tried to recover control of her body.

Ignoring her, Kade captured her wrists, held them, and continued to clean the wound. "While I realize you're a woman," he tore the shirt into strips, "please try not to act so daft. You're a mess and if you refuse to do anything about it, I will."

"You don't need to do that."

"I don't want to make your injuries worse," he locked gazes with her, "but if you don't stop moving, I will be forced to hold you down. You're no good to me dead."

"I'm talking about the shirt, jackass," she said not bothering to hide her annoyance and anger. "There's a pile of bandages by the fire."

"Too late now," he said tearing another strip. "If you already have bandages prepared, why haven't you treated this? You've clearly the knowledge and skill. Are you really as stupid as you're acting?"

"I get it, you know. Why you want me alive." Faela's eyes narrowed. "What Daniyelan wouldn't want the prestige of bringing a mythical Gray under judgment? I get that, I do. But could you please spare me the condescending arrogance?"

"Darkness, you really aren't very bright." Kade released her wrists. "Think. Just think for a moment. Do I look like a Daniyelan on circuit?"

As he began wrapping the strips of cloth around her stomach, Faela stared up at him in belligerent silence. Kade tied off the strips with a tug and pulled down her shirt. He stood and without turning to look at her. "Just get some rest."

*   *   *

Clucking his tongue, Caleb kneed his stallion up the incline. Before he stepped up onto the loose shale shelf, his horse shook his black mane in protest.

"Hey now, Chance, we're keeping the ladies waiting behind us," he whispered into the stallion's twitching ear. "You don't want to get shown up by Rani now do you?"

With an indignant whinny, Chance picked his way up the unstable hillside. Caleb chuckled and slapped his horse's neck affectionately.

"You vain beast," he said with a disbelieving snort.

"Just like his master," Talise voice drifted from beside him as her nimble mare, Rani, passed them hugging close to the cliffs. "We still heading the right way?"

"Yeah," Caleb said increasing the pressure of his knees to make sure Chance stayed ahead of Rani. "But you saw the remains of that camp. He's not traveling alone any more."

"Worried things'll get complicated?"

"Nothing stays simple, babe. You know that."

"I can always dream," she said with a wink as she bent low over Rani's neck and whispered something, which caused the mare to gather her muscles and surge up the incline past Chance.

"Oh, no you don't," Caleb said to himself, because Talise had already cantered out of earshot and had nearly crested the top of the ridge.

With a sharp squeeze of encouragement, Chance bolted up the hill sending chips of stones and dirt tumbling behind him.

Though Rani had more agility than Chance, she could never hope to match his strength or endurance and he overtook her easily. Talise sat motionless as Rani pranced back and forth in agitation at the top of the ridge.

When Caleb pulled Chance up next to her, he said, "You cheated." When Talise did not respond to his accusation, his gaze swept the cliffs and surrounding forest. "What is it?"

Talise pointed ahead of them where the cliffs turned to the right. "Can't you smell it? It's coming from over there."

Closing his eyes, Caleb felt the slight breeze drift across his face. The wind brought with it the hint of an odor, a vaguely sweet odor that he could never forget. With a curse, he pulled his kerchief off his head and untied it.

"Corpses up ahead," he said as he draped the kerchief across the bridge of his nose and knotted it behind his head with a harsh tug. Leaning forward, the metal of his rifle grazed his left knee as he lifted the gun free of the saddle and pointed its barrel toward the ground as he checked the chamber for cartridges. Satisfied that the magazine was full, he placed the rifle back in its holster.

Already having removed the black kerchief tied around her forearm, Talise yanked some of her curls as she pulled the black cloth down to settle it across her cheeks. Nodding to her, Caleb unholstered his revolver and pushed back its hammer with a click as they rode toward the bend. Though not overtly armed like her companion, who resembled a walking armory, Talise had more knives tucked out of sight than all of Caleb's weapons combined.

As they reached the bend they saw the first of the bodies and Caleb thanked the Light that Talise had alerted him before the stench hit them unprotected. Riding around the carnage, Caleb did a full circuit of the surrounding area before returning to her. He nodded in confirmation that they were alone and released the hammer before returning the revolver to his hip. Dismounting, Caleb thumped Chance on the flank to reassure him. Though surrounded by corpses, Chance stood calm and still as he waited for his rider. Like his rider, he was accustomed to the smells of death.

Stacked under some low brambles the bodies had been stripped of any possessions that were light enough to carry. Caleb knelt next to the pile. "All their easily accessible gear and money is gone. Someone was very thorough."

"Look at this, babe," Talise said pointing to the blood streaking the ground and the cliff face. Blood had pooled just under the cliff, but before it had dried, it had smeared. "Whoever this belongs to didn't stay here."

"Yeah, but look at how much blood there would have been," Caleb said crouching next to the spot. "That person couldn't have lasted long." As he tracked the direction of the blood, he noticed it went toward a series of caves further ahead. "Or at least couldn't have gone far. Not with an injury that cost that much blood."

"Do you think our boy was here?" Talise asked straightening to look over at the bodies.

Caleb nodded, brushing his fingers over the bloodstains. "Yeah, but he couldn't have done this by himself."

"You sure about that?" Talise asked with an arched eyebrow.

Caleb whistled sharply. His mount trotted toward the cliff face and bucked his head. With a grim smile hidden by his mask, Caleb pounded Chance's neck. "That one died by red magic."

Talise eyes brightened. "Looks like we just found out more about his little friend. Now things are getting interesting."

"It's more than that," Caleb said as he swung into the saddle. "Someone else who wasn't with those poor dead blighters caught up with our boy and his friend here."

"They said they weren't hiring anyone else to bring him in," Talise said her eyes and mood darkening as she vaulted to Rani's back. "Do we have competition?"

Shaking his head, Caleb turned Chance toward the caves. "Doesn't look like another hunter to me."

"So we have two mystery guests and we don't know if the boy survived this fight. The bounty did say that they wanted him alive, right?"

"Like I said, nothing stays simple."

*   *   *

Kade paged through the leather book, but the words were still the same regardless of how many times he read them. He tossed it on the ground. Leaning his head back on the wall of the cave some of the dirt showered his shoulders as he tapped his thumb against his arm and stared at the bright forest outside.

No one had ever described Kade as compliant and this forced inactivity had frayed his nerves to the point of snapping. As a direct result, he now sat alone listening to the dripping of water echoing from the depths of the cave.

After her collapse, Faela and Kade had reached an uneasy truce. As their injuries continued healing, they had little energy left over and most of the time Kade just slept. While awake though he continually fought the increasing urge to satisfy his curiosity about her, but she provided no openings. This morning over breakfast he decided to make one, which was why he now sat alone in the cave.

While his breathing had improved, his injury still throbbed and, now, felt agonizingly itchy. With the recovery of his bag, he had already mended the tears in his and Faela's overcoats to keep his hands busy, but he had finished that project yesterday, which left him alone waiting for Faela's temper to cool with nothing constructive to do.

He stopped drumming his thumb and grabbed his whetstone from his bag and tossed it straight up. Catching it out of the air, he removed his knife and started sliding the edge of the knife down the stone in short, quick strokes that only stopped when he flipped the blade to sharpen its opposite edge.

Lost in the rhythm of metal against stone, Kade's eyes shot to the entrance of the cave and he reversed his grip on the hilt so its edge faced out paralleling his forearm. Within the same heartbeat he crouched on the balls of his bare feet. He felt a stab of pain and his breath rattled in his chest from the sudden movement.

The intense light that streamed into the mouth of the cave created even darker shadows inside. Moving within the veil of those shadows, Kade inched toward the entrance and tucked his body against a hollow created by centuries of water erosion. It was shallow, but with the aid of the shadows and the brightness of the day, it should be enough.

He kept his knife arm relaxed and he waited. Though the intruders said nothing, Kade heard their approach and counted only two. He saw a large silhouette of a man pass in front of the cave at the furthest point from him.

He led with a revolver as he stepped into their camp. Backlight by the sun, his face was obscured, but beyond that hindrance he wore a black kerchief. He signaled over his shoulder and his companion entered close to Kade's hiding place. Gauging their movements, he knew he had to strike first if he were to have any chance against them in his current condition.

Without another thought, he struck. In a single movement he pinned the companion's arms to her sides with one arm and pressed the blade of the knife into her throat. "Who are you?" he asked in a flat, but commanding voice that compelled obedience.

His captive remained still; even her heartbeat remained calm and steady. Before Kade had uttered a word, the man across from him already had his gun leveled at his head, but Kade was no fool. He kept his captive's face positioned so it shielded his own, which proved complicated given her short stature.

"You okay, babe?" the man asked in a bored, even lazy tone muffled by the cloth, but his amber eyes burned.

"Never better," she answered with equal disinterest. "He's injured. Fairly severely if I'm any judge."

"Do you want help or just an audience?" he asked releasing the hammer of the revolver before holstering it.

"I always want an audience," she said with excitement as her wrists and ankles glowed with golden light.

Kade's eyes narrowed as he felt the build up of yellow magic in his captive. Only one person he had ever met used yellow magic offensively. Peering through her dark curls, he examined the man across from him and found what he sought. A long ragged scar peeked out from under the man's auburn hair. As he felt his captive's muscles gather, he knew it was too late to say anything that could stop her. Stepping to the side, he released her and tossed the knife to the ground. The metal sparked as it hit the rocks.

Holding his palms at chest level, he prepared for her attack. The woman pivoted on her closer foot like a dancer and launched into a twirl that whipped that leg up and around in a golden arc that would have shattered his jaw had it connected, but it didn't.

Kade diverted the impact with his forearm as he swerved back, but the momentum still jarred his shoulder and knocked him into the wall of the cave with surprising force given her size.

Shaking his head to clear the spots blinking in front of his eyes, Kade let himself slump to the ground and said with a whistling hiss, "Hail, Talise. It's been awhile."

Tugging the cloth off his face, Caleb said, "Hawthorn? Thrice-damned darkness, what're you doing here, mate?"

"At the moment, bleeding on the ground. You?" Kade asked with a pained grin as he rubbed his chest. "Darkness, Talise, remind me not to pick a fight with you again."

"Oh, Lior forgive me," Talise said dropping to his side. "I didn't realize it was you, Kade."

"That was pretty much my intention." Kade coughed, but luckily there was no blood this time. He hadn't damaged Faela's repairs. He silently thanked the Light for small mercies. He didn't want to face her wrath after wrecking what she had mended.

"Damn, you look like death," Caleb said. "What happened?"

"I ran into some bandits, then your wife there tried to decapitate me. Got sloppy, that's all."

Caleb whistled. "You must've. I thought I taught you better than that. Now you're making me look bad in front of my woman."

"I think we came across the remains of your friends a little while back," Talise said with a fiendish smile. "But don't listen to a word he says. He doesn't need your help to look foolish. He does just fine on his own. Don't you, babe?"

Caleb struck an indignant pose. "Do you see how I am thus abused? I don't know why I put up with you, you Deoraghan wench."

"I'd remind you," she said smiling with a pure sweetness, "but we've company."

"Talise, I'm shocked and appalled at your lewd behavior."

"That's not what you said last night."

Accustomed to their banter, Kade ignored it. "When did you get my message?"

"Message?" Caleb asked crouching in front of Kade. "Who'd you leave it with?"

"At your cabin, I left it at your cabin." His head still felt fuzzy. "I was just there last week." His palms flat against the floor, Kade scooted himself up into a sitting position. "You didn't get my message?"

Talise shook her head and tucked some of Kade's hair behind his ear in a maternal gesture. "It's been weeks since we've been back to the cabin, love."

"Then why'd you come looking for me?" Kade still looked confused.

"I think you addled his head a bit, imp," Caleb said with a chuckle watching Kade's eyes lose focus for a moment. "We weren't looking for you, mate. We're on a job."

At those words, Kade's eyes darkened, though his posture remained relaxed. From their first meeting in the clearing, Kade had known Faela was running from something, but the thought that someone wanted Faela enough to hire Caleb and Talise Murphy sparked a flash of anger in him.

While he did believe that she would have died without his help, he knew with just as much certainty that he would have died without hers. She could have left him. After his discovery of her secret, all instincts of self-preservation should have forced her to leave, but she hadn't. She had stayed. He was grateful to Faela for saving his life, but this protective reaction troubled him.

Caleb didn't miss his reaction either. "Who's our bounty to you, Kade?"

"It doesn't matter." Kade tried to shake the unease in his stomach. "I won't get in your way." But the words sounded flat even to him.

Talise and Caleb shared a look, but chose to take Kade at his word. He was not a man easily swayed. Once he had chosen a course, he rarely deviated.

"Why aren't you in Montdell, love?" Talise asked in concern. "What was so important that you went to the cabin?"

Kade didn't bother to mask the tortured ache reflected in his eyes. "I need your help."

CHAPTER SEVEN

Water engulfed Faela's head, blurring the world around her into muddled swathes of color. The watery barrier dampened all sounds of life as if they were trying to reach her from the depth of a cavern. Lifting her face out of the clear stream, she whipped her hair back like an unrestrained animal, tossing water droplets in every direction. The liquid streamed down her back, soaking her, cooling her instantly.

When she had stormed out of the cave, she had given the excuse that she needed to get clean, but more than anything she needed space and she needed to think. She had spent the last few hours making her way up the vertical rock face to the east of the cave. The physical challenge had pushed all other distractions from her mind and she was able to focus. Once she made it to the top, she was drenched in sweat and her mind was clear. She knew what she had to do.

Below the cliff, she flopped down on the grassy bank and closed her eyes reveling in the breeze that chilled her skin as it dried the water. Her muscles burned pleasantly from the exertion of the climb. Almost feeling content, she hummed a bawdy tavern song she had learned from her brother as a little girl. When her father had caught her singing it, he had been furious. The void in her chest tightened at the thought of her father.

The melody dropped into a minor key and its tempo slowed as it carried her thoughts to Sammi. Since the attack, she had directed her energy toward healing, which left nothing for their daily visits. He squealed as she touched his mind with hers. She simply enfolded him in impressions of affection and love. *I'm sorry I've been gone so long, lamb.*

Sammi just babbled and showed her images of cats, and a stuffed lamb she had left him, and of Ianos sitting at a desk, the skin of his face drawn as he coughed. His thoughts turned warm and solid when he thought of Ianos. Faela smiled.

Sammi was very fond of her former teacher and mentor. Faela barred her concern at Ianos' appearance from her son and held his mind close and touched it with a farewell kiss. *Mama loves you, Sammi.*

Faela released the contact with regret. All she wanted was to float in her son's innocent joy and wonder about the kittens he had seen. She leaned over and stared at her hazy reflection in the water. Just as she could not escape her eyes, she could not escape her own memories.

Splashing the water to dispel the image, she stood. Faela had fought with herself all morning as her body fought with the cliff, but she had finally resolved her conflicted feelings. "Kade should be fine on his own now. It's time I left."

Faela slipped her clothes back on and tied her hair into a knot on top of her head. Walking back to the cave, she heard voices and saw two horses tied to a fallen log. One of the voices was Kade, while the others held familiar timbres. Faela circled around the horses until she could see within the cave without being seen herself. Kade sat propped against the wall as he gestured to a man and a woman both dressed in black whose backs faced her.

Kade spoke in rushed, low tones. "I don't know how deep it goes in the Order, but many feel it is the only solution to the chaos that followed the war. But the price they are willing to pay is too much."

The man in black cut off Kade. "You can stop skulking out there, girl."

Wary, Faela approached, her footfall had been light enough that the passing breeze should have masked it entirely.

The look of regret in Kade's eyes made her freeze.

"I'm sorry," was all he said.

Faela felt her lips go numb. Nikolais had found her.

"For what?" the man asked confused. "Who's the wench, Kade?"

The man turned toward Faela and she made a choking noise as her voice caught and she took an involuntary step backward, her eyes wide in horror. Caleb stared stupidly as if he had just been slapped, then stood clumsily and marched over to Faela who took another step back.

He grabbed her shoulders halting her retreat and shook her. "It's been a year, a year. Where in the nether-blasted depths of darkness have you been, Ella?"

Kade was on his feet to intervene, when Talise grabbed his elbow to stop him. He looked down to question her, but when he saw the tears glistening in the corners of her eyes, he felt more confused than before.

"Caleb?" Faela's voice sounded like a lost little girl. She stood frozen looking up at his furious face as silent tears streaked her cheeks.

Crushing her into a protective hug, Caleb rested his cheek on top of her hair. "Blessed Light, I was so worried, Ella."

Faela wrapped her hands around his waist and buried her face into his chest. Her voice muffled, she said, "I'm sorry, Caleb."

"Why didn't you find me? I don't care how bad it was, you know you can trust me. You know I would've taken care of it. Darkness, Ella, Nikolais has been out of his mind trying to find you. Ethan's all but given you up for dead. Where have you been?"

All of the shame and fear she had been carrying around bubbled up inside of her and she felt like her chest would burst. She put her hands on Caleb's shoulders and forced herself back. He let her go reluctantly. Unable to look at him, her eyes found the horses. "Caleb," she began.

Getting a good look at her for the first time, Caleb tilted her chin to the side and saw the deep bruises along her jaw, cheek, and collarbones. "Who did this?" he demanded in a quiet tone that caused the hairs on the back of her neck to prickle.

"Dead men," she answered with a fleeting rage that sparked in her eyes.

"Good," Caleb said brushing his thumb along the bruise on her jaw. "That's my girl."

Counting slowly, Faela tried to calm her racing heart and closed her eyes. When she opened them, she grabbed his hand, but the worry mixed with relief in his gaze caused her hands to quake. "I'm sorry, Caleb." She shook her head, alarm and dread warring inside her. "I can't. I just can't."

At that she dropped his hand and spun on her heels and ran.

The forest melted into a blur around her as she ran. The wind whipped against her face, pulling her hair out of its knot. Water dripped down her neck and between her shoulder blades.

Until she stood at the creek's bank staring into its water, she had not realized that her feet had taken her back there. She dropped to the grass and laid her head on her knees in defeat. Trapped in her own cyclical thoughts, she failed to hear Kade's approach. She never heard him approach.

"So, you're clearly not all right. So, I won't insult you by asking." He sat down beside her and left her silence untouched.

All the memories Faela had tried to keep buried had surfaced with the arrival of Caleb. Had it not been enough that every time she passed a reflective surface, her eyes reminded her of the line she had crossed? Now Kade, a near stranger, sat beside her in respectful silence, waiting to hear the sorrowful tale of how she had been wronged. Only Faela had not been wronged. Her own choices had caused it all and Caleb's sudden appearance would force her to make another choice.

"If you're waiting to hear some sob story, you'll be here awhile." Her eyes locked on her own reflection, willing away the man sitting next to her.

Kade only grunted and lay on his back, his head resting in his interlaced fingers. The silence descended between them again. Distracted, her hands dug at the clay of the bank and began shaping it. Soon she had a sizable lump that she formed and reformed, first into a star, then a dog, then a person, then a flower, then a lamb. Her sculpting failed to banish Kade's presence as she wrestled with her indecision.

Exasperated, she balled the clay and threw it at Kade taking care to hit him in the thigh far from any of his injuries. "Go away!"

Kade started in surprise at her assault and found her face flushed in anger and he laughed. "Aren't you a little old for temper tantrums?"

"Stop laughing."

"Or what? You'll take your lump of clay and go home?"

"No, or you'll tear open your injuries, you jackass. Don't give me that look. I know you have a good bit of talent for red magic.

You know better."

"You going to tell me what all that was about?" He stared up at her from his reclined position.

"No." Faela curled her knees back into her chest and rested her chin on its shelf.

Kade nodded. "You ready to go back?"

"No."

"Will you ever be?"

"No."

Faela rose to her feet, gray eyes starring back from the water condemning her. She spun to escape her reflection.

"Are we going back now?"

"Yes."

Through a break in the canopy of leaves, an eagle wheeled toward the cliffs above the mouth of the cave. Kade's eyes slid from the careless aerobatics of the aerial predator to his companion. Faela kept stride with him even though the rigidity of her back and the occasional tensing of her hands betrayed her hesitance to return to the cave where they had left Caleb and Talise. The thick silence between them had only deepened since leaving the brook.

His thoughts circled the questions presented by this woman like the eagle moving ever closer to the rocks. People had always been simple to Kade, their motivations straightforward. Instead of answering his questions, spending time with her just produced more. He had known Caleb since he was seventeen and this woman he stumbled across in the woods had some deep relation to him. A relationship Kade had known nothing about. This ignorance disturbed him.

As they reached the clearing in front of the cave, Caleb knelt holding Chance's hoof, dagger in hand as he cleaned his shoe. Relief spread across his face when he spotted Faela beside Kade. One-handed he returned the dagger to its sheath on his forearm. Taking a deep breath, Faela wrapped her arms around her ribs as she lifted her gaze from the ground to his face.

She broke the stalemate. "I know this is stating what is

beyond obvious, but we need to talk."

Stoic, Caleb nodded, but said nothing.

Kade cleared this throat. "I'm going to see if Talise needs any help." Neither acknowledged that they had heard him. They stood in silence as several minutes passed, each waiting for the other to begin.

"Before you ask where I've been, there are some things that you need to know." Faela watched the sun streaking through the leaves and took a deep breath. "First, you're an uncle, Caleb."

As Caleb shot up from his crouch, his volume rose with him. "I'm a what?" He had expected to hear some shocking things from his little sister to explain her disappearance, but this possibility had never crossed his mind.

Faela's mood shifted with her weight and she put her hands on her hips. "Will you try to keep your voice down?" Her gaze darted toward the cave, then back at her brother. "Yes. You're an uncle. I have a son. His name is Sammi, well Samuel."

Caleb blinked, recovering his voice. "When did this happen? *How* did this happen?"

"Do you really need to me to explain the how?" Faela quirked her lips to one side recovering her humor for a moment.

Caleb proceeded oblivious to her response. "Who's the father? Darkness, Ella, were you unfaithful to Nikolais? Is that why you left? Wait." Caleb's eyes widened and he looked from Faela to the cave.

"No, will you let me explain." Frustration started overtaking her remorse and guilt as her brother continued concocting his own version of events.

"Is Kade the father? Oh, I am going to beat him within an inch of his bloody life." With that Caleb started toward the cave.

Faela supported her voice with the full force of a performer's diaphragm. "Will you shut up and let me explain! Darkness, you are impossible sometimes, you know that? Sammi is Nikolais'." She said the last name with regret and no small amount of bitterness.

Crossing his arms across his chest, Caleb stopped. "If the boy is Nikolais' son, why did you disappear, Ella?"

Faela looked into her brother's bright eyes and knew she might risk everything if she told him the whole truth. He would eventually forgive her this creative truth telling. After it was done, she would explain all of it, just not today. She had made her decision.

"Not long after the wedding, I found out I was pregnant. Nikolais wouldn't let me return to the Tereskan temple in Kilrood. He felt that I should stay, now that I was the head of the House." She avoided mentioning their father's death and focused instead on her inheritance of his responsibilities. "But I just wanted to leave the management of the House affairs to Ethan or Deborah. You know that Father had been grooming them to take his place. He knew I couldn't renounce my vows to the Orders to run the House."

Faela then began to spin the next series of events as she spoke. "Regardless of whether I ran the House or not, I wanted to return to Kilrood to visit Ianos. I wasn't sure how my gifts would be affected by my pregnancy, since so few of mind healers live past childhood and since he practically raised me, Ianos is the closest thing to an expert that exists. The night I told Nikolais that I was leaving to consult with Ianos that was the night I realized what kind of man he really is."

Caleb's jaw tightened. His scar pulled his mouth into a grimace, but he said nothing.

Faela closed the distance between them as she rolled the sleeve of her shirt up to her shoulder. Rotating her arm out, she exposed the tender skin under the upper arm. Running its length almost down to her elbow was the shiny puckering of a long burn in the shape of a blade. "He shoved his dagger into the embers, grabbed me by the shoulder, and forced me onto my knees." Her voice lost its dancing cadence and slipped into a flat monotone. "He told me that I was his and would do as I was told. He took the dagger out of the fire, twisted my arm and held the blade to my skin. I can't remember for how long."

Faela skimmed the burn with her fingertips, then dropped her arm to her side and started unrolling the fabric. "He told me that now I could never forget that I was his and always would be."

Caleb's throat muscles strained and his hands flexed into fists as he absorbed his sister's story.

"I would have killed him where he stood. An aneurism is so easy, just the tiniest pressure to a vessel in his brain. Or let him hemorrhage internally, just a few slices to a couple key arteries in the abdomen. It would have been slow. It would have hurt." Her eyes glimmered the ghost of red as the corner of her mouth jumped into a smirk. Then she sighed, dispelling the haze.

"But I couldn't. I could feel his blood in my growing baby, but I would never allow him to touch my child. So, I ran. Ianos hid me until Sammi was born. Since then I've been leaving a trail leading Nikolais as far away from Sammi as I can. I couldn't contact you without the possibility of alerting Nikolais. He knows you're the first person I'd turn to you if I were in trouble. I'm sorry, Caleb. I couldn't risk it."

Dragging his hands down his face, Caleb sighed. "You sure can pick 'em."

Faela's lips pursed as she shook her head. "Thanks for that."

"Ella." Caleb waved a hand to the side cutting her off. "Just shut up, will you?"

She nodded mute as Caleb paced, his nostrils flaring. He drew one of the curved, long knives at the small of his back and started twirling it from hand to hand as he stalked. Sheathing the knife, he withdrew the two-handed sword slung across his back and preceded to turn the nearest tree into firewood with impressive efficiency and savagery. Exhaling with a burst of air, he stopped as abruptly as he had begun.

"Well, some things are starting to make sense now." Caleb sheathed the sword with a sliding hiss.

Faela's brows drew together in concern. "What things?"

"I had some suspicions. After you vanished, Nikolais hired several bounty hunters. No one at the House knows about it." He grinned, his scar twisting the expression into something predatory. "But hunters can gossip worse than washerwomen and I know a couple of these hunters by reputation.

"I didn't want to think the worst of the man you married, but when he hired them, Ella... Let's just say, they don't care how damaged the goods get as long as the goods make it back to the client. The more I looked into your disappearance, the guiltier Nikolais appeared. Do you know that he's running the House in your name? He's been claiming that you've been ill."

Covering her mouth with her fingers, she chewed on her bottom lip. She dropped her hand and shrugged. "I wish I could say I'm surprised. He got what he wanted."

"Ella, Ianos could have hidden you indefinitely. Darkness, he's the Scion of the Tereskan Order. Nikolais could never have gotten to you. " He trapped her silver eyes with his amber one. "It's because you're Gray. That's why you left."

She winced at the word. She had hoped that connection would elude him. It was a vain hope, she knew that, but that hadn't stopped her from hoping all the same.

"Yes."

"Damn, there hasn't been a Gray in living memory, Ella. I always thought they were just a metaphor for breaking the vows. You of all people know how dramatic and flowery Lusicans can be." His eyes alight, he snapped his fingers as he wove his own version of events. "You did something the night you left Nikolais that broke your vows and turned you Gray. And since you're Gray now, you can't come home without fear of being brought under judgment by the Daniyelans."

The band constricting her chest eased as he steered the conversation. For once grateful for his presumption, she left his assumptions uncorrected.

"So, if Grays actually exist, then you're looking for the Shrine."

"Give the boy a prize."

Affording Caleb and Faela some privacy, though his curiosity burned like a furnace, Kade walked the short distance to the cave and found Talise staring at her interlaced hands.

"Did you find Faela?" Talise bent forward, her chin resting in her cupped palm.

"Yeah." Kade gratefully set his aching head against the cool wall of the cave. As he slid to the floor, he watched Talise from under his dark eyelashes. "She's not your bounty is she?"

Talise looked up in surprise. "You thought she was our bounty?"

"Why else would you be looking for her?" Kade asked in an

attempt to get more information on the woman with whom he had been sharing this cave.

"By Lior, you mean you don't know?" Talise laughed her blue eyes causing the rest of her face to sparkle as well.

"Clearly, I don't," Kade said tossing a small pebble at the petite nomad.

"You mean to tell me that you fought side-by-side with Caleb for over a year in the war and he never once mentioned his little sister, Ella? I find that very hard to believe."

"Faela is Ella. Caleb's Ella?" Kade felt like someone had just punched him in the gut.

"I know that I'm stunning, but it's not polite to stare, love. I'm an old married woman after all."

"That woman," he pointed outside the cave, "that infuriating woman is Caleb's crazy little sister, Ella?"

Talise eyes darted to the entrance of the cave as if wanting to join the discussion in the clearing. "She's his sister in more ways than just blood, Kade, which it sounds like you've already figured out. Well, she's his half-sister technically, who incidentally has been missing for the last year. Speaking of which," Talise said her eyes flashing, "what are you doing here with her, my friend?"

Kade furrowed his brow. "I'm not sure there's anywhere I could hide, if you two wanted to find me. You couldn't find her?"

Talise shrugged. "It was like she fell off the world. Caleb went a little mad for awhile." Her eyes darkened as she tapped her fingers on her thigh remembering that time. "It's been a bad year."

That's when they heard Caleb's voice, trained to command the attention of soldiers in the chaos of battle or cut through an angry crowd of villagers, bellow in disbelief. "I'm a what?" Followed by the hurried rise and fall of Faela's voice.

"Oh dear." Talise pursed her lips and shook her head. "Knowing those two, this is going to get much worse before it gets better."

Just then they heard Faela yell. "Will you shut up and let me explain!"

Talise winced. "If you had any doubts that they're siblings, that should be proof enough. So how did you, my friend, end up here in this cave with my sister-in-law?"

As Faela and Caleb strolled into the cave, Kade noted that no trace remained of the tension that had gripped both of their bodies. Instead they walked inclined toward each other with an unconscious openness born of a lifetime of familiarity.

"Faela!" Talise sprang toward Faela as if to tackle her, but she seemed to expect this reaction from the slight nomad and braced her stance to absorb the impact. Faela returned the hug with enthusiasm. Talise pulled away and frowned when she registered Faela's eyes. "Well, that certainly explains a lot."

"Caleb can fill you in on the details later." Faela squeezed the older woman's hand in reassurance before she let go.

"Speaking of which," Caleb interjected, segueing the conversation, "are you two the only ones staying here?"

"Yeah," Kade answered automatically, "we are now."

"Now?" Caleb inquired with his arms folded across his chest.

Faela sat down amongst her nest of blankets. "It's a long story," she said with an exasperated chuckle.

"We have time," Caleb stated the levity gone from his voice.

As Faela, who had been trained by the Lusican Order as a performer, began to tell their story her temples shone with golden lines. Starting with how Kade and Jair ambushed her near Ravenscliffe, she finished with Jair's exit the day before yesterday. When her story ended, the yellow lines faded into her skin.

Talise had been watching Caleb the entire time having already heard Kade's version of events.

A look of accusation crossed Caleb's face and he reached over and punched Kade hard in the arm. "You darkness-blasted git, you're the one who erased Rafferty's trail. Do you know that you cost us four days? I couldn't figure out how it had vanished at that creek. If I didn't know better, I'd think that boy knew who to find to save his own skin."

Kade smiled. "You're the one who taught me how to track and how to hide my trail Caleb. What did you expect?"

"Against me," he muttered, "you're all against me."

Faela looked from Talise and back to Caleb. "You've been

hired to catch Jair?" she looked genuinely concerned. "I mean, I know he's a terrible thief, but what in the name of the Light could he have done to warrant someone dishing out the small fortune you two charge?"

"You know we can't tell you that, Faela," Talise said with a wink. "It's one of the many reasons we're worth that much coin."

"Do you know where he was heading when he left?" Caleb asked both of them, but specifically directed the question to Kade.

"I couldn't say," Kade said, "I was barely able to hold up my head when he left."

"Kade, I want to help you," Caleb said clearly torn between conflicting duties, "but I can't just run off with my bounty still out there. It might not seem as important, but our reputation is the foundation of our operation. I can't just abandon a contract. Do you think he'll come back?"

"Not if he values his life," Faela said with a snort. "Though he was unconscious during the fight, he did see Kade's handiwork. Anyone with any lick of sense wouldn't come back after getting on Kade's bad side twice."

"Well, I'm not comfortable leaving Faela here with those injuries," Talise interjected. "I think the first thing we need to do is get her back to the cabin so she can heal up before she continues on."

"Continues on?" Caleb asked his wife in confusion. "I'm not letting her out of my sight until we get this thing resolved."

"Babe, look at her eyes. She's been marked. You skulking over her as a bodyguard won't change what she is or where she has to go."

"It'll bloody well keep anyone from trying to drag her back to Finalaran," Caleb protested.

"Why can't she just stay with you?" Kade asked trying to subdue his excitement at finally getting answers.

"My guess," Talise said with a flash of blue in her eyes, "is she's searching for the Shrine."

"Caleb, how did you ever manage to land such an intelligent woman?" Chuckling, Faela shook her head at her brother.

Rubbing his chin, Caleb struck a dramatic pose. "My stunning good looks naturally."

"I'll say." Talise growled low in her throat.

"But the Shrine is just a story. It's a myth." Kade objected, focusing on Talise's earlier statement.

"You mean like someone being Gray?" Faela interrupted, the side of her mouth quirked up.

"Yes," Kade answered reflexively, "Well, no. But the Shrine isn't an real place any more, if it ever did exist. It was destroyed."

"That's not precisely true," Faela said chewing on her bottom lip.

"What isn't true?" a voice asked from the entrance of the cave.

All eyes turned to see a tall, thin boy standing in entrance with a goofy smile and a full pack that had various objects hanging off its sides. At his appearance, Kade burst out laughing and Faela buried her face in her hands and groaned.

Walking into the cave, Jair set down his goodies. "You going to introduce me to your friends, fairest Faela?"

Caleb stared incredulously as his bounty walked toward him holding his hand out. "Hail, friend, I'm Jair Rafferty."

Blinking Caleb looked at Kade and asked, "Is he serious?"

Jair looked confused. "What's wrong?"

"This is," Caleb said in disbelief. "This is so wrong."

Faela lifted her face out of her hands. "Jair, this is my brother, Caleb, and his wife, Talise."

"That's brilliant," Jair said with a grin. "So, you really do have a brother. That's reassuring. I mean I know you lied to Kade about going to visit him, but it's nice to know you actually do have a brother. The honor is mine, Caleb."

"Okay, now I'm starting to feel guilty," Caleb said to Faela. "Make him stop."

Faela sighed. "Jair, my brother is a bounty hunter."

"Well now, that's a bit intimidating," Jair said with a laugh. "But I promise that I have been nothing but honorable toward your sister."

"I'm not sure using her as a human shield counts as honorable," Kade pointed out with a wicked grin as he watched everything unfold.

"So that doesn't bother you?" Faela asked Jair. "That he's a bounty hunter?"

"Should it?" Jair said looking from Faela to Caleb.

"By Lior, this is painful to watch," Talise said standing up. "Jair Rafferty, you are bound by law. We're here to transport you back to Lanvirdis."

At that Jair's face paled. "Oh."

Jair sat staring at the swirling patterns made by the lichen clinging to the rocks of the cave as Caleb knelt tightening the slipknot around the boy's hands. With a tap of his fingers on the rope, Caleb's eyes flared orange and the rope glowed with a fiery light that faded like ash.

When he had finished, he brushed off his hands and stood. "Hawthorn, you know how you owe me for the rest of time?"

Kade lifted an eyebrow. "Rest of time, eh?"

"Your words, mate."

"Not precisely."

"Details." Caleb waved his hand to dismiss Kade's interruption. "Look, I think I figured out a way to complete your errand, but things have gotten a tad more complicated." His eyes settled on his sister's wavy hair. "I'm not at liberty to give you the details, but you remember Dwight and Mal?"

Kade nodded, his eyes gaining a wary light. "Nasty blighters."

"No doubt. Well, those two charmers have been contracted with Ella here as the target. I want to help you, but I can't leave her unless I know someone's watching her back that I trust won't betray us."

Kade knew how much Caleb had lost over the years and now that he knew Faela was his little sister, he couldn't imagine what would happen to him if he lost her too. He didn't intend to find out. He owed Caleb more than his life.

Locking Kade's eyes with his own, Caleb's disappeared under a fiery haze. "Keep her safe."

"You have my word." Kade stood and clasped Caleb's forearm. For the briefest of moments, cords of fire encircled their linked arms then faded.

"When I've finished, I'll come for her and you can go. There aren't that many left who I'd entrust this to."

Caleb's words summoned Kade's memories of the war and their friends who had never returned. He and Caleb had been the only two to make it home, so much had been sacrificed. Kade picked up the sienna leather-bound journal and thought, *Never again.*

He handed Caleb the logbook, which he tucked away before turning to the bound and dejected Jair. "You, mate, are worth no small amount of coins to me. I've fulfilled half of my contract on you, but I will complete the rest after I've finished this favor for Kade." Caleb looked over to Kade. "Oh, right, that's the rest of my price. I need you to hold on to him until we're done. We'll be able to move faster without having to haul him after us."

Jair's head shot up with a panicked look of dismay. "No, please. Don't leave me with him. I promise I won't make any trouble."

"Sorry, mate," Caleb said shaking his head, "but you won't be able to keep up with the pace I intend to set and I refuse to have you riding behind me and you sure as darkness won't be riding with my wife."

Caleb crouched down so that he was eye-level with Jair. "Now, I'm sure if you behave and don't try to run, you'll have nothing to worry about. My contract states that they want you back alive, but if you do try to run again, you should know that it was a little fuzzy regarding where the line is between dead and alive. Now I know that Kade will have no qualms with maiming you and judging by that smirk he's wearing, I think he's looking for an excuse. Are we clear?"

Jair nodded in hurried agreement. Talise tried to repress her giggles sharing a knowing look with Faela over his head, so as to not break the air of menace that Caleb had created.

"Good," Caleb said as he untied Jair's restraints and broke the simple binding spell he had cast with a puff of smoke. "Now, who's going to feed me before we're off?"

CHAPTER EIGHT

Steam from a stopping train billowed across the wide avenue as Kimiko wended her way around the busy traffic between the rail yard and the wharf. Wagons, single riders, carts, and foot traffic all congested the road moving goods and people between these two transportation hubs of Montdell. Eve would have preferred to find a less crowded area to begin her search, but the river would provide her with information much faster than any other means.

The pier echoed with hollow thuds under Kimiko's hooves as they rode past various riverboats and wooden cranes used to move heavy cargo between the wharf and the vessels. Eve didn't mind the smell of the docks. To her, the cool, sweet smell of the water felt alive, but she did mind the metallic aftertaste in the air from the rail yard.

Spotting a secluded edge along the pier, Eve pulled her horse to a stop and dismounted. She knelt down and leaned over the edge. The tips of her fingers broke the surface of the water. Her eyes flashed a bright emerald green and matching lines appeared across her nose and onto her cheeks. The green light raced down her arm and through her fingers. Eve's senses followed the light into the water.

Connected to the pulsating life of the river, she released her senses and raced through the water soaking in information at a rate she could hardly process on a conscious level. The interplay of life and death, growth and decay, surrounding her seeped into her bones, invigorating her, lending her its strength. She searched, searched for a single blaze of life. A faint wash of color caught her attention. Kaedman had crossed the Bramm at Davenford.

Eve withdrew her hand from the water. Her fingers dripping, a smile played on her lips. "Thank you for being my eyes and ears," she sent to the living beings of the river. She opened her almond shaped eyes as the green glow receded.

"It's only a matter of time, Kaedman."

*   *   *

The steamy vapors of Sheridan's tea made her cheeks feel damp as she inhaled its minty smell. Sitting cross-legged in an overstuffed chair with a brown-and-navy crosshatched pattern, she nestled into its high back and raised her eyes to Silvia who sat with her one good leg propped up on her desk.

Before she spoke, Sheridan took a sip of her drink. "This is going to take forever," she said tapping her finger on the rim of the mug. "You do realize that."

"That it is, girlie. I don't think Tomas expected Eve to tear out of here like darkness itself were chasing her." Silvia lifted a stack of papers and started leafing through them. "I'd say starting with the interviews would be the most effective use of your time."

Picking out one of the sheets, she waved it Sheridan. With a shimmer of purple, the paper was gone from Silvia's hand and rested in Sheridan's.

As she scanned the paper, Sheridan snorted. "This is going to take me all over the city. Silvia, I'm going to need help. Otherwise, this will take me over a month to investigate properly."

"Tough, I'm swamped with Hawthorn and Burke gone. Trying to keep these seekers in line and pick up the responsibilities of two other Daniyelans has stolen what little sleep I used to get and I'm not sure the council can really handle me normally, much less when I'm even crankier because I've had no sleep. There's a reason they have me herding the trainees, not on the council. I've never had the patience for politics."

"Have you called anyone anything scandalous yet?" Sheridan asked with a mischievous waggle of her eyebrows.

"Would you consider telling Lady Pratt that her name said it all scandalous?" Silvia asked folding her arms across her chest.

"Silvia, I think I love you," Sheridan said with a huge grin.

"I don't think that council ever thought they'd miss Hawthorn, but I don't think they realized how tactful he could be when he wanted."

"The key phrase there being 'when he wanted.' But I think I may have discovered a solution to both our problems, m'love."

Sheridan leaned forward. "The seekers here are all within a year or two of their journeyman circuit. They've received all the basic training from the temple that they need. They're just here to learn what locally stationed Daniyelans duties are and to help out with the simpler tasks and assignments.

"Let them shoulder more responsibility for the day-to-day tasks and let me steal one or two of the eldest to assist me in the investigation. The sooner we sort this all out, the sooner you won't be the only avowed Daniyelan stationed in Montdell and the sooner you can forget about the council. What'd you say?"

"Well, I'll say this for you, girlie, that mind of yours never quits," Silvia said in a grudging compliment. "I'm not sure I can spare more than one of the elder seekers for this plan to work, but I'll give you one of the least incompetent I've got. Use Wiley Kemp. The only reason he hasn't started his journeyman is because we're so shorthanded and he's been hovering nearby ever since you arrived this morning."

Sheridan finished the last of her tea and stood. "Well no use in dallying, I'll start here with any of the staff and seekers who last saw Kaedman and Gareth. Where do you think I'll find Wiley?"

"If I'm any judge he's in the hall right now," Silvia said pointing at the door with her dagger, which she had just used to break the wax seal on a letter.

With a twinkle in her eyes, Sheridan opened the door to find the young man walking quickly in the opposite direction away from Silvia's office.

"Oi, seeker Kemp," Sheridan called down the hall in a louder voice than necessary. His ears a bright red, Wiley stopped and turned around with a lopsided smile.

"Yes, Sister Sheridan?" Wiley asked jogging back toward her. "How can I assist you?"

"How indeed," Sheridan said with a wicked grin and a wink. "You and I, my fine fellow, are going to be spending quite a bit of time together."

*   *   *

Swaying in the saddle, Talise's eyes traced the lines of Caleb's back as her mind wandered. She would follow this man wherever her led, into darkness itself should it be required of her. That did not mean, however, that she would follow blindly. Nudging Rani's side lightly, she brought her mount to ride abreast with Chance.

"We've been riding hard for two days," she stated simply, keeping her eyes on the plains ahead. "There is a very short list of reasons why you'd delay collecting a bounty and doing a favor, even for Kade, isn't one of them, babe."

"We have to do this, Talise."

"And what exactly is this ominous 'this' that you're refusing to explain?"

"Not refusing," Caleb corrected, "just being discrete. I don't want Ella caught up in any of this."

"You could've told me after we left," Talise said inhaling the warm, flowery scent that rolled over the wide-open plains stretching out before them. Traveling across the plains always made Talise feel free. She hated the closed-in suffocation of towns and cities. She belonged out here.

"We're paying a little visit to the Scion of the Nikelans."

Talise arched an eyebrow, but gave no other visible reaction. "Great, prophets."

"It's happening again, Talise. This time he's after Kade." The laugh lines around Caleb's eyes seemed to tighten with the phantom pain of memories he would sooner forget. "Where else can we go?"

"So, you think he's responsible for what happened to Kade? You don't seem surprised by this."

"Should I be after Stantreath?"

"That wasn't your fault, babe," Talise reminded him once again. "Does Kade realize what's going on?"

Caleb thumped Chance's neck as if to reassure himself more than the beast. "You heard him. He asked me to take his logbook to Tomas."

Talise sighed. "Merciful Lior, he has no idea."

Caleb shook his head. "I'm not sure if the legends about the Nikelans can be trusted, but this is the first solid evidence we've gotten in nine years. We have to try."

"It's worth the risk, Caleb." Talise responded to his unspoken fears.

Rani and Chance's ears flickered and snorted uneasily as an unseen voice shrieked from behind them. The voice came from a thick grove of brambles that reached higher than a man's head. "No, Dathien! We need to be heading more to the southeast. What do you mean there's a briar patch in the way? I don't care if there's a wall in the way; we have to go southeast." The voice paused. "Well, make a path through then."

Caleb and Talise had stopped to listen to the one-sided argument and exchanged questioning grins at the disembodied voice's commands. When the voice didn't continue, Caleb chuckled. The tension of their previous conversation had broken.

"Besides, there's at least one thing to be happy about," Talise said as they started riding again.

"What's that?" Caleb asked with a sidelong glance at his wife.

"You don't have to worry about Faela any more. We know that she's alive."

"That doesn't mean I can stop worrying," Caleb said with a grimace.

*   *   *

Rattling over the cobblestones, the wagon rocked as its wheel splashed into a hole filled with muddy water. The muck splattered across the toe of Eve's boot. With a grimace, she looked down at her once clean brown boots and back up at the bar in front of her. The soot that caked its windows made seeing inside difficult at best, but one of the panes closest to her had shattered at some point. In this section of Davenford, she knew the cause could be anything as innocent as a stray elbow or as intentional as a patron's forehead. The glass had yet to be replaced, but did reveal some of the bar's deserted interior.

Turning she scraped her boot against the doorjamb. Eve's grimace transformed into a smile of anticipation. No matter how many times she had to visit dives like this in the course of her duties as a Daniyelan, the thrill still felt the same. Squaring her shoulders with the challenging hint of a smile, she swaggered into the bar.

The Broken Fork was a bar situated on the edge between the

legitimate business of the Davenford dockyards and its more legally creative ventures. It was still too early for the more legally precarious of the two, but not too early for Eve to get the information she needed.

Since arriving in port only a few hours ago, after a day stuck on a steamer, she had learned that the owner of The Broken Fork was a familiar contact of Kaedman's. Any time he passed through Davenford, Kaedman paid a visit to Abe to keep him honest. At least, that's what her last informant had told her.

It took her only a moment to adjust to the dim light of the bar given the overcast day outside. The tavern was empty. Gliding soundlessly across the warped floorboards, Eve passed the scattered tables covered with upended chairs and the long bar on her way to the door under the staircase.

She rapped on the door twice for courtesy as she pushed it open. Behind a desk covered in stacks of ledgers and papers, a man several years older than Eve sat holding a stylus. His cheek had a stain of ink across it and his fingers were splattered with dark, wet speckles.

The incongruous bookishness of the man was not startling because of his surroundings, but because of his disfigurement. His blonde hair was pulled back in a ponytail that revealed a puckering scar that started on his forehead and wrapped down and behind his left ear. On the hand that held the stylus, his last two fingers stopped abruptly at the first knuckle joint.

At the sound of her entry, the man looked up through his fingers as his head rested against his palm. The intense detachment of his gaze did not surprise her. She knew that look. It was the same look she had seen a thousand times from other veterans of the war. This man was a survivor.

"Can I help you, lawman?" he asked depositing his stylus into its holder. He settled back in his chair with a creak and folded his hands onto the desk.

"You're Abe Hancock," Eve said bluntly tugging off her gloves.

"That wasn't a question, Sister," Abe pointed out without breaking his gaze.

"No, it wasn't," she agreed as she tucked her gloves into her belt. "I have been charged by the Daniyelan Order to find someone and I need information. Information that I hear you have."

"No offense, but if half the rumors in this town were true then the magistrate would have nine mistresses and twice as many bastards." Abe leaned forward. "And I have it on good authority, that he only has three bastards."

Eve grinned and placed her hands on the desk as she leaned in toward Abe. Even with the scars, he was an attractive man. "Well then, let's dispense with the pleasantries. I need to know when the last time you saw Kaedman Hawthorn was."

At that name, Abe dropped his gaze and pushed back his chair. "I ain't got nothing to tell you then. Sorry you wasted your time."

Coming from behind the desk, Abe grabbed Eve by the elbow and led her out of his office. Though Eve was by no means a short woman, Abe still stood taller and broader than her. With his size advantage, Eve complied for the moment.

"You can find your information somewhere else," Abe said shoving her toward the door, "because you'll find nothing here. Good day, Sister."

He turned on his heel and marched back toward his office. Now that he had released her, Eve's eyes burned with orange fire and she flicked her wrist. Bands of flame encircled his chest making him halt. Walking around her captive with the deliberate click of her boots against the wood, she trailed a finger across his back beneath one of the flaming restraints until she stood in front of him.

"I'm sorry, ser, but that's not how this works," she said with an intent grin. "You don't get the option to refuse my questions." She held her hand out palm up in front of his face. Twirling her fingers in toward their center, a sphere of fire appeared in her hand, but it did not burn her. "Do you know what this is?"

Abe gave one curt nod. "Yes."

"Then you know what happens if you lie," she said her eyes matching the flames. "If you lie to me, this will burn you. If you tell me the truth, you will remain safe and unharmed. I have no wish to hurt you, Abe Hancock, but I need you to answer my questions. Will you answer them without this?"

"Lady, I don't plan on answering them even with your blasted spell," Abe said with an indolent glare. "I don't betray my friends."

Eve sighed as she perched on the nearest table. With another flick of her fingers, one of the restraints lifted and she grabbed his hand and thrust it into the fire. His hand remained unscathed. "We'll start with something easy for a baseline, because I'm fairly certain I already know the answer. How do you know Brother Kaedman Hawthorn of the Daniyelan Order?"

"I met Hawthorn during the war," Abe said with a snarl as he watched his one undamaged hand within the fire. "He saved my life more than once."

"How did you first meet?" she asked watching his eyes instead of the fire.

"He was a battlefield healer working with the Tereskans. He was just a kid, but war doesn't care about that. He patched me up after one of the Greenie's cavalry caught me with his saber, nearly sliced my head open."

"So you feel a sense of loyalty to him for that? For saving your life?" Eve asked her hand still encircling his wrist.

"Gratitude, yeah," Abe said indignantly. "But, no, not loyal. Any Tereskan could've patched me up. There was a girl working with him who could've done it, his partner. She was healing guys just as busted up as I was or worse. Cute little thing too, pretty long brown hair, big brown eyes, all arms and legs though. She never should've seen any of that." He narrowed his eyes as he looked at Eve. "Actually, she had a thin, turned up nose like yours. Looked a lot like you. Could've been your kid sister."

Though shocked, Eve's face remained impassive despite the shiver running down her spine. "What did her call her?"

"Dani, I think. Sweet kid."

Her throat dry, she swallowed, but continued her questioning. "If that's not the incident in which he saved your life, when was it?"

"A couple years later, he wasn't with the Tereskans any more. I think he said his training with them was over. He was a full blown, honest-to-goodness Daniyelan fighting in the war now. He was a good healer, but his real skill was in dealing out death. I don't ever want to be on the receiving end of that boy's wrath.

"I had been taken prisoner by the Virds after the battle at Goran Pass. Hawthorn's unit had been sent in to intercept us before we reached Lanvirdis. Apparently, someone important was in the train. He never told me; I never asked. All I know is that during the fight, the Virds started slitting prisoner's throats.

"I was about to buy it when Hawthorn, by himself, took out our guards. There were eleven of them. I owe him my life, Sister. You can burn my hand off if you want, but I have what's left of the other because of that boy."

Eve's eyes saddened. "I'm sorry, Abe, but this fire doesn't just burn you if you lie. You will tell me what I need to know."

Abe returned her gaze with cold hatred. "Don't do this."

"When did you last see, Kaedman Hawthorn?" The fire deepened from a light yellowish orange to a raging maelstrom. His jaw clenched, Abe remained silent. She could smell burning hair. "Answer the question, Abe Hancock," she commanded.

"Five days ago," he said panting. His eyes widened as the pain receded.

"Where was Kaedman Hawthorn heading?" she asked, a small glimmer of relief rushed through her as he answered her.

"East." Beads of sweat ran from his temples down to his jaw.

"Where to the east?" she said clarifying the scope of her question.

"He crossed here at Davenford heading into the forest in the foothills south of Ravenscliffe." His breathing came in quick bursts.

"What did he hope to find there?" She furrowed her brows unable to fathom Kaedman's motives.

Abe shook his head. "I don't know."

Closing her palm, she extinguished the flame and released his wrist. "Thank you for your cooperation, Abe Hancock." She hopped off the table and walked to the door. "I apologize for the inconvenience." Stopping over the threshold, she snapped her fingers and his bonds disappeared like ash.

"You're not her," Abe said in a raspy voice as she walked through the door.

Looking over her shoulder, she paused. "What do you mean?"

"His partner, the girl healer with Hawthorn, you look like her. Thought you might be her for a moment, but you're not. You're not her."

Eve said nothing, nor did she leave. She stood in the doorframe staring at this man. "Why do you say that?"

Abe laughed. "Because no one who stood by his side and saw what they saw together could be hunting him for the Daniyelans. Not with the way they worked together. No way."

Looking at the rise and fall of the warped wood of the floor, Eve pushed down the resentment flaring inside her. "You met my twin, Sheridan," she said as she spun and strode out in the damp afternoon.

*   *   *

The gentle breeze that had stirred that afternoon had been gaining strength. The air seemed electrified and the forest darkened as iron clouds crowded the shrinking sky. This promised to be a memorable storm.

Faela's worried her bottom lip between her teeth as she watched the clouds expand as they stacked higher into imposing thunderheads. Although they had left the cave several days before, their injuries had yet to fully heal. Watching Kade in her periphery, she noted that his complexion still appeared sallow and he coughed with a rattling wheeze from deep within his chest. Her own skin still felt cold and clammy from chills that she seemed unable to shake.

Searching her memory, Faela recalled the small town of Dalwend not too far to the northwest. She would have preferred to avoid any towns, especially Dalwend, but as if to make its point, the wind blew her hair across her face with a chilled gust.

She glared at the sky and considered their options. *If we go there, someone will recognize me. But instead of hiding, if I make my visit obvious, I can send Nikolais in the wrong direction for a while.* Satisfied with her solution, the corner of her mouth tugged up slightly. *And I know exactly who will help me.*

Tightening her grip on the strap of her pack, she bit her lip as she smirked. "Lads, we need to change our direction slightly."

Whistling an upbeat tune, Jair stopped and looked over at her. "How come?"

"With the severity of our injuries, Kade and I can't afford to be caught in this storm all night," Faela admitted grudgingly. "The chance of his lungs sickening again is too great to risk and I'm still susceptible to fever.

"Dalwend is within a couple of hours of us to the northwest. The town sits along the Auchneid River, but is fairly secluded otherwise. No matter what we decide we'll be caught in this rain and I'd like to find shelter and get warm food into us as soon as we can. There's a tavern there with the best spiced lamb stew in any country I've been to."

Kade snorted low in his throat. "Do you think it's wise given your situation to be in a populated area like that?"

"No, I don't," Faela conceded as she kicked a stone into a scrubby bush. "But frankly, I don't believe I have much of a choice. Any other options are unacceptable. We're in the middle of the plains. My rain shelter is barely big enough for two of us much less three and all the healing we've done in the past week will be pointless if we spend the night out unprotected from this storm. And I don't know about you two, but I could use a strong and hot mug of mulled wine right about now."

Kade chuckled at this as the first swollen splotches of rain darkened the ground and the wind began to howl.

The raging wind outside the Otter's Tale slammed the door shut. Faela shook her overcoat in a vain attempt to dislodge the water that had soaked into every bit of her that had been exposed to the elements. Her companions looked no better than she felt. Jair bore a striking resemblance to a cat that had accidentally fallen into a washbasin and Kade looked as though he would be drier if he had jumped into the river the tavern bordered.

Jair approached the bar and asked the young girl with black braids and full lips, "Miss, is there somewhere my companions and I could change into something that hasn't spent the better part of the evening being submerged in this deluge?"

The girl giggled. "Down the hall and to your left is an empty room. Feel free to use that." She bobbed her head then scurried into the kitchens.

"You first, Faela," Jair offered as he gave an awkward and yet somehow graceful bow.

Once they were all settled and dry, they gathered at a round table close to the hearth. Kade and Faela both pulled their chairs so that their backs faced the wall. Faela had tucked her hair up into her hat that sat low on her forehead.

"You ever go anywhere without that hat?" Jair asked as he lounged in the chair across from her. "Where'd you get it?"

"I've had it for quite some time. I realized quickly that people become more than a little anxious and suspicious if you're always hooded indoors. Makes them uneasy, as if you're trying to hide something."

Faela focused on the relief that she felt at being warm and dry. She knew that if she allowed herself to feel her anxiety at being around people, she would attract the attention she was attempting to avoid.

"'Cause we have nothing to hide," Kade remarked with a wry grin resting his arm across the back of his chair.

Faela smiled. "Sometimes hiding in plain view is more effective than skulking about."

A woman whose dark hair was held back by a bright green kerchief weaved through the tables and arrived at theirs. She had the same pouty lips and delicate bone structure as the girl Jair had spoken to earlier. "Can you believe this here storm?" she asked with a forced cheerfulness. Without waiting for an answer to her pleasantries she continued. "Something to warm ya?"

"Might there be any of your father's marvelous lamb stew?" Faela asked leaning into the edge of the table. "I can't remember the last time I got to eat a good stew."

"Course!" the girl responded with a slight indignation at the implication and peered at Facla with curiosity.

"Wonderful. We'll each have a bowl and a mug of mulled wine."

Faela placed several coins on the table and the girl scooped them off its surface and nodded. Where her sister had scurried back to the kitchen, she sauntered.

Kade leaned back in his chair with feigned indifference, yet he had already noted the position of every person of the sparsely populated the room. "In exchange for your brother's assistance, I agreed to guard you, but to do that I need to know where we're going and why."

"Well," Faela said as she interlaced her hands and rested them on the table, "once the storm passes we'll continue to head northeast."

"You are so enlightening," Kade interjected with a raised eyebrow. "The mystery is solved."

"If you would let me finish." Faela scolded him with mock indignation. Kade waved at her to continue. "Thank you. You may have figured out some of this, but let me fill in the gaps for you."

At this, Jair leaned forward with interest. Navigating around the tables their server returned with a laden tray. She placed the food and drinks on the table with a practiced efficiency and was on her way before they could express their thanks.

Faela wrapped her hands around her mug and inhaled deeply, allowing the rich and spicy aroma to settle in her lungs. Sipping the wine, she savored its bite as its fiery warmth spread in her belly.

When she looked up, Jair had nearly finished sopping the remains of his stew from the sides of the bowl.

Sheepish, he stopped with a hunk of stew-soaked bread in his mouth. "What?"

Faela grinned. "Not a thing, Jair. Nothing at all."

"So there was something about you closing a gap or something, Faela," Jair reminded her.

Searching the depths of her mug, Faela sighed. "Very few within the Orders know anything about the man I seek. His name is Gresham. The only reason I know about him is because my teacher chose to share this information with me. Due to the erratic nature of my gifts, I was under the direct apprenticeship of Ianos, the Scion of the Tereskan Order. I was sent to him while I was still very young and he oversaw my training."

At that moment, a man with dusky skin and raven black hair that had frosted at the temples approached the table. Peering down at Faela's hat, he asked, "Mistress Rafaela?"

At the sound of that name, Faela went rigid and forced herself to breathe evenly as she raised her head. "Nathan!" She sighed with relief. *Right on time, old friend.*

Kade and Jair exchanged puzzled glances.

"Let me get a look at you, girl." The man's grin encompassed his whole face. "Oh, I guess I shouldn't be so informal anymore."

Faela pushed her chair back and Nathan swept her into a bone-crushing hug.

His face grew somber and serious. "We were right sorry to hear about what happened to your father. Aren't many like him. The Merchant Houses won't see another of his kind for some time."

Walling away her emotions, Faela nodded once. "He is missed, Nathan."

"But from what I hear, House Evensong will remain just as strong with you leading now, Rafaela. But I swear I heard you've been ill for the last year?"

Faela covered her wince with a shrug. "Ethan and Nikolais are managing the House's affairs for me, but that is not information that leaves the House. I mean it, Nathan."

"Our tavern would be struggling to keep ourselves fed, never mind our customers, were we allied to a different House. I know where my loyalty is owed." His tone lightened. "'Sides, who would I tell?"

That's what I'm counting on. Faela snorted and smiled with genuine happiness. "Sure, Nathan."

"Oh, Nathan, these are my companions, Jair and Kade. We're headed to the western foothills to meet with some trappers."

Nathan nodded to each of them in turn. "Anyone in Mistress Rafaela's company is welcome at my hearth. May the Light shine on you, sers. But I'm needed in the kitchen. I just had to see for myself, because I knew it had to be you, Rafaela, when I saw those coins and my girl, Sara, described you."

He hugged Faela one final time and moved swiftly out of the room. Faela flopped back into her seat with an unreadable expression on her face.

"So, you're Rafaela Durante, the eldest daughter and heir to House Evensong." Kade had an amused smile on his face. "Your family has quite the reputation even outside the Merchant

Houses."

"Your name is Rafaela?" Jair's face froze in a look of confusion.

"Hush," Faela said her voice low, "keep your voices down. Many of the merchants and traders in Dalwend are allied with Evensong. Now, I trust Nathan, which is the only reason I used those coins, but I'd like to avoid that happening again."

Kade nodded. "Fair enough. Though, this does answer quite a few questions that Caleb refused to discuss over the years."

"Caleb uses his mother's name out of respect for our father. It's not well known that the Darius Durante had a bastard." Faela sighed. "We weren't exploring my lineage though." A haunted look ghosted across her face and was replaced by a look of resignation as she once more took up the tale. "Shortly after I violated my vows to the Orders," she said touching her temple with her fingers, "I went to Ianos for guidance and sanctuary."

Unable to continue for a moment, Faela took several slow sips of her wine. Kade licked the stew off of his fingers and leaned back with his mug in hand waiting for her to continue.

Blinking, Faela stared at the nicked table and resumed her tale. "It was then that he told me of a Tereskan named Gresham who was a redeemed Gray."

Kade's grip on his mug faltered for a fleeting moment before regaining his composure. "That's not possible. There would be records, confirmation that the legends are true."

"Would you say that what you see sitting across from you is impossible as well? I'm learning to regard that word as relative these days. Any way, Ianos also told me that Gresham knew the location of the Shrine of Shattering and that I must find it."

Faela's memories washed over her and the tavern retreated far from her mind. She closed her eyes trying to physically force away the pain they contained as she remembered the last time she had held her son in her arms.

"It exists?" Kade asked skeptically once his mind slowed enough for him to speak.

Wrenched away from her reminiscing, Faela stretched her legs, her heels scrapping across the wooden floor. "That is what I intend to find out. Unfortunately, there are several complications. Gresham has no set circuit that he rides, because he technically is no longer a Brother of the Tereskan Order."

"I suppose there isn't a way you could track him without his blood?" Kade inquired.

"This isn't common knowledge, even within the Tereskans, but almost like a chronicle of people, the Tereskan Scion maintains a vault containing vials of blood from anyone that has served in the Orders. I don't know its extent, how long it's been around, but Ianos did have Gresham's and he allowed me contact with his blood.

"However, I can only search for his signature at sunrise and part of him seems to have changed on a foundational level since the sample was taken. Because of this, I can't pinpoint his location. I only get a vague sense of direction. Before I was injured, I believe I was only a day or two behind him, but now I don't know. Now, you both know as much as I do about our destination."

"Wait. Hold on." Jair held up his hands up. "Let me get this straight."

Having presented them with an explanation straight from a Lusican's fanciful legend, Faela waited and braced herself for his inevitable disbelief.

"Your name is Rafaela?"

Despite the pain the conversation had dredged to the surface, Faela laughed at Jair's apparent fixation.

"Yes, Jair, that is the name my parents gave me."

"But, your name is Rafaela," Jair repeated again as if the repetition would somehow change its truth.

"Of all the things you just learned, this is the one you have trouble accepting?" Faela chuckled as she swallowed a mouthful of stew and sucked on the back of her spoon.

Kade sipped his wine and merely watched as he digested this new information. They were seeking a person who by all rights should not exist in the hopes of finding a mythic place from the oldest legends.

CHAPTER NINE

After having spent a dry and warm night at the Otter's Tale, the three had returned to the road well before the sun rose to make up for lost time. They had stopped at dawn for Faela to confirm that they still headed in the right direction and Gresham's pulse had turned further to the east, but still pointed unwaveringly north.

Though the storm had passed, the countryside bore evidence of its presence. The Auchneid River had flooded in several places leaving piles of debris in its wake. Limbs had been torn from trees and several smaller trees had been uprooted entirely.

As they walked in companionable silence along the muddy banks of the river, Faela began singing quietly under her breath. The faintest hint of golden light danced at her temples. As the simple melody rose, red light swept across her eyes. Jair bounced down the trail with a content smile on his face. As if a fresh breeze had blown back long-drawn curtains, Kade's lungs felt open and free. Faela's song seemed to draw each man's feelings into a mood of hopefulness.

"What are you singing, Faela?" Jair asked from behind her.

Faela shook her head as if to clear it. "Oh, I didn't even realize I was singing. It's just habit, sorry."

With the absence of the song, the morning seemed to dim and the ache in Kade's chest returned.

"Aw, I didn't want you to stop," Jair said crestfallen. "I wanted you to sing louder so I could hear the words."

Kade sniffed at Jair's complaint, but gave no voice to his own desire for Faela's song to continue. Instead, he settled into an easy stride at her side hoping the sensation would return.

Tucking her hair behind her left ear, Faela spotted a bend in the river. "We need to leave the river now and start following the road."

After several hours of continued hiking, Jair began to

complain. "Can we stop for lunch, please? I'm begging you, I'm going to starve."

Faela snickered at Jair's one obvious weakness. "We can in a little while, but we need to—"

Looking up to see why Faela had paused, Kade realized that Jair and Faela stood still and stared at the path ahead. On the path stood a young woman, not yet out of adolescence. She wore flowing midnight blue robes that puddled on the ground, hiding her feet beneath the swathes of fabric. The breeze blew her hair back in a dark wild mass of curls. Her small delicate jaw was set with strength and determination. Her most striking feature, however, was the contrast of her dark skin with her eyes, a startling blue that covered even the pupil and seemed to flicker like unbound fire.

The girl's voice drifted on the wind. "Hail travelers, I greet thee in the name of the Light." Suddenly, the girl went rigid and blue lines seared the back of her hands. Her light soprano resonated as it deepened weaving with the earthiness of an alto, the still depth of a tenor, and the thunderous vibration of a bass. It seemed to spin around the girl and race through the trees.

"Seven shall come to undo what was done.

From Shadow revealed, three destinies sealed.

Daughter of Night shall succumb to black sight.

He who guards Time out of Fire shall climb.

Son of the Earth shall hail her lost worth.

Speaker of Truth, guide to the three, trust in that which only you see.

Keeper of Truth, watch and protect, never dismiss all you suspect.

Twin branches extend, a choice here resolved,

Either shall end betrayed or absolved.

From death shall be life; the world formed anew.

A promise was made; redemption pursue."

As the final word faded from the air, she pointed to Faela. "You are the one that I seek." The girl took a step forward, got entangled in her robes, and fell flat on her face.

Faela, Jair, and Kade stood staring at the tangled heap of dark hair and blue robes lying on the road before them, unable to speak or even move.

A hideously high-pitched shriek came from the pile. "Dathien! Every time, every time, it doesn't seem to matter how much I plan, or how careful I am. It always happens," the girl muttered under her breath. She looked up her face scrunched in frustration. "Dathien, I tripped on my robes again."

A man of average height with dark hair and a ruddy complexion appeared on the road next to the pile. Placing a book back into his bag, he leaned on a staff, looked at the heap of fabric and smiled.

"Don't just stand there, Dathien." She pouted. "Help me."

Dathien grasped the girl's wrists, pulled her off of the ground, removed a twig that had gotten lodged into her thick hair, and kissed her on the forehead. The girl giggled and hugged the man.

Kade cleared his throat. "Based on that rather dramatic entrance, it seems safe to assume that you're a Nikelan. But might I inquire exactly who you are and why you're here?"

The girl looked back at the three travelers in surprise as though she had forgotten them. Looking at Faela, she asked, "Could you remove your hat please?"

"Why?" Kade and Jair asked at the same time.

"Humph, that's none of your business," the girl retorted. "If you could please, remove the hat."

Transfixed by the swirling of the girl's blue eyes, Faela's hand went to her hat and pulled it off, revealing her own eyes, the color of the moon.

The girl let out a whoop of joy. "I found her! We found her, Dathien! And you doubted me when I told you to go through that briar patch."

Dathien chuckled. "Mireya, love, before you do a celebratory dance, we should give them an explanation. They look more than a bit lost."

The girl waved the man away absently, too pleased with herself to notice the puzzlement on the travelers' faces. In the midst of her triumphal dance of joy, Mireya stopped, then looked back at Dathien. "Did I prophesy?"

Dathien nodded.

"Same as last time?"

"Word for word."

"Good." She plunked herself on the ground on a particularly soft and wet clump of moss. "You may proceed."

Turning back to the trio, Dathien shook his head. "You'll have to excuse her. She's always a little distracted after a prophecy. You may want to sit down, this is a little complicated."

Faela stumbled off the path and sank to the muddy ground, pulling her knees against her chest. She had not spoken a word since she had first laid eyes on Mireya. Jair walked over to Faela's side and leaned against a tree. Kade hovered at the edge of the cluster, neither joining nor removing himself as he assessed the situation.

"My name is Dathien Grier." The man introduced himself. "And you've already met my wife, Mireya. Mireya, as you, ser, already figured out, is a Nikelan oracle. For the last year, since the first time she spoke the prophecy you just heard, we has been searching for someone. From her exclamations, I would assume she has found what was calling her. Namely you, miss," he said addressing Faela.

"Why would she be drawn to her?" Kade pointed to Faela with his chin.

"That I cannot answer," Dathien crouched on the ground next to Mireya, who blithely twirled a violet with her fingertips.

"Wait a minute," Jair interjected, "you two are married? She's old enough to be married?"

"Common practice with Nikelan oracles and their Griers," Kade answered without thinking. "At least that's what the legends say."

Dathien smiled and nodded confirming Kade's explanation.

"Ooh, did you hear that, Dathien? We're legendary. I don't feel very legendary."

"So does that mean that the prophecy is about Faela?" Jair asked again.

"In part," Mireya chimed in, while still studying the flower. Discarding it, by throwing it over her shoulder, Mireya tilted forward, staring unabashedly at Faela. "So, your name is Faela."

Faela nodded without speaking.

Mireya sighed. "There are many things you need to know and

I'm sure you have a lot of questions. I'll explain as much as I can and if you're still confused, I'll try again. Dathien says that sometimes my explanations aren't actually explanations. Words and I don't really get along." Mireya looked at the clouds, her eyes glazed as if far away.

"Mireya," Dathien prompted.

"A year ago," she continued as if she had never stopped, "after the first time this prophecy came upon me, I felt the call to leave the Nikelan temple. And let me tell you, it is not fun to be minding your own business and bam! Suddenly, you're on the ground. I have a lot of weird bruises. So, Dathien and I left. We've been following that call ever since and it led us straight to you."

"Straight?" Dathien challenged.

Mireya scrunched up her nose and stuck out her tongue. "So maybe not exactly straight to you."

"I seem to remember a jaunt around the entire continent that included a couple bogs where we lost our cart, a run in with a bear, and that briar patch a couple days back."

"Did I or did I not get us here?" Mireya demanded, ignoring the presence of the three travelers.

Faela cleared her throat. "Why?"

Mireya blinked like an owl thrust into direct sunlight at Faela's query. "Why, what?"

"Why were you called to me?"

"Oh," Mireya responded brightly, "because you're the first Gray of the prophecy of course."

"Did you say the first Gray?" Jair assumed he had misheard the young oracle.

"Yes," she said, annoyed and turned to address Faela. "I'm here to help you find the Shrine of Shattering."

Kade tensed at her words, a shiver running across his skin. "That seems to be coming up a lot lately for a place that doesn't exist." His sardonic tone hid the hope growing in his heart.

Faela blocked her vindicated smile behind her arms. "You know where it is?"

"Well," Mireya evaded wringing the extra fabric of her sleeve in her hands, "not the precisely exact whereabouts, if you want to get technical."

"What?" Jair exclaimed. "Then how do you propose to lead Faela?"

"Well," Mireya hedged, squirming uncomfortably, "I've never done this before, so I'm not exactly sure. But I'm sure it'll come to me."

Kade's face clouded at Mireya's response and obvious lack of experience. Keeping his vow to Caleb was going to prove more complicated than he had imagined.

"All that I know is that I have to help you in any way I can." Mireya sighed. "As a Nikelan, the Light has sent me as your guide to help you down your path."

"Talk about the blindest leading the blind," Jair said under his breath as he saw something fly at his head. "Ow!" The offending projectile lay at his feet. Picking up the small slipper, he turned to the fuming Mireya. "Does this belong to you?"

"Look here, you, you tall person! I happen to be an oracle of the Light." Mireya's small hands clenched at her sides in fury. "Regardless of the fact that I might not understand the overall plan thingy, does not mean that I don't know what I'm doing. So there."

"Can't argue with that," Kade commented to no one in particular.

"Ishi bah!" Mireya blurted in frustration.

"I'm sorry, m'lady, was that gibberish?" Kade asked in a polite tone that would have put most diplomats to shame. "I must be rusty."

Mireya's teetered torn between attacking Kade with her other shoe and the desire to not fall over in the process.

Amused by the young woman's reaction, Faela smiled then felt a wash of pity for the girl. "Kade?"

He turned at the sound of his name and looked down at Faela. "Hmm?"

"I know it's your natural state of being, but do try not to be a jackass."

Kade looked at her through his dense eyelashes.

"Leave her alone."

He shrugged indifferently, but ceased his torment of the girl

"If you don't know where the Shrine is," Faela asked, "how are you going to help me?"

"I am here to advise you on your journey," Mireya's eyes glazed over as they lost their focus. "There are many choices ahead of you that will lead to different ends. For now, I am here as counsel. At least, until I start feeling nudges."

"Nudges?" Kade asked.

"Um, well, that's what I call them," Mireya responded. "Call them hunches if you want. They've never led me wrong."

"Just through briar patches," Dathien said with a crooked smile.

Mireya glared at her spouse with a look that spoke of promised retribution.

"If I start going off this path you're talking about," Faela suggested, "then you'll get a nudge?"

"That's one way of looking at it." Mireya scooted toward her, excited that someone seemed to be catching on.

Faela chewed on her bottom lip, processing all she had heard. "All right, you can come accompany us. We're heading north to find a redeemed Gray named Gresham."

"Excellent!" Mireya crowed with jubilation as she vaulted off the mucky ground to dance again.

Faela blinked at the gyrating girl in front of her.

Jair leaned over to Faela and whispered, "I mean, I know you're a good cook, but why's she that excited?"

Mireya whirled manically on Jair. "Because I know where we're going!"

"Yeah," said Jair, "she just told you — north."

"No, you ninny," Mireya said as if she addressed a particularly dull rock. "She's going in the right direction. I just got a nudge."

"You sure that wasn't Jair poking you?" Kade asked skeptical.

"I did no such thing!" Jair demanded, looking hurt at the accusation. "I would never invade the personal space of a lady."

"Just Faela's." Kade quipped.

"Well that's different." Jair fumbled.

"Are you implying that Faela isn't a lady?" Kade said, twisting Jair's words.

"Stop using my words against me," Jair protested helplessly.

"What do I need to do, Mireya?" Faela asked ignoring the men arguing over her head.

"Find this man. This is the start." The girl's eyes focused beyond the forest to a place few can see. "You still have far to travel."

*   *   *

More than a week had passed since Caleb and Talise had left the cave and, finally, they had arrived at the border of Vamorines. The moors of northern Nabos dropped away in a sheer cliff face down to the churning water below. A wooden and iron bridge ran across the deep chasm but disappeared into a shimmering wall of blue light, the Boundary.

Since the time of the Shattering, Vamorines had been protected by the Boundary. No one strayed into the lands occupied by the Nikelans without an invitation if they wanted to ever leave again.

"Subtle," Caleb observed the rippling blue curtain that plunged down to the roiling waters below.

"So," Talise said looking at Caleb and back at the Boundary, "I guess we just ride across?"

"Well, we aren't going to get there by sitting here any longer."

Neither spoke a word as they prodded their horses into a trot and rode into the magical barrier. Passing through, they found themselves enveloped and suspended in the blue light. They could no longer see or feel the bridge beneath their horses. They could no longer tell up from down. They had stopped moving.

A clear and firm female voice surrounded them, coming from every direction and yet from none. "Why have you crossed the Boundary into my domain? Only the foolish choose this path without cause. Speak."

"We seek an audience with Nikela's Oracle, the Scion of her Order."

In the pause, a lifetime passed or a heart beat only once for all they could tell lost within that light.

"What would you seek from me?" the voice finally asked.

Caleb fished Kade's log out of his bag attached to the saddle behind him and held it aloft.

"I request an audience to present to you evidence of an infection that is rotting the Daniyelan Order from within. The Brethren have returned."

The voice fell silent again and they both felt as if something unseen examined them and that if they failed to meet its standards they might find themselves trapped within this space between spaces forever.

"Be welcome, friends."

As the words faded, so did the shimmering mist around the bridge and they saw in the distance the ruins of a expansive white city that ended abruptly in a steep cliff that dropped into the sea. Half of the ruins lay submerged in water. Before them sprawled the broken skeleton of the ancient city, Gialdanis.

A gentle breeze, laced with the salty tang of the sea, glided through the cavernous room. The gossamer curtains billowed and shimmered like warm ocean waters. While glittering light swirled around the room, the afternoon sun fell across the white marble floor. Leather-bound volumes stitched together by hand, scrolls faded as if stained with tea, and disintegrating fragments protected within blue canvas sleeves hid the walls.

Small, round tables ran parallel to long tables that seemed more at home in an alehouse than a library. The chairs scattered around them like lost children clashed in wood and style, yet all were upholstered in some shade of blue. The blending of the scattered light with the blue and white accents made the room appear to float underwater.

Hunched over a battered table in the corner stood a slight, almost frail, woman with silver hair that swept past her knees. She wavered for a moment as if in pain. Tucked within the shadows of the shelves waited a man with hair the color of iron that fell down his back in a loose braid. His hooked nose gave the impression of a falcon as he waited. Straightening, the woman smoothed her hair away from her face with deft and precise movements.

"It's costing you more," the man stated, his upturned eyes hard, but not cold, "every prophecy is costing you more."

"Whose was it?" the woman asked, her voice regaining its gentle strength.

"Mireya's, the one she received before they left."

"Its resonance..." the woman trailed off as she shook her head as if denying something she refused to even acknowledge. Her eyes strayed past the open doors to the balcony.

Striding out to the balcony, the woman surveyed the cliff that plummeted hundreds of feet to the crashing waves below. Amongst the scattered rocks at the cliff's base were white stones with lines too regular to be natural. As her gaze moved further to the sea, the individual rocks began to resemble the vestiges of buildings. The rubble of these once white structures of immense size and scope were battered by waves as they had been for thousands of years.

The man shadowed her, but offered no empty words of comfort. He simply watched. Grasping the rail of the balcony, she soaked in the destruction that lay before her, a testament to beauty, to folly, a reminder and a warning.

"Though I am a bit older than when we first met, no prophecy has ever possessed such a terrifying resonance." Clasping the banister tighter, she continued. "Mireya is a vessel of great change." Her eyes flickered to the decimated city submersed in the ocean before her. "I can only pray that Lior will see fit to spare her, if only in some small fashion."

"Jha'na—"

"Don't, Vaughn. Please don't call me that right now."

Vaughn stepped behind the Nikelan Scion and enfolded her in his arms. "Rivka, you know who and what we are. We are servants of Lior, at his mercy. As you said, we are vessels."

"But Mireya is so young."

"And strong. You've seen the depth of her ability to channel and that was just the surface of what she's capable of. No ones can match her receptivity. No one that you nor I have ever seen."

"Her prophecy will change everything. The choices of the seven in that prophecy will either remake this world or shatter it."

Their eyes both strayed to the sculptures on top of the half-sunken palace. The crumbling remains of three men standing with their shoulders barely touching created a triangle. The first man held a harp, the second a flower, the third a downturned sword.

"You know that this did not start with Mireya's prophecy, Rivka. This working began more than twenty years ago with a very disturbed and very powerful little girl."

The hint of a smile touched her lips and she sighed. "I miss Ianos' dry humor, especially these days."

The slight patter of bare feet on stone echoed through the chamber behind the two and they turned at the noise. A girl, who could be no older than eight, with guileless blue eyes stepped onto the balcony. "Jha'na?" she asked.

Rivka knelt and called the girl over. "What is it, sweetling?"

"The man and the woman from the Boundary are nearing the temple." She scrunched up her nose in distaste. "They're wearing all black."

Rivka kissed the girl on her forehead. "Well then, let us greet them properly. Go, Lynn."

Lynn grinned revealing a missing tooth and scampered back into the library. Rivka stood gracefully and smoothed her dress. She caught Vaughn's eye. "Shall we?"

*   *   *

Rolling off of the river, the breeze carried the stench of rotting sewage and water-soaked timber into every corner of the harbor. Including the alley where Sheridan crouched over a decomposing corpse. The buildings hunched in close hiding them within their shadows. Behind her, Wiley kept his distance looking a little white around the lips. Unlike Wiley, Sheridan knew the ravages of death all too well.

A red mist covered her eyes. As her hand hovered an inch over the bloated body, it came to rest over a series of lacerations on his chest that appeared to have been cauterized. Rocking back on her heels, she rested her arms on her knees and stared at the corpse of Gareth Burke or what was left of him.

Over the last several days since Eve left, Sheridan and Wiley had interviewed anyone who had seen or been in contact with Kaedman Hawthorn or Gareth Burke the week before their disappearances. This had led them all over Montdell from hospitable visits at the offices of council members to following scullery maids around the Reid's townhouse. Everything they had discovered pointed to Kaedman fleeing the city, while Gareth had simply vanished. Her investigation had gone no further and the lack of real progress had already worn Sheridan's patience. She was no closer to understanding each man's involvement with Nessa Reid's murder than she had been the day she arrived.

When it had become clear that Gareth hadn't left the city, Wiley suggested they check with the city guard. In a trade city like Montdell, unclaimed bodies caused little fuss. This was the fifth smelly corner of Montdell and the fifth body they had examined this morning, but there was no doubt in Sheridan's mind that these were the remains of Gareth Burke.

"He's been dead for over a week," she concluded after a few minutes, the red light dispersing. "Whichever of your guardsmen guessed he was tortured had a keen eye, captain."

She waved a hand to indicate the burns, the crushed fingers, and the minuscule slashes. Standing up, Sheridan looked at the innocent clouds gliding by in the sky and heard the shrill whistle of a departing train. It made the grisly scene before her seem even more obscene. She wiped her hands on her trousers. Catching Wiley's eyes, she motioned to the entrance of the alley. He nodded and they moved out into the sunlight.

"The person who did this was a fairly powerful Tereskan," Sheridan said in a low voice, "with intimate knowledge of how to prolong a person's suffering."

"A Daniyelan as well?" Wiley conjectured. He breathed more easily now that he was out of the confines of the alley. "Most likely a veteran of the war?"

Sheridan nodded, tracing the inside of her elbow with her fingers in a calming gesture. "Well done. That seems the most probable answer. But what does this evidence point to, seeker Wiley?"

Glancing over his shoulder back at the body, his brows furrowed as he considered the options and possible scenarios in his mind. "Well, the combination of Tereskan and Daniyelan training along with a person who served in the war points to only one suspect who would have been in Montdell when he was killed. At least that we know of."

Wiley avoided answering the question as he shifted his weight from foot to foot.

Though it pained Sheridan, she prodded him to finish his line of reasoning. "And who would that suspect be?"

"Brother Kaedman Hawthorn," he said reluctantly. "He's the only resident of Montdell that I'm aware of who fits the evidence. But I can't imagine why Brother Hawthorn would have done this. Whoever did that was filled with a consuming rage. Brother Hawthorn was always so controlled. No matter how many pranks we pulled, he never got angry." Wiley's shoulders hunched forward as he tucked his hands into his pockets, clearly unhappy with his own conclusions. "Sister Silvia is another matter entirely."

The memory of her sister's voice reverberated inside Sheridan's mind. *People can change.*

"We're Daniyelans, Wiley," she said in a saddened voice. "We don't have the luxury of allowing our own wishes and desires to change the facts of an investigation. Though this evidence is not enough to convict Kaedman of Gareth's murder, it does implicate him and we can't ignore that." Sheridan slid an arm around the gawky adolescent's boney shoulders to comfort him as well as herself.

"Yes, Sister," Wiley mumbled looking down at his arms.

"But," she said as she squeezed him, "in your analysis of the evidence you touched on something vital. You were quite right when you said that whoever committed this crime did so out of intense passion and wrath. As you also said, Kaedman is a steady and calculating man. If indeed he did kill Gareth, we must ask ourselves something: What could Gareth Burke have done that would cause Kaedman to lose control like that?"

Wiley nodded as he chewed on the side of his thumb. "Well, he was engaged to Nessa Reid. What if she had decided to run away with Brother Gareth? Jealousy and infidelity can cause the most rational person to break and do things they would otherwise be incapable of. So he killed her, then tortured and killed Gareth?"

"Possibly," Sheridan conceded, "but I never said Kaedman is

incapable of such ferocity, simply that his temper is very tightly controlled."

"So betrayal could have been enough to push him over the edge," Wiley said dejected once more.

Clearing his throat, the captain interrupted their speculation. "Sister Reid? One of my men found this next to the body." He extended a slender piece of metal. It was a throwing knife with a leaf-shaped blade.

Sheridan took the knife and ran her finger across the crusted blood on its edge. Fragments of images flashed through her mind. The thin face of a man with sable hair stared back at her. All emotion, all feeling was drained from those hollow amber eyes that glowed with a fiery light. Grimacing, she turned it over in her hands.

"Sister?" the captain inquired at the glazed look, as the red flashed over her eyes momentarily.

"I'm sorry, captain. I just recognized the blade type, that's all."

The captain gave her a dubious expression, but kept his thoughts to himself as returned to his guardsmen.

"I had hoped I wouldn't have to resort to this," Sheridan said more to herself than Wiley.

"To what?" he asked as he looked at the blade she spun in her hand. "Did you see something?"

Sheridan nodded. "I saw Kaedman." She handed Wiley the throwing knife. "This is his. He has them specifically made by a smith in Wistholt. I have no doubts now that Kaedman Hawthorn killed Gareth Burke. What we need to know now is why. It's not my strongest gift, I'm a popper, not a stepper, but I don't see any other way of discovering what really happened here. I'm going to have to time-fold. We have to find where Nessa was killed."

*   *   *

Her mount's tail swung in time with the clicking of her hooves as Eve lead her toward a weather-stained stone building that skirted the edges of Aberley and overlooked the Bramm River. The reins lay limp in her half-closed hand; the white mare followed without needing guidance. The horse's even gait created a rhythm that seemed to flow through her body and her movements matched her graceful cadence. Each step rose and fell with a hypnotic fluidity, making no noise.

Once Eve had left Davenford, it hadn't taken her long to pick up Kaedman's trail where he had doubled back out of the forest and headed north. Though his trail had diverted at several points, he had crossed back over his own path and kept heading north until she reached Aberley. She had ridden Kimiko hard trying to gain ground on her quarry and she was tired.

Reaching the tavern, Eve let the reins slip through her fingers. "Stay here, Kimiko, while I get a drink."

Whickering in response, her horse nuzzled the top of her shoulder pushing her toward the door.

"Trying to get rid of me, are you?"

Blinking twice, her pupils adjusted from the unrestrained sunshine to the dim light that came through the thick uneven glass of the common room windows. Dispersed around the room, stragglers lingered over the remains of their noon meal. Conversation ranged from the serious and apprehensive discussion of a group of farmers in the corner, to the raucous laughter and offbeat thumping from a table of traders stopped for a rest on their way to Montdell. Underneath the chorus of tankards hitting the tables and loud calls for more ale, beat an unmistakable rhythm.

That rhythm caused the delicate hairs on the back of her neck to tingle and her mouth to go dry. It was a familiar sound. Rubbing her clammy palms on the sides of her pants, she attempted to slow her breathing. It had been three years since she last heard this sound.

Leave, she commanded herself in an attempt to calm the maelstrom within her mind. *Leave now. It could be any Lusican.*

Turning, Eve could feel her heart beating in time with the rhythm. That familiar, comforting union caused her to pause. The panic rising within her clashed with the joy this music evoked.

No music has done this in three years, she admitted. *Not since he left.*

Closing her eyes, she turned her back on the door. Every sign of doubt receded replaced by a calm poise as she strode further

into the room. Weaving through the tables, she made her way to a
knot of men seated to the right of the potbelly stove.

In their midst, perched on a stool, a cloaked and hooded man
coaxed the notes of a bawdy drinking song from a worn lyre. The
pure clear notes produced a complex rhythm that soaked into
Eve's skin.

The smooth wood of the lyre appeared glossy from years of
use. Every curve, every nick in the surface of the instrument
summoned a memory. The musician's calloused fingers glided
over its neck exactly as she remembered.

As the last notes faded from the air, the inhabitants thudded
their tankard onto their tables and stamped their feet while calling
out the names of favorite tunes.

Well, I can't stand here forever, she thought with irritation, *and I
don't want to ruin everyone's lunch.*

Eve, supporting her voice, raised it above the din. "Don't ask
this worthless excuse for a minstrel to play those. He'd just
butcher them."

Betraying nothing, the figure smiled underneath his hood.
"You're just saying that because you have two left feet and can't
keep up with my playing, Eve."

Disappointed by his nonchalant reaction, she decided to
retaliate in turn. She placed her hands suggestively on her hips,
deep golden-brown eyes flashing. "Is that a challenge?"

Cheering, the nearby men began pushing tables and chairs to
clear a space for the woman. The sounds of boots stamping and
hands slapping wood thundered throughout the room. The
patrons wanted a show. Chuckling once, the musician began to
pick out the notes of a jig.

Eve shrugged out of her restrictive jacket and tossed it onto an
empty chair. She could feel the rhythm in her blood; she could
sense it tingling on her skin. Her hands began twisting
instinctively to the call within the music. The music seeped into
her, demanding her limbs respond, demanding that she dance.
Her hips began to move of their own accord. Her temples flared
with yellow light that covered her eyes as well.

The music carried her thoughts back in time.

The fire burned in the hearth warming Eve as she sat on the cool, slated wood floor. A young man leaned against her knees, plucking a playful tune from his lyre. The melody rose and fell with the rhythm of the blaze. She gazed quietly into the fire, watching the flames dance.

As the speed of his playing increased so did her dancing. Her joy in the dance overflowed into laughter. The patrons clapped in time with the music, urging Eve to surrender to the dance. The whirling movements swept her back to different time and place.

Eve walked next to a young man with auburn hair, their shoulders barely brushing. Strands of hair escaped from the ponytail low on his neck and fell in front of his eyes. He looked over at her and smiled. His green eyes were the color of a mist-covered moor splashed with the purest golden sunshine. They sparkled with a laughter that bubbled from deep within. With an absent-minded, but futile, gesture he brushed his hair out of his face. Grinning, she reached out and tucked the stray pieces behind his ear.

The interplay between her memories and the music enveloped her within their beauty. All thoughts were gone. All that remained was the rhythm, the cheering, the movement, the dance.

Abruptly, another memory overtook her senses.

Sunlight spilled through a high window and pooled around the wheat-colored hair on the pillow. The young woman's face looked pale like a porcelain doll. Her delicate hands lay folded on her chest. The absolute stillness of that chest was the only indication that she would never wake.

Jarring herself out of a spin, she froze and stared blankly above the hearth. "Nessa."

The music faltered then died. The patrons fell silent, waiting for more. When neither the dancer nor the musician continued, chairs scrapped the floor and excited voices filled the room about the performance and each performer.

The musician stared out from under his hood at Eve, and placed his lyre on the floor against the wall with deliberate care. She stood, her hand grasping her upper arm, chin raised as she fixed her eyes on a knothole in the wall. Dragging his hand along his jaw, he then wiped his hands on the front of his legs and rose from the stool.

With a shake of his head, he strode toward the open area where the dancer stood.

"Outside," she said, her eyes never leaving the knothole. Without waiting to see his response, she turned her back to him and walked to the bar.

As he watched the lithe woman retrieve her jacket, he shifted his weight. Before he could begin processing what had happened, several patrons slapped him on the back to congratulate him on winning the impromptu competition. He thanked them and moved toward the door. Throwing one more glance at the woman at the bar, he walked out of the tavern.

Eve attempted to focus her scattered thoughts, as she traced a never-ending circle with a single finger on the worn, sleek wooden counter.

"What can I get you, Sister?" an adolescent boy behind the bar asked. "No charge. You earned it."

As she pulled her arm through her coat's sleeve, a hard smile tugged at the corner of her lips. "Double shot of whiskey."

The lad nodded appreciatively as he turned to pour the drink.

He won't be there, when I get outside, she thought, trying to console herself. *If he is, I'll have no choice.*

The boy set the glass in front of her and nodded once as he moved on to the next costumer. She inclined her chin in response and pulled the glass closer.

Staring into the amber liquid, she thought, *Quick and painless as possible.*

She tossed the glass back, the whiskey pleasantly burning the back of her throat. Setting down the now empty glass, she moved away from the bar and toward the exit. She rested her hand on the hilt of her curved, long knife to keep it from trembling.

Stepping out of the tavern, she cast a quick glance for the musician. When she failed to see him, she let out the breath she had unconsciously held. A breeze clinging to the last fading scent of summer swept the tufts of Eve's hair into an invisible dance. Kimiko trotted over and whuffled into her shoulder. Her breath was warm and sweet. Eve caressed her brow as she let her thoughts drift away with the current of the river tumbling nearby.

Several lengths from the horse, the musician leaned against the wall of the inn. "You cut your hair."

At the sound of his voice, her heart dropped to her stomach. *You idiot, why didn't you run?* Keeping her tone level, she replied, "Yes, I did." But did not complete the thought aloud. *After you left.*

"What happened in there?"

"I forgot myself for a moment." Eve readjusted Kimiko's cinch. "That's all."

"You're tracking someone," the musician stated, rather than asked.

The muscles in her back tensed at the accuracy with which he still read her. She had forgotten how well he knew her.

"Yes."

"Personal or professional?"

Eve said nothing as she continued to inspect Kimiko's gear.

"I'm shocked. The righteous hand of justice, Evelyn Reid, is letting personal feelings influence her. To my knowledge, that has only happened once before."

"Stop it, Lucien."

"Why? Because I'm right?"

"Because you haven't the right."

Lucien's mouth twisted into a mocking smile. "You gave me that right long ago, Eve. Or have you conveniently forgotten that as well?"

"I forget nothing."

Lucien took a step toward her and Kimiko bucked, shying away from his advance. Eve looked from Kimiko and back to Lucien, her eyes narrowing.

"Why did I let you go?" she whispered. "Why didn't I turn you in?"

Lucien sighed. "I thought it was because you had faith in me. What happened to that faith, Eve?"

She loosened her knife from its sheath and twirled it, finding its balance. "I have to kill you now, Lucien. You know that."

Taking another step toward her, he paused for a moment then pulled back his hood, revealing a young face framed with strands of long auburn hair that fell out of a loose ponytail at the base of his neck, just as she remembered. Silver eyes stared back at her.

"Now do you understand?"

"You're Gray." Her voice had fallen to a whisper. The blade she had been clutching in her hand fell as her thoughts scattered. *This changes everything.*

"Because of the faith I thought you had, I..." He faltered, unable to look away from her. "I took this step."

"I don't know what you want from me, but I know that I can't give it to you." Dropping to a knee, her hand lingered, hovering above the knife for a moment. Hardening her resolve, she sheathed it and rotated away from Lucien in one fluid motion. "I'm sorry. I have to go. Don't follow."

"I can't let you. I've been waiting for years, hoping. Not even sure if I would have the courage to tell you when the time came. You can't just leave."

Unable to speak, Eve leaned against Kimiko, gaining more than just physical support from the contact.

"I've been waiting, Eve, all this time. Waiting to find the courage to face you as I am."

"It's a little late for vapid sentimentality," she said, with a jaded sneer, "don't you think?" Her rigid stance radiated an icy lack of emotion, as if the warm fire that burned within Eve had been extinguished. All that remained was an empty detached shell.

"I had hoped that at least you, of all people, would understand."

"Understand? Lucien, I am a Daniyelan. Why would you think I could have ever understood?"

"Because," he said, his quiet voice nearly masked by the rumble of the water, taking another step toward her, "you were the only one who ever did."

Kimiko bucked her head in agitation and backed further away from the approaching Gray. Eve took her mount's face in her hands forcing Kimiko to look at her and spoke in soft tones. She turned to Lucian. "Maybe once, but that was long ago in a different time, a different life."

"You're still that woman, Eve."

"You are hardly still that man, Lucien."

"That may be." He raised his eyes above her head, searching the clouds. "But you'll never know if you leave now. Can you live with that?"

"I've had to live with many unpleasant things." Her eyes were as frosty as her tone. Unable to say more, she stepped away from

Lucien and began leading Kimiko back onto the road.

"So that's it. You're walking away."

Eve said nothing as she continued her slow pace.

Cursing, Lucien closed the increasing gap between them and grabbed her arm. "Wait," he commanded.

Spinning out of his grasp, she used his momentum to hurl him to the ground with a thud. Her knee wedged between his shoulder blades, she twisted his arm at an unnatural angle behind his back. Lucien made no attempt to resist.

Whispering into his upturned ear, Eve seethed. "Never – never touch me without my permission."

"Moment of weakness?"

She released her hold and shoved him away hard as she rolled back onto her feet.

As she walked away, Lucien asked, "Let me come with you."

"You're supposed to be dead."

Lucien stood, silent.

"Sheridan will be joining me soon."

"She doesn't know?"

"No one knows." The agony in her eyes flashed and faded.

"Then don't tell her."

Eve turned toward him, an eyebrow arched skeptically.

"She won't be expecting to see me, if she thinks I'm dead."

"You should be."

Lucien sighed. "Then I won't come."

Her heart paused at his words, but she revealed nothing as she waited for his explanation.

"Lucien has been dead for three years," he said with regret. "Since you can't bring a dead man, how about letting a penniless Lusican come with you?"

"What are you suggesting?" She rubbed a palm on the side of her leg and cursed the hope rising unbidden within her.

Bowing with a flourish of his cloak, Lucien raised his eyes and when he did he had transformed with a shimmer of gold light. His dark auburn hair lightened and shortened to look like pile of thatch on his head. His nose bent crookedly and his pale skin gained a golden tan. "The name's Haley, m'lady. It's a right honor to meet you. I'm just a poor Lusican trying to get by and

I'm heading to Finalaran. Would you mind if a ruffian, such as myself, tagged along on your circuit? Safety in numbers, yeah?"

Eve barely managed to mask the smile created by the performance.

Lucien grinned, his silver eyes shimmering like starlight. "You have a notorious soft spot for minstrels, Evie."

"Put that smirk away," she chided, her resolve crumbling under the influence of Lucien's charisma. "You could convince me of almost anything, when you smiled like that."

Lucien's smile widened. "You won't regret this."

"I already do."

CHAPTER TEN

Faela's thumbs hooked into the back pockets of her trousers as she walked down the dirt road that led out of Oakdarrow. Swirling the dust on the avenue, the wind caught the wide brim of her hat lifting it back from her face. She uttered a curse and tugged it into place. Further ahead two men stood loitering in front of the blacksmith's yard. Kade leaned against the low wall that enclosed the forge area, while Jair paced, unable to dispel his nervous energy. Aware of Faela's approach, Kade kicked a stone at Jair.

"Ow, what was that for?" Searching for the reason for the projectile, Jair noticed Faela. "Well, was he here?"

"He was," Faela answered, a small smile played on her lips, "four days ago."

"Did he leave any indication of where he was heading next?" As he waited for Faela's response, Kade's hand searched for the bundle that lay at his feet.

"Were you able to get the herbs I requested?" Faela asked instead as the three moved back to the road.

At the edge of the village, a Merchant caravan kicked up clouds of dust as its wagons lurched buried under a mound of stacked goods lashed in place. Men garbed similarly to the traders rode at its perimeter, but the alertness in their eyes and the coiled relaxation of their posture suggested something else. Faela recognized mercenary guards in an instant. Most bandits avoided attacking any Merchant House caravans for fear of retribution from the Houses, who had never been known for their mercy toward thieves. That Merchant traders had to hire mercenaries to travel to a town like Oakdarrow concerned her.

Drawing a pale green, cloth package out of the bundle, Kade tossed it at Faela. With his longer reach, Jair caught it and handed it to her. Loosening the knot, she peered at its contents and smiled. Several of these herbs would ease Kade's and her continued recovery, but the others were cooking spices that she preferred to not have to live without.

"I answered your question," Kade pointed out.

"That you did." Faela tucked the packet into one of the many pockets scattered on her bag's exterior. "From what I was able to gather, his next most likely destination where we could catch him would be Kelso about three days from here heading—"

"North!" Jair declared with vigor.

"Actually, no." Faela chuckled. "He's heading further east now, but then, yes, north."

As a trader in tailored riding clothes gave instructions to the caravan's manager, he paused next to the three. Something tickled Faela's nose and she sneezed. The scent of sandalwood and myrrh drifted on the breeze. Jair's complaints faded away muffled as though she heard them from underwater. Along with the aroma came a barrage of memories and emotions, which overwhelmed Faela's mind.

The smell of sandalwood and myrrh floated from behind her as Nikolais' hands slipped across her stomach. He pulled her back against him and put his mouth to her ear. "I love you, Faela, more than anything in this world."

Her heart beat faster.

Nikolais' hand cupped her cheek as he traced her jaw with his nose. "Just this once, influence your father's feelings in favor of the Nightmist House representatives. You'd be helping him see past the Houses' silly prejudices and feuding."

It was becoming hard to remember to breathe.

Kneeling in front of her, Nikolais grasped both her hands as he looked into her eyes. "You know he'll never consent. I provide no advantageous alliance for the House. It won't matter to him that I'm the father of his grandchild, Faela. All he'll see is that I've disgraced his eldest daughter and heir."

Her fingertips were numb.

She knelt, the wool rug biting into her bare skin. Her hands were covered in blood as she wrapped the wounds with pieces of her skirt, but the blood wouldn't stop. No matter what she did, the blood wouldn't stop. She could feel the panic rising in her throat.

Faela could no longer feel her body.

As they passed the Merchant caravan, Faela had stopped.

"Faela?" Jair asked, but her eyes stared unfocused, seeing nothing. Kade arched an eyebrow at Jair. She trembled. Jair reached out to touch her elbow to steady her, but before he could lay hold of her, her knees buckled and she crumpled like a paper doll. Her eyes were open, but glassy and vacant of anything that resembled Faela. Kade dropped to a knee and felt for her pulse at her neck. Her heart raced erratically.

Several people from the caravan looked over with curiosity.

"Support her left side," Kade directed as he put his shoulder under her arm and slipped his hand around her waist. Jair helped to lift her to her feet. Her head lolled to the side, but her lips moved without sound.

"One too many pints for you, my friend." Jair projected his voice so that those passing by could hear. He caught the gaze of one of the caravan's wranglers. "Can't hold her ale, poor thing. Now, let's get you home, missy."

Kade and Jair kept Faela propped between them and continued down the road, leaving town. Once they were out of earshot, Jair asked, "What's wrong with her?"

Kade stared ahead, his eyes hard. "I don't know. I've never seen anything like this."

Under an ancient oak tree, Mireya sat on a large root that seemed to jump out of the earth. Her legs dangled, swinging like a pendulum. His staff resting in the crook of his arm, Dathien leaned against the tree's giant trunk. Before any sound heralded their arrival, Mireya's head shot up and her eyes flashed a brilliant blue. Turning, she saw Kade and Jair approaching with the immobile and limp Faela. She hopped off her perch, hitched up her robes, and ran toward the men.

"What did you do?" Mireya demanded hovering around them.

"We were coming back from town and she collapsed but," Jair hesitated, "she's not actually unconscious."

Now that they were away from any onlookers, Jair picked up Faela and carried her toward the trunk of the massive oak. He set her nestled against a grouping of roots. Mireya followed and sat, her legs crossed, next to Faela. In order to look into her catatonic eyes, she reached out and held Faela's face steady. They pulsed red in time with her fluttering heart. Faela's lips moved, but produced no speech. Mireya took Faela's hand in her own.

"Can you hear me, Faela?" she asked quietly as she rubbed the woman's drooping hand.

Faela continued to stare through everything.

"Oh bother," Mireya said in a spurt of frustration. "Dathien, help me."

Dathien knelt behind his wife and laid his staff on the ground beside him. Placing his hands on her shoulders, his wrists burned with sapphire lines.

"Faela." Mireya called to the woman, her eyes blazing blue and the glowing lines traced their intricate knot work on the backs of her hands.

Faela's body went rigid and her mumbling became audible. "Can't stop... quiet... just want ... make them..."

"Faela, what's not quiet?" Mireya asked.

"Make them go away." She begged in a terrified whisper and a tattoo exploded with a burst of crimson light on her chest.

At once, Jair and Kade's faces blanched as images and emotions one blurring into the next too fast to differentiate one from another assaulted their minds.

A woman in a gauzy green dress stood on a balcony bathed in moonlight, her cheeks stained with tears. His blood soaking into the wool carpet, a man with silver hair sprawled on the floor of a library, a dagger rolling from his hand. Dagger in hand, a man stood over a woman kneeling before a kitchen hearth. He pressed the burning blade to her upper arm. A scream tore from her throat. Dogs howled as a dark man explained that the crops would not be fit for harvest again this year. Chaos engulfed the inn as arrows rained down from the rafters. Screams cut off as the men around him died. A man rushed the boy, but another soldier pushed him out of the way as the blade caught him across the face. A mother clutched her two-year-old daughter in her arms as her youngest son watched from the porch. She fell to her knees looking up at the man. Her husband and eldest son would never come home.

Relentless, emotions hammered the men, guilt, shame, loss, loathing, despair, fear, panic, terror. All spinning and swirling like a cyclone that they could not escape. The images repeated, looping, trapping them. Dathien looked from the stricken men and back at Mireya.

Mireya's eyes narrowed and her voice deepened and filled the air. "Stop this nonsense and come back, Faela."

The incessant murmuring ceased and Faela blinked. Both Kade and Jair gasped as if they had been holding their breath the entire time. Jair doubled over, his hands clutching his knees for support. Kade sank wordlessly to the ground.

Faela registered the stricken faces of the two afflicted men and she shut her eyes to block out the image. "Darkness take me," she whispered, "not again."

*   *   *

"It seems really dry for Nabos at this time of year. Shouldn't we be drenched right now?" Lucien observed looking at the crisp blue sky. "Not that I'm complaining."

Eve grimaced at the dusty field they passed. The grass had withered to browns, instead of the rich greens typical to the end of summer in this once fertile country. Despite the storm that had passed through a couple days ago, the ground failed to retain the moisture. She knew this country was still recovering from the devastation of the war, but this destruction was new, different. The increasingly deteriorating health of the vegetation and creatures of Nabos worried her.

She lifted her water skin off her back and drained its contents. Midday had just passed and she would have to refill it for the fourth time today.

"This isn't normal," she snapped. Since they had entered this blighted territory, she felt as though her vitality had slowly leeched into the ground with every step she took.

"How draining has it been?"

"It must be causing havoc with the reconstruction effort."

"I didn't mean for those living in Nabos. I meant you. It's making me feel uneasy and I have a mediocre talent for green magic."

Eve raised an eyebrow at the self-deprecation then swallowed, unable to dispel the dryness in her throat. "It feels like someone has wrung all the moisture out of me. I feel like I'll crumble to dust if there's a stiff breeze."

Lucien grunted and nodded, as if he had expected as much.

"What could be causing this?"

"I've heard rumors in my travels," he said squinting his eyes at the stark sunlight beating down on them.

"Rumors?"

"Yeah, that this famine that hit southern Nabos isn't natural."

"And this is a side effect," she said with a grunt. "If its cause were magical, especially green, it's plausible that it's causing drought and famine, depending on how it happened."

"You never answered my question, you know." Lucien glanced at Eve out of the corner of his eye as she led Kimiko down the dirt-packed road.

"I just did," Eve said, purposefully misinterpreting his statement.

"No, you just answered my question about this." He waved his hand to take in nature surrounding them. "You never told me who you're tracking."

"That's Daniyelan business."

"It seems to be a bit more than that."

Eve quickened her pace as the village appeared tucked in the bend of the river as they crested one of the many low rolling hills of the plains.

Lucien sighed, but let the matter pass. He knew how futile it would be to push when Eve didn't want to reveal something.

"When we get to Dalwend," she said ignoring his observation. "I'll need to meet with the local magistrate."

"Yeah, doesn't seem like a big enough village to warrant anything more than an Daniyelan on circuit."

Eve nodded. "Restock our supplies while I'm gone. I shouldn't be long, but we need the rest."

Lucien grunted in affirmation and began constructing the glamour he would use once Sheridan joined them, turning from a redhead to a blonde once again.

As they got closer to the village, Eve loosened one of her saddlebags and threw it over her shoulder. She turned to Lucien and quirked a smile at his flawless disguise. "You always had a greater skill with glamour spells than I did. We'll meet at the Otter's Tale when I'm done."

* * *

The dank smell of moldering timber clung to the cellar. Sheridan rubbed her arms trying to increase the heat in her slender form. Small puffs of condensation accompanied her breathing. From the rafter above her, a drop of water fell and plopped brazenly onto her cheek. Wiping it away with indignation, Sheridan glared at the offending support beam and promptly sneezed.

"I hate being cold," she complained to no one.

Nothing about this cellar seemed remarkable to Sheridan. Barrels filled with flour and dried fruits were stacked in the far back corner. From just below the ceiling, sunlight peeked through the single small paned window. The slate floor implied the wealth of the building's owner, though it did little to keep the moisture out.

Nothing about this cellar indicated it as distinctive, but her investigations had led her here. Four days worth of hurling her conscious mind in and out of the past to sift for clues had brought her here. She had sent Wiley back to the temple. There was little he could do while she searched through the past.

Picking an unoccupied corner, she surveyed her view of the room. Nothing obstructed her sight entirely. She nodded once. "This will do."

As she prepared to stand in one spot for a lengthy period of time, she cracked her neck and loosened her shoulders. Intense violet lines seared across the tops of her cheeks. She blinked. When she opened her eyes, they shimmered behind that same violet sheen.

The water that dripped from the rafters suddenly froze in its descent. Sheridan's hands rose as she reached past the physical boundaries around her, searching for a specific signature. A length of what appeared to be transparent, shimmering silk lay in her hands and cascaded past her left hand onto the floor. It flowed like water. A stain of bubbly jade writhed several feet down the length. Lifting the liquid material, she touched the end of the length to the wash of dancing green and held them together. The room flashed with purple as if it had been thrust into the heart of an oddly colored sun. Sheridan did not blink as the room re-focused before her.

With her hands bound at her back, a slight woman with wheat-colored hair stood in a simple jade-colored dress, her posture rigid with fear. A stocky man, in the orange uniform of a Daniyelan, paced around the room looking for something.

"Gareth," the woman said with deliberate slowness, "why have you brought me here?"

"That's none of your concern."

"I should think it is of grave concern to me." Though her voice was patient, her hands shook.

He stopped moving for the first time since Sheridan had entered. He blinked as if the woman's statement confused him. "Just trust that I'm protecting you, Nessa."

She spoke each word with care to keep her voice steady. "Protecting me from what?"

A man appeared at the top of the cellar stairs. His features obscured by a black kerchief and hood, he waited.

Scurrying up the staircase, Gareth grasped his arm, his voice hushed. "Well? What of the vote?"

The veiled man shook his head. "He used his veto."

At hearing the news, Gareth cursed and pushed his stringy hair back.

"You pushed him too far. We are not pleased with the prospect of losing such a valuable asset." The man's eyes swept down to Nessa. "Clean this up, before it gets worse."

Gareth nodded and the man disappeared from the landing.

Nessa tried to keep her breathing calm, as Gareth descended back to the cellar.

With a click, Gareth unsheathed his dagger and sighed. "I'm so sorry, Nessa. This was not the result I'd hoped for."

"Really, Gareth, did you think I wouldn't be able to find you in time?" An arrogant voice echoed in the cellar as it stressed the final word.

His spine straightening, Gareth turned and saw a man in Daniyelan combat gear step out of the shadows of the stairway. Flexible leather armor fit close to his body while twin, curved blades crossed on his back.

"I mean, really, mate. Who thought the 'do what we say or we'll kill the girl' was a good plan?"

"Kaedman!" Nessa's voice carried a deep sense of relief.

"You all right, love?" Though he spoke with a playful tone, his eyes simmered with restrained anger.

Before she could answer, Gareth finally spoke. "I thought we agreed, Kaedman. This law would ensure the safety of the country."

"I had nothing against the proposed law, Gareth." Kaedman uncrossed his arms, flexing his fingers in toward his palm. "Have I not supported and encouraged similar measures on the council?"

"Then why veto it?" Gareth yelled as his temper frayed. "You knew of its importance to the Brethren."

Sheridan's breath caught at the name and the images rippled like the surface of a pond. Reasserting her focus, the room smoothed again.

"Yes and had they simply sought my support instead of trying to force my hand, I would have gladly given it."

"You know better than most, Kaedman. These lands can no longer be trusted to govern themselves. This was too important to risk your opposition. Or must we lose another Scion, another generation to their folly?"

"But to violate Taronpia's sovereignty," Nessa said, her eyes wide with shock as she looked from Gareth to Kaedman, "what you suggest is treason."

Gareth's lips curled into a sneer. "My loyalty is to the Orders, to the Brethren, not some petty king or council. They exist only because we allow them to. No king exists that has not been confirmed by the Scion of the Daniyelans. We are the determiners of justice. What law exists without us?"

"Heresy," Nessa whispered. "You are servants of the Light. You ensure justice, you do not create it."

"If I have the strength to enforce it, it becomes just." Gareth sighed. "As your deaths will be just. What's the sacrifice of two to keep millions safe? That's all this test required of you, Kaedman. To see if you understood that sacrifices must be made to attain lasting peace."

"I understand the meaning of sacrifice, Gareth." Kaedman's jaw tightened.

"But don't you see, Hawthorn? Why we did this?" Gareth's gaze settled on Nessa. "No matter the choice you made, you proved yourself true to our cause. For the greater good, you were willing to sacrifice sweet Nessa here."

Kaedman removed one of the short, curved blades from his back with a soft scrapping sound.

Gareth smiled, his eyes hollow and empty. "Oh, and the moment you entered you triggered a time lock on the this room. Don't think us so naïve." As he said the final word, his eyes disappeared beneath an oily black smoke.

Kaedman swore, but before he could close the gap between himself and Nessa, Gareth twisted his hand and released a roiling black sphere of light. It smashed into Nessa's chest, lifting her from the ground. She hit the wall with a moist crunch and fell to the floor motionless.

Already running, Kaedman unsheathed his second blade. Gareth twisted his hand again and a second ball formed and rocketed toward Kaedman. Each blade glowed in Kaedman's hands and ignited into flame as his eyes shimmered with orange. Crossing the blades in front of him, the black fire splashed against the shield and forced Kaedman back several paces. When he lowered the blades into an offensive stance, Gareth was gone.

Sheathing the blades, he dropped to next to Nessa. Reaching under his armor for the vial hanging there, his eyes glimmered red as he checked her. She was alive. Laying her on her side with her cloak balled under her head, he brushed her hair aside and kissed her forehead.

"I'll be back," he promised. His eyes unyielding and cold as iron he raced out of the cellar taking the stairs two at a time.

"Kaedman, it burns." Nessa moaned, reaching out to him with outstretched fingers. Coughing, blood dripped from her mouth and pooled on the ground. She coughed more blood, her whole body shuddering, and then the coughing ceased. Her body lay still.

Tears stained Sheridan's cheeks as she lowered her hands and pulled apart the two sections of the watery material. The images around her dissolved. Now, she knew.

* * *

Faela sucked on her index finger and considered the flavor. "Needs more rosemary," she decided after a moment.

Mireya peered over Faela's shoulder. "What're you making?"

"The simplest food to keep us moving down the road — soup." Unable to locate her bag, she called, "Jair, you now have a mission."

"Ooh, I like missions," Jair responded with an eager hop over some firewood.

"Find my bag." She ordered as she swept her hand to indicate the disorganized chaos of the emerging camp. "It's somewhere in this mess."

"I shan't fail you." Jair vowed solemnly, his fist placed firmly over his breast.

Faela chuckled as she stirred the floating contents of the pot.

"Where'd you learn to cook, Faela?" Mireya sprawled haphazardly on the ground. She gnawed on her thumbnail then rolled onto her back. "They tried to teach me at the temple — once." Mireya shuddered at the memory.

Faela smiled, the gesture softening the constant tension of her features. "It was my teacher, Ianos. My father never cooked. My mother did, but I left home before she could teach me."

"Ianos taught you to cook?" Mireya looked confused. "But isn't he the Scion of the Tereskan Order?"

Faela nodded. "But he wasn't always Scion. Everyone's story has to start somewhere. His was as a baker's son. He used to tell me how he missed getting up before the sun, so that everyone would wake to the smells of breads and muffins and pastries. He always wanted to go back there after a new Scion was appointed." Her smile remained, but her eyes saddened.

Blissfully unaware, Mireya asked, "So why'd he teach you to cook?"

"Ianos believed that one of the greatest gifts we were given by the Light is food and that sharing a meal with another person is one of the most significant endeavors of human interaction. Also, I couldn't boil water without burning it."

Jair returned with a jubilant crow. "Success!"

He presented Faela with her bag on one knee. "Your bag, m'lady."

"Thanks, Jair." Faela began searching for a set of small, carved wooden boxes. Finding a pear she had bought from an orchard in Oakdarrow, she tossed it to Jair. "For your troubles."

"Your kindness is only exceeded by your loveliness." As pear juice trickled down to his wrist, he flopped next to Mireya. He shook his head in denial. "I refuse to believe that you couldn't cook."

"It's true; I was beyond horrid." A conspiratorial smile spread across Faela's lips. "When I was little, after I had first come to live at the Tereskan temple in Kilrood, Ianos would attend to his duties within the temple with me tagging along. Usually with my hair horribly disheveled and my face filthy. I had a tendency to find the smallest and dirtiest places to hide. Any way, he always started our days in the kitchens."

Dipping her pinky into the pot, she sucked off the broth. "Kade and Dathien, if you lads don't want Jair to eat your share, I suggest you finish setting up camp later."

Dathien appeared behind Mireya and sat propping his legs on either side of her and rocked forward, draping his arms across his knees.

Kade stepped out of the shadows of the trees. "We've ensured that everything's secure. We were merely enjoying the silence."

Faela quirked her lips to the side at his choice of words and handed Jair a lightweight wooden bowl, steam rising from its contents. The smell of burning wood settled into the back of her throat. The smell was familiar and reassuring. She could feel some of the strain in her muscles relaxing.

"Well too bad, because Faela was telling Jair and me a story," Mireya declared as she smiled up at Dathien and snuggled against his bent leg. Dathien winked at her and smoothed her hair back. "She was telling us how she used to begin her days as a seeker in the Tereskan temple."

Kade settled against his pack with a bowl in hand. "By all means, don't let me interrupt."

"So why did he insist on starting your day in the kitchens?" Didn't you have an eating hall?" Mireya asked as she waved the spoon Dathien had handed her in the air.

Faela shook her head. "Ianos refused to allow anyone within the temple to serve him breakfast if he could help it. He preferred to make his own. Starting his day cooking centered and grounded him he said. But more than that, he used to remind me that this morning ritual connected us to every human being. That no matter how seemingly important or insignificant a man was, we all started our day the same and by making our own breakfast we would remember that we are no different than any other man."

Faela ate several spoonfuls of the soup as Jair asked, "So where does the horror part come in?"

A bit of wild onion, that Mireya had found, stuck to her lower lip, Faela licked it curling it into her mouth. "Well, one morning Ianos didn't wake me and I found out that he had been summoned by an Amserian, because of some emergency concerning an old friend, the night before and was still resting. I was twelve at the time and decided I would make breakfast for him." Faela smiled into her bowl and chuckled. "He always made it look so easy."

"What'd you do?" Mireya hugged her knees to her chest.

Faela's fingers brushed a rectangular scar on her palm. "Let's just say that the cooks managed to put out the fire eventually. After that, Ianos decided for my own safety and that of the entire temple he needed to teach me how to cook." Faela smiled and looked at Kade. "Of course I've heard some interesting stories about your journeymen year. It really is so nice to have a face for all of Caleb's stories you know."

The corners of Kade's mouth twitched in the firelight.

"Something about you sneaking out of a tavern dressed as a serving girl?"

"I had no choice," Kade asserted, punctuating the air with the butt of his spoon.

Jair choked on the cured meat he had been swallowing and began coughing violently. Water streaming from his eyes, the coughing turned to laughter. "You did what?" Jair managed to say amid his gasps for breath.

Faela's eyes sparkled as she sucked on the tip of her spoon. "I could tell the story as Caleb told me, however, we both know how his stories grow with each telling, don't we, Kade?"

Kade snorted, a dangerous choice given the food currently in his mouth. "It was his blasted fault. Did he tell you that?"

Just as Dathien's staff was never far from his side, neither was his slow smile that now turned into a grin. Wiping the corners of his mouth with his thumb, he observed, "It will only get worse the longer you keep us in suspense."

Jair nearly bounced with curiosity, which he could contain no longer. "So what happened? Why'd you have to sneak out? What color was the dress?"

"You will pay for this." Kade promised Faela as he glared at her over his bowl.

Faela simply chuckled and waited for the storytelling to begin.

Kade sighed and began recounting his tale to his dinner. "It was about five months before the war ended. We had been sent to infiltrate deep into Nabos to smuggle out a contact. Caleb decided we'd be less suspicious traveling in the open than keeping to the woods, because no one knows the forests and foothills of Nabos like the natives and he didn't want to get caught out there."

Dathien nodded as he ate. "Their woodsmen and trappers are ferociously territorial."

Jair gazed into the dancing fire. "The women are worse than the men." As if he had just realized that he had spoken aloud, he hurriedly added, "Or so I've heard."

"The tempers of Nabosian woman are legendary." Faela redirected Jair's slip out of sympathy for the boy. She knew what it meant to have secrets that you wanted to stay buried.

"Exactly as you said, Dathien." Kade allowed Faela to shift the focus from Jair, but watched the younger man. "We were staying in this small village pretty far from any of the fighting, when a band of mercs hired by the Nabosians stopped in town on a resupply mission.   And unfortunately, this particular band of mercenaries knew Caleb from a judgment he had mediated that condemned one of their numbers."

"Oh dear!" Mireya leaned forward in rapt attention. "Were you discovered?"

Despite himself, Kade grinned. No storyteller could resist an audience like Mireya. "Had we been discovered, it's likely I would not be here right now. But Caleb had a plan."

"He always has a plan." Snorting in a very unladylike fashion, Faela dragged the back of her hand across her mouth. "The sticking point is always whether he can pull off his grand schemes."

"Don't I know it." Kade shook his head. "Yet somehow he always makes it through. Now Caleb insisted that since all the men in Nabos had been drafted to fight in the war, a kid like me would raise suspicions traveling alone. The only solution, he claimed, would be for him to meet me in the woods while I rounded up our supplies dressed as a serving girl."

"You still haven't told me," Jair pointed out helpfully, "the color of the dress."

Remembered bitterness colored his tone. "It was brown."

"Would you say it was more of a taupe or a mahogany?" Jair inquired, stroking his chin. "And bows, did it have any bows? Please say that it had bows."

Mireya covered her mouth trying to block the escaping giggle as she pictured Kade with a big blue bow in his sable hair. Clearly not amused, Kade raised an eyebrow and fired a small pinecone at Jair's arm. Jair yelped in surprise and pulled Faela in front of him as a shield, ducking his head behind her back.

"Again?" Entertainment crept into Kade's expression. "You're really hiding behind her again."

"She was handy?" Faela's coat muffled the sound of Jair's voice.

"You know, Jair," Kade kept his tone casual, "you're never going to find a woman to put up with you, if you keep insisting that they're all fat."

Jair's face shot out from behind Faela's shoulder. "I did not!"

His reward was another pinecone, this time to the chest. Jair yelped again and dove back under cover. Kade chuckled at the boy's flair for the dramatic.

"I'm out of ammunition, Jair. Leave the poor woman be." Kade rubbed his hands together to remove the dirt. "Come to think of it, I believe Caleb's plan was the only solution to his boredom, not our escape."

Jair settled back to his position next to Faela, hands poised ready to deflect any further airborne attacks. "I can't decide which is worse: a ravenous pack of sisters dressing you up because they thought it made their only brother look pretty or that."

"Ravenous, eh?" Faela bit her bottom lip to hold back her laughter.

"Oh, I'll take his abuse," Jair said jerking a thumb to where Kade reclined, "over their's any day. Being the only boy with three older and two younger sisters does not do good things for your manly pride." Jair's usually friendly face clouded with a gloom as he thought about his family. "Faela?"

"Yes?"

"What happened today? What'd you do to us?"

Setting her bowl down on a half-buried stone in front of her, she swept a tangle of hair behind her ear. How to answer this inevitable question had hung over her head all throughout their hike that day. "Something that used to happen to me no fewer than a dozen times a day when I was a child. It's why I was packed off to Ianos when I was four. I have a rare form of red magic."

"Of course," Kade laughed at how dense he had been, "you're a mind healer. I had wondered why the physical healing took so much out of you."

Twirling a pear in her hands that she just rescued from her satchel, she smiled down at the fruit and tossed it to Kade. "Give the boy a prize."

"So, I'm still lost." Jair raised his hand as if waiting to be acknowledged. "Anyone else? Anyone? Just me?"

"Don't feel bad, Jair." Faela's eyes crinkled as she smiled. "Few of us survive childhood. Our gifts are erratic in nature and can cause trauma that most never recover from." Guilt washed over her face as she looked at Jair and Kade. "I'm so sorry, Jair, Kade. I haven't lost control like that in years."

"I'm still not sure what even happened." Jair threw his hands in the air in exaggerated frustration.

"My barriers slipped. There was a physical trigger, a smell, it recalled—" She paused, running her senses along her barriers. Her eyes glimmered with a ghost of scarlet as she added another layer to the weaving. She would not be taken by surprise a second time. "It recalled a strong memory. Have you ever been to the coast and gotten caught in the tide? You tumble over and over unable to break free, trapped in the current. It's like that, just inside my own mind, memories evoking emotions, which feed into each other.

"Most mind healers are unable to return after a few of these attacks." She drifted off as her fingers followed a thread in her shirt down to its hem. "Unfortunately for you, my ability isn't to be taken lightly, even with my current, diminished abilities." She pointed to her silver eyes.

"Had that happened before I turned... Well, I would have most likely drawn in the minds of the entire town and linked them within my own. Everyone's worst memories, worst fears flowing in an endless cycle." Faela turned toward Mireya and Dathien her eyes shining with curiosity. "I still don't understand how you remained unaffected."

"Uh, I'm a Nikelan," Mireya said as though that explained everything.

Dathien rubbed her upper arm and kissed her hair. "Love, that doesn't actually answer her question. Though the Nikelan oracles do have a Grier partner to protect them, they don't really need it. As the channels of the Light, they are protected by the Light."

Mireya smiled cheerfully as she ripped off a chunk of tack bread with her teeth. Her mouth full, she said, "Once, I fell off a cliff."

Chapter Eleven

Seated close to the fire, Eve could feel the chill in her hands beginning to thaw from the moist, cold air outside. She stretched her fingers as she studied Lucien across the table. The glamour he had woven for Haley, his minstrel disguise, looked nothing like the man she knew. Where Lucien's skin was pale like cream, Haley's was golden like clay. Where Lucien's nose was a sharp plane, Haley's was crooked as if it had been broken repeatedly. Where Lucien's hair was auburn and fine, Haley's was blonde and thick. And his eyes, Haley's eye were black, sparkling pools where Lucien's had been the color of a rolling meadow before — before they had changed to the color of moonlight.

"Can't keep your eyes off of me, yeah?" Lucien turned giving her a wicked grin.

Eve cocked an eyebrow, but refused to respond to jibe. There was nothing to say. Nothing she was willing to let herself say at least. She twisted in her seat, searching for the innkeeper, or a serving boy at the least. The inn was empty was except for a few older men playing kings and scions in the corner.

Never one to waste silence, Lucien said, "You know, I haven't played a game of kings and scions since the last time I lost spectacularly to you. I've never had a head for strategy games."

"Of course not, life is the only strategy board that holds your attention. Why waste your energies when winning fails to present a big enough challenge or pay off?" There was not any bitterness to her observation, just a statement of fact. "You've always seen people as the only pawns worth maneuvering. Getting them to play the roles you've chosen for them."

"Naturally. Carved figures can't decide to move to the right, when you've placed them to the left. But people, people are unpredictably predictable. It's all a matter of the correct pressure and leverage applied at the right time."

Eve shook her head. "You haven't changed a bit. It's that

kind of thinking that caused the mess you're in."

"What can I say? I am a man of conviction and consistency."

Pushing her chair back, she stood.

"Hey now, no reason to leave," Lucien protested. "I'm not that bad."

Her hand resting on the table, Eve leaned forward. "No. You are. But this has nothing to do with you. I want some food before we leave Dalwend. So, I'm going to find some, you narcissist."

Lucien ran his hand through his disheveled hair in a habitual gesture she had seen him do thousands of time before. Despite the alien appearance provided by the glamour, he still moved like Lucien. The clashing juxtaposition of the painfully familiar with the markedly unknown disoriented her. She shut her eyes and shoved away from the table.

"It's not narcissism when you're right," he called after her.

Eve approached the bar and bent over the counter to see if she could locate any of the help. There was no one there, but she heard voices coming from the doorway leading into the kitchens. She caught snatches of voice muffled by the door. Then she heard someone crying out in pain.

"We know she was here."

Sweeping the door open, she saw two men adorned with weapons. One held a young woman with black hair cut bluntly to her ears. A bruise had already begun to blossom on her cheek. A large man with the same coloring stood by the oven, a cleaver clattering from his hand onto the wooden floor.

All eyes fastened on Eve as she interrupted the scene. Collecting her thoughts in the time it took her to exhale the breath she had just taken in, she smiled brightly.

"So this is why I've been waiting to eat. Well that's reassuring. I remembered such good things about The Otter's Tale. I'm glad to see that things haven't gone downhill, because of the recent troubles here in Nabos."

The two men watched Eve stride farther into the room who still wore the uniform of a Daniyelan.

"Good sers, do tell me exactly what you think you're doing?"

The taller of the two with dingy blonde hair and a raised scar across the bridge of his nose and cheeks spoke. "We were coming in from stabling our mounts and startled the young miss here and she tripped and hit her face against the chopping block there. I was just helping her up, you see. Frightened her father good too. Made him drop his cutter there."

He ran his hand against the girl's hair. "Right as rain now, you are, miss." He let her go and she scrambled to her father's side. He lifted her chin to examine her injury.

Eve's throat itched. He was lying, but she had no desire to endanger the innkeeper or his daughter.

"Yes, and you were just leaving." The bearded man's voice rumbled as he picked up some steaming bread that was cooling on racks. He wrapped it in some cloth and handed it to the shorter man wearing a wide-brimmed hat. "Here's the food you asked for. It should last you to Oakdarrow."

The scarred blonde smiled widely. "Thank you, Nathan. Nikolais will be pleased to hear you were so helpful. You'll want to put something cool on that cheek, miss." The man nodded to Eve. "Sister." Then the two men exited out toward the stables.

Once they were out of earshot, the girl burst into tears and her father drew her into his chest and held her tightly.

Eve's eyes darkened along with her tone. "Who were they?"

"My thanks," Nathan said as he turned his head to look at Eve and saw her garb. "Well that explains why they ran out of here fast like. Bounty hunters, they were bounty hunters."

"Who were they looking for?"

Nathan paused longer than necessary to recall the information. "Some woman who stole something from a Merchant House," he answered rubbing his daughter's back in comforting circles.

Eve held back the derisive noise rising in her throat. Nothing Sheridan ever did irritated her as much as the Merchant House's political intrigues. She spent more time dealing with the aftermath of their infighting than she'd care to remember. Looking at the bear of a man, Eve knew he hadn't lied to her outright, but neither had he told her the truth. "Why did they come to you?"

"Guess they tracked her here. She left heading west but a few days back, the night after the big storm."

Eve didn't like being lied to, but the last thing she wanted right now was to get caught in some feud between Merchant Houses. "I'm guessing you didn't catch which Merchant House had contracted them?"

Nathan's arms tightened reflexively at the question. He knew. He just didn't want to believe that his own House would ever put a bounty on Rafaela. "Can't say I did."

Eve sighed as she tousled her short hair with a free hand. "Do you request my aid in this?"

Nathan shook his head. "They're gone now. No lasting harm done." Regardless of what Rafaela had done, he did not want the Daniyelans after her too. His one comfort was that he had sent the hunters searching for her in the wrong direction. He had sent them east to Oakdarrow.

*   *   *

"Sometimes, you just have to do things the old fashioned way," Sheridan said as she surveyed the meticulous living quarters. Not so much as a paper jutted out of place. No books slid ajar on any of the bookshelves, which lined the walls. Every available surface of the cramped apartment served a purpose.

"By the Light, you'd have to be this organized just to fit everything in here."

Sheridan pulled out the desk chair and flopped into the seat as she dug her watch from her jacket to check the time. She had left Wiley to organize her notes four hours ago. Clicking the watch shut, she returned the nicked, but well polished silver timepiece back into her pocket.

Enjoying the afternoon light streaming in the window above her, she opened the desk's drawers rummaging through their contents. She found stacks of neatly filed papers. Flipping through the pages of correspondences, they all appeared to be the ordinary sort of paperwork for a Daniyelan. She found reports on judgments within Montdell, new laws passed by the council, and new marriages, all to be entered into the archives at Finalaran.

Letting the files fall to her lap, she picked up another stack, which contained nothing more than personal letters from acquaintances and family. Had she not witnessed the incident in the cellar, she would hardly have associated this seemingly efficient and stable man with the Brethren.

"Not like I was expecting to find a book called *How to Join the Brethren with Ten Simple Virgin Sacrifices*, but this, this is so," she wrinkled her nose, "sterile."

Discarding the papers onto the desk, they spilled across its surface in a mess. Throwing her long hair into a hasty braid, she wandered over to the nearest bookshelf. She ran a finger along the spines of the books closest to the desk. They displayed titles like *The Magic of Color: the Divisions and Properties of the Spectrum*, *Orange Magic: the Fires of Justice*, *Yellow Magic: Artistic Expression as a Channel*, and *Purple Magic: the Folds of Space and Time*. Past the books on the nature and properties of magic were books of mythology and legend. Sheridan crouched down and drew out a volume titled *Roland's Legends*.

Thumbing through its pages, Sheridan remembered how she would ask Kaedman to read her this tale every night after her father had died during the first years of the war. He would tease her about being the only person who took comfort in hearing the legend of the destruction of Gialdanis. Regardless of his protests, he would always read her to sleep every night, until the nightmares passed. Brushing her fingertips across the chapter heading "The Banishment of the Light Mages," she sighed. She snapped the book shut and shelved it.

The next section she explored caught her attention. "Well, what have we here," she said as she tugged off a volume entitled *Separating Truth from Tale: Nikelan Oracles* and folded onto the floor with her legs crossed. Tossing her braid over her shoulder, she rested her chin into her palm and opened the book.

The first page read: *One of the most enigmatic Orders remains the Nikelan Order of blue magic. Few outside of the Scions have ever encountered a practitioner of blue magic or seen any form of this magic used. While tradition claims that they are the oracles of the Light, its channels, and the living embodiment of His divine will, the empirical evidence to support this claim is insubstantial. Tradition relies upon conjecture at best and legend at worst. All Scions declined to comment or assist in the research of this work, though all claim familiarity with the*

Nikelan Scion and trust her prophecies. Their unwillingness to discuss the methods of the Nikelans raises many questions, which this work will endeavor to answer.

Sheridan flipped forward several chapters, until she found one called "Explanations for Alleged Prophecies." Skimming down several paragraphs she read: *The eyewitness accounts, regarding the prophecies for which the reclusive Nikelans are famous, seem to describe an event similar to a disease of the mind caused by pressure in the brain, which compels the victim to speak in nonsensical patterns and then have no recollection of these episodes later. Another plausible explanation for this phenomenon could be the ingestion of certain fungi, which produce fantastic visions in the subject, which others present are unable to see.*

"Well if nothing else, he was definitely an academic," she said as she skimmed the rest of the speculative work on the blue magic. While she read, the light had receded from the room with the sun's descent toward night. With a regretful noise, she returned the tome to where she had discovered it.

Scanning the shelves on the adjacent wall, she saw practical instruction guides for the different schools of color, theories on the subjective manifestation of color abilities, copies of the charters of each Order and nation. She even found a treatise on why the breeding programs of the sixth century had failed.

With a heavy sigh, she sat on the bed and surveyed the square room and its furniture placement with the wardrobe next to the bed, the desk under the window, and the bookshelves filling any open space in between. Reclining back on her elbows, Sheridan dropped her head between her shoulders.

"C'mon, Gareth. With as conscientious and intellectual as you seem to have been, you had to keep something, some record."

Sheridan's head snapped up and her gaze swept the room again. Her eyes shimmered indigo.

"It's square."

Levering herself into a standing position, she ran to the hallway and into the adjoining room. Its width exceeded its depth by ten feet or more. She ducked out of the room and passed Gareth's room to check the one on its left. The dimensions were the same.

"One more," she said as she swung her head around the

doorjamb of the room across the hall to find the identical rectangular construction – the same construction of all quarters in a Daniyelan temple.

Excited, Sheridan returned to Gareth's room. To the casual observer, the furniture pressed against the walls gave the room a cramped feel and hid the fact that eight feet of the room had vanished.

"Clever." Sheridan grinned. "Now this is more like it."

Using her limited purple ability for time folding over the last week had stretched and exhausted her. But this, the use of purple spatial folding, this is where Sheridan shined.

Placing her palm flat on the wall over the headboard of the bed, her eyes glowed indigo and a matching light pulsed like waves over her hand. A gap existed between the walls. With a flash of indigo, Sheridan disappeared from where she knelt on the bed and appeared in the same posture on the floor of a small cell.

A small slit of a window near the ceiling kept the room in shadow. Snapping her left fingers, a soft orange flame appeared in her hand. It illuminated the room in an instant, driving all the shadows from the corners. With a flick of her wrist, the light floated suspended in the air and followed her as she inspected the room. The walls had no doors, no seams to indicate a passageway. Gareth, who had never demonstrated any ability for purple magic, could have kept this secret indefinitely.

Unlike the quarters she had just left, this room was in disarray. Books were cantilevered in a precarious stack on a sturdy, compact worktable. Intermixed with polished, stone bowls, papers sprawled across its charred tabletop, covering sooty black grooves. Sheridan picked up the top book from the pile. It bore no title, but it had a black binding. She knew this book. Every child learned of this book as part of their final weeks as a seeker in any of the Orders as a warning. These were the writings of the heretic, Simon Nightfall. This was black, the magic of darkness. The magic, according to the legends, that sundered light magic into its separate colors.

Given what she had witnessed in the cellar, it didn't surprise her to find his philosophies here, but it did provide her with further evidence exonerating Kaedman. Slipping the book back onto the table, she riffled through the letters strewn there. She shuffled the letters from front to back, skimming their contents. They were letters from the Brethren, many of which mentioned Kaedman.

"This can't be right."

Sheridan's brow knit together as she checked and rechecked what she had read. The earliest letter mentioning Kaedman dated back to the war. Thrusting her hand out, she leaned against the wall for support. The Brethren had begun watching Kaedman while they had still been training together. They had maneuvered his early admittance into his journeymen post during the final year of the war. As she continued reading, her face blanched.

"Blessed Light, the Brethren control the Daniyelan Order."

At that moment, she felt a harsh, fast tug at her heart that drove the breath from her lungs. Her eyes widened in shock.

"Eve, stop!" Sheridan cried out to her sister, hundreds of miles away.

Fixing the image of her sister's face twisted with fury firmly in her mind, she reached for Eve and folded their locations together so they overlapped. A crushing pressure descended around Sheridan. The indigo light from her eyes engulfed her body. With a pop, she was gone.

*   *   *

Caleb drew off his riding gloves and tucked them into his belt. The entry hall of the Nikelan temple glimmered where the sunlight fell across the white marble. Soaring four stories above where Caleb and Talise stood, the ceiling arched as though it bore none of the weight of its marble structure. Breathless at the grandeur of the hall, Talise's hand covered her mouth as she spun on the ball of her foot to soak in the beauty of the architecture.

As Caleb approached a large bowl recessed into the floor, he heard the delicate trickle of running water echo up into the hall's vaulted ceilings. Gazing into the pool of water, chips of mother of pearl and glass of varied hues of blue lined its bottom where a mosaic formed concentric circles moving inward. Beneath the water, the lines seemed to swirl, pulling the observer toward the center.

Talise joined Caleb, slipping her hand around his waist. Instinctively, Caleb drew his arm across her shoulder. Before looking into the pool, Talise traced the lines of his disfigured, yet rugged face with her eyes and smiled to herself.

As she admired the reflecting pool's beauty, the circles seemed to pulse and the bottom of the bowl appeared to deepen, drawing her with it. Her eyes flashed azure and she heard a nightingale singing behind her. She turned to find the bird and the temple was gone.

A fire burned in a large hearth and crumpled on the ground before it lay Faela. Her body unmoving, the stones around her glistened dark and wet. The nightingale's song stopped. The vision changed and she saw a small boy of the Tribes sitting alone in a meadow. He was crying. A man in uniform picked up the boy and walked away from her. She tried to catch him, but with every step she took, they moved further away.

Talise blinked and the images dissolved around her. She still stood, with her arm encircling Caleb's torso, gazing at the glittering mosaic of the pool. He inclined his head toward her to speak when the sounds of footsteps signaled that they were no longer alone. At the intrusion of the sounds, Talise's vision receded in her memory, the details fading into a haze.

A familiar voice carried across the hall. "I see you have found Nikela's Mirror. It was built by the hands of the first blue mage, my Order's first Scion. Nikela was quite the artist before the Shattering of magic. You are not the first to be drawn by its power, Caleb Durante Murphy and Talise Murphy of the Lightwind Tribe."

Turning to face the voice they had heard at the Boundary, Caleb and Talise saw a slight woman with silver hair that cascaded past her the small of her back. She wore a simple blue cotton dress belted with a wide swath of sea green brocade. Her beauty seemed ageless, but laugh lines deepened at her sapphire eyes and smiling mouth. Behind her stood a man with a watchful gaze and deep black hair, streaked with silver, swept into a long braid.

Caleb's eyebrows rose. "Mage? But there are no more mages, not since the Shattering."

"A decision made by the first color mages, including Nikela. To avoid the arrogance that caused the destruction of this city, they established the Orders and we became known as Brothers and Sisters. Whether you call a spade a chicken or a spade does not change what it is. Those blessed with the ability to see and control the colors of life are mages. I call a thing what it is, not what we wish it to be. But where are my manners, I am Rivka, the Scion of the Nikelan Order and its temples and this is Vaughn, my Grier."

Caleb's mouth quirked up. "I guess it would be foolish to ask how you know who we are."

Rivka's eyes crinkled as her smile widened. "We were aware of you long before you came to our Boundary, Caleb." Stepping toward Talise, she held out her hand, which Talise took in her own. "It is always good for the children of Vamorines to come home, my child."

Unblinking, Talise stared at the Scion and spoke in a whisper. "I had heard you still served, Rivka Peacemaker, but I never thought I would ever see you myself, jha'na."

Rivka squeezed her hand. "It has been a very long time since anyone has called me that."

"Oh, come now, Rivka," Vaughn said from the chair he lounged in, his long legs stretched out in front of him. "Didn't I call you that last night at dinner? When I asked you to pass the Vinfirth red, I believe."

Rivka smiled, but otherwise ignored her spouse. "You've come a long way to speak with us. You have made some grave accusations, Caleb Murphy."

Fetching Kade's logbook from the bag slung across his back, he gripped its edges with both hands and spoke the ritual words. "I believe that Tomas Segar, Scion of the Daniyelan Order, is a member of the Brethren. I bring evidence of his corruption and seek the discernment of the Scion of the Nikelans. I seek judgment by the Light itself from the only one vested to remove a Scion. He is no child of the Light."

Rivka nodded. "I shall hear this evidence. Continue."

"I served in the Daniyelan temples for many years before my banishment," Caleb began. "I completed my journeyman year before Nabos began testing the borders of Isfaridesh and Mergoria.

Shortly after I was assigned my first circuit, Nabos began claiming their border towns as part of Nabos' historical territories. It wasn't long after that the Nabosian council and king executed the Daniyelan mediators. The rulers of Nabos had clearly betrayed their people and I had sworn an oath as a Brother of the Daniyelan Order to uphold justice.

"It was my duty to serve the people and I fought. The conscripted soldiers from the other nations all had a Daniyelan commanding officer." Caleb curled his fingers around the logbook more tightly. "I was a very successful officer. After the assassination of the Phaidrian Scion in Lanvirdis, Indolbergan joined the war though they were safe from the Nabosian's expansionist measures. It was clear that the king of Nabos and his followers had to be removed. I fought. I led. And unlike most, I lived as did many of the men under my command."

Caleb drew in a slow breath as he listened to the clear trickle of the water. "I was a good soldier. Because of this, seven years into the war I was removed from my post and given a new command. This new command was comprised entirely of Daniyelans. Tomas was my immediate superior; I reported directly to him. Tomas served as Benjamin's head of intelligence back then. Before Benjamin died in battle and Tomas became the new Daniyelan Scion. We were sent on many missions. Missions which I'm now certain Benjamin never ordered."

Rivka's face remained impassive as she noted the rigidity with which Caleb held himself as though he recounted these events to a superior officer. His formality tried to mask the pain these events held for him and it would have worked one someone with less experience than the woman standing before him.

"You knew the man, jha'na," Caleb said as he laughed, his eyes downcast with remorse and nostalgic longing. "Benjamin was a man who inspired loyalty and devotion. Tomas said the orders came from Benjamin, so I followed. We assassinated key figures in the Nabosian regime. My men, my men died. They sacrificed to retrieve information on supply routes, fortifications, battle plans. We ambushed supply trains, poisoned waterways, blighted farmlands, kidnapped-" Caleb broke off, then cleared his throat.

"I had begun to suspect the origin of our orders, when a

seventeen-year-old boy was assigned to my command. The men I led were all seasoned veterans as Daniyelans and in the war. This boy had yet to finish his journeyman year.

"But this boy," Caleb said, his eyes glinting with a weary pride, "this boy was extraordinary. His name was Kaedman Hawthorn. Kade learned fast, not to just survive, but to thrive. He never hesitated and was wickedly lethal. They say that Daniyelans are the living weapons of the Light. In this boy, it was true. Kade was a weapon. They sent him to me to sharpen, but how they intended to wield him I never discovered. We were sent on a simple retrieval mission after we had completed a several-month guerrilla campaign."

The muscles in Caleb's throat constricted before he regained his composure. "The war was coming to a close and Tomas' information led me to believe it would be clean and easy. My team went in to extract a contact from a small coastal town in the north of Nabos, Stantreath. Easy, he had said."

Caleb raised his gaze and long suffering rage simmered in his eyes. Guilt and loss were plain in the set of his jaw. "They were slaughtered. They were waiting for us with who I thought at the time were renegades from the Orders using black magic. Kade and I were the only two to survive. When we returned, I began investigating Tomas and my unit's orders. I found nothing conclusive enough to publicly accuse the new Scion of my Order, but I did discover that Benjamin had known nothing of our existence.

"When Tomas asked me to lead this team, he told me that Benjamin had formed it and chosen me. He had lied to us and my men were dead. Apparently, my investigation ruffled some feathers, because after the treaty was signed at Kilrood and the war ended, I was blamed for the catastrophe at Stantreath, stripped of my command, and banished from the Orders.

"In the nine years since Stantreath, I have collected information on Tomas and his cohorts. I now know that the men at Stantreath were members of the Brethren and this," he held up Kade's tattered logbook, "is Kaedman Hawthorn's Daniyelan logbook on the council at Montdell. It chronicles the influence of members of the Brethren within the Daniyelan Order and how they have been manipulating the legislation of the councils to give increasing civil authority to the Orders. Kade's observations are disturbing and recent events in Montdell implicate Tomas' involvement. Gareth Burke, the other Daniyelan attached to Montdell, openly spoke of the Brethren with Kade on many occasions. Gareth Burke was also Tomas' second cousin. Gareth tried to recruit Kade for the Brethren and failed."

Caleb strode to Rivka and placed the logbook in her hands. "Jha'na, if Tomas succeeds, every country will hand over their sovereignty to the Daniyelan Order. As we rode in, I saw the ruins of Gialdanis battered beneath the waves. A place I dismissed as a legend. But if the legends are true, the last time mages ruled our society was nearly destroyed and magic itself shattered. I have seen and done horrific things, I would not dream of denying that. But I will not stand by and watch our world burn a second time to the same folly that threw this city into the sea. Read this and decide."

Rivka's pulled the logbook to her chest, her thoughts heavy in her blue eyes. "You are a good man, Caleb Murphy. I will investigate this further, but there is a weighty price I must ask of you."

"I am yours to command, jha'na." Caleb's voice was soft, but firm.

"I do not think it a coincidence that you are Rafaela's brother. Just as she was chosen by Lior, I believe you too were chosen."

"My sister?" Caleb's eyes darkened dangerously at her mention, but what shocked him more was her invocation of the tri-fold deity of his wife's people, the Deoraghan. "What does Ella have to do with this?"

"Your sister is a key. If the Brethren knew the significance and potential of her gifts, this world would enter a time of darkness deeper than the Shattering, deeper than the Cleansings of the Deoraghan. If you want to protect this world, you must protect that which is precious to Lior. You are a guardian, Caleb. That is your mission now. I will deal with Tomas should your allegations prove true.

"This is a difficult task I ask of you both." Rivka looked from Caleb to Talise and back. "You did not betray your men, Caleb. You have spent many years on this quest for justice, which is the truest sign of your loyalty to Lior. Nor is leaving Tomas' punishment in my hands a betrayal of their memories. But you must heed me when I tell you that this is not your battle to fight."

The tops of Rivka's hands glimmered blue. "The weapons that can win this battle have been chosen, but they are still being forged. Should your sister, Rafaela, lose anyone else, I see a splitting of her path. Do you understand my meaning?"

Arms crossed, Caleb's eyes were still dark as he examined the Scion. "I understand."

Rivka tapped a finger on her chin, considering the man clothed in black. "But will you obey?"

Sinking to one knee, Caleb placed a closed fist over his heart in the formal gesture. Orange light covered his eyes and lines seared his forehead as he spoke the binding words. "Before the fire of the Light, I swear it shall be done." The fiery glow flared and disappeared, sinking into his skin like embers turning to ash.

"As always I must ask too much." Rivka's thoughts drifted to Mireya's laughing smile that made her face glow like the sun shining through amber glass. "Well, before you go, may we offer you the hospitality of the Nikelan temple for the evening? You must be very weary."

Caleb rose, but Talise stepped forward to answer. "Yes, we are, jha'na. Thank you."

"Vaughn?" Rivka turned to where he husband had observed silently.

"Already gone." He winked at Rivka and left through a door in one of the archways.

"While Vaughn finds one of the girls to show you to your room and the kitchens, I must satisfy my curiosity. What did Nikela's Mirror show you, Talise?"

Talise shot a glance at Caleb out of the corner of her eye. Though the details had faded like a forgotten dream, the silence after the bird's song stopped filled her mind. "I'm not sure what I saw, jha'na."

"You saw something?" Caleb asked looking from Talise to Rivka. "I didn't see anything. Why didn't I see something?"

Rivka motioned for Talise and Caleb to follow and headed for the archway Vaughn had disappeared through. As she walked, she answered Caleb's question. "The Deoraghan are the true children of Vamorines, exiled after the destruction of Gialdanis. They carry the sight in their blood, a blessing to some, a curse to others. You do not have the sight, so you see nothing but a pretty reflecting pool when you look in the Mirror, but the blood of our people runs true in Talise."

They had entered a hallway that felt claustrophobic after the lofty arched ceiling of the entry. The walls here had been paneled with dark woods where tapestries depicting scenes from their world's history hung at regular intervals. The colors had faded, leeched away by the passage of the years, but the details of the massive weavings remained sharp and clear. As they passed each, Caleb tried to identify, which stories they featured. One depicted the destruction of the Gialdanis as the ground cracked and fell into the sea.

"Did it feel like you had just awoken from a dream that you immediately forgot?" Rivka inquired of Talise.

The colors of the next hanging looked brighter than the others to Caleb. It showed the Cleansing of the Deoraghan by the Orders and the signing of the treaty at the Battle of Twinning Pass. Caleb examined it, wondering which figure was supposed to be Rivka.

Talise nodded. "It did. The more I try to remember, the further it seems to slip away from my mind. All I can recall is a songbird's melody being silenced."

The hall came to an end. The last tapestry showed the seven founders of the Color Orders, each standing in a shaft of colored light at the Shrine of Shattering. The Shrine his little sister now searched for.

Rivka nodded as if she had expected Talise's explanation. "I have seen this before, but it could mean any number of things." Leaving the hallway, they entered a large dining hall. "You will remember when you are meant to."

A plump girl with curly red hair, in a blue dress similar to in cut to Rivka's, approached them and bobbed her head. "Jha'na, Vaughn Grier asked that I show your guests to their quarters. Mistress Talise, master Caleb, if you would be so kind to follow me, we've already seen to your belongings and mounts."

"My thanks, Leigh," Rivka smoothed the girl's hair with an absent gesture. "I wish we could offer you hospitality for more than this night, but I understand your desire to have already left. Lior keep you from darkness, my children."

Talise pressed her palms together and held them at her breast while she bowed her head. "Ashalioris guide you."

Caleb pulled Talise away, his hand around her waist, finishing the blessing. "And Tallior guard your way, jha'na."

Rivka held her palms together at her breast returning the gesture as Leigh led the bounty hunters past the tables and through the arch in the opposing wall. "I know you're there," Rivka spoke into the silence. "You might as well say what you're thinking."

Vaughn joined her watching the trio disappear from sight. "You've known for the last decade, Rivka."

"No, I've suspected Tomas. There is a difference, Vaughn."

"We've always known that Ben's death was no accident."

"Yes, but we could never prove Tomas was involved. Otherwise, he never would have been confirmed as Scion."

"Whether it is true, that boy believed every word he said."

Rivka sighed and rested her head against Vaughn's arm. "Yes, but who of us hasn't deceived ourselves without ever realizing it? Caleb was earnest; it's true. But I cannot depose a fellow Scion on hearsay, no matter how sincere the accuser. We must be certain."

Vaughn grunted agreement and twirled a lock of her hair with a finger. "When do you want me to leave?"

"I should say now, but I'm tired. I'm tired of sending so many children into the darkness. Tonight, I need you here."

"Then here I shall stay."

CHAPTER TWELVE

Lucien perched on the stone boundary fence at the edge of Oakdarrow.   He sat polishing his lyre or at least that's the impression he projected to any passersby.   His rag ran across the grain of the wood in rhythmic circles, but his eyes were busy elsewhere, which caught every shift in Eve's posture, every change in her expression.

She stood at the town's smithy gesturing about an inch above her head indicating a height to the man in the leather apron. Though short in stature himself, the man's compact build showed the expected strength of his trade. The man nodded and turned Eve's shoulders toward the stables between the smithy and the wall and pointed past Lucien with the flat of his hand. Lucien's stomach tightened at the man's casual contact and his gaze darkened, but his hands continued without so much as stutter. Eve shook the smith's hand and returning the gesture he pat her arm soundly.   As she trotted to the wall, her good mood almost palpable in the air, Lucien's eyes glimmered golden as the tension in his face smoothed into a lazy affability.

"News on the hunt, oh great trackeress?" Lucian asked without looking up from his instrument.

Eve's mouth quirked into a smile. "As a matter of fact, yes."

Lucian dropped his rag in mock surprise. "Wait. You're talking to me about your secret mission? Be still my heart."

Eve hopped onto the wall and butted his shoulder with her own. "Don't be a jerk."

"But I'm ever so good at it," he observed without a trace of humility.

"You won't hear me contradicting you."

"You cut me, Eve." Lucien held his fist over his heart. "You cut me deep."

Eve grabbed his fist and pulled Lucien off the wall with her. "I can feel him. He was here and not long ago."

"So, it's a he, yeah?" Lucien poked for more information while hiding the uncertainty that flared inside him. "You're not hunting a jilted lover, are you? Should I be jealous?"

Waving away his jesting, she commented offhand, "There's never been anyone else. But I need you to get Kimiko from the inn, while I check something out."

Lucien smiled at her admission, but still felt a pang of insecurity. "Good information from the smith?"

Eve nodded, but seemed distracted. "Without a doubt. Francis is an old friend. He recognized Kae—" She broke off realizing what she had almost said. "The target of my investigation, he recognized the target of my investigation."

Lucien forced his muscles to remain relaxed, keeping any sign of his anger hidden from her. He knew the name she had almost spoken. He now knew that she hunted for the one man he hated, the man who had always disapproved of Lucien as well as their relationship – Kaedman Hawthorn.

He needed to get away from her before his composure cracked. Grinning, he dropped her hand. "I'll meet you at the grove east of the wall."

Waving, she vaulted over the stone fence. Drawn to the eastern outskirts of the village, her skin felt electrified. The energies around her licked at her like the cresting waters of a flood. Pausing, she inhaled and opened her eyes, which shimmered green. She could see the coursing green energy of the oak grove before her. Instead of flowing healthily like blood in veins, the energies had been torn and hemorrhaged across the ground. Someone had savaged this forest.

To her left, the leaves of an ancient, gnarled oak reaching toward the sky shook in the breeze, a brilliant crimson. Instead of the robust energy of a tree at the end of summer, this tree's energies had faded to that of a tree preparing for the long sleep of winter. Eve dropped to a knee beneath the tree's root system that dove in and out of the ground around her. She dug her fingers into the dry dirt between the roots of the oak. Her hand splayed within the soil, she traced the energies to the center of the incident. Just a few feet from where she knelt, the energy had funneled through a single person.

Her eyes snapping open, Eve blinked and withdrew her hand. "A channel? Here?"

Rubbing the dirt between her fingers, she strode over to the spot where the channel had stood. She could feel where the energy from the grove had burst through the soil and into the person, but the channel had not been the one to use the energy. The energy had been thrown back toward the oak. Following its course, the traces of its overflow centered around one of the roots.

Fading glimmers of red splashed all over the area. It had fueled red magic, but Eve had never seen an aftermath like this. Though the sun beat down on her back warmly, she felt cold, isolated. As though this spot consumed anything warm and living. Crouched, she extended her senses and saw the scarlet energies had seeped deep into the earth. Prodding the shadows left by the magic, she sucked in a breath and lost her balance as a wave of terror and shame engulfed her.

She lay in the dirt with a twig digging into her cheek; the contact had broken. Propped up on her forearms, she heaved herself off the ground and stepped back from the tree as she wiped the dirt from her face. "By the Light, what happened here?"

Her hand skimming her short hair, she looked at the seemingly peaceful grove that masked a hidden torment. Steadying her nerves, Eve collected her internal energy and the green light veiled her eyes again. She kept a safe distance from the treacherous marsh of red magic and searched for other signatures. Near where the channel had stood, she saw a distinctive blend of purple and orange.

Before she moved closer to confirm, she saw a dusting of blue next to the marsh. This glint of blue caused her to stop. Shifting her gaze, the blue seemed to fade. She wiped her eyes with the back of her hand and looked again. No trace of the blue remained.

"Great, now you're seeing legends. What's next a mage?" Eve commented under her breath.

Refocusing her efforts on the purple and orange traces, she touched them and saw Kaedman's face, as though in a memory, but this face was not the face of the man that she remembered. His eyes were bruised with exhaustion and she had never seen his cheeks so hollow. "You should be haunted by what you've done, Kaedman," Eve said her voice tinged with bitterness.

"So, you are searching for Hawthorn," said a flat voice behind her.

Startled by the voice, Eve flinched. She had been so engrossed by her investigation that she had not heard Lucien's approach. Looking over her shoulder, she saw Kimiko trying to shy away from his hold on her reins.

Eve took the lead from his hands, which he gladly surrendered. Patting Kimiko's blaze, she also surrendered. "Yes."

Lucien's face was unreadable. "Why?"

"I need him for questioning in an ongoing investigation."

"What did he do?"

"That's all I'm willing to tell you, Lucien." Eve tugged on Kimiko's reins lightly as she headed for the road.

Lucien put his hand on her shoulder turning her toward him. Her soft brown eyes glistened with tears. She had drained her energy to read the grove and the backlash from the residual red magic had demolished her emotional control. Everything she had walled away washed over her, her grief at Nessa's death, Kaedman's betrayal, her mistrust and love for Lucien. Everything she had tried to ignore, to pretend did not exist came rushing over her.

He brought his free hand to her cheek. "Eve, what did he do?"

She blinked and the tears rolled into his fingers. Her voice breathless, she whispered, "He killed Nessa."

Without a word, he drew Eve into his arms. She didn't fight him this time. Instead she sunk into his chest and wrapped her arms around his back. Her face buried into his neck, she let the tears she had held back for so long fall.

*   *   *

Once again, Faela found herself drawn to water, to its rumble, to the clarity it brought her. Still and silent, she listened as she sat cross-legged on a granite boulder that had lichen creeping up its side. Behind her, the forest rustled as its inhabitants transitioned from day to night. In soft purple streaks, the twilight reflected off the water that raced down the river in front of her. Just soaking in its soothing rush, Faela rested her cheek on the rough canvas that clad her knee.

Lost in the sparkling waters of the Foster River that crashed around protruding rocks, Faela doubled over to grab her bag from the springy ground below. Elbow deep into the satchel, her fingers found their quarry. She smiled with wistful nostalgia as she pulled out a small, pale green scrap of fabric. She let the blanket settle onto her lap, which it barely covered. Her fingers twined in the soft fabric, she began humming the refrain from Sammi's lullaby and her eyes faded behind a red mist.

Neither man moved as Kade and Dathien watched the rabbit nibble on the purplish berries hanging off the bush in front of them. Just a little to the left, if it moved just a little to the left they too would soon eat. The rabbit hopped toward a large cluster that happened to be to its left. It made a high-pitched screech when the trap snared its legs and whipped the scrawny animal into the air.

"Nicely done," Dathien observed revealing his hiding place as he moved toward the rabbit that thrashed in its captivity.

Kade stretched his legs and back as he stood. "It shouldn't have taken that long for something to wander into that trap."

"This is unusual? You know these moors better than I do."

Kade nodded as Dathien unsheathed his knife and slit the animal's throat ending its agony. Something brushed the back of Kade's neck. Swatting at it, Kade frowned. There was nothing there. He felt it again. Kade turned to identify the cause. Nothing was there. Then the contact returned and with it came a sweet, childlike melody – a song.

Stealing a glance at Dathien, the other man had almost finished skinning the rabbit and nothing about his focused efficiency indicated that he had heard anything. Kade felt a pure, uncomplicated love wash over him as the music continued. He blinked, shocked by the intensity of the emotions. Words soon accompanied the music. As though he thought it himself, he heard inside his mind a feminine voice, a familiar voice singing. *Shine, shine like the sun. Light will come and night be done.*

Without knowing how, he knew the music came from the river. Just as surely as he knew where the music originated, he also felt a compulsion to find its source.

"Dathien, you take that back to camp. I'm going to see if I have any luck by the water."

One-handed, Jair grasped the dead branch sticking out of the briars and pulled, but the wood refused to budge. The vines growing around it and up the tree had entangled the branch. Tucked under his other arm, the results of his scavenging balanced precariously. Jair looked at the dry branch and tried to gauge how firmly it was wedged into the jagged shrubs.

Though the leaves around him remained still, he felt the passing touch of a breeze that carried the faintest hints of a melody. It did not carry the sound of a song so much as the memory of one.

Though Jair would have sworn he had never heard it before, it reminded him of his mother. The way she would laugh when he couldn't stop himself from smiling when he tried to lie, that no matter what he had done, she still loved him. Jair let the thought pass without examining it too closely as he put down his firewood. He had decided to try wrestling away his prize from the brambles.

Walking along the riverbank, Kade strained his eyes in the dwindling light. Though the song had ended, the emotion tugging him forward remained. As he climbed a small rise, he saw a rocky outcropping ahead. He heard unrestrained laughter carry across the running water. Sitting on the rocks, he saw Faela smiling. He had never seen her features so bright and relaxed. The joy radiating from her smile caused him to pause before approaching. In that moment of hesitation, he stepped onto a pile of debris washed ashore from the river's last flooding.

Alerted by the crunching sound, Faela dropped the cloth in her hands, her features returning to the cold mask he had seen so often. Her hand had dropped to the dagger he knew she kept in her boot and her eyes glowed a dangerous dark crimson as she faced him.

"Oh, it's just you." She let out the breath she had held and her posture relaxed though her face remained unreadable. Without another word, she surreptitiously stuffed the cloth into her bag.

Kade grinned. "Just me? Just?"

Not rising to the bait, she asked instead, "Do you need something?"

Kade leapt from rock to rock until he reached hers and sank down next to her. "So, what's with you and sitting by running water?"

Faela just stared at him her mouth slightly open at his brash intrusion. "Did I say, 'Please join me; won't you sit on down'?"

Kade's grin widened. "I'd love to."

"That's not what I—" Faela broke off making an irritating sound in her throat. "Forget it. What's the point anyway?"

Undeterred by her reaction, Kade asked again, "What started this fascination with rivers?"

Faela just sighed, resigning herself to his presence. "It reminds me of home."

"Which one? Kilrood or Finalaran?"

"You know, it's a little disturbing that you know that."

"Everyone knows that the Tereskan temple is on the shores of the Kurinean Sea in Kilrood. Plus, you're a Durante of House Evensong, so that means you're from Finalaran and the Dalibor River cuts the city in half. Anyone who knows the Merchant Houses would know that. So, let me see if I understand. You find a basic grasp of geography and deduction disturbing? Anyone ever tell you that you're paranoid?"

Faela spoke enunciating each word clearly. "Caleb Murphy is my brother."

"Ah, you do have a point," Kade conceded. "So which is it?"

"Both, I guess. I've always lived near water," she explained. "Everything seems too quiet without it. Half the time without even realizing it, I find myself seeking it out. I usually don't even know that's what I was doing until I'm already there."

As she tucked her knees under her chin, Kade smiled watching her out of the corner of his eye.

"What about you?" she asked scrapping her heel against the rock as she readjusted. "Do you sneak up on people for fun all the time or is it just me?"

"Who says I'm out here looking for you?" Kade deflected her comment.

Faela rotated her face, her cheek resting on her boney knees, so he could see her skepticism.

Without missing a beat, Kade found a plausible excuse. "I promised your brother, but since you keep insisting on disappearing, I am forced to find you. It's not my fault that you're unobservant."

Faela rolled her eyes, but her mouth jumped as she tried to repress a grin.

Kade's deep brown eyes captured her own, though her instinct was to look away, she did not. The pleasant warmth spreading in her stomach offset the unease in her mind. It was nice to not have to hide from everyone.

"You know your eyes shine like moonlight on water when you smile. You should let yourself do it more often." Kade felt the same warmth lap at his mind and grinned as it confirmed his suspicions.

A cold bitterness sliced through her as his words evoked memories of Nikolais. He had loved the color of her eyes before, before everything shattered. "There's not much to smile about," she whispered as the warmth froze.

Sensing the shift in her emotions, he tested his theory. "Light will come and night be done."

Faela's head snapped up. "Where did you hear that? Did Caleb tell you?"

"No," Kade stretched out the word. He could feel her panic like spikes jabbing him. "I heard it from you. It's what drew me to you earlier. You were singing it, weren't you?"

Faela's brow drew together in disbelief. "But you weren't here. I never saw you."

"You're right. I wasn't. I was about half a league from here trapping with Dathien. That's when I heard it." Kade tapped his temple. "I heard it in here."

Faela buried her face into the sleeves of her coat. "Oh, no."

"I also felt, I felt joy, affection, love, and sadness, but you were trying to hide the sadness."

Tangling her fingers into her hair, she berated herself. While they talked, the half-light of dusk had deepened to full dark. She raised her head and pressed her chest into her tented legs, humming low to herself. Her temples pulsed with golden lines and her eyes glimmered red. She touched his cheek and his heart quickened as he felt her fear as though it were his own while the image of a stuffed lamb abandoned on a rocking chair formed in his mind. He could smell the tang of salt in the air that blew through the open window.

Looking into Faela's eyes, he described what he saw. "It's near the sea. There's a rocking chair with a lamb on it, a stuffed lamb."

Faela's hand wavered where it touched him and the colored light cleared like smoke. She moved to pull her hand away and he caught it with his own.

With guilt rippling around her, her eyes searched for forgiveness. "I am so sorry, Kade. It was-"

Too late, Kade dropped her hand and twisted just as a tall woman with cropped brown hair leapt onto the rocks and threw a right hook at his jaw whose force ground bone against bone. Standing over him, the woman removed a curved blade from its scabbard.

Orange fire licked along the blade and engulfed her eyes. "Miss me?"

*   *   *

Though night had fallen, Eve had refused to stop when Lucien had asked. As she led Kimiko through the forest, he hung back giving her space. They must be getting close. Otherwise she would never risk her horse turning an ankle in an unknown wood in the dark. Remembering how annoyingly observant Hawthorn was, Lucien began preparing the glamour for his persona, Haley. His hair shimmered from a deep auburn to the color of straw and his nose bent as if he had been on the losing side of a bar fight, while his jaw retracted and rounded near the chin. The golden light faded from his eyes and temples when the transformation completed.

Eve stopped Kimiko and waited for him to catch up. She turned to look at him and took an instinctive step back at his appearance and punched him in the chest.

"Darkness take you, Lucien! Warn me before you put up a glamour."

When he spoke his voice rumbled, its pitch had lowered. "Sorry, Evie. From your fidgetiness, I figured we must be close to Hawthorn. I didn't want to risk him recognizing me. He always notices way too much."

Eve caressed his cheek once without thinking. "No, that's good. But don't call me Evie. He'll suspect something if you do. Like you said, he notices too much. He's close now, very close." Reins in her hands, she pointed where the forest began thinning ahead. "This way."

From the direction that Eve indicated came the low thunder of water. Lucien watched her back as she wended Kimiko around the densely wooded forest. The muscles of her neck and shoulders bunched hard and tight. Her fingers played with the reins as they always did when she had too much nervous energy. She was wound like a coil ready to explode. Eve had always been tightly controlled, but Lucien has never seen her like this.

The desire to make the tension inside Eve melt away felt like an itch he couldn't reach. He moved his hand to push a stray hair behind his ear before he realized his hair was too short to do so. With Nessa dead, however, there was nothing he could do except stay out of her way and he knew it. That didn't mean that he liked it. As much as he hated Kaedman Hawthorn, he couldn't deny the man's skill or his lethality.

Lucien dreaded the idea of Eve opposing him. While her height matched Lucien's own, her lithe build looked like a delicate willow swaying in the wind. She seemed so breakable to Lucien right then. He had an unshakable faith in her abilities, but that didn't stop him from fearing for her safety. Hawthorn was not a man you antagonized unless you had good reason and Eve had a reason that no amount of charm could persuade her to abandon, no matter how badly he wanted to protect her.

They had reached the edge of the forest and he could now see the river tumbling on its way. Seated amongst a rock field, a man leaned toward a woman deep in conversation. Lucien recognized Hawthorn's profile at once. Eve had dropped Kimiko's reins as the woman touched his temple and he covered her hand with his own. Her face blank of all emotion, Eve sprinted toward the pair.

*   *   *

The warm bite of blood filled Kade's mouth. Rubbing his jaw where Eve had hit him, he spit the blood into the river. He rose with deliberate care and positioned himself so that he blocked Eve's view of Faela. A stolen glance told him that she had already pulled on her hat that had rested on the rocks. Though Kade knew without a doubt that Eve's attention fixated on him alone.

"Eve," he said in way of acknowledgment. Not even a full foot filled the space between the two Daniyelans.

"My name? That's all you have to say?" Eve clenched her fingers around the hilt of her long knife in order to keep her voice from shaking with the rage filling her. "Clearly, you don't even miss Nessa," she accused, waving her blade at Faela who had yet to move. "Is this why you killed her, Kaedman? To run away with this tart?"

Eve took a step toward Faela, but Kade mirrored her movement blocking her way. "No, Eve."

"Well, she obviously meant nothing to you from what I just watched. She's not been dead three weeks, Kaedman – three weeks." Eve closed the gap between them. Kade stood only a few inches taller than the woman before him.

Locking his eyes with her flame-filled ones, he advanced forcing her to take a step back. "When you were eight Eve and you accused Sheridan of stealing your copy of *Roland's Legends* simply because you had seen her reading the day before, I thought you would grow out of jumping to wild conclusions based solely on your own perceptions. I see that you have not. Where is Sheridan? Why isn't she with you?"

Eve's breathing quickened, but her hand remained steady as it gripped the hilt. Her control finally broke and she yelled drowning out the roar of the river. "Don't you dare tell me, tell me, about my sister, you darkness loving traitor. She trusted you, loved you like a brother, and this is how you repay her? By killing our cousin? By murdering your fiancé?"

The fire on her blade flared and surrounded her hand as well in response to her anger.

"You must calm down, Evelyn," Kade warned watching the fire. "You know what will happen if you lose control."

Despite the rock biting into her ankle, Faela did not move, but watched Kade and the Daniyelan woman, her mind trying to understand what was happening. This woman had just accused Kade of murdering his fiancé. Faela had no doubt that Kade would kill when he had to, but this was different.

She could feel his regret, his guilt, his pain. Kade had been running, just like she had. She had known there had to be a reason. Why should this information feel like she had been punched in the gut? Faela's shock and mistrust hit Kade harder than Eve's right hook, but he would not look at her. He wanted to explain, but he would not draw Eve's attention to her. It could wait.

At that moment Mireya, Dathien, and Jair broke through the line of trees. Staff in hand, Dathien's eyes swept over the scene assessing the situation as he approached with caution.

Hiking up her skirts, Mireya pushed past him and marched over to the rocks. Dropping them, she put her hands on her hips and faced Eve demanding, "Who are you? And what do you think you're doing?"

Mireya's blue eyes shone with her irritation. With one look at her eyes, the flames consuming Eve's blade and hand extinguished. Her fingers lost their grip and the blade clattered onto the rocks. Faela grabbed the sword and joined Dathien and Jair.

"A Nikelan?" Eve whispered, her rage transformed into confusion.

"You haven't answered me, Daniyelan," Mireya said with more authority than someone her size should be able to command.

"Sister Evelyn Reid of the House of Fireglen."

"Well, Sister Evelyn Reid of the House of Fireglen, what did you think you were about to do, hmm?"

Regaining her composure and her righteous anger, Eve gestured toward Kade. "Taking a fugitive into custody."

"That's not what it sounded like to me, Evelyn Reid."

"I'm sorry," Eve said her ire rising, "but what business of yours is this, Nikelan? What concern of yours is this man?"

Mireya's confidence wavered. "Um, he hunts for me for one."

"Hunts?" Eve raised an eyebrow. "So, what right do you have to stop me from fulfilling my oath to justice?"

Mireya gnawed on her bottom lip and looked to Dathien who stepped to her side. "What are the charges against him, Daniyelan?" His voice was quiet and steady. "What laws of the Light has he violated?"

"He murdered a daughter of the Noble Houses of Montdell, Nessa Reid."

"What proof do you bring against him?" Faela questioned, speaking for the first time since Eve's arrival.

"I do not have to prove anything to anyone but the Light." Eve tried to peer into the moon lit shadows cast by the brim of Faela's hat. "You weren't wearing that when I first arrived."

She made to move toward Faela, when Kade stepped in front of her and swept Faela behind him with an arm. Eve's eyes and right hand ignited with orange fire.

"You kill Nessa, but you protect her?" Her voice dropped to a deadly growl. "By the Light, you will pay for this, Kaedman Hawthorn. I swear by the burning flame of justice, you will pay."

With that Eve, placed her open palm against his chest, which exploded with fire that engulfed them both. Kade stumbled and blood seeped through his shirt from his chest wound. Mireya shrieked and back away from the inferno. Faela looked down at her hands and saw the flames begin to appear. Closing her eyes, she hummed a single note and the flames extinguished.

Without a moment of hesitation, she wrapped her arms around Kade's back allowing the flames to flow over her. The full force of her voice behind the note this time, the flames turned scarlet and disappeared.

When the fire vanished, a loud crack and a flash of purple exploded throwing Eve, Kade, and Faela apart. Faela landed hard knocking the air from her lungs with Kade crumpled at her feet. Where the trio had been, stood a woman like, but unlike Eve. Her hair was braided like brown silk down to her waist.

The woman whipped her head around until she spotted Kade bleeding, sprawled across Faela's legs. "Kade!" she cried and rushed to his side.

Faela had already started moving. Kneeling next to him, she lowered her ear to his mouth. She felt his warm breath and heard his thought, *Darkness, she actually tried to bind me.*

Blinking, but too relieved to be shocked by the mental contact, she rested her forehead on his chest for a moment. "Can you sit, Kade?"

He nodded but said nothing as he lifted his head. Now that Faela could see her clearly, the woman looked like a reflection of Eve, except for the hair.

Kade put a hand on the woman's forearm and squeezed, a genuine smile on his mouth. "Sheridan, you're here. Good."

Sheridan winked. "Someone's got to save your hide."

Pausing, Sheridan stared at Faela supporting Kade. The force of the fall had knocked Faela's hat off so that it hung down her back. Distracted by Kade's possible injuries Faela looked up without thinking and their eyes met. Sheridan grinned with a laugh of surprise, but said nothing.

Convinced that no lasting harm had come to Kade, Sheridan surveyed the riverbank and spotted her sister who had clambered back to her feet. Sheridan pushed off the ground and advanced on her sister and slapped her across the cheek with a sharp crack. "Eve, what in the name of the Light were you thinking? I told you to bring him back so we could question him, not bind him. He can't stand trial if he's dead. Darkness, Eve, you could have killed both of you! Then where would I be?"

Eve stared at her twin her mouth agape in shock. "But he's guilty. He never denied killing her once."

Sheridan smiled cheerlessly. "That's where you're wrong. Gareth killed Nessa, not Kade."

Before Eve could respond to Sheridan's revelation, Mireya watched the twins and her eyes glowed like burning sapphires and lines of blue seared her hands.

Her voice expanded and boomed across the river, "Seven shall come to undo what was done. From Shadow revealed, three destinies sealed."

At the multiple voices speaking as one, the twins froze facing one another and turned to see Mireya's eyes staring at them without seeing them as she recited the prophecy. Her head tilted to the side as she concluded. "From death shall be life; the world formed anew. A promise was made; redemption pursue."

As the voices faded and the light withdrew, Mireya blinked as though she had no idea what had just happened. Dathien put a hand to the small of her back as she began to wobble unsteadily.

"Was that what I think it was?" Sheridan asked the corners of her lips twitching with excitement.

Jair tapped his chin thoughtfully. "If you thought it was a Nikelan prophecy, then you get a cookie." Jair craned around Dathien so he could see Faela sitting on the ground. "Faela, do you have any cookies?"

Sheridan tried to repress her amusement at the lanky man. He seemed to Eve unusually comfortable with what had just occurred as though Mireya had merely skipped a stone across a pond, instead of acting as a channel, becoming the voice of the Light.

"Ohh, so I prophesied then?" Mireya asked leaning into Dathien's support. "That would be why I'm dizzy. I thought I was just hungry."

Kade had managed to get himself into a sitting position with Faela's help. "So what does it mean? You haven't prophesied, since you first saw Faela."

Eve had stood stunned since the prophecy had interrupted Sheridan, but the mention of the woman she had found with Kade in connection with the prophecy peaked her curiosity. She wanted to know who this woman was.

Dathien supplied a theory. "I'd say more of the seven have arrived. Though they don't look very tree-like, there's no denying that they're twins."

Looking up through her hair, Faela added, "And they're not alone." She looked at Eve, her face impassive. "You can tell your friend to come out now."

Eve looked over into the forest with a scowl. "Haley, bring Kimiko with you."

Sheridan cocked her head to side questioningly at her sister as a man with a tumble of straw-colored hair and a round face exited the forest trailing a horse behind him. Though Sheridan kept her suspicions to herself, she couldn't help feeling confused that someone traveled with Eve. It made her stomach twinge.

The man approached the group and the horse trotted past him to Eve in a hurry to return to her master. Faela helped Kade stand and turned to look at the man she had sensed in the forest. When she saw his face, hers blanched and she took a step back.

"Faela?" Kade questioned her reaction.

The man Eve had called Haley swept through the group and strode purposefully up to Faela who stood her ground. He grabbed her shoulders and stared at her.

"Hey now," Jair protested. "Let's keep our hands to ourselves, ser."

Haley ignored Jair and continued staring at Faela.

It was Faela who finally broke the silence. "So, I can see we have something in common, but would you please mind letting me go. You've got a pretty good grip there."

Haley dropped his hands, but made no move to give Faela more space. "How? How can you be-"

"A Gray? I doubt I'd have to explain to you. Your name's Haley?" Faela asked her voice calm.

The man blinked and his face transformed with a grin that coaxed a smile from Faela in response. He swept his traveling cloak around him as he bowed low before her. "The name's Haley, miss. I be a Lusican minstrel that this fine Daniyelan woman agreed to let travel with her. Kind soul that one. Well, kind when she ain't out for holy vengeance that is. And who might you be, lovely?"

"I'm Faela. The ebony beauty with the impressive bass voice is Mireya and the one holding her up is her Grier, Dathien. The gangly one who needs a haircut is Jair. This is Kade."

Mireya had been staring at the churning water when she rejoined the conversation. "Wait. Faela, you just said Gray."

"Welcome back, darling. I surely did."

Jerking her thumb at Haley, Mireya asked, "He's a Gray?"

Faela nodded once.

"Oh, goody!" Mireya clapped her hands together and flounced over and shimmied her way between Faela and Haley. Her nose scrunched up, she peered up at his face and promptly sneezed.

Rubbing her finger under her nose, Mireya sniffed. "Well, he's definitely a Gray."

"Does that mean that he's part of the prophecy?" Jair inquired.

"How many Grays do you usually run into randomly in the forest?" Mireya asked with a snort. "He must be."

"Well, so far my track record is two," Jair said holding up two fingers that he turned to look at and then hold them out for Mireya to count. "Yeah, so far two."

Kade had to keep restraining the urge to pull Faela away from the minstrel. Something about him bothered Kade, but he couldn't discern what it was. Though this man was a Gray, he was not like Faela.

"Well, if he's the second of the three," Mireya tapped her finger on her chin, "then he'll need to know where he's going now."

"Where he's going?" Eve found her voice. "What do you mean where he's going? Who are you people?"

"With us," Mireya explained, as though the question were extremely silly, "to the Shrine of Shattering of course."

"To where?" Sheridan blurted out in disbelief.

"I did say the Shrine of Shattering, right Dathien?" Mireya turned for confirmation from her husband. "I said it out loud?"

"You did."

"Oh. Have you not heard of it?" Mireya looked with concern at Sheridan.

"No, she's heard of it," Kade answered for his flabbergasted friend. "You just told her that her childhood daydreams and fantasies just came true."

"So it's a real place? You've been there?" Sheridan's questions tumbled out in a rush of words.

"Well, no," Mireya said slowly.

"It's not real?" Sheridan fired back. "Then where are you going?"

"No, it's real. I just haven't been there," Mireya explained, "yet."

"Not this again," Kade interrupted to interpret Mireya's half answers. "Look, we're heading for Kelso. There's a man there who's a redeemed Gray. He has information. He knows how to get to the Shrine."

"Why do we need to go there?" Haley asked. "Why do I have to go with you?"

"Because that's where Faela is going and the nudges haven't told me that she's wrong."

"Any cosmic forces poking you now?" Jair asked.

"Other than the prophecy, nope."

"So will you come with us, Haley?" Faela asked, her arms interlaced across her chest.

"Wait," Eve interrupted finally regaining her mental footing. "Just wait a moment. You're not going anywhere. Kade has to return with me to Finalaran to stand trial."

Sheridan turned to her sister. "I told you, Eve. He didn't kill her. He doesn't need to stand trial and the murderer is dead. There will be no trial."

Eve's jaw clenched in a hard line as the wind blew the water misting from the river into her face. "What proof do you have? How do you know that he didn't kill her? You're just trying to protect him." *Like I tried to protect Lucien.*

Her eyes darkened as she approached her sister, she pulled Eve close. Sheridan spoke so that only Eve could hear what she said. "Had Kade done what you assumed, I would be the first to bring him to Finalaran. Never doubt my resolve, Evelyn. I won't discuss this now, but trust me." Sheridan's expression softened as she looked at her twin. "Just trust me for now, Eve. He's innocent of Nessa's death."

Eve sighed, though her eyes still burned with rage. "Fine."

"We need to figure out what's going on here. Why is there a Nikelan wandering in Nabos? How is it that not only is this woman a Gray, but also the man you're traveling with and what in the name of the Light is this prophecy and what does Kade have do with all of this? We need to stick this out, Eve."

Eve nodded her assent. "I said, fine, Sheridan. We'll at least stay with them until they reach Kelso. How could there be a redeemed Gray running around the countryside without the Orders knowing about it? Something doesn't add up here. There's something about that Gray woman. I don't trust her." Eve glanced at Faela out of the corner of her eye.

Faela stood behind Kade with a hand flat on his chest while she prodded the flesh between his ribs. He shook his head at the question she asked too quietly for them to hear. Her face was focused, ignoring everyone else around her but the man she examined. Nodding her head, she stepped away from him with a satisfied expression in her eyes.

Closing her fingers in toward her palm, Eve narrowed her eyes at Kade as the briefest hint of orange flashed across them. She pulled her closed fist back and Kade stumbled as though he had lost his balance. She smiled to herself imperceptibly. *The binding worked. Now you can't escape me, Kaedman.*

Steadying Kade, Faela's eyes found Eve and the silver had darkened resembling cold and hard granite.

CHAPTER THIRTEEN

To fight off the growing cold of the night, Sheridan scooted closer to the fire. Her hands tucked under her armpits, she slid her feet until they nearly touched one of the flaming logs.

"Let me see if I understand," she began looking at the people sprawled across the camp. "You don't know why you're on this journey?"

"That's not exactly accurate," Mireya corrected. "I know that I'm supposed to aid Faela and apparently Haley here now too."

"Okay, so why are we finding this Shrine?" Sheridan ran her fingers rhythmically through a strand of her hair. "I mean, don't get me wrong. I'm thrilled with the prospect of finding it, but I'm more than a little obsessed with the old legends."

"A little obsessed would be owning a bookshelf dedicated to the legends. But you," Kade said poking at Sheridan with the toe of his boot, "you have every manuscript you've been able to borrow, trade, and steal concerning these legends."

Sheridan looked injured, but her eyes sparkled. "Not my fault! You're the one who filled my head with these stories when we were kids. Not responsible! It was all you."

Kade chuckled and threw a pebble at her. "Spoiled rotten that one."

"I'd like to point out that if I'm spoiled, you're to blame. But really, who could say no to this face?" Sheridan's lower lip protruded and trembled pathetically.

"Someone with the same face," Eve suggested.

"Oh, that's just cheating," Sheridan accused. "So," she turned her questioning to Faela who was using Jair for a backrest, "why is it so urgent that you get to this Shrine?"

"I have my reasons." Faela felt anxious with so many new people in their camp. Though these people knew that she was a Gray, they did not know why. In fact, none of them knew and Faela still didn't know how her companions would react to the news of what she had done. If she had to tell them she would, just not yet, not tonight.

"Really? That's all you're going to give me?" Sheridan leaned forward, her elbows resting on her knees and spoke each word slowly. "You have your reasons?"

"That's right." Faela chewed on her thumbnail, giving every indication that she intended to give nothing more as she glanced at Sheridan and Eve's uniforms.

"That irritates you, right?" Sheridan asked Kade. "I mean like really irritates you?"

"She's got a right to her privacy," he shrugged.

Sheridan squinted an eye at Kade. "You would never let me get away with that."

"Yeah, because you have no right to privacy."

"Tyrant."

"Brat."

"So, I get why Mireya and," Sheridan paused, biting her inner lip, "Dathien, right? Why Mireya and Dathien have to go where she's going. But what's the story, Kade? Why're you going?"

"Repaying a debt." Kade gazed into the fire.

"Well that be terribly tragic sounding," Haley interjected from his seat against a tree. "Sounds like a story be in there."

"There's always a story," Eve said almost to herself, "isn't there?"

"What's your story then?" Jair asked resting his chin on Faela's shoulder looking at Eve and Sheridan and then back again. "But first, since tonight seems to be introduction time, my name is Jair and I'm a fan of eating."

"Yeah, be careful what you leave out or it just may end up missing," Kade warned. "And by missing I mean, he'll have consumed it without chewing."

"I chew!" Jair objected. "Sometimes."

"Oh yeah," Sheridan straightened up, "I just realized that I never actually introduced myself. I'm Sheridan Reid and I am also a fan of eating."

"A bigger understatement has never been uttered," Eve said to no one in particular.

"Actually," Kade said pointing two fingers at Jair, "you may have met your match in this one. Be wary when she gets to the food first, because there may be nothing left for you."

"That happened once," Sheridan protested. "And I definitely asked you if I could have your share beforehand."

"I wasn't there. How does that count?"

"Not my fault."

"It never is."

"Uh huh," Sheridan said pleased with herself. "Now you're catching on, such a bright boy."

"You were introducing yourself," Jair reminded her.

"Ah, yes. Well, I know it will come as a shock to you, but the one sitting over there all grumpy-like is my twin sister, Eve."

Eve merely crossed her arms and raised an eyebrow.

"She's usually very pleasant." Sheridan leaned toward Faela and Jair and spoke in a loud whisper so that everyone in the camp and several woodland creatures outside the camp heard. "You just caught her on a cranky day."

"You seem to have recovered your humor," Eve observed.

"Well, clearing someone from a murder investigation tends to put a little spring in my step, don't you know."

"When did you and Kade meet?" Mireya asked pulling her cloak in more tightly.

Sheridan looked at him and framed his face with her fingers and thumbs. "Since before the Shattering of the Light? Okay, so not quite that long ago, it just feels that way. I think I first met you when I was, what, five?"

"Sounds about right," Kade nodded. "You were all pigtails and flashing people with your dresses back then, such a lady. Wouldn't stop following me if I remember correctly."

"Hey, it's not my fault that no one else wanted to catch frogs with me. And I am a lady, I'll thank you."

"At least you don't wear pigtails any more," Kade left the implication hanging in the air.

Sheridan's face didn't change as she leaned over and punched Kade in the arm as hard as she could.

"See what I mean?" Kade said laughing as he rubbed his arm.

"We met when Eve and I were sent for temple training and since Kade's gifts and my own mirror one another, we were tracked together."

A look of understanding dawned on Faela's face. "So you're an Amserian as well," she addressed her revelation to Kade.

"Yeah, he is," Sheridan interrupted before he could answer. "He just wishes he were a popper like me."

"So were you in Montdell before you popped here?" Kade asked.

Sheridan nodded. "I had continued the investigation, while Eve was supposed to find you for questioning."

Jair's eyes bugged out at this news. "You were in Montdell? How'd you get here so fast? That's hundreds of leagues away. I never knew Amserians could pop that far."

Sheridan's grin widened. "Want to see?"

Sheridan stood up and Jair removed himself from his duty as Faela's backrest. Placing a hand on his shoulder, Sheridan's eyes glowed indigo and the light oozed out until it surrounded her and Jair as well. There was a quick increase in the air pressure and a loud sucking sound like swirling water down a drain and they were gone.

From far away they heard a yelp and then a splash followed by a cackle of laughter. Two or three heartbeats later, the air pressed down around them again and in a flash of indigo light they were back, but Jair was now soaking wet and Sheridan perfectly dry.

Kade took one look at them and shook his head chuckling. "I warned you about her."

"Woman! You dropped me in the river," Jair protested wringing out his drenched right sleeve, when a thought seemed to occur to him and he twisted his left sleeve over Sheridan's head. "See, that's river water."

Sheridan yelped and danced back from Jair's reach wiping the water that had trickled onto her forehead. "That's cheating!"

Jair blinked. "I'm sorry," he began as though she didn't understand and then increased his volume, "but you just dropped me in a river."

"It's not my fault that you lost your balance," Sheridan said her face the picture of innocence.

Jair narrowed his eyes. "My vengeance shall be slow and involve paper cuts, many paper cuts."

"Should I be worried?" Sheridan asked Kade over her shoulder.

Kade shook his head.

Jair continued as though no one listened. "And lemons. Oh yes, I shall have my lemony revenge."

"You're still talking?" Sheridan asked. "I promise this is not a tragedy."

"Says you! It's freezing!"

"Let me show you another trick," Sheridan said walking toward him.

Jair put up his hands. "Oh no, you don't. Fool me once, shame on you. Fool me twice, shame on you for tripping me while I tried to run away."

Sheridan laughed once at that. "I like this one. Can we keep him?" Sheridan directed her question to Eve.

Despite Eve's suspicions, she couldn't help but smile at Sheridan's antics. It had been too long since Eve had gotten to see this truly manic side of Sheridan. She had missed it.

Her only response was to say, "Sheridan, just do it before he freezes."

At that, Sheridan pounced on Jair who squealed like a little girl. Her hand flashed with purple light and all of the moisture in Jair's clothing was bone dry in an instant.

"Handy, right?" Sheridan said grinning.

"Where'd you learn to do that?" Jair asked his jaw slack with wonder.

"It's just a little trick I picked up working as a battlefield healer." Sheridan shrugged and folded her long legs underneath herself as she sat.

"When you were eleven," Kade added.

"It hadn't stopped raining for eight days. My socks were soaked. I," Sheridan said holding her hands up and shrugged, "improvised. I just moved the water back to the river. It's where it wanted to be anyway, just putting things right."

Jair nodded never taking his eyes from her. "Yeah, I'm pretty sure you're mad."

"By that you mean brilliant and winsome, of course."

"Of course," Kade answered his tone wry.

"So you conveniently changed the subject and never finished answering my question, good ser." Sheridan targeted Kade.

"Who're you doing a favor for?"

"Caleb."

Both Sheridan and Eve froze where they sat, but Eve spoke first. "You're helping that traitor?"

Half a heartbeat behind her, Sheridan asked, "Caleb's mixed up with this too?"

"I'm sorry, Eve was it?" Faela said her tone low. "But what did you just say?"

"He's talking about a traitor to the Daniyelan Order," Eve explained matter-of-factly. "He disgraced himself and was stripped of his rank in the Orders at the end of the war. If he's involved, nothing good will come of this."

"I see," Faela said a strange look in her eyes. "Well, then, I guess we disagree on what constitutes a traitor."

"He was tried and thrown out of the Order by the Scion himself, Tomas Segar. There can be no disagreement regarding that bastard's guilt."

Kade felt Faela's fury like standing next to an open forge and readied himself to intervene if necessary, but Faela reined her anger back as she rose without a word and left the camp.

"Evelyn," Kade reprimanded, "you need to learn to hold your tongue."

"I spoke nothing, but the plain truth." Eve said without any guilt. "I see no fault."

"That woman," Kade gestured after Faela as he stood, "is Rafaela Durante, Caleb Durante Murphy's little sister."

"Oh, Eve," Sheridan said in barely more than a whisper.

Kade just shook is head as he trotted in the direction Faela had started walking. "You never think."

* * *

Faela grabbed a low-lying branch of the elm and pulled herself up. Levering off of her torso, she brought her feet under herself to stand on the branch. Just as she reached for the next branch, she saw someone jogging below her. She swung her knee over the branch and lifted herself up to sit on it. She rotated her back to rest against the trunk. The man stopped under the tree and pivoted scouting in every direction.

Faela's nose tickled and she sneezed. Alerted by the sound, Kade found her and lay his hand on the first branch. She waved halfheartedly before she stared through the canopy of the forest out to the stars above, ignoring him.

"Can I come up?"

Without looking back down, she beckoned for him to join her. Kade swayed holding the branch as he brought a foot to meet his hands and stepped up into the tree. He slung his arms over the branch Faela used for her seat.

"You always look for somewhere to run?" Kade asked looking out into the forest from their high vantage point.

Faela finally tore her gaze away from the sky to glare at him. The leaves shuddered in the wind, which cut through Faela's shirt. She leaned forward to tuck her bulky overcoat closer around her body.

"It's a better alternative to what I would have done had I stayed," Faela admitted, her voice still had a sharp edge.

"He's not a traitor, Faela," Kade finally turned back to her. "I was there, in Stantreath. He wouldn't let me testify."

Faela's face fell slack, the anger diffusing around her like steam. "You were there?"

Kade nodded. "Your brother saved my life. It wasn't the first time." Kade snorted. "This was different though. I didn't think any of us were going to make it out."

Faela held her breath as he continued. Laying her head back against the tree's ridged bark, she played with the fraying cuffs of her coat.

"They weren't supposed to be there. We were supposed to be walking into friendly territory. Did you know that? It's why they got so many of us in the first attack. But a moment before the ambush, Caleb got this odd look on his face and shoved me to the ground. He was fast, just not fast enough. That's how he got the scar on his face. He was protecting me. Your brother would have gladly died to save his men, Faela."

Faela's eyes shone with tears.

Smiling with regrets about events he could never change, Kade grabbed for her hand. "He betrayed no one."

Faela returned the pressure. "I know he didn't. It's just that a lot happened today and I couldn't, I just couldn't brush off what that horrible woman said."

"She's not horrible," Kade objected. "Eve is just a little tactless regarding what she views as the truth. To her, it's irrational to be offended by what she considers a statement of fact or truth. She's a little single-minded sometimes and she just lost someone very close to her. Just give her a chance. I think you'd actually like her."

Faela made an unladylike noise of disbelief as she wiped the unshed tears away with her thumb.

"She's typically the friendlier, more good natured one, while Sheridan... frankly Sheridan can be a lot to take. You just caught her in a manic mood tonight."

"What'd you mean?"

Kade laughed. "Well, she's very opinionated, but she's usually afraid of offending someone. My guess is that her curiosity overcame her reticence. You and Mireya present a mystery for her. You're puzzles for her to try to solve."

"I'm a puzzle?"

It was Kade's turn to laugh. "You are indeed, Rafaela."

Faela's eyes darkened as she turned her head revealing some flakes of bark caught in her hair. Kade could feel her withdrawing into herself. "You don't like your given name?"

"Not many people call me that. That's all. You just surprised me."

"No, that wasn't surprise I felt. That was guilt. Who calls you Rafaela that makes you feel guilty?"

Faela looked at Kade's intent gaze that seemed to find whatever he sought. Trying to evade him would be futile and she was worn out from hiding. "The only person who calls me that was my father."

"Was?" Kade asked his dark amber eyes continued hunting for her reactions.

The guilt spread to shame and she chewed on her thumbnail. "He's dead."

Bringing the pieces together, her reticence to discuss herself, her clear fear at seeing Caleb despite his devotion to her, her evasion when talking about her family, Kade nodded. "I see."

Faela realized that he did indeed see and her guilt flowered into grief as her eyes shimmered with tears. "I killed him." Faela managed to force the awful truth past her lips. "It was me. I did it."

Kade still held her hand in his and twined his fingers through hers. He had no intention of leaving.

*   *   *

They had followed the Foster River south for several hours, when the town of Moshurst came into view at the river's headwaters. Like many of the towns in Nabos its main industry was agriculturally based. Farms surrounded the land approaching the village, but this close to the ample forest Moshurst also had a thriving lumber trade. A mill with high smoke stacks thrust into the sky sat on the river near the line of the forest. Signs of a healthy timber industry spotted the landscape, but no smoke rose from the mill.

Trailing behind the rest of the party, Haley walked with Faela. When Faela and Kade had returned to camp the night before, Haley noticed that the girl had been crying. Her demeanor, however, had an easiness that she had previously lacked. She seemed almost relieved, though sadness still clung to her like a shadow. What a girl like this could have done to turn Gray fascinating him. He wanted to know more about her. He had to know what crime she now paid for.

"So, you been to Kelso before, yeah?" Haley asked companionably as he brushed his hair out of his eyes.

It still caught Faela off guard that he made no attempt to hide the mark of his corruption. "I haven't actually."

"I would've bet you had being a Durante and all. More proof that I should stay far from gambling."

"I never spent that much time with my family after I was sent to Kilrood. Many of my travels were with," Faela paused as though she changed her mind. "They were for my journeyman training with the Tereskans."

"When were you at Kilrood?" he inquired, his face relaxed in an easy smile of interest. "I grew up there."

"I spent nearly all of my training with the Tereskans," Faela commented offhand surveying their surroundings. As they got closer, the mill dominated more of the landscape. "Hold on."

Putting two fingers in her mouth, she whistled shrilly once. The party stopped and turned to see the source of the noise. Faela motioned for everyone to wait and swung her bag off her back to dig inside. Her fingers brushed Sammi's first blanket and kept searching until she found her hat. Jair took the opportunity to drink from his water skin and offered some to Sheridan who removed her wool jacket before taking a swig. Pulling out the hat, she set it in place low on her forehead.

"Sorry, let's keep moving."

Haley looked at the hat and tugged on its brim. "Inconspicuous, lass."

"You don't seem overly concerned with anyone noticing you," Faela observed.

"People see what they want to see," Haley pointed out. "The trick be making them believe that what they want to see really be there."

"Oh, and how do you do that?" Faela found it natural to talk with Haley. Maybe it was his infectious smile. Maybe it was his easy laugh. Maybe it was that when she looked at his eyes, the silver looking back at her didn't condemn her, didn't pity her. Haley just accepted what she was.

"Oh no, tricky lass. I'll not be fooled into revealing the secrets of my trade." Lucien surprised himself. The smile he gave Faela was genuine. He liked this quiet woman. He didn't have to try with her. He wanted to lighten the melancholy that hung on her whenever her attention wandered, so he took it upon himself to dispel as much as he could. Though he wanted to know if her story matched his own, it didn't matter in the end. What mattered to Lucien was that they shared something he could never explain to anyone else. They were connected.

Faela smiled. "So you grew up in Kilrood? Where about?"

"Gallows Way," Lucien found himself telling her the truth without reservation.

At hearing that name, Faela stumbled and Lucien steadied her by the elbow.

"Careful now, lass."

"My thanks." Faela nodded as she looped her thumbs through the straps of her pack. "I'm sorry. It's just I used to go down there to help with the children after the first frosts, not to mention having to set some broken bones."

"Aye, the lil' uns down there always got lung sick in the winter. And well, the seasons don't change the men down in the Way. They'll get drunk and hit anything that makes the mistake of getting too close."

Faela looked at the jovial minstrel somewhat differently knowing that he had grown up in one of the roughest districts in Kilrood. Ianos had tried so many times to help out those living in the slums, but nothing he did seemed to effect any lasting changes. Men still drank and still beat their wives. That is when they stuck around Gallows Way at all. The most notable attribute of Gallows Way wasn't the bar fights, but the orphans.

Every year Ianos would go down to the Way to provide food and clothing to the parentless and abandoned children. Many feared adults and hid when he visited. When Faela was still a little girl, he started bringing her with him and more children began to show themselves. She still dreamed about their bruised, thin, and haggard faces.

Ianos had managed to persuade several, who exhibited magical gifts, to come to the temple to receive training, but so many of those children had been orphaned because of the war and knew little outside the Way and refused his offers.

She glanced at Haley trying to imagine him as a child. She wondered if she had ever seen him in her trips down to the Way. She wondered if he had ever seen her.

"But what would I have to sing about without a little tragedy in life, yeah?" Lucien didn't want Faela to feel sorry for him. He had escaped from the Way, when Philip had found him and brought him to the Lusican temple in Kitrinostow. Philip and the Lusican Order had saved his life. A fact he had never forgotten.

"Love and kittens?" Faela suggested as the bank of the river started sloping up the hill.

Lucien chuckled his gaze drifting to Eve's back as she and

Sheridan talked quietly, their heads close together. "Aye, love."

As they passed the mill, it became apparent that it had not operated in quite some time. The metal of the saws showed a dusting of rust. Kade cautiously approached the buildings with Sheridan and Eve only a step behind.

"What happened here?" Faela asked as the rest of them entered into the empty dirt-packed courtyard grooved with ruts from heavy wagon wheels.

Kade disappeared through the wide opening of the mill. "Anyone here?"

Only the reverberation of Kade's voice answered him. Sawdust covered the floor in piles that had been blown into the corners and against the defunct equipment. A series of metal chains swung in the breeze filling the place with a clanking rhythm that masked the footfall of the twins behind him.

His hearing muffled, Kade slipped a throwing knife out of his belt as he moved further into the building. The chains hung from the rafters to help lever timbers onto the conveyor. Passing behind the conveyor, Kade saw that the mill had been stripped of anything not welded in place. All the tools were gone, but he could see where the steam pump, that had run the conveyor, had been pried out. Cabinets hung open emptied of everything, but the ever-present sawdust. There was nothing that indicated the presence of people. No one had used this mill for months.

Sliding his knife back in its sheath, he turned to Sheridan and Eve who had fanned out to investigate the rest of the building. "Find anything?"

Eve shook her head, wiping her hand against her thigh to remove the sawdust. "Nothing here. This place was stripped efficiently."

"Scavengers?" Sheridan suggested as she ducked her head under the slats of the staircase.

"No," Eve drew the word out as she rotated on a heel to take in the entire room. "No, this was too systematic, not rushed. Those cabinets over there weren't left open." She pointed to the row of storage behind Kade. "Look, you can see how the hinges are cracked. That's from time and the elements, not clearing this place out."

Kade nodded in agreement. "You've always had a good eye for the details, Eve."

Eve smiled, her face brightening for a moment as she forgot about the past three weeks before she recalled the image of Nessa's motionless body and the coldness in her chest returned. She pivoted as only a dancer could and said, "We should keep moving and get to the town. They should be able to tell us what happened."

Sheridan grunted her agreement. "Though it needs some love, this equipment would still function and there's still plenty of timber to fell. You can see how they staggered their harvesting so that the forest would continue growing. I see no reason for this facility to have been abandoned."

The trio came back outside to find Jair perched on the fence that surrounded the courtyard. His brows drawn together in concern, he kept scratching behind his ear. Faela and Haley examined the water wheel and discussed something intently, but the river and the water wheel hid their conversation. While Dathien roamed near the tree line, Mireya sat on a rock, chewing on some jerky with a far away expression.

At their approach, Jair hopped off the fence and captured Kade's arm whispering, "Can I talk to you?"

Never having seen this affable young man so serious before, Kade nodded and they detached themselves from the twins.

When they arrived at an acceptable distance, Jair scratched behind his ear again and said, "There are no animals here."

"What?" Kade asked skeptically. "How do you know?"

"They're gone; they're just gone." Jair tapped his fingers against his crossed arms in rapid agitation.

Even when he had caught Jair in that clearing, the young man had remained calm and good humored. Seeing Jair this anxious raised some serious concerns.

"Okay, let's talk to Eve. She'll know for sure." Kade raised his voice. "Eve, we need your help."

Eve cocked her head in question, but jogged over with the fluid grace of a gazelle. "What do you need?"

"Can you check for animal life?" Kade asked without further explanation.

Eve raised an eyebrow, but complied. She breathed in deeply through her nose and closed her eyes. When she opened them again, they glimmered with green light and she gasped as though something restricted her breathing. The light flickered and faded.

Kade steadied her with his arm. "What did you see?"

Eve blinked and looked at Kade her face tight with panic. "It's gone. It's like a desert where there had once been a lake. There should streams of life, of energy here, but it's just the faintest trickle. It's like someone dammed the flows, redirected them somewhere else." Her large topaz eyes widened and she clutched at Kade's coat sleeve. "The town, Kaedman, we have to check Moshurst. If the green magic has been diverted away from this place, first the animals would have left, and then no new crops would have grown. There would be famine, starvation, and then people would start getting sick - very sick, Kaedman. We have to warn them."

Jair's face whitened, the color draining with each word Eve spoke.

"Do you think that's why this place is empty?" Kade asked her.

"Um, yeah, probably, but we need to get up there - now." Eve's urgency had caused her volume to increase attracting the rest of their party.

"Eve, think it through," Kade said forcing her to meet his gaze. "If the mill has been abandoned then what are the chances that there's anyone in the town? This mill was the livelihood of this place, with it gone, what would they have had to trade?"

Eve shook her head obstinately. "Even if you're right, we need to check. We have to make sure that they've left."

"What's going on?" Sheridan asked as she joined them.

"Somehow someone shifted the flows of green magic here, Sheridan."

Sheridan's shoulder blades pinched together. "How is that even possible? I've never met anyone who could channel that much energy without burning themselves to dust."

"I don't know," Eve said shaking her head, "but how doesn't matter right now. We'll figure it out later. What matters is making sure that the people living here know how much danger they're in. We can't just stand around here debating this. I'm going."

At her final word she pushed her way through the people around her and whistled once. Kimiko came trotting toward her and, without slowing down, Eve vaulted onto her mount's back and swung her around toward Moshurst. Whispering in her horse's ear, her eyes sparked green and the horse jumped into a gallop as though chased by darkness itself. Eve rode up the hill toward the village without a look back.

"She's right. If anyone is still there, we need to evacuate them," Kade agreed.

"Why?" Faela asked confused by Eve's sudden exit. "What's going on?"

"Someone's upset the balance of green magic here," Sheridan explained combing her long hair back from her forehead.

"That's even possible?" Faela asked in surprise. "I thought that much contact with the energy would consume its wielder?"

"Whether it be believable," Haley said shouldering his bag, "don't matter. If that woman says it be true, it be true."

Faela could see Kimiko's gait eating the distance between herself and the town as Eve arrowed along the path of the river. As Eve past the first buildings of the town and left their sight, a look of pain crossed over Kade's face and he clutched at his chest as he fell to his knees.

"Kade!" Sheridan cried and caught him before he pitched into the dirt.

The wrenching pain that pulled Kade to his knees washed over Faela like the memory of a broken leg and she inhaled too quickly at the sudden sensation. Trying to push though the pain, Faela walked with deliberate care to join Sheridan. Traces of orange light glowed on Kade's chest.

"That reckless fool," Sheridan whispered then looked up at Faela. "I saw you checking him after I popped in; are you a Tereskan?"

Faela nodded. "I am."

"I've had Tereskan training, but Eve bound him using a Daniyelan binding spell. If he goes too far from the person he's bound to, his heart will stop," Sheridan explained. "I need you to keep his heart beating while I retrieve Eve. We can't move him like this. Can you do it?"

Scarlet light bathing her eyes and hands, she placed her palm over the orange lines that pulsed with increasing intensity. Humming a low, rumbling series of notes, Faela found his fluttering heart and breathed in and out slowly until her breathing and his heartbeat matched her own.

Opening her eyes, she nodded. "Go."

Sheridan squeezed Faela's shoulder and stepped back from them as indigo light enveloped her and she vanished with a pop.

Faela returned her attention to Kade who slumped into her shoulder for support, her hand held up his chest. Her humming transformed into singing quietly in a rhythm that matched her heartbeat. "Shine, shine like the sun. Night will end and day will come."

His heart beating at a normal rhythm, Kade's eyes found hers as she sang. *Saving me again, eh? We really need to find a better way to spend our time.*

Faela concentrated on keeping their hearts in time and did not respond, but sweat trickled down the sides of her face as she continued the song. Jair paced inside the yard, his hand shoved deep into his pockets. Faela's lips paled as the orange magic fought against her to claim control of Kade's heart. The scarlet light around them flared and Faela's hand shook. The orange light intensified and Faela's song stopped as she cried out in pain. Her hand had burns across her palm.

Without a second's hesitation, Faela put her hand back on Kade's chest and began singing again. Seeing Faela's burns, Jair stopped his pacing and dashed to her side and knelt behind her to support her. She was running out of energy. If she continued much longer, she would soon lose consciousness and Kade.

Jair closed his eyes and reached around him to help her. Eve had been correct; where there should have been rivers of energy there were only tiny trickles. Jair expanded his reach farther and farther until he reached where he knew the magic would be, his hometown, Garon. Jair found the barrier he had erected all those months ago. With a burst, the barrier tumbled and the magic rushed back into its natural courses. Pooling its energy within himself, he channeled it into Faela.

Gasping as the energy rushed into her, Faela hesitated and regained her focus making use of the new resources pouring into her. The lines of the binding faltered as scarlet from Faela's hand enveloped Kade's chest. His spine arched and he bucked away from Faela. With Jair steadying her, Faela cushioned Kade's violent tremors and held him upright. All the while her voice remained strong and true, weaving the rhythm that kept Kade's heart pumping one beat after the other.

Somewhere far away, Faela heard the clamoring of hoof beats getting louder and louder as each second passed. As Jair directed what energies Faela needed, he siphoned away the excess energy so that it returned to the channels in the land around him. He saw the pooling of magic that sped down the hill in the form of Kimiko and the twins, though the horse's energy had threads of green magic that linked her to Eve. While he focused on keeping the energy flow from overwhelming Faela, a part of his mind recognized Kimiko as Eve's familiar.

Sounding far away, he heard voices that seemed to echo from the bottom of a well. Sheridan slid off of Kimiko's back, making directly for the trio. Eve vaulted to the grass without making a sound when she landed. Where her sister had run, Eve approached with wary steps. Kade's breathing had slowed from its rapid pace now that she had returned. The color in his cheeks returned as well as he lifted his head off of Faela's shoulder.

"You had no right, Eve," he said in a choked voice. "You had nothing substantial."

Arms folded across her chest, the lines around Eve's eyes strained. She leaned her weight onto one leg where she stood. "You fled. What was I supposed to think?"

"Think what you like," he responded coughing, "but think before you act."

Sheridan crouched behind Kade, taking his weight from Faela who fell back into Jair. "Eve, a binding spell can only be removed by one on the Daniyelan council in Finalaran and only after the person has passed the Trial of Fire."

"I know," Eve said her voice even.

Sheridan shook her head. "I knew you were going to try. I could feel you building the spell all the way from Montdell. It's why I came, to stop you from doing something so blasted reckless." Sheridan couldn't look at her sister and instead concentrated on the skeletal remains of the rusted mill. "I thought I made it in time."

"Well, he's fine, isn't he?" Eve directed her question to Faela.

Faela pushed her hair back, contempt clear on her face. "He is now. But I almost lost him. I had used all my reserves. He was going to die."

Pushing off of Jair's leg, Faela stood. Her energy had returned thanks to Jair's efforts, so she stood without so much as a tremor. "Do you understand, Daniyelan?" Faela continued to close the distance between her and Eve. "Life might mean little in your Order, but mine is sworn to protect it." Faela's eyes flashed a dangerous crimson. "And that vow is the only thing protecting you right now."

Sheridan had her arm under Kade's back to help him as he struggled to make it to his feet to intercede, but before he could say a word, Mireya spoke. "Rafaela Durante, you will stand down."

Faela turned toward the commanding voice and Mireya did not look her short nineteen years. An ancient authority infused her. Opening her mouth as if to protest, she thought better of it and closed it again. Averting her gaze from Eve, Faela returned to Jair who stared at one of the deep ruts in the yard.

Eve licked her lips and approached Kade. She lowered her voice. "I'm sorry, I won't leave like that again."

"Oh," Kade said smiling without any mirth, "you're right about that."

When Faela knelt next to Jair, she was unsure what to say. She had never experienced anything like what had just happened. The energy he had given her seemed endless. She put a hand on Jair's shoulder as she crouched in front of him. At the contact, she felt a wave of guilt knock the air from her lungs.

"Jair?" she questioned peering into his bowed face. When he raised his eyes, they were silver.

"By the light," Faela breathed and fell back onto the ground to sit across from him.

"It's my fault," he told her, his voice shaking. "I did this."

Faela reached for his hand to reassure him. "Jair... what?" Too many questions swirled in her mind. All she managed to ask was, "What happened?"

The people standing around them noticed the change in the tall boy's demeanor, but didn't interrupt their conversation.

Jair choked down back his emotions and replied, "The green magic, it was my fault, its absence."

"How is that possible?" Sheridan murmured her large eyes wide.

"You?" Kade scoffed in weak disbelief.

Jair nodded miserable. "I never knew it was unusual," he explained. "My mother just taught me to mold the energy I saw everywhere when I was six. She found me stealing energy from her garden to make a tree age a sapling into an old tree. Because my mother could do it, I never knew everyone else couldn't."

Eve's eye lit with recognition. "You were the channel I saw evidence of in Oakdarrow."

Jair nodded again and glanced at Faela unwilling to reveal her secrets to this woman. "I didn't know that's what I was until the Phaidrian Order came looking for me about six months ago."

"You're a channel?" Sheridan's shocked turned into excitement. "Okay, honestly, Kade, you collect the most interesting people."

"Why were the Phaidrian's looking for you?" Faela asked rubbing her thumb in circular patterns over his knuckles.

"They said that I had upset the Balance. I had no idea what they were talking about. When they questioned me as to how I had done it, I had no answer. They threatened to send my mother and sisters to work as indentured servants unless I told them what I had done. But I didn't have the answers they wanted to hear.

"I told them that all I had done was help siphon off some of the energy to help the crops grow in Garon, my hometown." Jair kept his gaze on his and Faela's hands. "There had been a battle just outside our town during the war. It left the land sick. I was just trying to help. I didn't know it would do this. I didn't know it would hurt the people here."

"How could you not know?" Eve asked looking down at his bent head.

"I mean, I knew that the energies would be a little low in the areas I had redirected it from, but I didn't know that it would do this."

"Oh, Jair," Faela said quietly, "upsetting the Balance is an offense punishable by death. It takes a very powerful channel using black to do it. That's why Caleb and Talise were hired, isn't it? The Phaidrians hired them."

Jair nodded. "When they threatened my family, I ran and made sure they were safe and hidden, then I went in the opposite direction. I didn't think I had done anything wrong - until now."

Mireya sat next to Jair and rubbed his back with her hand. "Jair, that's why you just turned. Do you know that your eyes are gray now, just like Faela's?"

Jair raised his head to look at the girl next to him. "What?"

"It's true. You just released the green magic from where you had redirected it, didn't you?"

Jair nodded.

Mireya smiled. "That's why you're a Gray now. By trying to alter the harm that you've done, you renounced the black you used. Don't you see?"

Faela squeezed his hand again. "She's right, Jair. You're one of us now."

Jair smiled and Faela wrapped her arms around his neck in a hug. He hugged her back and rested his chin on her shoulder.

"We'll figure this out together, Jair," Faela promised in his ear.

CHAPTER FOURTEEN

"Okay, so being with these people is like being caught at sea in a storm," Sheridan confided to Kade. "Is it always like this?"

Once tempers had cooled, the party had left the mill to head up to the abandoned village. Faela, Haley, Jair, and Mireya all talked in front of them, while Eve led the way with Kimiko and a silent Dathien. At the top of the hill, the buildings that comprised Moshurst huddled above the river's headwaters. Even at this distance, they could see the cattails from the marsh that stretched out below the town.

"Life is a bit of a whirlwind with a Nikelan around," Kade admitted as he watched Faela and Jair.

"Did you have any suspicions that Jair was a channel?"

"Oh, we knew he had done something," Kade chuckled remembering Jair's face when he had realized why Caleb and Talise had come to the cave.

Sheridan looked at him significantly and gestured for him to continue as she took in deeper and deeper breaths the further they hiked up the incline.

"Caleb had been contracted to retrieve him." Kade slowed down his pace when he noticed Sheridan was winded.

"Thanks for that," she said with an appreciative wink. "You know how I hate hiking, all that sweating. I'm horribly out of shape."

"You're out of shape because you're lazy, Sheridan. Didn't you just finish a circuit?" Kade asked shaking his head in amusement. The closer they got to Moshurst, the more Kade felt the hairs on the back of his neck prickle. After spending the last weeks traveling away from inhabited areas, he was accustomed to the absence of people. That absence though was to be expected; this was not. This abandoned husk should not be empty.

"I'm not lazy," she argued. "I'm inventive and efficient. It's not my fault that I lose all that travel time by popping ahead of Eve to the towns I know. We can finish a circuit twice as fast with my method."

"Only to be defeated by a gentle hill," Kade mused philosophically.

Sheridan poked him in the side between the straps of his pack in retribution. "Getting back to the point. How'd you know Caleb was contracted to collect Jair?"

"Because Caleb and Talise caught up to him over a week ago after he had already crossed my path."

"How'd that happen?"

Kade narrowed his eyes in remembered annoyance. "He stole my clothes while I was bathing in a creek."

Sheridan's laugh rang down the hill behind them. "Okay, even if he is a Gray, I like that boy."

"You've always been so sympathetic to my suffering," Kade said in a monotone.

"You can take care of yourself," she said with a dismissive wave. "How does Faela fit into this farce?"

"When I was chasing Jair, he found Faela and used her as a shield."

"How does that," Sheridan asked, pulling her hair off her neck and up into a ponytail, "add up to you all traveling together?"

"It didn't. Faela took Jair with her, because she was convinced I'd do him harm if she left us alone."

"A distinct possibility," Sheridan conceded. "Smart girl."

"I realized after they left that he had stolen more than my clothes. He had also pinched my circuit kit, which had my logbook from Montdell."

"This explains why you went after them, but not why you're still with them right now," Sheridan pointed out as she stopped for a moment to catch her breath.

They had reached the edges of the town now. The streets were empty. Only their approach and the noise of the nearby river disrupted the silence. There were no birds, no dogs, no children, no signs of life, just the wind and the water.

"When I caught up to them, they were being attacked by bandits. I helped. In the process, I got hurt."

"Scrap-on-the-knee hurt?"

"Sword-through-the-right-lung hurt."

"Ouch."

"Yeah, just a little. I'm just grateful that the itching has finally stopped."

"Lucky for you, she's," Sheridan said nodding in Faela's direction as they walked between the abandoned buildings, "a Tereskan."

"Aye," Kade responded watching Faela examine the debris-strewn street looking for any sign of inhabitants. She had stowed her hat earlier. Since they had met, he had always seen her mask herself before entering populated areas. Her quick and sharp movements betrayed her anxiety at being exposed, but she made no move to hide herself here.

Returning his concentration to Sheridan, he continued his story. "My recovery took longer than I would have liked, but it was probably faster than it should have been and I'm beginning to see why." His gaze slipped to Jair's long back.

"I get that you had to stay with Faela while you were healing," Sheridan prefaced, "but that doesn't explain why you're still with them."

She didn't voice the rest of her question. Why had he run from Montdell in the first place? Her investigation had uncovered Kade's involvement with Gareth Burke's death, but not the extent of his involvement, nor his motivations. She had many things she needed to ask, but this was not the time.

"Patience, girl," Kade admonished tugging on her hair, just as he had when she would pester him with her questions as a child. "I'm getting to it."

Sheridan arranged her face into a mask of virtuous perseverance. "See, this is my waiting face."

"Mmm, right," Kade eyed her skeptically before telling her more. "Caleb and Talise tracked Jair to where we were recovering."

"We?"

"Yes, we. Faela had been injured pretty badly herself during the attack and had drained herself healing me."

"Tereskans are completely mad." Sheridan shook her head in amazement. "I swear, they're all a few apples short of a bushel."

"What does that say about us then?" Kade asked raising an

eyebrow significantly.

"Hmm," Sheridan considered, "maybe there's something about handling magic that rots the brain? Or at least common sense, maybe?"

The main thoroughfare of the village, like everything else they had encountered, was starkly empty, but the usual signs of an abandoned human settlement simply could not be found. Plants and animals should have begun reclaiming this village, but there was nothing but dusty streets without so much as a weed or a rat to mar its surface. Only bits of branches and other dead plants blew across the road.

"Looks like everyone's cleared out," Eve called back to Sheridan and Kade.

"Satisfied?" Sheridan asked her sister holding her thumb up in question above her head.

"I'd like to check a few of the buildings first," Eve said rocking onto the balls of her feet.

"Just to make sure no one moved in once the townsfolk moved out," Sheridan said illuminating her sister's thought process.

"Sounds like a plan. Will it be safe to get water from the wells here?" Kade directed his question to Eve whose eyes flashed green momentarily.

"Not yet." She shook her head. "Whatever Jair did, things are equalizing. It should be safe soon, but don't drink any standing water. The water from the river should be safe. Running water tends to remain stable with an unbalancing of the green. It has its own equilibrium, being neither alive, nor static."

Most of the signs that should have hung outside each establishment proclaiming the proprietor's trade had been removed. Eve entered a building with large windows patch-worked together in leaded diamond crisscrosses. From its proximity to the center of Moshurst, she assumed it was the town's tavern. When she pushed its door open, a layer of dust billowed out into the street.

Haley broke off his conversation and jogged over to the tavern. "Exploring in pairs might be a good idea, yeah?" Haley suggested. "Never know what you might find." When Eve snorted skeptically at his proffered help, he clarified his motivation for exploring.

"Me? I'm hoping for some ale."

"It's not a bad idea, minstrel," Kade agreed. "No one should go off alone. Just stick together until this place is behind us."

Jair and Faela continued down the main avenue toward the well in the center square of the town. Shimmying off her water skin, she took a swig and handed it to Jair who drained its contents and handed it back to her.

Kade watched his two companions and considered what he had witnessed of each. Given her own injuries, Faela had risked her life without a second thought when she healed his chest wound. Before that, she had taken a complete stranger as a traveling companion to ensure his safety. Jair had always had a cheerful attitude regardless of his circumstances. He had helped Faela without any clear benefit to himself time after time.

Yet, both this man and this woman had violated the most basic and sacred laws of the Light and they were forever marked for that exploitation. They were fugitives running from the justice of the Daniyelan Order, the Order entrusted with enforcing the laws of the Light, his Order. Jair had committed a taboo that Kade previously would not have thought possible, upsetting the balance of green magic, the very energy that fueled their abilities. Faela was responsible for the death of her father and while Kade still did not know how, it had to involve her unique gift for red magic. Regardless of how contradictory this information might seem, he knew it all to be true.

Following Faela and Jair, Sheridan picked up their previous conversation. "Hold up. If Caleb caught up with you, why is Jair here?"

"It's why I'm here now."

"Which means?" Sheridan prodded both verbally and physically.

"I was looking for Caleb," Kade admitted, "when I left Montdell."

Sheridan said nothing to this revelation, but waited for him to continue as she drug the soles of her boots along the street to kick up small clouds of dust.

"I don't know how much you uncovered in your investigation, but you need to know that Gareth Burke was a member of the

Brethren. I never believed they truly existed, until Gareth used Nessa as leverage to ensure I vetoed a law on the council for them." He paused. "I'm sorry, Sheridan. I underestimated him. He managed to kidnap her during the council session. I tracked him, but I was too late. When I confronted him, he killed her. Even though I didn't kill her myself," Kade looked at Faela who had just elbowed Jair in the side for whatever he had said, "her blood is on my hands."

Sheridan cleared her throat before she spoke. "I know, Kade. I saw the confrontation."

"I should have made sure she was stable before I left."

"You couldn't have let him escape."

"Was it worth her life though?"

"Kaedman," Sheridan took him by the elbow and made him look at her. "You couldn't have saved her. I examined her body and the black magic he struck her with had twisted her insides. Whether you stayed by her side, she would have died."

Before Kade could answer her, he heard a familiar voice call out, "Hey there, little bit."

"You and your grand entrances," Faela said with a disapproving cluck of her tongue.

Turning from Sheridan, they both looked to where a man and woman dressed in black sat on the rim of the well, their feet dangling freely.

"I mean, really, Caleb?" Faela said with a shake of her head. "How long did you know we were in the area?"

"A couple hours," he conceded.

"And you decided to just kick back and wait for us to come to you?"

Caleb nodded, his mouth wide in a grin. "Pretty much. But c'mon, you have to admit. It makes us seem mysterious and enigmatic, like we knew you would be here before you came. Try to deny that you're impressed." Without waiting for a response, he continued, "See, you can't. Because words cannot describe how awe-inspiring we are."

"There are definitely no words to describe you," Faela agreed with his statement in part.

"Well, she looks better than she did when I left her with you,"

Caleb peered over Faela's head to Kade, "So, you're safe."

"When you last saw her, she was trying to fight off a poisoned wound," Kade pointed out. "If she didn't look better, she'd be dead."

"Which is why you're safe," Caleb explained. Seeing Sheridan with Kade, Caleb's knuckles flexed one after another in a wave. "What is she doing here?" he directed his question to Kade.

"Tomas sent her and Eve to investigate the matter we discussed."

Caleb didn't bother to hide his obvious anger at this news. "Eve is here as well?"

Kade nodded.

Caleb swore colorfully, suggesting that Tomas do several anatomically impossible things in rapid succession. "Kade, we need to talk," he said getting up to usher Kade aside. When he stood, he saw Jair for the first time.

"You've got to be kidding," Caleb said looking from Jair's eyes to his sister's. "No, you've got to be kidding." Turning on Faela, he demanded his voice rising, "How did *this* happen?"

"So you didn't know why the Phaidrians had hired you?" Faela asked wincing on her brother's behalf.

Caleb looked at his sister impressed. "You always were too blasted smart for your own good, Ella."

Attracted by Caleb's ranting, Mireya and Dathien entered the square. Caleb turned at their entrance hand on grip of his revolver, which promptly fell to his side when he processed what he saw.

"Well," Caleb backed up against the side of the well and draped an arm over Talise's leg and addressed her, "this is starting to make more sense, wouldn't you say?"

Talise nodded a secret smile playing on her lips that matched the light dancing in her blue eyes.

"Mireya made something make sense?" Jair questioned. "I think that's the first time those words have ever been uttered with sincerity."

"I guess we don't have to sneak away to talk, Kade, because the news I bring concerns all of you, if she's here. I didn't go to Finalaran like you asked," Caleb confessed his free hand resting on the hilt of the knife at his waist. "I went to the Boundary of Vamorines."

Kade gave no audible response to this revelation, but Sheridan felt his muscles tense at Caleb's declaration.

"Kade, I went to see Rivka Peacemaker to bring formal charges against Tomas."

It was Sheridan, not Kade who exclaimed, "You went to the Nikelan temple?"

Caleb leveled the woman with a stony gaze. "I formally petitioned the Nikelan Scion to strip Tomas Segar of his rank and office within the Daniyelan Order and to appoint a new Scion. Clear enough for you?"

"On what grounds?" Kade asked as Sheridan just stared mouth agape in disbelief.

"As a member of the Brethren."

"Oh," Sheridan said in response, but not in shock, but as an epiphany. "Oh, that's not good. That means it's true."

"What's true?" Caleb and Kade asked at the same time.

"I discovered a hidden room in Gareth's quarters. The room housed books by the Brethren, spells, rituals, and letters. He had instructions from the Brethren to recruit Kade. They'd been following his career since before the war."

When her words confirmed what he had feared, Caleb's eyes darkened and the air around him sparked with orange crackles of light.

"For the Brethren to pull off positioning Kade where they did, I knew they had to have influences high up within the Daniyelan Order," Sheridan continued unaffected by Caleb's quiet fury. "There was also something shady about Eve and me getting this assignment. The instructions we received from Tomas, the fact that we were chosen at all given our close relationships to the victim and suspects, none of it made sense, unless–"

"Unless Tomas orchestrated the whole thing to either turn me or get rid of me," Kade finished for her.

Sheridan nodded. "He knew how Eve would react."

Faela's gaze mirrored her brother's. "Sounds like he was counting on it."

"Counting on what?" Haley asked as he and Eve joined them.

"Hail, Evelyn Reid of the most noble of the Noble Houses," Caleb greeted the woman who looked as though she had seen the dead, "but not well met, I'd wager."

"Come to collect your prize, bounty hunter?" Eve demanded refusing to use his name.

"Alas, no," Caleb admitted with exaggerated sorrow. "As much as I'd like to fatten my purse a little more, that young lady," he pointed to Mireya, "has a higher claim than mine."

"What did Rivka say?" Kade asked bringing the discussion back to Caleb's confession.

"She said she would investigate my claim."

"That was all?" Sheridan pressed for more information.

"No, Sheridan," Caleb said locking eyes with her, "that was not all. But unfortunately, I'm not sure you should be privy to that information. It doesn't concern you."

"That might not be entirely true," Mireya interjected walking toward Caleb.

"Care to elaborate, little one?" Caleb invited.

"Sheridan and Eve have a role in the prophecy. If you spoke with Rivka, then you know something about it, yes?"

"I know that I've been given a duty to fulfill," Caleb evaded.

Mireya cocked her head to the side and touched Caleb's cheek lightly and the back of her dark hands flared with blue lines. "Yes," she said, her voice far away as she looked at Caleb's face, but seemed to see through him. "You are the guardian. You must protect that which is most precious."

Her hand dropped and she blinked her eyes refocusing on Caleb. "Do you understand?" Mireya asked him.

Caleb's eyes slid over to Faela. "I'm beginning to."

Motioning with his eyes to a wind-scoured building across the square, he stood and left the crowd around the well. His hand still resting on his weapon, he took in a breath preparing for what he had to tell his sister. Taking the hint, Faela detached herself from Jair and joined her brother. The others watched with curiosity, but none intruded on their desire for privacy. Though Eve clearly disapproved of their departure.

"What is it?" Faela's irritation and nervous fidgeting made it obvious that she preferred her question to remain unanswered.

"Ella, I think I understand what Rivka charged me to do."

"Which is?"

"Is Sammi still with Ianos?" Caleb asked ignoring her terse question. He knew she wasn't upset with him.

"Yes," Faela said slowly, "why?"

"I know you think that you're going to find some kind of resolution by finding this Gresham, and I'm not saying you won't or that you shouldn't. But there's something much bigger going on here, Ella. Something I can't stop and something that you're caught in the middle of."

"I," Faela began shuffling her weight from foot to foot.

"Look, just listen, okay? On our way back from Vamorines, I stopped by The Otter's Tale. Remember the hunters I told you about? They roughed up Nathan's eldest, Sara, looking for you. He thought he sent them heading in the opposite direction from you."

Faela's throat felt dry.

"They told him that you had stolen something from Nikolais and he just wants it back. So, he sent them to Oakdarrow."

Repressing a moan, she clutched the fabric of her coat. "No. I wouldn't tell them. I wouldn't tell them where he was."

Caleb put a finger under her chin forcing her to look at him. "I don't think you would."

"I'd die first," Faela promised, the same hardness that had been in Caleb's eyes now resided in hers.

"That's what I'm afraid of, little sister. Which is why I'm going to see Ianos, so I can move him somewhere safe. You won't know where, so you won't be able to tell. I'm to guard that which is most precious, right? This has to be what Rivka meant."

Faela nodded unable to speak. Her throat felt thick, but she held back the tears stinging her eyes.

"You need to stay with the Nikelan girl and do whatever it is that you are meant to do, Ella. I'll keep him safe. Okay, love?" When Faela did not respond, he repeated, "Okay?"

Faela gulped and nodded forcing out the word. "Okay."

CHAPTER FIFTEEN

Over the past century, Lanvirdis, the capital city of Nabos and the home of the Phaidrian Order, had changed only marginally. Though evidence of the last war still marred its buildings and outer walls, which bore the charred scars of countless sieges. The reconstruction of Nabos had begun over a decade ago, but piles of rubble still littered the base of the walls. The remains of the buildings outside the protection of the walls gave a silent testament to the destruction wrought by the war.

Vaughn leaned back in the saddle to take in the ingenuity of the walls surrounding the city. Easily twenty feet thick, the walls were hollow and filled with a mix of loose stone, which allowed the structure to move with the earth tremors that plagued this coastline. This barrier that withstood the upheaval of the earth itself had repelled invaders century after century and good men and women of the Orders had died before these walls trying to liberate their comrades held prisoner within.

Though he had little fear of being seen, Vaughn entered through the trader's gate where the traffic would be heaviest this time of day. No living citizen of Lanvirdis would recognize Vaughn. It had been well over a century since he last entered those gates, gates that still stood as they always had. While Vaughn preferred anonymity, the mission Rivka had sent him on demanded it.

He thought back to his last night with his wife before he had left their home. On the terrace overlooking the bay, they had shared a bottle of red wine from the Vinfirth region of Isfaridesh. The bay had once been the center of the grand, sprawling city of Gialdanis several millennia ago, long before Vaughn had been born. The antiquity of the city made even his nearly four hundred years seem short in comparison. Rivka never liked it when their duties forced them apart, but he had to leave. No one else could be trusted with this task. As her Grier, it was his responsibility to be the eyes and ears of his Scion.

Vaughn's wandering thoughts turned toward Tomas Segar and the first time they had met, when the Daniyelan council had elevated him as Benjamin's successor. To Vaughn, he seemed a charismatic and passionate young man, if a little ambitious. His installation process had gone smoothly enough, but Benjamin's death had never sat well with Vaughn.

He had known seven Daniyelan Scions in his lifetime and few had displayed Benjamin's quiet leadership. During the war, Benjamin had evaded or foiled countless assassination attempts by the Nabosians. His understanding of strategy seemed as much a part of him as his own skin. He knew where ambushes would be set, where to reinforce troops, and when to sacrifice. For Benjamin to fall to a stray arrow seemed unlikely at best and treachery at worst. It was that nagging suspicion of treachery that had never quite left Vaughn and now a decade later he rode into Lanvirdis to finally investigate that suspicion.

As he entered the dirt-packed streets just inside the Trader's Gate, the dust churned around him. Soon the dirt gave way to cobblestone streets that widened to make room for two carts to drive abreast. Though Lanvirdis was the seat of the Phaidrian Order, Tomas had visited regularly from Finalaran to aid in the reconstruction effort after the war. All these years later he had become an established institution within Lanvirdis. It had been a simple matter to find him.

Vaughn had played spy for Rivka many times before this mission and he knew where to begin. If you wanted to know the simple and uncensored truth about the current happenings of Lanvirdis, you went to the taverns down at Diarmid Bay Harbor.

Vaughn's horse, Mesa, picked his way carefully through the throng of people who crushed into one another and into the brick buildings to make room for the horses, carts, and carriages moving along the avenue.

Vaughn caught sight of a young boy navigating through the sea of bodies. He had to look twice before he realized that it was not a young boy, but a girl. Her hair spiked around her head like a purplish black sea anemone and dark streaks of cinder smudged her face.

She tripped and bumped into a man wearing a tailored tweed suit and a rounded felt hat. The man helped her up and she rewarded him with an innocuous smile. Patting her on the back after he righted her, he continued on his way. Vaughn's mouth drew into a smirk as he watched the girl move in the opposite direction of her mark toward a narrow alley between a baker's and a butcher's shop. Her fingers never once going for his money purse that she had slid under her shirt.

Wheeling Mesa's head toward the alley, Vaughn cut off the girl's escape. Instead of altering her course, the girl aimed for the horse. Vaughn smiled again; she was audacious.

"Mighty fine beast there, ser," she commented her voice lower than he expected.

Vaughn leapt off his horse's back and reached behind the girl to where she had hid the money. The girl cursed in surprise at his proximity. With one deft movement, he removed the purse and dangled it in front of her.

"I believe this belongs to the gentleman you accidentally fell into," Vaughn said to the flushed girl.

She glared at him, then blurted out, "How'd you see? No one ever sees me lift."

"Sweetling, I've seen it done a thousand different ways," Vaughn said the corners of his eyes crinkling when he smiled. "I almost missed it, but your hand off stumbled enough for me to catch it."

The girl sucked in her bottom lip and eyed him. The cuffs of his shirt tapered at his wrists with a series of four bone buttons. She had seen women who worked as domestic help wearing shirts like this, but never on man and certainly not one who could spot a pickpocket. "How's an upstanding gentleman like you know about the lifting lay?"

"Because for one, not everyone starts out upstanding," he answered as he flipped a gold coin across his knuckles and back. "And, two, looks, as I'm sure you well know, can be very deceiving."

At that Vaughn flipped the coin up and caught it in his palm. Pushing it up in between his forefinger and thumb, he held it in front of the girl's nose. "You return this purse to the man you lifted it from and this is yours. Honest pay for honest work."

"I'd make five times that lifting another purse," she lied as naturally as breathing in.

"Well, you lost this one. So, if you don't want it to be a total wash, return it or I will."

The girl didn't stare at Vaughn, but at his horse. Mesa was strong, well fed, and his coat shone from a recent grooming. Vaughn insisted on currying Mesa himself every night, even when they were home at the temple, but she didn't know this. To her, the horse simply seemed content and well tended. She looked back to Vaughn and had no doubt that despite the crowd he would catch her before she made it two shops away. She held out her hand. "Fine."

"His name is Mesa," Vaughn said noticing her examination of his mount. He tossed her the purse, which she caught without looking and burrowed through the mass of people. He watched her as she wriggled her way to the man she had lifted the money from. The man looked shocked, but shook her hand and reached into the purse to reward her. She held up her hands waving away his attempt to repay her and she disappeared back into the crowd. A few moments later she emerged behind Vaughn who tossed the coin over his shoulder.

As soon as the first coin left his hand another appeared. "Feels good to make honest pay?"

The girl ran her hand along the horse's flank as she walked back into Vaughn's sight. The horse whinnied happily and turned his head to nuzzle her.

She shrugged her shoulders at his question. "Not as much fun. No challenge."

"To not have been caught by either the city's guards or the Daniyelans yet, I'd wager you have your ear to the ground. I could use someone with that kind of information and discretion during my stay. My name is Vaughn."

The girl ran her hand up and down Mesa's nose bridge, but did not respond to his offer.

He held up the other coin and explained, "For your name."

"They call me Wes," she answered skeptical of his generosity. For all her big words, Wes hadn't seen this much money in a year's worth of lifting.

Vaughn took her hand and put three silver coins in it. "I'll be staying down at the Harbor at the Vine and Reef."

With that, Vaughn vaulted back onto Mesa and took the reins from Wes. "Come by around dusk if you want a hot meal," he told her as he turned his mount into the alley that angled downhill toward the wharf.

*   *   *

The smell of dank wood and oily smoke blew into the street from the door of the Vine and Reef Tavern. Vaughn landed on the ground, his boots splashing in water that had collected from the gutters, but hadn't evaporated this close to the wet air of the harbor. The stagnant, slime-filled water coated his boots as he strode into the tavern. A minstrel, perched on the counter of the bar, picked out a haunting lament on his guitar that matched the flickering of the oil lamps on the walls and the chandelier that hung opposite a second floor balcony.

A thick murky smoke swam lazily near the two-story ceiling of the building as the sounds of chairs scraping the floor and tankards hitting tables filled the room. The bar was filled with longshoremen from the docks who wanted some fun before heading home to their families and boisterous sailors who had just come into port. Scanning the occupants, Vaughn saw a group of sailors sitting at a table playing Four Card Brag. Vaughn smiled and headed straight for their table.

Lifting his purse, he tossed it on the table mid-hand. "Can I buy in?"

The sailor's looked at the size of Vaughn's purse and their grins widened. One with a pockmarked face motioned for his friend next to him to make room. His friend, a man with skin the color of chocolate, spun a chair in Vaughn's direction, which Vaughn caught and twisted to face the game. Settling into the chair, he stretched his long legs out in front of him as he leaned into its spindled back.

The first hand Vaughn watched, happy to listen to the sailors' gossip without asking any questions. He just played his hand while reading each of the men sitting around him.

"So," said the pockmarked sailor as he dealt four cards face down to each of the players. "I told Marcus, if he be wanting me to stay on, I get five percent cut straight off the top."

A man wiped his nose with the back of his hand and barked a laugh. His face was sun-and-wind burned from years of working on the exposed deck of a trawler. He sniffed. "What you should've asked for be some time with that woman of his."

All the sailors responded with grunts and laughs of agreement. "Be that as it may," the pock-marked one continued, "we be scheduled to head back down to Kilrood to transport this load of grain for the Scion."

The red-faced man reorganized his cards left to right and back again, adding, "I normally don't stand for fetching for the Orders, but the Scion be doing right by the people here. Sending the surplus crops to help those in Kilrood after that storm that wrecked the coast is real decent. Leon nearly lost the *Light's Maiden* in that blow."

Vaughn continued to listen, hoping to determine which Order's Scion they discussed in such glowing terms.

"Aye," the dark-skinned man agreed pulling a card out of his hand and rapping the table once with his knuckles. "The Daniyelan man be a great man. Providing for those down on their luck."

Vaughn placed the first wager tossing two bronze coins into the center.

"What about you, stranger?" asked the pockmarked man. "You be a quiet one. What brung you to Lanvirdis?"

"Time," Vaughn replied sliding his cards face down on to the table. "Harvest's almost here. Checking the market."

"A farmer, yeah?" remarked the red-faced man. "Must be a big farm." His gaze rested significantly on Vaughn's purse.

"Farms," Vaughn replied offhand. "You seeing or not?"

The red-faced man snapped his cards together and tossed them on the table. "Out. It'd be a shame to waste good coin that could get me more ale on a hand like that."

Stroking his chin, the dark-skinned man moved his hand to his purse and threw four bronze coins into the pot.

The pockmarked man waggled a finger at his friend. "Oh no,

you'll not be taking me again. Out."

"What about you, farmer?" the dark sailor asked titling his head causing some of his dreadlocks to spill over his shoulder.

"You only live once," Vaughn commented tossing two more coins to join the growing pile. "So how long's the Daniyelan Scion been in Lanvirdis?"

"Seems like he's here every time we lay anchor in this port," commented the red-faced man. "Been nothing but good for Lanvirdis after them Virds almost wrecked this fine city."

"One of the best harbors along the coast," agreed the pockmarked man. "Ain't no trade go in or out during the war. Darkness blighted blockades sunk anyone caught smuggling. Ain't a good time to be a sea dog, I tell you that."

"So how much is he paying for the surplus grain that he's sending for aid?" Vaughn inquired.

"Paying?" The pockmarked man laughed into his mug. "It be 'donations' only, friend. This ain't the place to try selling it."

Vaughn kept his expression appropriately concerned for a businessman, but repressed his true apprehension. All of the towns he had traveled through on his way to Lanvirdis had failing or weak crops this harvest. It had yet to turn into a famine, but there would be shortages this year that every country would feel.

Yet, here in Lanvirdis Tomas advertised a surplus and took control of the grain supply in the name of aid for the struggling towns of Mergoria. Even without the shortage, Tomas as the head of the Daniyelan Order had no jurisdiction to seize these goods. The Daniyelans enforced the laws of the Light. They were the hand of justice, not charity.

"Well, friend," Vaughn said laying down his cards to show a prial of four fours. "Let's see what you have."

The dark-haired man cursed elaborately and threw down a purple running flush eight high. "Best bloody box in the game. That's some darkness-blessed luck, farmer."

Vaughn merely smiled and swept in his winnings when he saw a small figure dart into the room. Wes had come for her meal.

Nodding to the men, Vaughn stood and hooked his purse back onto his belt. "Sers, enjoy the night."

The men mumbled something after him as they returned to

their drinks and complaining about their latest voyages. Vaughn caught Wes' gaze and motioned her to a table near the warmth of the hearth.

"Nice to see you again," Vaughn told her as he sat draping his arm across the back of his chair. "Keep your hands to yourself since we last met?"

Wes eyes, the eyes of a survivor, kept darting around the room as if she expected a trap. She shrugged noncommittally, her arms across her chest, her hands shoved under her arms. She saw no cause to tell this man that she had lifted three more purses that afternoon. With the harvest coming, people flocked to the capital city for one final trip to sell and buy goods before the snow settled in for the year, which made it her most bountiful and profitable season as well.

"I thought not," Vaughn observed with a smile. He motioned the young serving boy over with a flick of his fingers. The boy with curly black hair wove his way through the packed tables in the low light with an efficiency born of repetition.

"What it be?" the boy asked without any preamble or pleasantries. He was used to dealing with a gruff and narrowly focused crowd. The Vine and Reef's patrons came to drink and gamble, not to talk with the help.

"Mulled wine and your lightest ale and two of whatever the catch-of-the-day is," Vaughn ordered without hesitation.

The boy grunted and bobbed his head in affirmation. "That be the cod."

He turned on his heel and disappeared back into the sea of tables to the yells of, "Oi! More stout, boy!"

"Stop your yelling, Hank," called one of the few feminine voices in the pub from behind the bar. Lifting her head to peer over the counter of the bar, a woman with pale blonde hair streaked with silver said, "It's on its way. Darren has more than you to worry about."

"C'mon now, Meggy," Hank pleaded. "Don't be cruel. A man's got to drink."

"There's plenty to drink out in the harbor, if you'd like to go for a swim," Meggy observed dropping the wooden crate she had been searching for onto the counter with a thud. "I can show you the way, if it's too dark." She flashed the man a wide, toothy grin. Hank and his tablemates roared with laughter and went back to their conversation.

"So, Wes," Vaughn said his attention switching back to his own table. "What do you hear about the grain markets?"

Wes looked at him for a moment before beginning. "You want to know about grain?"

"That's what I asked, isn't it?"

Uncrossing her arms, Wes started tapping the edge of the table with her thumb. "Been real scarce."

"I hear there's been a surplus."

"Bleeding lies that is," Wes said her eyes still roaming the room. "That's what I been hearing too, but it ain't true."

"How do you know?" Vaughn asked his eyes watching her constant fidgeting. This girl was clearly uncomfortable staying still for any stretch of time.

"People don't notice me," Wes returned her gaze to Vaughn again and considered. "Well, normal folk don't. I hear things, see things."

"What kind of things?"

"Well for one there be these storehouses down by the local Daniyelan temple. They're supposed to be for the grain donations." She snorted at the last word. "This time of year, see, lots of folk from all over Nabos come here to sell and buy. Ain't half of the folk who typically come to Lanvirdis been showing up. Ain't no grain coming into the city. I don't know what be in those storehouses, but it ain't relief for no one."

"What about the Daniyelan Scion Tomas Segar? What do you hear about him?"

"That pretty boy?" Wes made another unattractive noise in the back of her throat. "Aye, that one. You'd think he were the Light embodied the way women in the market prattle on about him. How he be doing right by us after our good-for-nothing king got all the men folk killed in his war."

"You don't trust him?" Vaughn asked. "Why?"

Wes laughed at this question. " I ain't trust no one, ser. But him, he got a cruel look to him. I knew a man who used to run the street kids like him. Seemed all pretty talk and smooth like.

But he used to take the girls for himself, little ones too," Wes' gaze moved toward the door, "too little. They come back all beat up on saying how it were their fault for not being good. He had a look in his eyes when he smiled at us. Like he knew we was his. Not many caught it, but I saw it. Your man, Tomas, he got the same look. So, no, I ain't trust him."

Vaughn nodded. "You've a sharp eye, Wes. Trust it."

"I heard you at cards with those sailors," she said evading his advice. "You ain't a farmer. No way, no how."

Vaughn smiled again. The boy slid their plates and mugs onto the table and Vaughn handed him some coins. The curly-headed boy bit them and pocketed the currency without a word.

"Like I said, Wes, you've a sharp eye."

CHAPTER SIXTEEN

Faela rummaged through the cabinets in the kitchen of what had once been Moshurst's inn looking for a frying pan, hoping for a frying pan. Mireya had begged to be able to stay in the town for the night. They had agreed once Eve had deemed it an acceptable risk with the green magic steadily returning.

Yanking open the double doors of the cabinets by the ovens, she stuck her head inside and crowed jubilantly. "Success!"

Pleased with her find, she stood spinning the cast iron pan by its handle. When she heaved the pan onto the chopping block in the middle of the large kitchens, she saw Jair leaning against the doorjamb. Pulling her hair off her neck and into a knot at the crown of her head, she said, "What can do for you, darling?"

Jair shrugged and entered into the kitchen switching his weight between his feet looking generally awkward. "Nothing. I don't know."

Faela pat one of the dusty counters. "Keep me company while I cook. But before you do, can you light the oil lamp hanging from the wall. I won't be able to see anything soon."

Jair looked around for flint and when he failed to find any, Faela said, "My bag, right-side front pocket."

Finding the flint, he struck it and ignited the wick of the lamp, oil still sticking to its glass bottom. He turned the dial and the flame leapt bathing the room in its dancing glow. After tucking her flint back into its pocket, he hopped up onto the nearest counter, his long legs pulled up into his chest, the balls of his feet teetering on its edge.

Faela filled the silence to try to take the edge off of Jair's mood. "No soup for us tonight. We get to have food cooked like real, civilized people."

"Oh?" Jair's voice perked up at the mention of food. "What're you making?"

"I don't know yet," Faela admitted searching the kitchen for inspiration. "Something that requires a pan though."

Jair actually smiled. "Why?"

"Because, I never get to use one on the road." Hefting the pan in her left hand, she pointed it at him. "Would you want to carry this while hiking all day? I think not."

"Faela?"

"Yes, darling?" She busied herself searching to see if any food had been left that she could add to her list of assets. In some barrels tucked against the corner were some shriveled potatoes. The barrel next to it held withered green apples. "I think I can do something with this," she said to herself, bending into the barrels to retrieve her ingredients.

"How long have you," he trailed off uncomfortably, "how long... I mean, when did you..."

Faela peered out from under the crook of her arm, still rummaging through the barrels, and finished for him. "Have I been Gray?"

Jair nodded.

Palming three apples and then five of the small potatoes, she untucked her shirt to use as a basket and dropped in her findings. "Over a year now."

Jair's now silver eyes widened. "A year?" His voice cracked.

Faela gave him a half smile. "That's right."

"So, you've been on the run for a year?"

"Off and on, yes." Faela deposited her tubers and fruit on the counter next to the pan and continued her scouring for more hidden treasures.

"What," Jair broke off, "what did you do?"

Faela froze and pushed back a stray lock of her hair that curled slightly in the cool moisture of the kitchen. "Something unforgivable."

"As bad as upsetting the very Balance of magic?" Jair asked skeptical.

"In its way," she evaded. "The scope of the crime does not make it any less horrific." Faela breathed in and paused before exhaling. "I betrayed everything I held dear, everything I had sworn I would be, for a man."

Jair crossed his arms over his tented knees and rested his chin on his forearms listening.

"You're aware of who my family is?" Faela asked as she removed her belt knife and started chopping the potatoes.

"One of the Merchant Houses of Finalaran?"

Faela nodded and continued. "One of the largest. While the other Merchant Houses frequently do whatever is necessary to ensure their own success, anything from ambushing caravans to assassinating individuals viewed as problems, House Evensong has typically been immune, because of our size, our allies at court, but mostly because of our reputation. The Houses are ruthless in their practices to get what they want, to cement alliances, to secure trade routes, to ensure trade agreements." She punctuated each point with a chop of her knife.

"My great-grandfather was particularly merciless. Should a rival House attack any of our caravans, the force sent would be annihilated, save for one to take a message back, to let them know who had done this. The ones allowed to die were the fortunate ones. When the one he spared would return to his House his tongue would be intact, but that was about it. Many times, he would be branded with the crescent moon and the harp."

"Your family's seal, like on the pendant you wear," Jair observed.

Faela fingered the chain around her neck. "Yes. Since that time, House Evensong grew in numbers and strength. My father was a good man, gentle even. He lacked the ruthlessness of his grandfather, but the other Houses still feared our name. The Houses have long memories and one particular House had not forgotten."

Faela stopped chopping and wiped off the starchiness that clung to the blade of her knife with the bottom of her shirt. "One of the last attacks another House made against Evensong, before my great-grandfather's death, was led by the heir of that House and he was the one who was spared. Apparently, they never forgot.

"You have to understand, I learned this history only after this," she said indicating her eyes, "happened. But while in Kilrood I met a boy from this House. Though at the time I didn't know it, he was the nephew of the head of his House." Faela could not bring herself to speak his name aloud.

"He was charming, sweet even." The ghost of a smile played on her lips as she remembered that time in her life. "I never knew many people my own age. Even my parent's thought I was quite mad as a child. I only ever spent time with my siblings and Caleb was already in training in the Orders when I was born. I have a little sister. Did I ever tell you that?"

Jair shook his head. "You don't talk about yourself."

Faela pushed on the handle of the knife slicing through another potato. "You're right, I don't. She's two years younger than me. She'll be twenty-four next month actually. Her name's Deborah. I was taken to the Tereskan temple in Kilrood when I was four. So I only saw her when I came home." Faela paused then amended. "When it was safe for me to come home. Deborah's a shrewd girl. She'll make a good head of the House, if Ethan ever gives her a chance."

"Ethan?"

"My cousin," Faela answered pushing the pile of diced potatoes off to the side of the block. "Though Eve was blunt in her statement, she wasn't incorrect when she called Caleb a bastard. We have the same father, but we have different mothers. Caleb's ten years older than me and I'm the eldest of my mother's children. Caleb's mother was a good woman and I don't think our father ever really got over her death.

"But our father couldn't marry her and she knew that. He had to be available for alliances with other Houses. She died in childbirth with Caleb. When our father finally married my mother, Caleb was already training in the temples. But he always made time to visit me. Even when I was in Kilrood." Faela smiled.

"He would bring me baubles and books from his travels. However, because, Caleb isn't the legitimate son of our father, by Merchant law, he can never inherit the House. I could inherit, but I renounced my claim."

"Wouldn't it fall to Deborah then?"

"Legally, she does have the strongest claim, but Ethan has a head for Merchant politics and management. Plus, he was father's Second and as a blood relation, he does have a claim."

Jair snapped his fingers at Faela. "Didn't that innkeeper in Dalwend say that you were the head of the House now? How can that be if you renounced your claim?"

Faela picked up an apple and sliced off the bottom. She set the apple on its now flat side and began quartering the fruit. "This brings us back to the boy I met. As I said, I've never had a lot of experience with people my own age. I was naive." The force of her last cut embedded the knife into the wood of the block. She levered the handle to remove it. "He convinced me that he loved me. He convinced me to use my gift to influence my father's trading decisions toward certain parties. And I did as he wished.

"I did it, because I was a gullible, idealistic child. I knew what repeated uses of my gift would do, but I ignored what I knew and I did it any way." Faela rolled another apple into place with the tips of her fingers. "Should I choose to, my gift allows me to affect the emotions of others, to make them feel what I feel. I have to be very careful not to get trapped by the person's emotions, their thoughts. Repeated contact is dangerous." She pointed the knife at Jair. "Think about it like this. When I cut into the wood, if I cut in the same place what happens?"

"The mark in the wood gets deeper and wider," Jair answered.

"Exactly. And after every cut, hitting that same fissure becomes easier and easier. It's the same way with my gift. Grooves, pathways are deepened, widened with each contact. After a while the contact no longer needs to be made deliberately. Unless I consciously block those pathways, my emotions begin to affect the person I'm linked to."

"So linking to your father was taboo?" Jair asked trying to wrap his mind around the explanation. "How is that unforgivable?"

"The link wasn't unforgivable," Faela corrected, "just inadvisable. What happened because of that link, that's what was unforgivable. I made many bad decisions. I don't excuse them. They were my choices, no one else's, and I made them. For several very complicated circumstances, I was convinced that my father was in the way of my happiness. I began to think that it would be better if he were gone. About a month after my thoughts turned this direction, my father committed suicide."

"You can't blame yourself for that." Jair spoke slowly.

"No, Jair. I'm not blaming myself. I know that I did this to him. This isn't empty guilt over something that I couldn't control.

What I did, manipulating my father's emotions, is a violation in every sense of the vows that I took to the Tereskan Order. There is a reason there aren't many like me, Jair. Most people can't control it. They can't keep themselves separate from the people around them. It's dangerous for anyone like me to allow contact.

"But more than that, Jair, I used black. I used the magic of darkness to manipulate my father. There's a reason why people fear Grays, Jair. We all have been touched by darkness at one time. We can't be trusted. I was not the one who put the dagger in my father's hands, but I might as well have with how I violated his mind."

Motioning with her head to the cauldron peeking out of her bag, she said, "Can you fill that with water and start a fire in the stove." With her elbow, she pointed at the potbelly stove across the room." I want to smash these potatoes and I need to be able to boil water to do that."

Jair jumped off the counter and grabbed the cauldron. Standing next to Faela, he hugged her with one arm. "You don't have to hide, you know."

Faela lay her cheek on his chest, her hands still busy cutting the apples. "I know. Now get going. This meal isn't going to cook itself."

*   *   *

Talise and Kade sat talking at a table near the hearth where Caleb was starting a fire. The last rays of sun melted away as they fell in murky diamonds through the dirty glass panes. Faela and Jair had disappeared into the kitchens to make dinner earlier and the sounds of conversation and chopping drifted to the dining room. Using his own clear voice as the baseline, Haley sat on the floor by the hearth tuning his lyre. Eve and Sheridan sat at a table leaned toward one another in deep conversation.

"Okay, so it's later," Eve announced to Sheridan as her gaze found its way to Kade's back. "Explain to me why I shouldn't drag Kaedman back to Finalaran tonight."

"This situation is much more complicated than we originally thought," Sheridan prefaced before she started her explanation. "I can tell you definitively though that Kade is innocent of Nessa's death."

"Based on what evidence?"

Sheridan looked down at her own interlaced fingers. "I saw it."

"You time-folded?"

Sheridan nodded, her tiny braids sliding into her face and falling over her shoulders. "I found the cellar Gareth took her to, where she died."

Eve took in a deep breath and leaned in on her forearms. "You better start at the beginning."

"Gareth was a member of the Brethren. He had a hidden chamber in his quarters at the temple. You can only reach it by popping."

Eve drew her eyebrows together as she traced a pattern on the table with a fingertip. "But Gareth never trained at Wistholt. He had no purple magic."

"Apparently, he did. The room was sealed. In the room were letters, instructions from the Brethren. He also had a copy of Simon Nightfall's teachings. His instructions were to persuade Kade to become sympathetic with the Brethren's cause. There was a specific vote on Montdell's council that the Brethren wanted Kade to veto. It was important enough for them to tip their hand. Gareth told Kade that if he didn't veto the legislation, they would kill Nessa."

"I imagine that went over well," Eve commented with a snort.

"Gareth kidnapped Nessa. Brought her to that cellar. Kade tracked Gareth faster than Gareth had anticipated. When Kade rejected the Brethren's offer, Gareth killed Nessa."

"Why didn't Kaedman just step using his time-folding?" Eve asked still skeptical of Kade's innocence.

"Because it doesn't work that way. While I can only see the past, he can actually go there, but that doesn't mean he can change anything. The best he could do was watch it happen again."

Still unsatisfied with Sheridan's answers, Eve asked, "But if he got there before Nessa was killed, what prevented him from stopping Gareth?"

"Kade couldn't have known that Gareth would use black to

attack Nessa and not him. Gareth knew who he was dealing with. He knew he couldn't win in a head on fight against Kade. There's nothing Kade could have done to save her, but he went after Gareth.

"I found Gareth's body before I discovered his hidden room. He had been killed and someone had taken their time. The most troubling thing about the letters I found is that the Brethren had stared watching Kade back before the war. I don't understand what game they're playing. Not yet at least."

"So he had no part in Nessa's death?" Eve raised the question again.

"He was not the one who killed her, but she was put into the situation because of her ties to him." Sheridan reported honestly, pushing her hair out of her face with her fingers.

"I see," Eve reclined back into her chair, her hand covering her chin and mouth as she absorbed what Sheridan had just revealed to her.

Out of the corner of Sheridan's eye, she saw Haley strumming his lyre and for a moment she could have sworn that his hair glimmered auburn, but when she turned to look at him directly, his hair was still the color of hay.

"So what do we know about Kade's previous ties to the Brethren?" Eve asked recapturing her sister's attention. "Why were they coming after him?"

Sheridan shrugged. "No names were mentioned in the letters except for references to 'Hawthorn.' The only person we know for certain had ties is dead." Sheridan set her chin into her cupped hand and her eyes slid to Kade chatting with Talise as Caleb joined them. The fire popped as air pockets cracked in the wood. Though he sat with a relaxed posture, Sheridan could spot at least three weapons on him within easy reach and she knew that if she saw three, he had just as many concealed. He appeared to be in comfortable conversation, but she could see the tiny adjustments of his gaze that never stopped assessing the room.

"Eve, look at him," Sheridan suggested. "You really have to ask what they could want with him? He's one of the best fighters I've ever seen, but more than that, he's a stepper. Those who've walked the halls of the Amserian temple in Wistholt are few and those of us who can wield purple are usually poppers, not steppers. I can only watch the past. I can't interact with it. But Kade," she puffed her cheeks and blew out the air, "he can go there."

"I know what a stepper does," Eve interrupted.

"Well, then you should understand why they would want him. It seems obvious to me. Beyond his color blending, when that man is determined, he will get what he wants. He's a powerful ally. And well, I wouldn't want to be the one facing him on the other side. I'd recruit him too."

Eve grunted, but said nothing as she watched Kade listening to whatever Caleb was saying.

"You're letting your personal attachment to him get in the way of analyzing the facts," Eve concluded after they sat in silence for some time.

Sheridan's voice became flat. "What do you mean?"

Eve traced the grain of the wood with her pinky as she began. "The Brethren have been trying to recruit Kade for years, what's to say they didn't succeed?"

"That's absurd."

"Is it? Let's look at the facts," she paused for emphasis, "objectively. You found letters from the Brethren saying they were trying to recruit him for over a decade. Kade flees Montdell after Nessa and Gareth's deaths. Kade is discovered in the company of not one, but two Grays. And the second Gray," Eve laughed without humor, "was black for the majority of the time they were together."

"You were traveling with a Gray yourself," Sheridan pointed out.

Eve flinched for a fraction of a second and someone who was not her twin would never have noticed, but Sheridan knew her sister. Waving away Sheridan's objection, she replied, "Whom I ran across while tracking Kade."

"Who you were granting safe passage without any talk of bringing him back to Finalaran for judgment." Sheridan caught her sister's eye. "What aren't you telling me, Evelyn?"

"I hadn't decided what to do yet," Eve wavered. "What would you do when a legend walks into a bar?"

Sheridan couldn't help but laugh. "Make sure you have a good punch line for that set up."

Eve tried not to smile, but failed. "Darkness, Sheridan, this is serious."

"Oh, I know that it is, but really," tears were building in the corners of her eyes from her laughter, "he walked into a bar?"

"Will you let me finish?"

Sheridan covered her mouth and nodded, trying to stop laughing.

"When he fled from Montdell, he went looking for," Eve lowered her voice so it wouldn't carry, "a convicted traitor and bounty hunter who happens to be the brother of one of the Grays. This does not add up to him being pardoned."

"He didn't join them, Eve," Sheridan shook her head with absolute confidence. "He wouldn't."

"See," Eve said jabbing a hand at her sister. "This is what I'm talking about. You're compromised. You can't see the picture these pieces create. You won't, even if they are staring you in the face. He may not have killed Nessa, but he is far from innocent. I just need more time to find out what his angle is."

*   *   *

With a wary eye, Caleb watched the twins speaking earnestly in the opposite corner. They clearly disagreed about whatever they were discussing and he did not have to stretch his imagination to figure out the subject of their conversation. Turning his attention back to his own table, Caleb joined Talise and Kade's discussion of the new kicks she had learned the last time they had met up with her Tribe.

"See, it's all in the carry through," Talise explained twisting her torso to illustrate. "You aren't exerting that much force yourself, but using the force of your own weight to increase it."

"It makes sense," Kade admitted. "But you can break the jaw of man who's standing with it? At your height?"

"Easily," she said her curls bobbing as she nodded.

"As much as I love to hear you talk about crushing bones, babe," Caleb interrupted, "Kade needs to know more about our visit with Rivka, while we have him to ourselves"

Kade crossed his arms and settled back into his creaking chair. "So, you accused Tomas."

"Aye, and she didn't seem all that surprised by it."

"Well, she is the Nikelan Scion," Talise said thoughtfully. "Would anything surprise her?"

"What evidence did you bring to her?" Kade asked.

"Stantreath for one."

"You suspected him of being behind Stantreath?" Kade's eyes sparked orange momentarily then faded. "For how long?"

"Almost immediately." Caleb slid his hands across the tops of his legs.

Realization passed over Kade's face. "That's why you refused to let me to testify in the trial."

Caleb nodded while watching the fire crackle and spark. "I didn't want him to associate you with my suspicions."

"What did she say?"

"That she would take it from here and that I was released from my obligation to the men who died and that I had a new mission."

"If you suspected Tomas even before the trial," Kade said thrusting two fingers at Caleb, "you must have spent the last decade collecting evidence."

"That's right," Talise answered for him.

"But why now? Why did you go to the Nikelan Scion now? What changed?"

"Your logbook, what happened in Montdell with Gareth. You gave me a concrete connection back to Tomas."

"Back to Tomas? If there had been a clear connection, I would have seen it."

Caleb grinned. "With all the cards, yes, you would have, but you didn't have all the cards. How much did you know about Gareth?"

Kade shook his head. "Only what I knew from our time together in Montdell. I never served with him before then. He was private and so was I. I saw no need to pry. It worked well."

"Gareth Burke is Tomas' cousin, but more than that Gareth worked as one of Tomas' aids during the war. Among many others, he brought me the orders for both your deployment to my unit and the orders for Stantreath. When you told me about his involvement with the Brethren, you pointed me to the bridge I'd been searching for."

Though a reserved man at times, Kade rarely found himself at a loss for words, but this news left him mute staring at his former mentor and commanding officer.

Caleb hunched forward, his characteristic mirth gone from his face replaced with earnest seriousness.   "Kaedman, you cannot trust anyone within the Daniyelans, especially those two."   Only his eyes drifted to the twins. "Eve's first loyalty is to the Orders, she will not hesitate to bring you to Tomas, mark my words."

"Sheridan will make Eve see reason," Kade argued.

"You can't risk it, Kade.   Eve sees me as the perversion of everything she holds true, because of my conviction at the trial. And by association, even if Ella weren't marked as a Gray, she would already be suspect in Eve's book.   Look at who you're associated with."   Caleb locked gazes with him.   "You know how her mind works. Tell me that these facts lead to your innocence in her eyes."

Kade sighed. "I can't deny it, but Sheridan won't turn on me."

"Eve's her blood, Kade."   Caleb's eyes flashed dangerously. "That ain't the kind of tie that breaks easy.   Even knowing what Ella did, I'd still defend her to my last breath."

Kade considered the sincerity of his friend's declaration and did not doubt a word of it. But he wondered if Caleb really did know what she had done and if he did, whether he would still be as vehement in his protection.

"She may be Sheridan's blood," Kade conceded, "but I'm just as much Sheridan's kin. She won't betray me."

Caleb shook his head.   "You're a blasted stubborn fool, Kaedman Hawthorn. Don't say I didn't warn you."

"I won't deny I'm stubborn and I may be a fool, but I trust her with my life, Caleb."

Caleb nodded and lowered his voice. "It's one of the things I admire about you, mate, but don't let your blind spot for Sheridan put my sister in danger. One other thing that Rivka told me is that there's something special about Ella. There's something she's got to do, but I have my orders.   Talise and I leave in the morning."

"I wasn't planning on leaving her, Caleb," Kade cut him off, "even if you stayed."

Caleb stopped for a moment watching Kade, studying his friend's motivations. "Be careful there, Kade."

"Caleb, she's got a Nikelan following her around," Kade brushed off Caleb's suspicions. "You're right when you said that there's something she has to do. I don't know what it is yet, but I intend on seeing this through. Your sister's fiery, I know that, and deadly when the need arises, but she isn't exactly levelheaded when it comes to her own safety. I'm not leaving her unprotected."

Kade failed to mention his other reasons. Reasons which might incite Caleb's over-protective meddling. Caleb didn't need to know that he could feel Faela's emotions as though they were his own and at times could hear her inner thoughts like a whisper. Nor did he need to know that at the moment, pangs of bitterness and shame, her constant companions, plagued her. Nor did he need to know that Kade had to keenly subdue the urge to storm into the kitchen to eliminate whatever roused those feelings.

Jair swung the kitchen door opened and poked his head out. "Dinner's coming soon."

"Excellent," Haley exclaimed from the floor, lyre in hand. "Thought me stomach might strangle me guts soon."

Caleb gave a sharp laugh at that before turning back to Kade. "See that you don't."

*   *   *

Kade lay on his back as the straw poked him through the mattress. His head resting in the crook of his arm, he stared at the slanted ceiling of the room. He had gotten stuck sharing a room with Jair who had passed out as soon as his body hit the mattress and had snored vigorously for the last hour. With sleep kept far from his grasp, Jair's snoring left Kade alone with his thoughts. So much had happened in the past weeks. So much that he didn't want to think about. But at night in the place between wakefulness and sleep, the thoughts came unbidden.

Though he was glad to see Sheridan, the way she looked at him when she thought he was being high-handed was identical to the look that Nessa used to give him. Their brows wrinkled and the left corner of their mouths turned up in the same way. He loved her as he loved Sheridan, like a little sister. He had known her just as long, though not nearly as well. Gossip had always circulated in the Noble Houses as to which he would make an offer to, Sheridan or Nessa.

He cared for them both, but he would never trap Sheridan like that. Her family would expect her to start producing heirs immediately and she would be pressured into renouncing her ties to the Orders. Being a member of the Orders was a part of Sheridan's identity and he would never take that from her.

Nessa's parents, however, had been trying to marry her off since she was sixteen. He closed his eyes and he saw her standing on the balcony overlooking the gardens in Montdell keep. Her hair shone like threads of golden silk in the sun as she leaned on the banister and glanced over her shoulder to laugh at him.

He opened his eyes to banish the image. He had succeeded in keeping her out of his thoughts by concentrating on getting justice for Gareth's crimes. But now that the deed was done, nothing kept the thoughts away. When he closed his eyes again, he saw her lying on the floor of that cellar. Blood dripped from her mouth as he rolled her onto her side, her eyes blurred with pain. Nessa had died alone and it was his fault.

Jair inhaled noisily like something had gotten caught in the back of his throat. Covering his ears with his hands, Kade swore and lurched over the side of the bed. Without bothering to put on any shoes, Kade slid on his trousers and left the room.

He descended the stairs and left the tavern without a sound. As Kade wandered the streets of Moshurst, the moonlight fell in long, bright strips. Save for the wind, silence filled the empty streets. It would take time for this place to heal from what had happened.

It was a year ago, on a night much like this, when Nessa had come to him her face streaked with tears. Maybe if he had stopped himself from meddling, she would still be alive. Maybe if he hadn't tried to rescue her, she would still be alive.

Kade looked up to discover that his feet had brought him to the headwaters of the river. His mouth twitched in a half smile.

"Now isn't that odd," he told the water.

His thoughts turned from his guilt over Nessa's death to Faela's affinity for water. Stretching his arms over his head, Kade lowered himself to the grass and watched the river tumbling away from him. He shook his head comparing Nessa's vibrant optimism to the melancholy that shadowed Faela's every move.

Faela, a woman who, by all accounts, he should have returned to Finalaran the moment he knew she was Gray. Though to be fair, during that moment, he had been preoccupied by a collapsed lung. Since that time, however, his understanding of justice had begun to shift. Of one thing he was confident. Even if Tomas were not as Caleb claimed, he would not have turned Faela over for judgment. This fact troubled him and made him question what that said about his character.

He had told Caleb that he would not leave Faela unprotected and he meant every word, but where he belonged in this grand scheme nagged at his mind. Mireya had already found her three Grays from the prophecy. Even Sheridan and Eve had a purpose and the Scion of the Nikelan's herself had given Caleb and Talise a mission to fulfill. Everyone fit into a larger plan, everyone except for him. If Eve tried to force him to leave, he knew he would fight to stay. Though he couldn't even explain to himself why.

He had no doubts about Dathien's ability to protect Faela, but his first responsibility was Mireya's protection. Jair would try, but he seemed to have little training or experience. While Sheridan had seen more combat than anyone ever should, it was as a healer, not a fighter, though she did have good instincts and training. He could trust Faela to Sheridan, if he were certain of her stance regarding the Grays, but she was still undecided. If Caleb had to leave, Kade couldn't deny that he was the best chance of getting Faela to Kelso and wherever else her destiny led her from there.

Kade could choose to help. He didn't have to be mentioned in some prophecy to make the decision to aid them. He had sworn his life to uphold the laws of the Light. If a Nikelan, the voice of the Light, said that this woman needed to find the Shrine of Shattering, then it would contradict his own vows to abandon her now.

Kade picked up a pebble and tossed it in the air. Catching the pebble one-handed, he laughed. "My, I am good at convincing myself that there are good and legitimate reasons for my own selfish desires."

Even before Oakdarrow, nearness to Faela had reduced the ache in his chest. An ache he knew came more from losing Nessa than from his injury. Since Oakdarrow, since the link, he could no more willingly leave Faela than he could willingly cut off his own arm. It was time to stop trying to delude himself into thinking his primary motivation came from anywhere else.

His thoughts returned to Jair and Haley, the other two from the prophecy. He had always known something more lurked beneath Jair's awkward and affable surface, but he had not imagined the raw power that Jair possessed. Haley, the self-proclaimed minstrel, however, was more than he appeared. Jair had broken the most basic taboo of the Orders in altering the Balance and as much as he had a hard time believing it, Faela was a kin-slayer. Both of these were grave crimes. Kade could not fathom what a Lusican minstrel could have done to become a Gray. Haley's story contained some gaping holes that stirred Kade's paranoia.

The sound of a twig cracking alerted Kade to someone's approach. His hand went for the knife that wasn't there as he turned to face the noise. Eve stood hands empty in front of her.

"Jair's snoring wake you up too?" Kade asked his face relaxing.

She shook her head and walked up to the water's edge. "No. The binding woke me when you left the tavern."

Kade nodded. "Sorry, didn't mean to wake you. I didn't intend to walk this far. I just found myself here."

"Just like you found yourself in the cellar?"

Kade's gaze darkened. "No, I tracked Gareth there."

"So you claim."

Kade looked down at his hands, callused from consistent practice and use of his weapons. "I'm sorry, Eve. I loved Nessa like a sister. I never wanted any harm to come to her."

Her back muscles spasmed at his words, but she continued to look at the running water. "Like a sister? Then why were you marrying her?"

"To save her."

"Well, you certainly did a stellar job of that," Eve said her voice cruel and cold.

"Eve, you were born in a Noble House." Kade's voice was quiet. "You know the expectations your Uncle had for her."

She said nothing, but wrapped her arms around her stomach.

"She was going to be married for money to a man widowed twice already. She came to me in tears the night she found out. She said she'd rather marry someone she knew would treat her well, someone who cared about her. So, I offered."

Her mouth slightly agape, Eve turned her face toward him. "You made her an offer out of pity?"

"No," Kade said his gaze resolute. "Compassion and affection."

"Nessa deserved more than compassion." She bit off her words.

"You're right, she did," Kade admitted. "But it's what she wanted and I was happy to give it to her."

Eve looked at the moon its reflection blurred and broken in the running water. "Why did you run?"

Kade drew in a breath and exhaled with a sigh. "I had to ensure the information I had gathered on the Brethren got to Finalaran."

"If that's true," she said giving his story the benefit of the doubt, "then why did you head southeast instead of southwest toward Finalaran immediately?"

"I didn't know who Gareth had been talking to. I didn't trust him not to have a set up to implicate me in Nessa's death."

"You implicated yourself just fine without any help from Gareth," Eve interrupted.

Kade rose to his feet without a word and turned to go back to the inn. His feet were wet from the grass, causing the dirt on the roads to cake the bottom of his feet.

I really should have put my boots on, he thought to himself concentrating his irritation at the dirt rather than Eve.

"Kade, wait. You didn't answer my question," she called after him.

Without turning, Kade said, "You've already made up your mind. Find another target, Eve. I'm done for tonight."

As he strode through the canyons of the abandoned streets,

the wind swept down them with a biting chill. Wearing only trousers, he shivered in the cold, but felt no urge to slow down, though he knew Eve followed. He just wanted to wash the dirt from his feet and try to get some sleep. Finding the water pump outside the kitchens, he scrubbed the filth off of his feet in the spurting spray.

When he was done, he looked up and Eve stood holding a rag, which she tossed to him. He caught it and dried his feet to keep from repeating the incident.

"My thanks," Kade told her. When he finished, he gave her back the rag.

Eve's expression softened. "Let's try this again when I haven't just woken, okay?"

Kade nodded. "Deal. Now let's see if I can manage to sleep with the growling coming from Jair."

She actually smiled at this. "I could hear it all the way down the hall."

Kade led Eve back into the inn, his hand on her back. Cloaked in the shadows of the stairs, Lucien watched, his fists clenched and his eyes sparking golden.

*   *   *

Caleb and Talise had left for Kilrood before the sun had fully crested the horizon that morning. Regardless of the route they chose, whether traveling by train back down to the Bramm or riding east to Lanvirdis to catch a ship down the coast, they had a long journey ahead of them. Faela's heart fluttered thinking about Caleb's warning. She had known that Nikolais had sent bounty hunters after her, but she had tried to convince herself that his main concern wouldn't be Sammi. She knew it had been a foolish hope, but that didn't stop her from clinging to it.

The sun sat just above the line of the horizon now. It was time. Faela closed her eyes as she felt the rhythm of her blood pulsing inside her. Harnessing that rhythm, Faela wove a note around that anchor and reached. She did not have far to reach. The pulse she sought, Gresham's signature, was less than a day's walk away. Just as she had predicted, he had gone to Kelso.

Before the sun set on this day, she would meet the man she had spent the last several months tracking. At times it felt like chasing a shadow, but now she would have proof that forgiveness was possible.

Releasing the vial around her neck, she opened her eyes and smiled. "He's still in Kelso."

"You mean, we'll catch up with him today?" Jair asked strapping on his pack, his hair still ruffled from recent sleep.

I believe we will," Faela answered her voice somewhat unsure. Whether they would intercept him today did not cause the wavering in her voice, the prospect of facing him did.

Misinterpreting her hesitance, Jair reassured her. "We will, Faela."

Flashing him an appreciative smile, Faela turned to the rest of the party standing in front of the inn. Their packs filled, they waited for her to begin their hike. Within an hour of Caleb and Talise's exit, the rest of the party prepared to depart.

"He's still in Kelso. Everyone ready?" she asked of the group and was rewarded with a series of affirmative responses. Less than a month ago, she had thought she would face Gresham alone. Looking around at the large group chatting and yawning as they made their way out of the skeletal remains of Moshurst, Faela shook her head in disbelief.

"Hurry it up, Faela," Kade commanded with a smirk as he walked down the street backward. "We got people to meet."

CHAPTER SEVENTEEN

Situated at the crossroads between the northern coastal cities of Nabos and the railways that ran from Montdell to Lanvirdis, Kelso more closely resembled a small city, than a town. Many of the towns of Nabos during the war had erected walls to protect them from invasion and Kelso was no exception. Just as Faela predicted, they made it to Kelso before nightfall. Spreading like spilled ink as the sun set, the waning light stained the bottoms of the clouds with oranges and purples.

To keep out the cold wind, Faela had draped a wide tan scarf around her head and neck. It was nice to have a legitimate excuse to hide her face for once. This close to Gresham, to answers, she refused to leave anything to chance.

Approaching the gate, Eve took the lead. "Let me handle this."

Despite Faela's misgivings about Eve, she had to admit that a Daniyelan who wasn't a known fugitive had better odds of slipping them into the city unnoticed, so she swallowed back a retort and let the Daniyelan proceed.

"Hail and well met, gentlemen," she called, her voice inviting and relaxed, "we've been on the road all day and would love to wash the dirt from our throats with a nice pint. Could you direct us to the nearest tavern?"

Eve's conversational strategy seemed to work. One of the guards stabbed at the other with his elbow and whispered something, which caused the taller of the two to laugh.

The shorter returned Eve's easy smile and said, "Best place in town is the Tin Whistle, just three blocks past the livestock markets. You can't miss it. Best summer wheat ale you'll find anywhere these days."

Eve clasped the guard's forearm with a grin. "My thanks, friend."

When the man caught the cut of her jacket under her

overcoat, his eye widened. "Sister," he stammered. "Will you be wanting the magistrate?"

Eve shook her head, her stance still relaxed and open. "I'm not here on business, Sergeant. I'm just accompanying some friends."

The guard's posture relaxed somewhat, but still remained hesitant as he caught sight of Sheridan. "You'll not be wanting to stay at the Tin Whistle, m'lady. It's not a place for the likes of you and your friends."

"If it's good enough for you to recommend, then it's good enough for me and mine," Eve insisted winking at the guard.

"If you say so, m'lady," the guard relented uneasily, but stepped out of her way to allow them to pass.

"I do, and thank you Sergeant," she paused waiting for him to supply his name.

"Carver, m'lady. Silas Carver."

"Sergeant Carver," she smiled her face brightening.

Faela had never noticed how pleasant her angular features looked when she smiled. Her short hair made her appear sharper and harsher than her twin, but when she smiled her features looked refined, even delicate. "You've been a great help."

Sergeant Carver bowed clumsily, while his comrade stood in dumbfounded silence.

Eve retrieved Kimiko's reins from Sheridan and the party entered through a stone archway into Kelso's market. With the sun setting, vendors and traders without permanent storefronts were closing up their carts and booths for the evening. Those wealthy enough to afford permanent shops reached to light the oil lamps in their windows and outside their doors. The light of the setting sun mingled with the light of the lamps in long jumping shadows.

Unlike the town they had just spent the night in, Kelso was wealthy enough to boast cobblestone streets instead of packed dirt and gravel. Faela had heard stories about crossroads towns like Kelso, but had never been to one. Any time her father had taken her with him on a trip, it had been by river and Kelso was a day's walk from the nearest waterway and she had never traveled by train.

With a squeal of delight, Mireya skipped over to an herb vendor where a young boy carefully carried baskets, too big for him to manage easily, from the street to pack them onto the back of their cart that had displayed their wares. The group had stopped, waiting for Mireya to return, when Faela felt a physical tugging.

At the sensation, she pushed back the edge of her scarf to increase her field of vision. When she did, she saw both Kade and Jair staring at her. The surprise in Jair's eyes and the suspicion in Kade's told her that they had felt it too.

"What was that?" Jair asked her.

"What was what?" Sheridan craned her neck to look back at them from the cart.

"I can't be sure," Faela said each word slowly, "but you felt it coming from the east, right?" She directed her question to Kade.

Kade nodded his agreement.

"Hey," Sheridan interrupted. "What's going on?"

"I think my tracer spell is telling me where to find Gresham," she explained. Though the spell would indicate the target's general direction, once in close proximity to the target, it should have dissipated entirely. Yet as she continued to stand there, the insistent tugging returned again, stronger this time.

"Okay, I definitely felt that one," Jair told her and Kade nodded confirming that he had as well.

Sheridan tucked her arms across his chest. "If that's just your tracer spell, why is Jair feeling it?"

Kade raised his shoulders indicating his ignorance. "Maybe it's a Gray thing?"

"Did you feel that, Haley?" Sheridan asked, but Haley talked with Eve oblivious to their discussion.

The tugging returned and this time it managed to upset Faela's equilibrium and she staggered into Jair who put out a hand to steady her.

"I have to go, now," Faela said regaining her footing. "Tell Mireya to hurry up or catch up, Sheridan. I'm not waiting."

Sheridan opened her mouth to argue, but Faela had already started walking in the direction of the tugging with Jair and Kade at her heels. They continued through the market, passing weaver's shops, ironworks, then butchers as they approached the livestock market. As they passed each shop, Kade noted their location within the city.

"I think we're heading for that tavern, the Tin Whistle," Kade remarked.

Within a block, the pungent smell of animal had blown down wind and away from the shops they now passed, tailors and cobblers and bakeries. As they rounded the third block they saw a tavern with a sign marking it as the Tin Whistle. The tugging led directly inside.

Faela inhaled slowly, holding her breath for a moment and exhaled gustily. "Here goes," she said more to herself than her companions.

Stepping through the doorway of the tavern, they entered a raucous room filled with men and women laughing, cursing, dancing, eating, and singing off key. Seated at the bar with his arm around the serving girl lounged the source of the tugging, a large, muscular man with a bushy beard and curly brown hair pulled back in a ponytail at the base of his neck. He looked barely out of his thirties. When they entered the room, the man's head perked up and he swiveled his gaze to the door.

When he saw the three of them, his eyes fixed on Faela and his mouth cracked into a wide grin. "My, you've filled out nicely, Rafaela."

"Tobias?" Faela spoke the name as if she looked at a ghost.

Patting the serving girl on the hip, he winked at her and whispered something in her ear. She giggled and hurried away back behind the bar. Free of his encumbrance, Tobias stood showing that his height matched Jair's, but his frame could have fit two of Jair inside it. He strode over and swept Faela into a paternal hug.

"I knew it would be you," he whispered through the fabric of her scarf, his voice tinged with sadness.

Faela stood stunned as Tobias enveloped her much smaller ribcage with his arms. Then coming to her senses, she put her hands between his chest and herself and pushed back to look up at him.

"Now you just wait a darkness blasted moment," she said, her face still displaying her shock. "You're not Gresham. I'm looking for a man named Gresham. You can't be Gresham."

Tobias smiled his dark eyes twinkling. "Rafaela, think for a moment. It will come to you."

"No." She shook her head, her face beginning to flush. "No, Ianos would have told me. He would have."

"Let me see if I can guess," Tobias offered, his eyes crinkling as he tried to keep from laughing. "Ianos took you to the vault in the crypt below the Tereskan temple in Kilrood. He gave you a blood sample to cast a tracer. He told you it would lead you to a man named Gresham who once served the Tereskans."

He lifted Faela's chin with a finger to force her to look him in the eyes. His eyes flashed silver then returned to their deep brown. "A man who was a redeemed Gray."

Faela's protested, her voice weak. "But your name isn't Gresham."

"Did it never occur to you that it might be a surname?" he asked smiling down at her.

"But your surname is," Faela's voice trailed off as she blinked and covered her face with a hand. Dragging her hand down her face, she made a disgusted noise. "I don't know what your surname is."

"I'm guessing it's Gresham," Jair added helpfully still several paces behind Faela, where he and Kade had claimed seats at the bar facing the pair.

Faela turned a look of loathing at him as Kade smacked him in the back of the head.

"Ow!" Jair exclaimed looking far more injured than he was. "What? I'm not wrong."

"And in no way are you helping," Faela said ruefully before turning back to Tobias. "I don't understand. Why didn't Ianos tell me I was looking for you?"

"He had his reasons, girl. Just as you have yours," he said nodding his head to indicate her eyes.

"His reasons?" Her pitch rising, Faela began to object to his non-answer.

"But let's find somewhere quieter to sit in here so we can talk," he said cutting her off. "It seems like just yesterday you were that skinny little girl with the dirty face."

The look he gave her was affectionate as he squeezed her shoulder. Walking over to the bar, he thumped the counter to get the barkeep's attention.

"Rick," he called to the thin man with large gold hoops in his ears. "Back room open?"

Not even trying to be heard over the crowd, he waved Tobias to go on back.

"Ladies first," he said to the trio, waving in the direction of a curtained opening.

Jair looked around for the rest of the party. "Um, Kade," he said stopping the other man with a hand before following Faela who had disappeared behind the plain canvas curtain. "How are they going to find us?"

Patting his chest directly over his heart, he replied, "Eve will." Kade too disappeared behind the curtain.

Not wanting to miss what would inevitably follow, Jair ducked after them through the doorway. A round, carved wooden table shiny from use and age filled most of the space in the room.

Already settled into chairs, Tobias saw Jair's admiration of the craftsmanship and the sheer size of the table. "It's used for card games that Rick would rather keep off the main floor."

Jair found a seat next to Kade who had pulled back a chair near Faela. A small black stove in the back corner blazed filling the room with heat. Faela sank into her chair enjoying the warmth like a cat in a patch of sunlight.

Her eyes never leaving Tobias, she remarked, "How is it that you don't look a day older than the last time I saw you?"

"It's all the ale and women," he replied. "Keeps me preserved."

"It's been twelve years since the last time you visited Ianos in Kilrood. I was fourteen and you still look exactly the same. Don't try to peddle that to me."

Tobias tented his fingers and watched her over them. "Never could back then either. You always were the suspicious sort. Guess I have your brother to thank for that."

"Is it because of being," she hesitated, "is it because of being like me?"

"Yes and no," he answered. When she threw him a murderous look, he held up his hands. "Whoa, I was going to explain. Rein it in, little miss. I would not be as I am, had I not turned Gray, but I am not as I am because I was Gray."

"Okay, that explained nothing to me," Jair interjected.

"Why don't we start where this began?" Tobias suggested. "But before you hear my story, I want to hear yours, Rafaela."

Faela had feared this would be necessary when she found Gresham, but she had never imagined it would be Ianos' old friend who used to regale her with wild tales of his adventures when she was a child. Forcing herself not to look at Kade, she had to decide how much she was willing to reveal, even to Tobias.

While she steeled herself to answer him, Tobias locked Jair with his gaze. "Yours as well, son. Don't think I didn't notice that you're one of us."

Jair swallowed and nodded under Tobias's gaze, but said nothing.

"Before I tell you," Faela prefaced, remembering what Tobias had whispered to her. "Why did you say that you knew this would happen to me?"

"Patience, girl," he said, melancholy tingeing his smile. "That's part of my story too."

Faela exhaled. "Fair enough. Well, there's no point in beating around the bush about it. I killed my father, Tobias."

Tobias put his hand to cover his mouth and leaned his weight onto his elbow resting on the table to listen.

All emotion erased from Faela's face, she spoke as though reporting something she had memorized without any understanding of what she said. "I abused my gift by violating his mind and free will by forming a link through repeated manipulations of his emotions. Eventually, my own hopelessness and selfish desires influenced him through that link and he took his own life. Because of the link, I felt him slit his arms clear from wrist to elbow. He was in his study. When I found him, he was dying."

Faela's voice finally caught. She curled her fingers around the arms of the chair and cleared her voice. "I severed the link and tried to repair the damage, but I was far too late. When I severed the link and reached for my red magic, I felt like I was being burned from the inside out. The next time I saw my reflection, my eyes had changed. I was cursed as a kin-slayer."

"No," Tobias disagreed. "You weren't cursed. Is that what you think this is?" He tapped her temple with two fingers.

Tears gathered at the corners of her eyes and she looked away from him to the stove. "What else could it be?"

Tobias's eyes carried a deep pain despite being offset by his absent smile. "Tell me what you think you know about Grays."

"According to *Roland's Legends*," Kade spoke up, "the first Gray was Simon's apprentice, Justin. After the Shattering, he had broken his vows to the Orders by wielding black magic, which was forbidden, but when Simon ordered him take the life of a Lusican seeker, Justin refused and used his orange magic to shield the girl nearly killing himself in the process. Simon fled and Justin had turned. He had become Gray."

"You know your legends," Tobias said complimenting him.

Kade folded his hands across his chest. "I knew a little girl who had trouble falling asleep."

"So what can we learn from this legend about Grays?" Tobias asked his gaze moving around the table to all three.

Jair surprised them by answering in a quiet voice. "You have to have used black magic."

"You are correct about that," Tobias replied. "But not all who wield black magic turn and become Gray. So what was different about Justin?"

"He risked his own life to protect another's life," Kade suggested.

"That's part of it, but it isn't the whole story," Tobias leaned toward them. "Dark magic steals its energies like a parasite. It latches onto other colors and uses them. But more than that it corrupts any magic it touches. All magic has two sides. Red magic is the most obvious, because it can heal and save life, but it can also kill and take life. Orange magic protects; it tracks, seeks out the truth. But where there is the power to protect there is the power to enslave. Yellow is the expression of magic through beauty and art, but it can also manipulate and lie. Green is the foundation, the fuel for magic, but it must be used carefully so to not alter the Balance of magic."

At this Jair's retreated into himself, his expression troubled, yet blank.

"Purple magic," Tobias laughed to himself, "has the ability to see through space and time and for some to move through either and with that comes the potential to destroy the very fabric of reality. I can tell you that I'm glad I was never called to Wistholt. I wouldn't want that responsibility."

"But blue magic doesn't have two sides like that, does it?" Faela asked.

"Of course it does," Tobias corrected. "Why wouldn't it? Blue magic is probably the most misunderstood, because of the Orders teachings."

"Their teachings?" Kade questioned, his brow wrinkling.

"Yes, their teachings. Only Nikelans have Blue magic, correct?" Tobias asked them.

"Right," agreed Kade.

"Wrong. More people possess blue magic than the Orders would like you to believe. That boy sitting next to you," he said pointing to Jair, "he has blue. It's not dominant, but it is there all the same."

Faela rocked forward in her chair, her mouth slack. "Blue?"

At the same time, Kade raised an eyebrow and asked, "Him?"

Tobias nodded. "How did you meet him, Rafaela?"

"He was being chased by Kade in the forest. I had just finished my tracer spell looking for you, when they ran into me near a clearing. Jair used me for a shield actually."

Tobias's eyes twinkled. "Jair, why did you run toward that clearing? You knew you'd find help there, didn't you?"

Jair opened and closed his mouth. "It was just a gut feeling."

"You get those a lot, don't you? Knowing where to be at the right place at the right time? That's untrained blue, boy."

Kade tapped a finger against his lips as his mind connected bits of information. "I never did ask you, Jair. Why did you steal my circuit kit?"

"Honestly?" Jair said sinking in his chair. "It seemed like a good idea at the time?"

"You took the one thing that would make me chase you and by getting me to hunt you, you were able to shake two of the best bounty hunters I know. I'm one of the only people alive who could confuse the trail well enough to confound Caleb." Kade shook his head laughing. "Darkness, you do have blue, Jair."

"Just as I said. Now, if you two are here," he said indicating Jair and Faela, "then there's a Nikelan somewhere nearby. Am I right?"

"Yes," Faela admitted slowly. "Her name is Mireya."

Tobias nodded, his smile widening. "Sweet girl. She's a favorite of Riv's."

"Riv?" Faela's pitch rose flabbergasted at the casual familiarity he used referring to the Nikelan Scion.

"Scion of the Nikelans," Tobias explained. "I know you've heard of Rivka, Rafaela. Ianos is a stickler about learning history. If Mireya is here, then there's been another prophecy and you're part of it, children. If Lior is moving in the world again, then your meeting was directed by him."

"You mean it was predetermined? Meant to be?" Kade asked his voice skeptical.

"No, I said you were directed. Jair didn't have to follow his gut."

"You clearly don't know Jair." Faela spoke only loud enough for Kade to hear.

"But he did. Lior didn't decide for him. He just nudged him."

"You sound like Mireya," Jair observed.

"I've spent some time with Nikelans," Tobias said cryptically.

"Lior?" Faela asked realizing what he had said after he repeated the name. "The tri-fold deity of the Deoraghan? What does he have to do with this?"

"That is for you to discover, my girl," Tobias said with an infuriating smile, "not for me to tell."

Faela rewarded him with a withering glare and finally asked, "So what're the two sides of Blue? Since you refuse to answer my other question."

"The blue opens a channel to the infinite, which enables those with it to see the future. Some are possible futures, but there are certain events that will occur. Knowing the future can be a terrible burden. It can be used powerfully for good, but when someone with blue presumes to understand what future a prophecy will create and tries to bring that interpretation into being instead of allowing Lior to guide them..." He left the implication unsaid.

"Any magic can be used for the Light or corrupted by darkness. But black," Tobias paused, his fingers drumming the tabletop, "black magic is inherently self-focused. There's a reason why those in the Orders are called Brothers and Sisters. They are meant to serve the people of this world, not exploit or enslave them. But that has not always been the case in our history."

Tobias looked beyond the three to a darker time haunted by the ghosts of his past.

Something troubled Faela and she chewed on the inside of her bottom lip. "Tobias, what did you mean by 'another prophecy'?"

"Well, I told you I would tell you my story, and I will." Tobias looked into Faela's eyes reassuring her fears that he was just putting her off again. "But we still need to hear this young man's tale."

Jair squirmed in his seat, shifting his weight from side to side. "I didn't know what I was doing," he began.

But before he could continue his story, Mireya peeked her head through the curtain. "There you are," she admonished and said back into the front room of the inn, "They're back here."

She jerked the curtain back and walked into the room. "You know, it's not nice to go running off without even a word, when I was just trying to find some nice herbs to brew some tea to help you wake up in the morning."

Mireya's rant was cut off when she realized the three were not alone. Spotting Tobias Gresham sitting with his back to the stove, she squealed with delight and rushed around the table and threw herself into his lap. "Tobias!"

"Am I the only one who doesn't know this guy?" Kade whispered to Faela who suppressed a laugh.

Behind Mireya, Dathien crossed the cramped room in a few strides.

Tobias extracted an arm from the bundle of Mireya and clasped Dathien's forearm. "Looking well, mate. Have to fish this little one out of any ponds recently?"

"Well met, Tobias," Dathien replied with a slow smile. "No ponds, just briar patches and bogs."

Mireya glared balefully at her spouse, but snuggled in closer to

Tobias. "No complaining. I got us there."

Sheridan, Eve, and Haley entered the room hesitantly, clearly feeling out of place. Unfazed, Sheridan marched to Jair's side and fell into the chair next to him with a wink. Eve trailed after her with Haley at her side. They each sat unsure of what was happening.

"I'm sure you did get where you were going, child," Tobias answered stroking her arm, "by taking the most direct path possible regardless of the obstacles in your way."

Dathien and Tobias shared a knowing smile of memories and mutual experiences.

Mireya looked over to Faela. "Tobias brought me past the Boundary to the Nikelan temple in Vamorines when I a little girl."

"Aye," Tobias affirmed. "You were a wee little thing too. I couldn't take my eyes off of you for a moment or I'd find you up a tree or in a pond or feeding a chipmunk or petting a wolf."

"They never bit me," Mireya protested.

"Of course not, dear one," Tobias agreed kissing her hair.

As if something had just occurred to her, she sat up. "Wait, what are you doing here?"

"He's who I've been tracking," Faela answered.

"Oops," Mireya flushed a bright pink.

"Oops?" Faela repeated, as the heat of the room finally required her to peel off her overcoat.

"You didn't know," Dathien told her.

"But I should have," Mireya argued. "I knew Tobias's surname is Gresham. I just never thought..."

"Don't worry, Mireya," Faela reassured her. "He's known me most of my life too."

"Whole life actually," Tobias corrected.

Faela's brows knit together at the revelation as she draped the coat over the back of the chair and pushed her foot against the edge of the table.

"But we'll get to that. Right now, Jair was about to tell me how he joined our ranks."

All eyes turned to Jair who slouched down further in his chair and hooked his ankle across the top of his thigh.

"It's a good thing this isn't awkward at all," Jair said, his voice cracking. "Any way, like I was telling you before we were so rudely interrupted, I really didn't know what I was doing. I was pretty young when the war broke out and my father was conscripted. I never went to any of the temples because the Brothers and Sisters of the Orders, who hadn't been forced to fight, had been expelled from the country. I grew up here, in Nabos, on a farm near Garon.

"My mother caught me playing with green magic one day. I had picked her daisies and kept them alive for weeks. It took her awhile to figure out who was keeping them alive. She had liked them so much and it made her smile. She didn't smile much after my father went to fight. One of my sisters ratted me out.

"Once she determined I was the culprit, she taught me the basics. Before the war, my mum helped out at the local Phaidrian temple with the little ones. She had some talent for green, but nothing out of the ordinary and not enough to take vows. I never knew everyone couldn't mold green magic the way I did."

Jair interlaced his fingers and opened his palms like in a child's game and just stared into his hands. Tobias once more did not interrupt, but allowed Jair to continue when he was ready.

Clasping his hands together, Jair sighed. "My eldest brother was eventually conscripted as well. I'm the youngest boy, but have two younger sisters. With da and Zane gone, my mum and sisters needed me to help run the farm. I never got any real training. The war was real hard on my village. There was a battle fought not far from it. Daniyelans and probably other Orders fought there too."

His eyes slid from Sheridan to Eve. "But the battle did something. It did something wrong to the land. All that magic in one place at one time, it wasn't right." Jair picked at the fabric of his pants, keeping his gaze down. "Afterward, nothing wanted to grow. No matter what we did, nothing would grow. That's how it started. Then the animals started having stillbirths."

His voice got real quiet and his brows knit together. Pushing his hair back with his fingers, he said, "Then people started getting sick. I could feel it. Everything was off. I kept our crops alive for a season, but I knew it couldn't last. I knew I wouldn't be able to keep it up.

"So, one night, I was standing on a ridge overlooking our fields and I followed the eddies of magic until they fattened and became pools and rivers and lakes. There was so much, I figured redirecting it wouldn't," he paused, "that it couldn't." He fell silent again starring into the creases of his palms.

"That's not true," he whispered. "I convinced myself it couldn't hurt anything, but I knew. I could feel it when I erected the channels to siphon the green magic back to Garon. I knew what had happened at the battle. I knew that the energies would renew themselves, but it would take time. I knew that I was damning another area to the same sickness plaguing my home.

"But my little sister, Emma, had just gotten sick. So, I lied to myself and said that it wouldn't be like it was for us and I did it. I took the energy and trapped it. It wasn't until the Phaidrian Order reestablished itself at Lanvirdis that my mother insisted I go for training if they would have me. I was only there for two years when they discovered what I could do and it didn't take them long to realize what I had done. They came when I was home visiting."

Faela extended her arm across Kade and pat Jair's hand in reassurance. He gave her a grateful, half smile.

"I still didn't really understand that there was anything unusual with what I could do. I thought all Phaidrian's could follow the flows like I could. They told me I had wrecked the Balance and it was affecting the green magic all over the world. I couldn't believe that what I had done could possibly have had that kind of impact. They questioned me, but I didn't know what they were talking about. They asked about something called the Brethren and why I had done it.

"When I didn't give them the answers they wanted to hear, they threatened my family. They said they were going to send my mother and sisters to work as indentured servants far to the southwest, high in the mountains at Wistholt.

"I'd never left Nabos. I couldn't even imagine my family being somewhere as far away as Wistholt in Indolbergan. They gave me a night to think it over. My family and I left that night. I left my mum and sisters with my uncle in Kilrood. Then I left, so they wouldn't be endangered any more."

Tobias shook his head. "Same mistakes again," he said in an

absent voice. "We keep making the same mistakes."

"The town we stopped in before here, Moshurst" Jair picked up his narrative, but his voice caught. "The same thing that had happened in my village had happened there. Only this time it wasn't because of a battle." He paused and curled his hands into fists. "It was because of what I had done."

Obscuring his mouth with his fingers, Tobias watched Jair's constant fidgeting movements, but kept his thoughts to himself.

"There were no animals, no people, nothing new grew there. The town had been abandoned. It's what would have happened to my home. When I saw it, I reached out and I destroyed the dams I had created. Like Faela said, it felt like I was burning to cinders. When I was done, she told me that my eyes had turned and that I was Gray now."

Tobias' mouth twitched into a smile that spoke of triumph and vindication. "Do you see the commonality between your two stories?" he directed his question to Faela and Jair. "Do you see what links them?"

"Other than our blatant disregard for the natural order and use of black magic?" Faela asked her tone dry.

"Turning Gray brings on a wicked bad case of heart burn?" Kade suggested.

Tobias gave a tolerant smile. "Funny. But what preceded each of their turning?"

Jair raised his tortured gaze from his intertwined hands. "We tried to reverse what we had done. It's like you said, black magic uses magic for itself, for its own goals and purposes. We tried to fix what we'd done without caring what it would do to us. We just wanted to make it right. Was that it?"

Tobias' smile widened and his eyes twinkled. "Precisely so. What you both did, trying to reverse the magic you had built was done so at great personal risk. Faela severing the link could have easily killed her or at least burned out her gift. You destroying the barriers you had created could have done the same. By dismantling the black magic you had constructed, you rejected that magic. The recoil that creates usually kills the wielder."

"So that was the burning sensation?" Faela asked, letting her foot fall as she scooted to the edge of the chair.

Tobias nodded. "It was the backlash of the energy. Dark magic takes, it destroys and it resists change with a tremendous amount of force. Have you never wondered why there have been so few Grays in our history?"

"It never kept me up at night," Faela admitted.

"Well, I did," Sheridan said, speaking for the first time. "And none of the books I came across ever explained what they were, except that they had all used black magic at some point. But it never explained why all wielders of black magic didn't become Gray."

"Not all people who use black magic and then renounce it become Gray," Tobias explained. "They don't become Gray, because they don't survive the process. Both Faela and Jair absorbed the energy when it recoiled. They had the capabilities to absorb it.

"You said you thought you would burn away, right? Well, were you unable to absorb the release of the magic you would have. The energy would have consumed you, leaving nothing behind. Only the strongest wielders become Gray, because they are the only ones who can survive the turning."

Faela and Jair looked at each other, then back to Tobias speechless.

"Do you know why your eyes turn to silver?" Tobias asked them. "Why all Grays are marked by the mirror eyes?"

Faela bit her lower lip. "Like I said before, I thought it was a mark of my curse. To never allow me to forget what I had done."

Sheridan smacked Jair's upper arm repeatedly. "No, no, don't you get it?" she said the words tripping over each other in her haste to verbalize her thoughts. "It's part of the absorption. It's so obvious. Why hadn't I made the connection before?"

"Because the Orders' stories about Grays that are told aren't meant to explain what they are." Tobias shrugged. "They're meant to be morality tales about what happened to bad, little magic wielders who use black magic."

"I'm still lost," Jair admitted.

Sheridan swiveled in her seat, tucking a leg underneath her thigh. "Okay, think about this way," she said gesticulating widely. "Think about what happens when you boil water. There can be things in the water that can make you sick. But when you boil it, the heat kills anything that might harm you. The heat purifies the water."

In the exact same intonation, Jair repeated, "I'm still lost."

"The colors that we harness to do magic, they're energy, just like fire," Sheridan gestured to the, unseen, but felt fire in the stove. "Just a different form of energy. Our bodies channel the energy and our minds shape it. With that much magical energy blasting through you, your bodies went through the magical equivalent of boiling water. Any impurities were literally vaporized.

"Well, not exactly," she corrected herself. "It's more like when lightning strikes sand. If it hits the wrong material it destroys it. But Grays, you're like sand. Instead of destroying you, the energy melts the sand into glass. The energy purifies it, changes it into something new, something reflective. Don't you see? It makes so much sense."

"Yeah," Jair said shaking his head, "not at all."

"Some of the magic leaks through us when we wield it," she said the words tumbling out. "Through our eyes and our skin. It focuses and collects itself in certain areas. Some have theorized that how we think of the magic determines how it manifests."

Sheridan shifted her body toward Faela. "Yours radiates from your hands when you heal, like most Tereskans. When I pop, it radiates from my collarbones because it's my center and I'm moving me. We all know that over time this seeping of magic permanently marks our bodies, like tattoos. Look at Dathien's wrists." She gestured with her palm open and pointed at Dathien.

Dathien held up his arms, the sleeves falling down toward his elbows. Dark blue lines crisscrossed around his wrists forming cuffs.

"How old are you?" Sheridan asked him.

"Twenty-nine," he answered, lowering his arms into his lap.

"See," she said waving her hands out from her chest. "From what I understand, from what I've read, a Grier's power is always present, right?"

Dathien nodded in affirmation.

"Because of that he is already marked. Those lines shouldn't be permanently visible for another ten, maybe fifteen years."

"What does that have to do with our eyes?" Jair asked.

"When you absorbed the backlash of black, it scorched every bit of color magic within you at the time, like when lightning strikes sand. It melted it all and reformed it into something fundamentally different and new. Instead of marking itself in your skin, it," Sheridan said snapping her fingers over and over grasping for a word, "purged your eyes, so to speak."

"Purged?" Faela said a hint of amusement in her voice.

"She's not wrong," Tobias said grinning at Sheridan's explanation. "Well done, young lady."

Sheridan looked pleased with herself, but more than anything she nearly vibrated with delight at this discussion on magical theory, few things got her this excited.

"Well think about it," Sheridan began. "The color in our irises changes as we use magic. Most people are born with green eyes and they change as the magic changes us. I have four color blendings, as do Eve and Kade. So we all have brown eyes now.

"Though Eve and I are identical twins, my eyes have indigo flecks around the pupil, but Eve," she said gesturing to her sister, "has golden flecks. Because where I have purple magic, she has yellow. So it follows that the silver eyes mean that at one point, all color was burned out of you."

Suddenly Faela's face froze in a look of horrified realization and she snapped her head up looking at Tobias. "Does that mean that in that moment we were completely colorless?"

Tobias nodded as he stroked his beard. "It does."

"How is that possible?" Eve blurted out half rising out of her chair. "No magic wielder can be colorless."

"Grays not only were at one time," Tobias corrected, "but the ability to be colorless remains within every Gray."

"Darkness take me," Faela whispered as she sagged in her chair her shirt bunching under her arms. "But what does that mean? To be colorless..." she trailed off her voice strangled.

Kade's eyes reflected the churning of his mind. "That means that Grays can absorb any magic used against them."

"That and so much more, my boy," Tobias said in a hushed tone.

No one spoke, trying to process the revelation. To be a colorless magic user was worse than blasphemy. To be colorless went against the foundations of the Orders teachings about magic. Magic infused every living thing in the world. The colors of magic were the threads that bound reality together. To be colorless meant that a person was nothing, a void. Worse than a void, to be colorless meant that person existed outside the structure of reality.

The implications left them stunned, everyone looking at something, anything other than Faela or Jair or Haley. Except for Sheridan, who chewed on her thumb as her mind tracked down each implication that watershed from this revelation.

"Darkness," Faela finally spoke, her voice an empty echo. "No wonder the Orders hunt down Grays to bring them to judgment and cleansing."

Tobias' eyes clouded at the final word she spoke, but it passed as fast as it had appeared so that Faela thought she must have imagined it. "The Orders fear that which they cannot contain and control."

At that statement, Eve's gaze locked on Tobias, her eyes guarded and suspicious.

Before she could speak, Faela pushed back her chair rising to her feet. She paced in her small section of the crowded room, then leaned into the corner, her forehead resting on the paneled wall. The cool, lacquer of the varnished wood pressed against her skin.

Inhaling, she broke the silence. "I thought I had been cursed, but this..."

Startling everyone in the room, she slammed the flat of her palm with a loud crack against the wall at the height of her face. "This is an abomination," she said in a choked whisper. Her nose touching the wall, she let her hand slide down until her arms hung at her side. In a dead tone, she said, "I'm an abomination."

Mireya slipped off of Tobias' lap and stood beside her. She slipped a hand onto Faela's back. "No. No, you aren't, Faela. Really, you just need to-"

Faela shook off Mireya's touch, whirling to face the girl. Her eyes glowing a dangerous crimson, Mireya took an involuntary step back from her.

"I need to what?" Faela seethed as she yanked back the scarf revealing her flushed face. The scarf sagged down her back. "What do I need to do, Mireya? Guide me. Counsel me. Tell me what to do. Tell me how I'm not a monster."

Faela advanced a step closer to Mireya with every sentence, until Mireya backed into the adjacent wall, next to the stove. Dathien half rose out of his chair, but one look from Mireya restrained him.

Mireya voice was small. "Faela, stop. You're scaring me."

Anger and loathing and guilt and shame rolled off of Faela in waves.

"This isn't you," Mireya said only loud enough to reach Faela.

Faela's eyes flashed and without a warning, she hauled back her left shoulder and with a scream of frustration threw all of her weight behind her fist into the wall narrowly missing Mireya. With a crunch, she shattered several bones in her hand. Tears in the corners of her eyes, her voice thick, she pressed her body in toward the wall and Mireya. "You have no idea who I am, little girl, or what I'm capable of."

No one in the room moved. No one made a sound. Until the noise of a chair scrapping the floor, as it was pushed back from the table, shattered the tension. Tobias stood behind Faela, who still leaned in toward Mireya, her knuckles ground into the wall. He covered Faela's hand with his own and pulled her away from Mireya whose cheeks were stained with silent tears.

Blood dripped down Faela's knuckles where the skin had split and ripped against the wood. Tobias flipped her hand in his to examine the damage. He did not try to extend any of her fingers that curled in unnaturally. Instead he rotated his large hand that cradled hers to see which joints and bones had taken the brunt of the impact.

He made an affirming noise in the back of his throat. "This is going to hurt, Rafaela. Are you prepared?"

She gave an apathetic nod as she stared through everything.

His hands glowing with red light that enveloped hers, he flattened her hand in his, straightening each one of the crushed fingers. Faela gasped with a sharp intake of air at the pain, but did not flinch.

"There," he said dropping her hand. "It's going to feel stiff for weeks and be sore for days." He lifted her chin with a finger, forcing Faela to meet his gaze. "That was a reckless, hot-headed, and cruel thing to do, Rafaela," Tobias reprimanded her, "and I understand completely. I did something very similar when I found out the same thing. Only I didn't hit a wall. What I hit, hit back."

Faela flexed her fingers and nodded with a choked laugh as she walked back to her chair and sank into it. "I don't understand. How can we be colorless?"

"For one thing, you aren't colorless," he amended. "The analogy young Sheridan used was a good one. When lightning strikes sand it melts the sand, but the individual grains aren't gone. They're still there, just in a new form. You've noticed that your power is diminished since the turning, correct?"

Faela nodded in affirmation. "I thought that meant I had lost the right to wield my magic."

"No, girl, that's not it at all. The process of turning is painful and it leaves scar tissue. During the healing process, your capabilities lessen, but you'll find your strength will return with time and practice."

"Tobias?" Faela asked looking at the blood still staining her hand.

He inclined his head to her.

"How old are you?"

"And now we come to it." Tobias checked over his shoulder and Mireya now stood next to Dathien whose arm encircled her shoulders. "As winter fades and the first crocuses of spring poke through the snow, I will reach my three hundred and seventy-first year."

CHAPTER EIGHTEEN

"That simply isn't possible," Eve objected with a definitive shake of her head. "You don't look older than thirty-five."

"So, you're going to tell me what is and is not possible about my life, young lady?" Tobias asked her with an amused smile. "I learned long ago not to restrict the world into what I believe to be possible, because that is precisely when the world surprises me."

Sheridan's eyes sparkled as she leaned forward eager. "Your name is Tobias?"

He nodded.

"But then your surname isn't really Gresham," Sheridan concluded. "That was her name, wasn't it?"

Tobias' eyes clouded visibly this time and lines of pain marked his face. "My, you do know your stories for someone who didn't spend any time at the Lusican temples."

"Whose name?" Jair asked then turned to Sheridan demanding, "How do you know all this?"

"What?" she asked defensive. "I like to read."

"The name she was known by was Gresham," Tobias began as a look of loss passed over his face. "It was the name she chose for herself to protect her nearest kin when she started the resistance, but her true name was Valaria Sagewind. Not many of the stories mention her real name any more. She was merely Gresham, one of the most feared of all the Deoraghan freedom fighters during the Cleansing. And she was my wife."

A look of horror spread across Faela's face. "You're that Tobias? The Deoraghan Tereskan who discovered how to remove a person of the gift? By the Light," Faela whispered through the screen of her fingers, "you started the Cleansings."

"To my eternal shame, yes," Tobias replied. "I started the Cleansings."

"So that's why you turned?" Sheridan asked propping one of her knees against the table and she leaned into it. "It's why you became a Gray?"

"Let me start at the beginning," he offered. "It'll make more sense if I start there."

Eve laced her arms across her chest watching the proceedings, but she remained an observer, not a participant in the conversation. The direction this discussion had taken set her nerves on edge. The disregard and apparent disrespect that this man, Tobias, showed for the Orders irritated her. Neither his attitude toward the Orders, nor the fact that this man was once a Gray engendered her trust.

Now he claimed to be responsible for one of the most notorious events in history. Eve was fairly sure he was mad, but looking around the table, she saw each person listening as though they considered his claims to be true, everyone except for Lucian, who while looking intent kept picking at the skin around his thumbnail. Eve hid her smile at his nervous habit. He didn't trust this Tobias either.

"Do you know why there aren't that many Deoraghan in the Orders?" he asked.

"Their potential is typically weak," Sheridan answered automatically as though being quizzed. "They don't have a lot of talent for handling magic."

"That is what the Orders have taught since the Treaty at Twinning Pass," he acknowledged. "It was their compromise."

"Their compromise with who?" Sheridan asked her voice holding a hint of a challenge.

"Talise," Faela interrupted with a smirk, "she uses magic in ways I've never seen. My brother's wife," she explained to the others, "she's a Deoraghan. She uses yellow magic combatively when she fights."

This stirred Eve drawing her into active participation in the conversation. "But yellow isn't a combative magic. It's artistic expression."

"Trust me," Kade answered. "If you've ever seen Talise fight, it's an art. You should be able to relate, Eve. It reminds me of your dancing."

Opening then shutting her mouth, Eve bit back the reflexive response that he knew that she didn't dance anymore, because it was no longer true. With Lucien's return to her life, when she felt the rhythm it no longer ached like an open wound.

"That's what I mean," Tobias said seizing on Faela's tangent. "The Deoraghan don't use magic in the ways you're taught in the temples. It's more instinctive, organic even. Whereas normally only one in ten people can handle magic, the majority of the Deoraghan can. Because of that, the magic is more a part of every day life in smaller ways. So, it's easy to convince outsiders that the Deoraghan have little talent for it. Dathien can attest to the falseness of that claim as much as I can."

"But without temple training by the Orders anyone with the gift to effect the flow of color magic is a danger to themselves and everyone around them," Sheridan argued. "The untrained don't know how to use the magic without possibly causing irreversible damage. I mean I hate to say it, but look at what Jair did."

Jair shrank back as if physical struck by Sheridan's words.

"Sorry," she said with a shrug, "but it's true. So how can it be that the Deoraghan have so many more gifted than everyone suspects."

"It was part of the treaty," Tobias explained. "The Deoraghan were free to train their own without interference from the Orders. They are no more untrained than you, young lady. They've just undergone a very different kind of training. But to understand the Cleansings and my story, we must go back to the founding of the Orders of the Light."

"That was more than three hundred years ago," Jair felt compelled to point out. "You're not that old."

"Not yet, boy," Tobias acknowledged. "Thousands of years ago before the Shattering, the center of the civilized world was the Gialdanis, the white city. It was a place of beauty and learning. It was the home of the light mages. Through their work the city advanced and prospered. Eventually the mages decided that their abilities allowed them to see more of life, to understand more, so it was their duty to rule the city, instead of serve it. It was for the greater good for the mages to take care of the people. But that much power over the lives of the people, in the hands of so few, is never good for the people. Shortly after the mages began ruling the city, an earth tremor tore open the western half of the city.

"No one at the time knew what had caused it, but it was the mages. They had tried to subdue light magic to their own wills. The eruption of the earth was a result of the Shattering. Half of that great city fell into the northern sea that night and the light magic was split into its separate colors. They were denied the ability to ever wield the unified light ever again. Only a handful of light mages survived the explosion. Of those remaining few came the first color mages. They wanted to ensure that no one else dared use magic as they had.

"The first mage with red magic was a woman named Tereska, orange a man named Daniyel, yellow a woman named Lusi, green a woman named Phaidra, blue a woman named Nikela, and finally purple, a man named Amser. Together they founded the separate Orders. They wanted to ensure no one experimented with black magic ever again. They feared the independent use of magic, because from that freedom came the potential for the misuse of magic, like they themselves had done."

"But the Orders were founded to serve the people of this world," Sheridan objected. "Not to maintain control."

"That is true," Tobias admitted. "The best way to ensure a selfless use of magic was to make sure that any who wield magic are taught to view their purpose as service, not rank or privilege. It suited their ends. But at the core, the Orders do teach control. Would anyone here disagree?"

"I don't see what's so wrong with that," Eve protested. "An uncontrolled gift is a menace. It's deadly."

"Self-control is important," Tobias answered, "but coerced control is not. Control based on deception is not. Trust me, I speak as one who believed the teachings of the Orders unreservedly and without question at one time. You must understand, I thought that anyone trying to live outside the Orders prescribed guidelines for magic was a threat. So much so that I sought a way to remove the gift from those who refused training in the temples. It's a horrifying process, but the process itself is nothing compared to my intentions for its use.

"I am Deoraghan, a son of the Tribes. I knew how strongly magic ran in the Tribes. I wanted to give the Orders a way to help them. I thought I was helping them." Tobias shook his head with an abiding sadness. "I was removing the danger they posed to themselves. I was ensuring that black magic could never destroy my people, the way it had destroyed Gialdanis. That's what I kept telling myself."

Tobias ran his hand along his jaw and through his beard breathing deeply as he recalled these painful memories. Despite the centuries that separated him from the events, he still remembered the faces of those women and children. The pain stabbed at him as sharp as if the events had just happened.

"Cleansing I called it," he snorted, "cleansing. It was a violation plain and simple. I raped the minds and souls of every person I 'cleansed' of the gift. I knew I was ripping away something that was essential to them, but it didn't matter. What mattered was protecting the world, protecting the Deoraghan from their own backwards ways.

"After a person is cleansed, they are never the same. Trying to remove a person's gift is like trying to remove a person's mind. Except with cleansing, they live. They can walk and eat and talk, but that spark of the individual, their likes and dislikes, passions and hatreds, they were wiped clean, just gone."

Chuckling without any amusement, Tobias continued. "The perverse thing is that cleansing can only be done by using black magic."

The shocked faces around the table confirmed that his companions were unaware of this fact.

"That's a little tidbit the Orders don't advertise about that particular punishment. In my arrogance of trying to cleanse my people of the taint of black magic, I began to wield it myself. One day, I was brought in to cleanse a group of Deoraghan that had been rounded up. They were only children. Why I balked at this when there was so much blood on my hands already, I do not know, but I did. I refused.

"Another Tereskan stepped in to do the job, but I stopped him. I protected the children and in the process it killed my comrade. When I threw the shield around the children, I felt as though my insides were on fire. Just as you experienced," he said gesturing to Faela and Jair, "when you each turned."

"What did you do?" Faela asked. "Where could you go? You

had betrayed your people, your family."

"For a while, I just wandered. Using my abilities to help the people I came across. Until one night I was traveling in the foothills north of Wistholt and I came across a group of refugees who were being hunted by the Daniyelans. A band of fighter from the resistance protected them. Their leader was a woman from the Tribes, a Deoraghan like me."

The smile that spread across Tobias' face was warm as he remembered that meeting. "It was the first time I met Valaria. I offered her my services. Many were hurt or sick. Valaria kept leading me to one person who needed my help after another. I could tell she was exhausted, but she stayed with me as I worked. It was nearly dawn when I finally noticed that she too had been hurt."

He shook his head with a grin. "She was such a stubborn woman. I insisted on healing her and she demanded I see to the next child and would brook no opposition or argument from me. We worked through the night and when morning finally came, she saw my face."

"She recognized you?" Faela asked.

He nodded. "My people knew who I was and what I had done." Tobias drew in a slow breath. "Valaria had lost her brothers when her Tribe was captured for cleansing. They resisted and were killed by the Daniyelans sent to bring them in. They were one of the first Tribes targeted. I had known that my life was forfeit for a long time and it seemed fair and right to me that Valaria would be the one to take it. I didn't beg for my life. I merely told her I could never make it right, even if I lived a hundred lifetimes."

He paused at this with a bittersweet smile on his lips. "I told her that I had no right to ask it, but if I were to die, I wanted to at least ask for her forgiveness. I should have died that night, but as you can see I did not."

"What stopped her?" Faela asked in a quiet voice. As they waited for his answer, the only sounds drifted in from the raucous common room in an indistinguishable mass of noise.

"When she had imagined avenging her brothers' deaths, she thought she'd have to force the person to admit what they had done before they died," Tobias explained. "She never imagined that the person would confess what they had done and ask her for forgiveness, but not mercy. I deserved to die; I knew that. It was my question that stayed her hand, but it was my eyes that stopped her. You see, the Deoraghan have their own stories about Grays."

"They do?" Faela asked startled by this revelation.

"We do indeed, Rafaela. They've fallen out of fashion in the Tribes in recent years, but in my day they were quite popular. Grays are not the abominations that the Orders paint them to be. In the Tribes, there are stories of Grays throughout history since the Shattering who were chosen by Lior, raised up as the defenders of the people, the hands of Tallior.

"Valaria knew these stories and when she saw me, she believed that I would save our people. But I was so ashamed of what I had done that I wanted no part in the resistance. I only wanted to help the people Lior put in my path, nothing more. After traveling with the refugees and the resistance for a few weeks, we were discovered."

"Oh no, who found you?" Mireya asked worried, caught up in the story.

"You know them quite well, Mireya," Tobias said with a knowing smile. "It was Rivka and Vaughn."

"The Nikelan Scion?" Kade asked dumbfounded. "She's as old as you?"

"Older actually," Tobias answered. "But she wasn't Scion yet. Rivka showed up and did the whole choir-of-one performance and told me that I was a part of her prophecy. To make a long story short, I wasn't the only one who was a part of the prophecy, so was Valaria. Though she had not yet turned, Valaria was also Gray.

Our purpose was to stop the cleansings and gain the Deoraghan their status as a sovereign nation to keep them safe from being enslaved again. Of course, we didn't know that at the beginning. It would have been nice to know that, but prophecy is a slippery thing as I'm sure you're learning. We did succeed." He paused. "But everything comes with a cost. Do you know why the Treaty of Twinning Pass was signed?"

Sheridan answered her voice subdued. "The son of the Daniyelan Scion was saved by Gresham..." Sheridan broke off unable to finish the sentence.

"We were there to negotiate terms, but someone on the side of Orders tried to provoke the resistance into fighting. Whoever it was fired an arrow into the resistance ranks; it killed a very dear friend of mine, Liev. He was one of our commanders. Someone decided they wanted blood for blood, so they fired at the son of the Daniyelan Scion who was the Orders' emissary. Like many Deoraghan, Valaria had traces of blue. She didn't see it in time to stop the soldier, but she did see it in time to knock him out of the way. The shot killed her instantly."

The room waited for Tobias to continue. He cleared his throat. Though the event had occurred hundreds of years ago, recalling it always reignited the pain.

"With her death, the treaty was guaranteed. Her valor and sacrifice convinced the Scion of the Daniyelans that the Deoraghan were no agents of the Darkness and deserved equal standing amongst the other nations. That is what Gray means, children."

Tobias held the gaze of each Gray in turn as he spoke. "It means pain. It means sacrifice. And it means loss. It is not an easy road Lior asks you to walk. But those who have not faced adversity already, would not be called to this life."

Faela and Jair could not look away from Tobias, but Lucien still sat hooded from the cold despite the warmth of the cramped room. He watched Tobias from under it. The Orders had given Lucien a home, a purpose, a family when he had nothing, when everything had been taken from him by the war. The way this man talked about them infuriated him. It took all his self-control to remain seated. Like Faela had said, Grays were an abomination. No sentimental tale would convince him otherwise.

"I cannot speak for your story, Jair, but, Faela, you asked what I meant by another prophecy."

Faela nodded shifting her weight. Now that the tale had finished, she noticed the twinges in her lower back and twisted to relieve the pressure.

"The night you were born a prophecy came upon Rivka about a little girl with the gifts of a mind healer who had the power within her to either heal or destroy the world. Rivka sent for me and I spent the next three years looking for that little girl. I found you just after your fourth birthday."

Bringing her legs up into her chest, she lowered her chin behind her knees and just stared at Tobias without speaking.

"Your parents were already worried that there was something wrong with you. You couldn't speak and would fly into rages without any reason they could discover. The only thing that would calm you was Caleb singing to you. He taught me your lullaby, before I took you to Kilrood. Though I have to say my singing didn't calm you immediately like Caleb's could. But it did work."

Gazing sidelong at Faela, Kade remembered the words of the lullaby he had heard in his mind that night beside the Foster River before Eve had found him, the lullaby she had sung to keep his heart beating when the binding was killing him. He didn't have to ask; he knew it would be the same song.

"You were the one who brought me to Ianos?" Faela said as if confused. "Why did you never tell me when you visited? Why did Ianos never tell me?"

"Very little good comes from knowing prophecies like that," Tobias explained with a gentle voice. "What good would it have done to tell a little girl that her life held that kind of destiny? I'm just thankful I found you in time."

"Before I had completely lost my mind, you mean," Faela said with a touch of bitterness in her voice and a melancholy shading her eyes.

"You're not wrong, Rafaela," Tobias said bluntly. "You know better than anyone the dangers and struggles faced by a mind healer. The only reason you survived past childhood was because Rivka sent me for you. With the rarity of those born with the gifts of a mind healer, your parents never would have recognized the signs and gotten you to the right people in time. I believe that it's no coincidence that Ianos has the gifts he has either. Without them you never would have survived adolescence, I'd wager, not with the strength of your abilities."

"Is that why you visited, Tobias?" Faela asked her eyes staring at the floor. "To check up on me for Scion Rivka? To make sure I hadn't gone mad and killed the entire temple?"

"Yes and no," Tobias answered truthfully. "Rivka wanted to

keep up with the progress of your training, but I wanted to make sure that you were safe and happy. But that is neither here nor there. This brings us to why you came to find me. Ianos told you to find me so you can find the Shrine, correct?"

"Yes, he did. He said that the key to my penance would be found there."

"He would phrase it that way," Tobias said mostly to himself. "What you must find is at the Shrine. You will find what you seek there, but only a Gray and a Nikelan can together unlock its hiding place within the Shrine. What I have told you is only a small portion of what and who you are. You will understand more once you arrive at the Shrine. You must travel northwest to the Boundary and enter Vamorines. Continue north once you cross the Boundary. Half a day's ride in head east and you will come to a peninsula. From there, Mireya will be able to find the Shrine. Trust me, you won't be able to miss it. Once you've found it, you'll know what to do from there."

"Could you have been a bit more cryptic?" Kade asked his voice dry.

"Information is not understanding," Tobias replied, his light-hearted tone replaced with sobriety. "You can give information, but you can never give understanding and what Faela needs is understanding. Do not make the mistake of confusing the two, son.

"Now, I don't know about you folks, but my throat is mighty parched and I'd wager you could use something in your bellies if you came all the way from Moshurst today," Tobias guessed getting to his feet. "I'll get Rick to send in some food."

"Yes!" Sheridan agreed enthusiastically. "I'm starving."

"Hey," Jair objected, "stay out of my head. That's what I was going to say."

"Of course it was," Faela said soothing his wounded pride. "Don't worry, Jair. No one here doubts your voracious appetite. Your position is safe."

"For now," said Eve her tone ominous.

Not expecting humor from that particular source, Faela's shock escaped as a laugh, breaking the emotional tension surrounding them. The laughter rippled around the room until it rendering them all breathless.

Tobias peeked back through the curtain with a mug in hand. Wiping the foam of the ale off his beard, he asked, "Did I miss something?"

*　　*　　*

Wes blew hot air into her cupped hands trying to unstick her fingers stiffened by the cold. Shadows kept the alley where she waited shrouded in a deeper darkness than the gas lit street she faced. Next to her stood the man who had hired her a few days back. Hired was a word Wes was unaccustomed to hearing attributed to her. Men didn't hire girls like Wes to sneak around storehouses and Wes had sworn that she would die before any ever hired her the usual way.

This man seemed different to her though. Different from the kind of men who ran in the areas of Lanvirdis she frequented. He kept his distance and his hands to himself. When he said he would pay her, he did. When he said he just wanted information that was all he wanted. But in Wes' experience, everyone was working an angle. She just hadn't pegged his, but she would.

"That's it," she said, pointing toward the small door in the side of the large rectangular brick building in front of them. "That's where the Daniyelans are keeping the grain."

Vaughn bobbed his head slightly and uncrossed his arms. "You have my thanks, Wes. You can go now."

"Whoa," she exclaimed. "You're not going in there are you?"

Vaughn looked down at her over his shoulder. "I am."

"Then you're crazier than I thought." She shook her head. "Ain't no one want to get caught breaking into Daniyelan property. I'll steal from just about anyone, but even I'm not stupid enough to cross the Daniyelans."

"Then I just won't get caught," Vaughn said to reassure her.

"It ain't that easy, Vaughn. You can't just walk on in there. They got wards, warning spells on their buildings. You can't just sneak in through a window or pick the locks."

"I appreciate your concern, Wes," Vaughn began.

"I ain't concerned," she objected, her hands tucked under her arms. "I just want to get paid."

"Fair enough." Vaughn removed a gold coin from his bag that he tossed to her.

Catching it easily, even in the darkness of the alley, Wes had it tucked away somewhere out of sight before a beat had passed.

"Well, you're on your own then," Wes said a little too fast, "'Cause I ain't crazy or stupid."

"I just needed you to get me here, Wes," he explained. "I can take care of myself."

She believed him. This man who had seen her lift a purse when no one else ever did, not since her first months of lifting, who carried more money than she had seen in her life, whose efficient movements told her to run rather than fight. She trusted his quick smile and few words. That was another concept foreign to Wes, trust.

"Fine," Wes said her voice hard, "get yourself strung up by the Daniyelans. I'm gone."

Wes shoved her hands back under her arms and spun on her heel to march back down the alley. When she looked over her shoulder, Vaughn had already disappeared.

A tiny smile tugged at Vaughn's mouth as the girl stalked away fuming. Her reaction to entering the storehouse told Vaughn more about its contents than a week of questioning workers would have. She was terrified of the Daniyelans in Lanvirdis. It wasn't unusual for people to be wary of the Daniyelans. People tended to feel nervous around anyone who enforced the law. Although Wes was a thief, her fear of retribution should never have been that intense. True, were she caught by a Daniyelan working her chosen profession, she would face judgment, but the judgment she faced would sentence her to work off her debt, nothing more.

As they had approached the storehouse, however, Wes had become increasingly agitated. She did not fear indentured servitude to repay her crimes; she feared for her life and for his. Daniyelans did not kill without due cause. They were called to at times, but they did not relish it or do it for the sake of expediency. Were the Daniyelans adhering to the proper role of their Order,

Wes had nothing to fear, but just restitution for her crimes. Not a pleasant prospect, but by no means fatal.

Something very wrong was going on here in Lanvirdis and Tomas seemed connected to it. Conjecture, however, provided no evidence he could bring back to Rivka. As the Nikelan Scion, she alone had the power to remove another Scion and to do so her case had to be unassailable. Vaughn needed proof of Tomas' violation of his vows. Nothing less could justify his removal.

Vaughn saw no visible guards outside the storehouse, but that was to be expected. As Wes had said, wards and shielding spells guarded the building. Nothing could get through without activating them. Even trying to dismantle the spells would trigger them. Slipping through the shadows, Vaughn reached the small, wooden door. The bricks around its frame were pitted and stained with streaks of rainwater. Dark, inky blue lines glowed encircling his wrists, the light bleeding through the fabric of his cuffs as he lifted the latch. The door opened without any resistance. Extending his senses, he felt the shielding wards remained undisturbed.

Grinning, Vaughn closed the door behind him gently to muffle the sound. Not even the strongest Daniyelan shielding spell could impede a Grier. Their magic existed to protect their oracle. They were living shields and, as such, their very presence nullified the effect of any shielding magic turned against them. The magic of a Grier was unique and less than a dozen lived at any given time. Vaughn was one of a handful of people who could breach Tomas' defenses undetected.

Sliding along the rough and gritty wall, Vaughn's gaze analyzed the storehouse. Crates were piled five high and covered most of the floor. Prying open one of the crates with the blade of his dagger, he saw that it was indeed filled with grain. He dug his hand in and scooped out a handful of its contents. Shaking his hand, he sniffed the grain. It smelled earthy with a metallic tang. The grain slid through his fingers and he tilted his hand letting it flow back into the crate.

About to dig further into the container, he heard the door he had just entered, creak open. Flattening himself between two rows, he inclined his head to peek between the columns created by the stacked boxes. Two men walked down the open row running down the middle of the storehouse. Both were hooded.

"Have you contracted enough ships to transport the supplies?" asked the taller of the two figures.

"We hired the last captain this afternoon. They should be ready to sail within the week."

"Excellent. We need to make sure this arrives in Kilrood in time."

"Yes, master," replied the shorter man.

Vaughn's eyes narrowed hearing the last word. He recognized the taller man's voice. It was Tomas Segar. While no law existed regarding their titles, no Scion would condone someone calling him master.

What are you playing at, Segar? Vaughn wondered as he tried to get a better view.

"Are our people in place? Ready to receive the shipments?"

"Yes, master. They are ready to strike at your orders."

"Excellent. After they have seized the Tereskan stronghold, you must ensure they do not harm Ianos. I need him alive. I trust that he will eventually see reason, but they may spread the rumor that the Nabosian rebels have killed him. That should be enough."

"Undoubtedly, master. With a massacre at Kilrood, the people will demand you remove Nabosian monarch and council. And with no suitable replacement they will hand over control of Nabos to you."

"I do not want the power, my dear friend. I simply want peace for each country, for this petty bickering to stop. I want the people to be safe."

Vaughn's nails dug into the wood of the crate at Tomas' words. This was far worse than he had feared.

"Of course, master," answered the smaller man. "We are the servants of the people."

"I hate to put Ianos through this," Tomas said, his voice holding genuine regret, "but he stubbornly refuses to see what must be done to keep the people safe. He forces my hand."

"Of course, master. You would never choose this unless there were no other way."

"Ianos is a gentle soul," Tomas observed, stopping by one of the crates to slide its lid in place. "As he should be as the Tereskan leader. His concern is healing, not ruling, but it is different for me."

Vaughn's jaw tightened at Tomas' words. Daniyelans enforced the law to keep the people safe, not to rule them. If those with the authority to use force against the people also ruled them, it wouldn't take long for the people to become the enemies of those rulers. The mission of the Daniyelan Order was to ensure justice, not to govern a particular territory. A cold knot of dread grew inside Vaughn.

Tomas wiped the dust from the grain off of his hands. "Mine is a heavy burden to make these decisions for the people. They cannot be expected to carry this weight. I would have everyone work together for the good of the people, but when they cannot see what must be done, what choice is left to me? This sacrifice of those in the Tereskan Order, their blood will forge a new world, a peaceful world. These deaths that are required for the preservation of society are regrettable, even tragic, but it is a necessary loss. I hate to make this decision, but I must do what I must for the good of all."

"The people, as always, are your primary concern, master."

"Listen to me, lost in my own thoughts." Tomas sighed. "Let us have this ugly business completed as swiftly as possible. Inform me the moment the shipment reaches Kilrood. Please make sure that the grain makes it to the proper facilities to be distributed as soon as can be. We don't want families starving in those coastal towns."

"Of course, master," answered the shorter man. "I will make all the arrangements, but we must return to the keep. King Phineas will be expecting your presence at the feast tonight."

"Naturally," Tomas said his voice filled with scorn, "that man would be having a feast while his towns starve with such a weak harvest this year. This is why I do what I must, Stanley, because no one else will."

Taking one last look around the storehouse, Tomas exited through the door and Stanley pulled it shut behind them.

His legs feeling weak, Vaughn leaned against the crates behind him. Running his palm down his face, he covered his mouth and exhaled.   Controlling the urge to leave the storehouse immediately, Vaughn waited to ensure no one would see his exit. Though no mention had been made about the Brethren, Tomas had clearly overstepped his bounds as Scion of the Daniyelans. By his actions, he had already abdicated his office as Scion. Now, he had to be removed.

Though what paralyzed Vaughn was the revelation that he planned a massacre at Kilrood, the heart of the Tereskan Order. Besides the Lusicans, they were the only other Order welcomed without question in every country.   No one turned away entertainers and healers, nor did they attack them. Tomas' plans exceeded mere avarice and ambition.   Tomas planned the overthrow of a fellow Scion and the sanctioned the murders of members of another Order. Despite the bloodshed and fighting Vaughn had witnessed over the centuries, he had never seen a Scion plot the strategic slaughter of another Order. Yet as he stood in the warehouse, he could not change Tomas' own words.

Ianos had to be warned, but Vaughn couldn't endanger the local temples. Word of this had to remain secret to keep them safe from Tomas' retribution. Only once he was behind the Boundary in Vamorines could Vaughn do anything for Ianos. Should they fail to get word Ianos in time, the world would suffer loss the likes of which had not been seen since the Cleansings. He had to return to Rivka immediately.

Convinced that Tomas would be halfway to the keep by now, Vaughn left his hiding place and slipped out the door. Keeping to the shadows, he made his way back down the alley where Wes had led him. When he approached the Vine and Reef Tavern, he found Wes pacing outside. Her head snapped up when she heard him step into a puddle.

"Huh," she said looking him up and down, "made it out in one piece, I see. Would've lost that wager."

Vaughn merely smiled and said, "As I said, I would be fine."

Wes shook her head and smacked her lips together. "Find what you was looking for?"

"More than I expected, to be sure," he answered without revealing anything. The less Wes knew, the safer she would be.

"Be needing me for anything else?" she asked kicking the toe of her worn boot against the ridge of a stone sticking up from the road.

"I'll be leaving tonight," Vaughn informed her.

"You be leaving Lanvirdis tonight?" Wes repeated trying to mask her shock. "I may be a cutpurse, but I don't want to meet the fellas outside these walls after the sun be down."

"Thank you for your help, Wes. You've done more than you know."

"What be so important that it can't wait until morning?" Wes said with a skeptical rise of her voice. "What was you looking for in those storehouses?"

"Leave it be, Wes," Vaughn warned. "The less you know the better things will be for you."

"Who are you really?" Wes asked her eyes narrowing.

Vaughn grabbed her arm and pulled her under the eaves of the tavern.

"Oi!" Wes protested as he easily maneuvered her out of sight.

Thinking back to Wes' self-espoused dislike of Tomas, Vaughn explained, "You've good instincts, child. Trust them. I can tell you nothing more without endangering your life further. I am sorry for that. But I must return to my lady with what I discovered immediately. I know I'm telling you something you would already do, but stay away from the Daniyelans here in Lanvirdis. Do not trust them."

Wes nodded, her hands tucked around her stomach. Catcalls, discordant singing, and laughter spilled into the street as a dockworker staggered out into the night. Vaughn stood blocking the patron's view of Wes until he turned the corner out of sight.

"You must forget that we met and what you did for me, Wes. Do you understand?"

She swallowed, her throat suddenly dry. "Ser, what was in those storehouses?"

Vaughn closed his eyes, his hand that rested against the wall closed into a fist. "Wes, you can't ask any questions like that. Promise me you won't go poking around after I leave?"

Her eyes shadowed, she pursed her lips to the side clearly unhappy with this request.

"Wes, promise me," Vaughn demanded.

"What if I don't?" she asked, her fierce independence asserting itself.

"Then you would leave me no choice," he said his voice quiet.

At those words, Wes' survival instincts were roused and she stood perfectly still, repressing the urge to run. She knew she didn't stand a chance against this quiet man.

Vaughn's face softened when he recognized her fear. "Wes, I'm not going to hurt you."

Her fear turned to confusion. "Then what?"

"I can't leave you by yourself here in Lanvirdis," he explained. "With your less-than-legal trade, if you get picked up by a Daniyelan the fact that I was here would get back to Tomas. I don't doubt that he would kill you and I cannot have that."

"Where you be taking me?" she asked sounding timid for the first time in their short acquaintance.

"I'm sorry, Wes," he said putting a hand on her head. "I can't leave you here. I don't have time to discuss this further. You're going to have to stay at the Phaidrian temple until I get back. You don't leave and you don't mention my name. Understand?"

Wes nodded, but something lay hidden behind her eyes as they left the harbor heading toward the city center for the Phaidrian temple.

CHAPTER NINETEEN

Faela sat on the servant stairs that led to the Tin Whistle's kitchens. Though it was late and most of the customers had gone home for the evening, the clattering of dishes and chatter drifted up to her hiding place. She pressed her back against one wall and propped up a leg against the other listening to the familiar noises. For so long, she had waited to find Gresham. She had spent so many nights away from her son for this. Placing her elbows against her thighs, she buried her face into her hands.

"You always did like small spaces," said a deep, rich voice behind her.

"Why didn't he tell me, Tobias?" Faela asked her hands.

She felt more than heard the large man sink to the floor in the hallway as the floorboards lifted a little.

"Ianos is nothing, if not a teacher, Faela. You know that."

"So what was he trying to teach me through this?" she pleaded, her voice stretched thin as she turned to face Tobias. "What lesson was this one?"

"Had you known that he sent you to find me, what would you have done?"

"I would have asked how in the name of the Light you could help me," she answered after a moment's consideration.

"And had he told you that I was a redeemed Gray, what would you have done then?"

Faela chewed on her bottom lip as she thought. "I'm not sure I would have believed him at first."

"So you would have obsessed over whether it was worth it to find me, no?"

Faela tapped her heel against the wall, remembering the thoughts she had entertained mere moments before Tobias arrived. "I don't know."

"Yes, you do." Tobias pushed her, his voice gentle.

"Fine," she admitted. "I might not have come at all."

"Why?" Tobias asked, peering down at her face. "What would have restrained you? What didn't you tell me earlier?"

She closed her eyes and crushed them into her palms again. Exhaling, she sat up, her back flush against the stairwell. "I have a son," she said with a wistful smile laced with bitterness. "His name is Samuel. He'll be six months old in five days." When Tobias remained silent, she continued. "He's the only reason I'm still alive, you know. After what I did, he was the only reason the guilt didn't destroy me. I knew I had to live for him."

"It may not have ended your life then," Tobias pointed out, "but you're still allowing it to consume you. It is destroying you, Rafaela."

"I have to carry it," she said with firm conviction. "I can never forget what I did – never."

"What you did is horrible, I won't patronize you by trying to deny that. But if you continue to cling to this guilt, it will destroy you."

"Then what am I supposed to do?" Faela asked with a caustic glare.

"Accept what you did," he began. "Grieve for the loss of your father. Accept that nothing you do will ever make right what you've done. I know it's a hard truth, but it's one you must embrace. Because what you did is a part of you. You must accept that this darkness is inside all of us. Once you accept that you must let it go. Let go of the past or become its slave. Those are your only two options."

"Just let it go?" she asked her voice rising with her skepticism.

"Yes, accept it, then let it go."

"What does that even look like?" Faela asked her hands splayed on her thighs.

"Don't hide from what you did and why you did it."

"It's not like I can really hide," she said gesturing to her eyes.

"But that's just it," Tobias said leaning across the hall. "You are hiding. You can't look at your own reflection without being overcome by your guilt can you?"

Faela chose not to answer, but looked down the stairs concentrating on the normal, domestic sounds of the kitchens.

"See? You're hiding even now." Tobias studied her face before he said, "Just as you were hiding why you killed your father from those boys earlier. You weren't hiding that from me."

Faela whipped her head back to stare at Tobias. "That's not true," she objected a little too forcefully. "Jair knows."

"So you were hiding it from the Kade boy then," he surmised. "Why?"

Faela was unsure she even knew why. She couldn't imagine why she would hesitate to tell him. He already believed her to be a pitiless kin-slayer, but for some unfathomable reason the thought of him knowing the truth made her numb with fear.

"I don't know," she admitted.

"Would you like to hear an old man's theory?" Tobias' eyes sparkled.

Faela repeatedly flicked her thumbnail against her index finger. "I'm not sure I'll like what I hear, but say it."

"Who is Samuel's father?"

"That's not a theory," Faela felt compelled to point out.

"Just answer the question."

"His name is Nikolais."

"And what role did Nikolais play in your father's death?"

"I believed the lies of Sammi's father." She refused to say his name aloud again. "He's the one who encouraged me to manipulate my father. Once my father was dead though and he had what he wanted," Faela broke off and looked up at the ceiling. "Well, let's just say that I wasn't what he really wanted. I left him while still pregnant with Sammi. Ianos hid me."

"So what angers you more, the fact that your actions led to your father's death or that you were betrayed?"

Faela's eyes hardened. "Careful, Tobias."

"That alone answers my question," he replied his eyes saddened. "You feel like a fool for believing that this man cared for you."

"Of course," Faela answered in exasperation. "But what does this have to do with this?"

Tobias looked at Faela sitting in the stairwell, her wavy hair shining like pale copper in the lamp light of the hall, her brows drawn together in frustration, her bottom lip tucked in between her teeth. She really couldn't see it, but Tobias decided against telling her.   He had always believed that revelations like this needed to happen in their own time. It wasn't his place to tell her what she had yet to realize.   He decided to take a different approach instead.

"Do you remember when you were a little girl and I would visit Ianos?" he asked rhetorically. "It was several years between my first visit and when I brought you to Kilrood from Finalaran. You didn't recognize me and you hid under Ianos' desk and he tried to coax you out, but you refused."

Tobias chuckled remembering the dirty-faced little girl with a thick braid of reddish gold hair peeking out from shadows of the desk. "Then I sat on the floor and told you that since you refused to come to me, I would come to you. Do you remember?"

A small smile tugged at her lips and her posture relaxed somewhat. "I do. I thought you were a bear who was going to eat me, but you made me laugh."

"And eventually, you came out," Tobias reminded her. "But, Faela, not everyone will come to you. You need to be willing to go to them from time to time. You need to be honest. You can't keep everyone at arm's length forever."

Faela took her foot off the wall and swiveled to face Tobias. "I'm not trying to keep Kade away, because I'm afraid of being betrayed."   She locked Tobias with her gaze.   "I'm afraid of betraying him."

"Enslaved, my dear," Tobias said shaking his head. "This is exactly what I meant. Until you accept who you are and what you've done, you will be trapped by it."

"Maybe I should be trapped," Faela suggested, "then I can't hurt anyone else."

"Rafaela, we all hurt people." Tobias's voice was sharp and cutting. "That's universal. We're all broken and those shards will cut those around us."

"Yes, but we don't all kill our fathers," she retorted.

"No," he admitted, then his voice turned cold. "Some of us commit genocide against our own people."

"That's not what I meant," Faela began then trailed off.

"Rafaela, if anyone here has the right to self-flagellation, it is me, not you," he told her bluntly. "It's a certainty that you will hurt every single person you are traveling with in some way on some level and if you keep closing yourself off in a martyred attempt to keep them safe from you, you will eventually explode and that explosion will be much worse than anything you're fearing."

Faela combed her fingers through her hair and closed her eyes. "I already have."

"Explain," he commanded.

"When we were in Oakdarrow, I smelled something that reminded me of Nikolais. It triggered an episode."

"Merciful Lior, what happened?"

"I linked Jair and Kade's minds to mine."

"Without Ianos to yank you out of the time stream to segregate you from any other minds, how did it end?" Tobias asked with real concern.

"Mireya," Faela smiled. "She commanded me back. I don't know how, but it worked."

"Have there been any side effects?"

Faela nodded, her cheek resting in her palm. "Kade can feel my emotions and I his. He's even managed to project his thoughts and pick out mine. It's not fading like I thought it would." She grimaced. "It's getting stronger."

"What about Jair?"

"I don't know, he hasn't said anything about it, but tonight when I was compelled to come here, to find you, both Kade and Jair were effected as well. They felt the same pull."

"My dear girl, this is troubling."

"See," Faela said then pointed to herself. "Causes problems."

"Regardless, you still need to be honest," Tobias reprimanded her, his tone softening. "Until you are and until you want to, you won't be able to let it go."

"Well," she said being honest, "I'm not there yet."

"Good," Tobias smiled. "At least you've acknowledged that."

"What a triumph," she said sarcastically.

"You need your sleep, child. You have many long days of travel ahead of you." Tobias stood and stooped over kissing her on the top of her head. He said into her hair, "Go to bed."

"Soon," Faela said her fingers intertwined in the chain around her neck. "I'll go soon."

"Where's Tobias?" Mireya asked as she wandered into the dining room of the tavern, her dark hair still big and bushy from sleep.

Kade, Dathien, and Faela sat at a table with a pile of sweet rolls in the middle. Mireya noticed the darkness ringing Faela's eyes, made even more severe by the mirrored reflection of her irises. Clearly she had not slept well, if she had slept at all.

Faela sat, her finger curled around a steaming mug. "As far as I know, he's still sleeping, the sluggard."

Scratching her head, Mireya plopped down into a chair across from Faela and grabbed a roll. She bit into its soft and hot doughiness. With a large hunk in her cheek, she asked, "Is that where everyone else is too?"

Kade answered as he set down his mug. "Sheridan went down to the market. She said she was tired of borrowing Eve's things. I'd wager collecting water tonight that Jair is still asleep."

"That's not a fair wager, when he's your bunkmate," Dathien pointed out licking the melted sugar from his fingers.

"What's unfair is that he *is* my bunkmate," Kade corrected.

Dathien smiled at that and passed his mug to Mireya who happily slurped the tea inside.

"I don't know about Eve and Haley though," Kade finished.

"Those two seem to be together quite a lot," Mireya observed then popped the remaining bits of the pastry into her mouth. "How did she say she knows him again?"

"Just said he was traveling with her from what I remember," Faela answered, her arm resting across the back of her chair as she sat at an angle facing Kade and Dathien.

"Huh," Mireya said with her mouth full of roll. "That seems odd. Eve doesn't seem the type to be chummy with any Gray."

"Indeed," Dathien agreed, but offered nothing more.

"We were just discussing the fastest route back to the Boundary with Dathien," Kade explained. "Do you have any suggestions that don't involve briar patches?"

"You take a man through *one* briar patch," Mireya muttered to herself. "I'd say retracing our steps, then head north from Oakdarrow to avoid the Auchneid woods. It should be the fastest route, if not the most direct."

Kade and Faela both stared at Mireya.

"What?" she demanded ripping apart another pastry with her fingers.

"That was so coherent," Faela stated with surprise.

"And accurate," added Kade with an equally shocked expression.

"And helpful," Faela said gesturing to Kade with an open palm.

Mireya scrunched up her nose, then shoved a large piece from her mangled roll into her mouth. After swallowing, she retorted, "I tramped around this continent for a year looking for Faela. I know my way around."

"Now," Dathien said with a sly smile at his mate.

Before Mireya could retaliate, Sheridan entered the tavern now sporting a pack of her own and a half-eaten snow plum.

Spotting the plum, Kade raised an eyebrow. "I'm going to the market," he said in a nasally imitation of Sheridan's intonation. "Really, the market, not back to Montdell to retrieve my things there."

Sheridan walked over and punched Kade in the arm before joining them at the table. "What? Eve's clothes are too tight and the prices were outrageous."

Unperturbed by her assault, Kade continued his imitation. "And I definitely never went back to my quarters at the Amserian temple in Wistholt to steal from the kitchens."

Sheridan tilted to the side and bit into the plum, the juices dribbling onto his exposed arm.

"Hey!" he exclaimed immediately reciprocating by wiping the juices on her sleeve.

To which she squealed and batted his arm away. "This was actually clean, you slob."

"You dripped on me, love."

Sheridan finished off the plum and chucked its pit into Kade's mug. Watching it successfully disappear into the rim, she let out a whoop of triumph. As she gloated, she licked the stickiness off her fingers.

Narrowing his eyes, Kade waved a finger at Sheridan in warning. "Remember well that you started this."

"It's not my fault you are undeniably jealous of my ability to return to Wistholt whenever I please. I was born this way," she said fluttering her eyelashes at him. "I wasn't the one who gave you the short end of the purple stick. Take it up with your mum."

"That gives me an idea," Faela said still smiling at watching Kade so at ease. His playful mood radiating from him energized her despite her lack of sleep. "Sheridan, could you pop us to the Boundary? We were just discussing which route to take there."

Sheridan shook her head, her freshly braided hair swaying. "It doesn't work that way. I've never been to the Boundary. I can't pop somewhere I haven't been."

Mireya paused from her feasting, her full lips pursed. "Then how did you pop to us from Montdell?"

"Okay, so let me amend. I can only pop to somewhere I've been or somewhere Eve is," she explained shoving a whole sweet roll into her mouth. "It's a twin thing."

"Well can you pop somewhere Eve's been?" Faela asked trying to grasp the limits of Sheridan's ability.

"We've never tried that," Sheridan admitted, but she had that far-away look in her eyes that meant that her mind was trying to solve something. "I don't know. It might work. I mean, I use her as an anchor when I pop to her. I know where she is in space and I just go there. I'm not sure how to adapt that to somewhere she's been that I haven't."

"Have you been to Oakdarrow?" Faela asked pushing aside the warning that Caleb had given her about the bounty hunters. No matter how they got to the Boundary they would be heading toward not away from the hunters Nikolais had contracted.

Sheridan shook her head again. "My circuits have usually kept me in the central and western portions of the continent, mostly to the northwest in Isfaridesh around Kitrinostow, the southwest of Indolbergan around Wistholt and the furthest east I've been is Mergoria to Kilrood, but never to the northeast to Lanvirdis. Even during the war, they kept us away from the front lines of the conflict as healers since we were still seekers. I haven't spent much time in Nabos before now."

"We can save three, maybe four days if we can pop near Oakdarrow," Kade calculated. "It's definitely worth a try."

Sheridan nodded though still distant as she thought through all the possible difficulties presented by an attempt.

"We could make it to the Boundary in four days from Oakdarrow," Dathien said mapping the journey in his mind.

"How much of a risk would be involved?" Faela asked.

"If I try to pop somewhere I haven't been, or where I don't have an anchor of some kind, I could be ripped apart or just disappear and never come back," Sheridan said dismissively, still lost in her thoughts, "or I could end up inside a tree. It would depend on what I did wrong."

Eve and Haley entered the tavern both smiling. Not an odd occurrence for Haley, but infrequent would be a generous description of Eve. As Haley stopped, swinging his head to watch Eve as she passed him, Sheridan caught them enter out of the corner of her eye and as the morning light hit Haley, she saw the movement of a dark copper ponytail. Turning to get a better look, she saw nothing more than Haley bird's nest of short, wheat-colored hair. She blinked her eyes a few times. That was the second time the light had played tricks on her. Instead of dismissing it, Sheridan tucked away her observations.

"Eve, I need your help with something," Sheridan said rising and taking her sister's hands.

"Um, okay," Eve said in a helpful tone.

"I need you to remember Oakdarrow."

Eve stiffened recalling how she had broken down in the field after coming into contact with that wild red magic. "Why?"

"An experiment," Sheridan explained. "I want to see if I can pop to a place I haven't been to, but you have."

Her discomfort at the memories evaporated and was replaced with concern. "Sheridan, that's extremely dangerous, isn't it?"

"Potentially," Sheridan admitted. "But I want to see if it's even possible first. I want you to picture a particular place in Oakdarrow. Remember how it looked, how it smelled, any textures, the temperature. Try to visualize and feel as much as you can."

Eve squinted at her sister skeptically, then closed her eyes and inhaled. She remembered the dust coating the back of her throat, the dry wind scraping over her skin as it kicked up that same dust. She remembered the ancient oak tree with its leaves saturated with the deep red of autumn instead of the early changes from green to yellow that should have been there. She remembered the dry smell of dirt and crushed leaves. She sneezed involuntarily. As she painted this picture in her mind, her temples glowed golden.

Sheridan smiled at this. "Good," she encouraged. "This is exactly what you need to do. Keep remembering each detail."

Eve barely nodded, adding the clouds high in the sky like streaks of a painters brush to her mental image. Still holding her sister's hands in her own, Sheridan's hands began glowing red and she closed her eyes. When she closed her eyes, she saw what Eve saw, not only saw it, but felt it as well. Sheridan's nose tickled and she sneezed just as Eve had.

Once the image fully focused in Sheridan's mind, a purple light flared from her collarbones and surrounded them both as an intense pressure descended on the room with a popping sound and the women disappeared. Kade felt his heart lurch and his lungs seize as if the breath were knocked out of him. The same physical sensation pulled at Faela.

Jair stood at the bottom of the stairs, his foot still in mid air. "What in the name of darkness just happened?"

Before anyone could answer him, the pressure fell again and with a flare of indigo light and a pop, the twins returned to the spot from which they had just vanished. Blinking, Kade shared a look with Faela. The pain had lasted less than a heartbeat. Faela's features hardened her gaze settling on the twins, but Kade gestured for her to say nothing so she held her tongue.

Eve opened her eyes with a grin. With a holler of delight, Sheridan threw her arms around his sister's waist to pick her up and spin her around. Setting Eve down, she kissed her forehead with a loud smacking sound.

"It worked!" Sheridan danced in place with absolutely no rhythm.

Kade shook his head at her antics, but his amusement was clear. "You may be twins, but, Sheridan, for all of our sake's, please leave the dancing to Eve. That is a travesty to witness."

Sheridan ignored him and kept shaking her rear with triumphant euphoria. "I can't believe that worked," she finally said once her dance had ended. "I can take everyone now. I'll be fairly drained though." Looking Jair up and down, she pointed at him. "You may have to carry me."

"Carry you?" he exclaimed.

"Hey, if I'm to pop you three days travel time, you can make the sacrifice of carrying me. Even if I am chubby," she claimed with a serious expression as she poked at her thin waist.

Kade nodded his agreement. "Yup, you're a heifer all right."

Jair looked at the both of them as if they had lost their minds. "She's a twig," he objected.

"Lies," Sheridan declared. "I am most definitely chubby."

"If you're chubby," Faela interjected, "then I must be frighteningly large." To make her point, Faela looked at Sheridan's narrow hips and slapped her curvy ones.

"You're not even chubby," Sheridan disagreed. "I am."

Faela looked to Kade for an interpretation.

"Don't even try to argue," he told her. "Even if you're right, you'll still lose. You're the chubbiest, Sheridan."

"That's right," Sheridan said with a triumphant grin.

"So I guess we should get everything together and leave as soon as possible," Dathien said looking around the room.

Faela agreed as she started up the stairs to collect her gear from her room.

Jair lifted the strap of his pack off of his shoulders with a thumb. "Already good to go." He sat down at the table with the remains that had been the pile of sweet rolls with a despondent sigh.

Taking pity on him, Eve told him, "You know, if you just poke your head into the kitchens, I'm sure there are more."

With an excited glint in his eye, he rewarded her with a dazzling grin and frolicked off in search of more breakfast. As Jair disappeared into the kitchens to beg for food, the rest of the party dispersed to their various rooms to collect their belongings.

By the time Jair found his way out of the kitchens with a pear and several pastries, his companions were scattered around the room in smaller clusters talking about divergent topics. Faela and

Dathien discussed the best way to braise mutton, while Eve nodded as Sheridan gesticulated wildly explaining how she had managed to get them to Oakdarrow and back in one piece.

"You ready to go?" Faela asked as she spotted Jair returning with his prizes.

Jair nodded since he had just bitten into the pear.

"Good," she answered with a returning bob of her head. "I guess we can start the process, Sheridan. Unless you need to rest from the initial popping?"

Sheridan shook her head. "Transferring just myself and one other person isn't that draining. I'm good to begin whenever you're ready. The only time popping wipes me out is when I have to take Eve, her beast, and me. Hauling all that mass at once feels like I just ran to wherever we just popped."

Mireya touched Faela's arm to get her attention. Looking over at the girl, Faela inclined her head in question.

"Do you know where Tobias is?" she asked her voice quiet as Sheridan flounced over to Jair to steal his food. "I want to say goodbye"

"I haven't seen him since last night," Faela said scanning the tavern. When her gaze reached the stairs, she saw Tobias talking with Kade. Kade nodded to whatever Tobias had said. Tobias' serious expression broke into a wide grin and he grasped Kade's forearm, a gesture that Kade returned without hesitation. Kade clapped Tobias' arm with his free hand and they descended the stairs to the rest of the group.

Kade came to stand with Faela and Mireya, but swung his pack to the front in order to lean against the wall behind them.

"Oh good," Mireya squealed skipping over to Tobias. "You haven't left yet."

"Not yet, sweetling," he said folding her into a hug.

As he hugged her, Faela asked Kade at a volume that would only reach him, "What was that about?"

Shrugging noncommittally, Kade swept his hand through his sable hair to tie it back into a ponytail. "Nothing worth repeating."

Faela squinted an eye at him in disbelief. "Right."

Before Kade could defend his honor, Tobias said, "Faela, come say goodbye to an old, cranky man."

Faela gave Kade a look indicating that this was far from finished, but complied with Tobias' request. When she reached the imposing man, he drew her into an enveloping hug much like he had Mireya. His mouth close to her ear, he whispered, "Don't isolate yourself from those who care about you, because of who and what you are. Don't make that choice for them. Embrace your strengths don't fear them. Otherwise," he said pulling away to look into her eyes and his mirrored her own with a silver glow, "well, you already know, my dear girl."

Faela simply nodded, not wanting to argue with him. "Thank you for everything, Tobias." She stood back with his hands still encompassing hers and she squeezed them. "Thank you for being honest."

Bringing her hands to his lips, Tobias kissed them. "May you find truth and understanding, Rafaela." Addressing the rest of the party, he said, "Safe travels, children, but I must leave you. I have much work to do and even more ale to drink."

Dathien stepped forward and clasped his forearm. "Safe journeys, Tobias. May Ashalioris see you safely home."

Tobias eyes crinkled and shone with a wistful, melancholic longing. "Yes, home."

When Sheridan folded space, it felt like the world was compressing around her and those in the nearby vicinity could feel its ripples. Experiencing those ripples did not prepare Faela for the reality of moving with Sheridan and her stomach roiled rebelling against the wrenching movement.

In a flare of dark purple, the tavern blurred around her and suddenly burst open into a field outside of Oakdarrow, the field where Faela had linked to Kade and Jair's minds. They stood beneath the reaching boughs of that same gnarled oak tree. At the memory, the nausea curdling in Faela's stomach rose to her throat. Stumbling away from Sheridan, she bent over one of the roots that plunged into the earth and emptied her breakfast onto the grass.

Faela had insisted on being transferred last. She had wanted Mireya and Dathien waiting on the other side at Oakdarrow when Eve and Kade were taken. The idea of those two alone together on either side of this journey did little to calm her nerves. During the process, there had been a disagreement between Sheridan and Eve regarding Kimiko. Their shouting had resolved when Eve realized that Dathien stood feeding the horse a carrot blithely ignoring the argument. She seemed satisfied to leave Kimiko in his care.

Over the course of that last half an hour, they had traveled four days. As she clung to the root, she tried to remind herself that gaining that time had actually been worth it.

"Please tell me I'm not the only one who got sick?" she asked wiping her mouth with the back of her hand.

"I didn't at the time," Jair answered trying not to look where she had emptied her stomach, "but I'm not feeling so good now."

Though Kade said nothing, he did look a little white around the lips. Sheridan, however, looked downright dreadful, her skin had a waxy sheen. Her sister had an arm around her waist barely keeping her upright.

"So, I got us here," Sheridan said her voice thin and feeble, "but I think I could sleep a week and honestly, Eve, you owe me for bringing that beast of yours. Do you have any idea how much Kimiko weighs? That is a lot of mass to pop on top of lugging about the rest of you."

Eve kissed her sister's hair. "You won't be complaining while you're riding her today."

Sheridan snorted. "If I don't fall off and break my neck that is."

"You won't," Eve said admonishing her.

"So is everyone whole, here, and ready to move?" Kade asked, color returning to his cheeks.

Faela patted Jair's arm and stood on steadier legs. "I feel better now."

Everyone responded positively, so Eve and Kade helped hoist Sheridan into the saddle.

"Thanks," Eve told him after her sister was situated.

Kade gripped her shoulder and gave her the kind of wink he usually reserved for Sheridan. Eve looked down to hide her smile, but Lucien caught her eyes when she raised them. Spinning around to break the contact, she grabbed Kimiko's reins and clucked her tongue to get her horse moving.

"Let's keep outside of town," Faela said pulling her hat out of her bag and tugging it into place. "We need to head north."

"Ah, just like old times," Jair said with a wistful sigh.

Only Kade and Faela laughed at this as Kade cast an eye to the position of the sun. He pointed back toward the town, "We can skirt it, but we'll need to head that way."

As they passed by the outer stone wall, Faela's toe caught on a rock and stumbled, but Kade was close enough to catch her hand with his and place another at the small of her back to keep her from falling.

"Blasted feet," she said with a laugh, "never do what they're told."

Helping her right herself, Kade's hands touched her not a second longer than necessary. Once he was sure she was steady, he moved to a respectable distance from her.

Hiding a grin, he replied, "Has any part of you ever done what you were told?"

Sucking in her lower lip as she thought, she shook her head. "Nope, not that I can remember."

As they passed around the corner and out of the sight of the town's main avenue, two men in black adorned with weapons stood by the blacksmith's yard. After watching the exchange, they disappeared into a small alley between the buildings that headed to the northern edge of Oakdarrow.

Eve walked silent as Haley and Jair discussed the latest ballads coming out of the Lusican Order. There had been a resurgence recently of the old songs about the Shattering. Jair and Haley had been vigorously debating whether tragic ballads needed to be in minor key. Behind them Eve allowed Kade to lead Kimiko while Sheridan rode regaining her strength.

"Kade," Sheridan said breaking their companionable silence. "This is as good a time as any to discuss what I found."

"Go ahead," he said as the afternoon sun beat down on them dispelling the chill in the air.

Taking a deep breath, Sheridan began to recount what she had discovered in her investigation regarding Nessa's death. She stopped after explaining what she found in the alley with Gareth's body. Kade waited for her to continue, his eyes roaming the rolling moors they crossed. Despite this route being the fastest to Vamorines, he felt his neck tingle at the lack of cover. He hated being this exposed.

Sheridan removed a throwing knife from her jacket's pocket. "He received no trial, no formal judgment as far as I can tell." She watched Kade's minuet reactions, but he merely continued scanning the wide expanse of the heath. "Unless you have a record of it in your logbook?"

"I no longer have my logbook," Kade reminded her.

"What happened to it?" she asked disturbed by this revelation.

"Caleb took it to the Nikelan Scion and I assume that's who still has it."

"That's why you went to find him?" Sheridan asked confused as her thumb stroked the leather of the saddle's pommel.

"Not exactly. I went to find him to discuss what happened in Montdell and what was happening with the Brethren in our Order." He shrugged. "Given our history, who better to ask? I wanted him to take it straight to Tomas and no one else."

"But clearly he didn't," Sheridan interrupted.

"No, because of the revelation you heard from him yourself in Moshurst."

Sheridan thought about this for a while as her thumb moved to tracing the ridges of the saddle. "When I went to the cellar, where Nessa died." She paused again considering her words carefully. "Gareth mentioned a vote on the council that he wanted you to veto for the Brethren."

Kade did not react; he just continued to lead the horse at a steady pace down the small dip of the moor. The withered grass crunched under his boots.

"He also said that you had assisted in such measures before, that you had gone along with Brethren positions."

"You want to know if there is any truth to his claims," Kade concluded for her.

Sheridan chewed on her thumbnail. "Yes."

"He wasn't lying," Kade admitted.

Sheridan nodded slowly as she processed this information.

"What did you do? What were these positions?" She refused to voice the apprehension that knotted her insides.

"You know what I did during the war, Sheridan, right? You understand how they used us?"

"You were part of a small unit under Caleb's command. You did whatever Scion Benjamin ordered you to do."

"Well, that depends on who you ask," Kade said with a humorless laugh. He led Kimiko around a patch of small scrubby bushes covered in green berries with splashes of red where they ripened.

"I don't follow," Sheridan conceded with an irritated flattening of her lips.

"It's not important," Kade said moving forward. "You need to understand that we did what was necessary to stop the war. That was our mission. But in completing that mission, I watched the Nabosians use children to protect supply trains heading for their troops. I saw fathers die."

He paused, remembering Henry's slow smile and limitless generosity, but the memory soon shifted to his sightless eyes looking up at Kade. The blistering made Henry's face unrecognizable. "Their children would never see them again. I don't have to remind you of that, Sheridan."

Remembering her own father's death during the war, Sheridan tightened her knees into Kimiko's side unintentionally causing the horse to whuffle in surprise. She thudded the horse's neck. "Sorry, beastie."

"After you lost your father, Sheridan, you refused to eat for two days." Kade's hand gripped the reins pressing the leather into his palm. "You were only seven. No seven year old should have their lessons interrupted to be told that their father died in the service of his king."

"And a nine year old shouldn't have to stay up with her every night to keep the nightmares away," Sheridan pointed out.

"I'll sleep when I'm dead," he said deflecting the comment. "Sheridan, the war destroyed families. Look at Jair's story, it destroys the land, entire villages. That kind of destruction should never happen."

"Of course, it shouldn't," Sheridan agreed. "I wish my father were still alive, but I would never have kept him from fighting and I don't regret working as a field healer for the Tereskans."

"That was a lot for Scion Ianos to ask of children," Kade said in a quiet voice.

"It was brilliant," Sheridan argued defending Ianos. "We learned how to use red magic fast and we were saving people, Kade. How can that be bad?"

"We saw things no children should see."

Sheridan narrowed her eyes as she heard in his tone what he really meant. "You mean I saw things I should never have seen."

"Your nightmares didn't end until you were seventeen," Kade said matter-of-factly.

"That's a small price to pay for the lives of those men and women we saved."

"That's what I mean," Kade replied. "I never want any other little girls to be afraid to sleep."

Sheridan sighed. "So what does this have to do with the Brethren?"

"Gareth proposed that I encourage the passage of certain laws placing more of the civil authority under the domain of the Daniyelans. What could it harm for the keepers of justice to decide what is best for the people?"

"What could it harm?" Sheridan asked her voice low. "Kade, you may be brilliant, but you're an idiot. What could it harm? Are you a farmer?"

At that question, Kade actually stopped walked and turned to look at her. "What?"

"I asked you, if you're a farmer. It's a simple enough question."

"You know I'm not. My mother was a member of the same Noble Houses as yours."

"Am I a farmer?" she continued without acknowledging his response.

"Is that rhetorical?"

"No," she said shaking her head. "Answer the question."

"Of course you aren't. I'm not sure you would even know which end of a hoe to use."

"Are you a tradesman?" she continued her questions.

"Sheridan, what are you trying to get at?" he asked his patience wearing thin.

"So, if you aren't a farmer, a tradesman, a tavern keep, a smithy, or a sailor, then do you think you could be thrown into their professions tomorrow and be able to do it as well as a man born with soil under his nails or salt in his lungs?"

"That's unlikely and gross," Kade said referring to her analogies.

"Irrelevant," she snapped. "Answer the question."

"No, I could not."

"Then why do you think you should be telling them how to run their farms, sail their ships, or keep their taverns?"

Kade slapped his free hand on his leg, dispelling the dirt dusting his trousers.

"Then if you can't run their lives better than they can run them, why would you ever want our Order to consolidate that kind of power over the people?" When he didn't respond, or object, she barreled forward. "Kade, we have authority over life and death as the enforcers of the law. When there is so much injustice in this world, why should we busy ourselves with trade squabbles and negotiations? Let the darkness-blighted Merchant Houses deal with that nonsense. We are to protect the people, Kade, not dictate their lives. Let the people make their own choices."

"But look what people do with their choices," Kade objected. "How can we enforce justice in a thousand small ways, but let the people make choices that endanger everyone's safety?"

"When our Order was founded, we were charged with the task of protecting the people of this world, to be the voice of the Light's justice for all people. How can we make broad decisions for all the people of each country because it is just for the majority? What about those in the minority? Who will seek justice for them if the Daniyelans are ensuring justice for most? That isn't what our Order was tasked with, Kaedman Wilfred Hawthorn, and you know it."

"What you propose is chaos," Kade's gaze swept over the wide vista in front of them that blurred the line between earth and sky as he ignored her invocation of his full name.

"What I propose is justice for every man, woman, and child in the world by ensuring they have the right to determine their own lives."

"What about them?" Kade asked pointing with the reins to Faela and Jair who walked with Mireya and Dathien. "Are they determining their own lives?"

"But their individual choices brought them to where they are, their choices. No one forced Jair to alter the Balance. No one forced him to try to restore it. If the Light uses those bad choices to accomplish something good and true, who are we to claim that their right of self-determination has been removed? Is it your right to take away their ability to choose to follow Mireya? When she showed up, did she force herself on Faela?"

"Not exactly," Kade admitted after a time of silence. "She told Faela she had been sent to help her and Faela agreed to allow them to accompany us to Kelso."

"So it was Faela's choice, right?" When Kade did not answer, Sheridan sighed gustily and tried a different approach.

"The Brethren's philosophies don't align with the Light, Kade. War is a horrible, ugly thing that should never happen, but the only thing uglier is to not fight back in the face of injustice. Out of great destruction can come life, Kade, just like a forest after a fire."

Kade still remained stoic as they crossed the hills. After several minutes, Sheridan broke the quiet by leaning forward and tapping his shoulder with the flat of the throwing knife. "Kade, what happened to Gareth after he left the cellar?"

"He disappeared almost immediately," Kade responded taking the blade from her. "But I recognized the traces left by his popping. Who knew the blighter had purple?"

"I don't think he did," Sheridan interrupted unable to keep her theory to herself any longer.

"But he did," Kade disagreed, "I saw it myself."

"No, I don't mean that he didn't pop. I mean he never had purple. I think he used black to do it."

"How's that possible?" Kade's voice was controlled, but insistent.

"Well, think about it. Black can touch and use any color of magic, right?" She didn't wait for him to answer. "So, if black can use any kind of magic, shouldn't a wielder of black be able to mimic any form of magic?"

"But the risk in using a magic you're unfamiliar with..." Kade trailed off, "especially purple. At best you might destroy yourself."

"At worst you could unravel the fabric of reality," Sheridan finished the basic lesson they both learned at the Amserian temple.

Kade shook his head in disbelief at Sheridan's theory. "It's possible. Regardless, I was able to track him. He was trying to flee by boat hoping that the water would displace any tracking I could do, I guess. It wouldn't have been very effective, but it would have slowed me down considerably. I found him at the docks. Catching him wasn't hard. Gareth was never very good at obscuring his trail. I didn't kill him at first."

His choice of words sent a shudder down Sheridan's spine.

"I took him back to the cellar with me to check on Nessa." Kade's voice though only a couple feet from Sheridan sounded very far away. "But when we returned, she was already dead. A life for a life, the Deoraghan say. I didn't want him to die quickly."

"So you questioned him?" Sheridan asked without any hope of a positive answer.

"To find out what?" Kade asked with scorn in his voice. "I knew that he guilty of kidnapping, extorting a member of the Orders, murder. What else did I need to know?"

"What about who had sent him? Who gave him his orders?"

"They didn't kill her," Kade said dismissing her questions. "He had. They didn't want her dead."

Sheridan shook her head. "No, Kade. There was a veiled man who came and spoke with Gareth before you got there. He told Gareth to clean up his mess. Kade, he meant Nessa. Nessa was never supposed to be involved from what I gathered from the conversation."

Kade said nothing to her assessment of the situation. He just kept walking his eyes ranging across the open, rolling hills they traversed. Ahead to the left the moor skirted the edges of the Auchneid forest. With a clear day and nothing to obstruct his view, he could see for leagues. Behind them near the tree line, he saw two riders heading north along the river.

CHAPTER TWENTY

For reasons that Mireya couldn't explain, she refused to camp under the cover of the nearby forest regardless of how convincing Kade and Eve's reasons were. After almost a half hour of arguing, they were setting up camp under the open sky of the unprotected moor, a fact that pleased no one, except Mireya. The sun had already set, but it had yet to turn to full dark. Under the gentle glow of the blue sky that contrasted with the darkness growing around them, they made camp. As they worked, the chirping of the bugs that lived in the grass provided an odd serenade.

Crouched in the dirt, Faela had clumps of loam surrounding her as she continued digging a fire pit. Jair and Sheridan had already left to hunt for firewood.

"Are you sure it won't rain tonight?" Faela asked again stopping her excavation of the soil.

"Sure as lightning bugs in summer," Mireya answered as she searched to add more rocks to the pile next to Faela.

Pushing the loose dirt up the sides of her small pit, Faela shook her head. "I don't like being out here, Mireya." She shuddered feeling as though unseen eyes watched her, but maybe it was just the singing insects watching.

Bent over, Mireya stood from her waist and put her hands on her hips. "We cannot stay in the forest."

Faela pushed her hair off her forehead with the back of a dirt-covered hand as she watched Mireya return to her scavenging as if that were the final word. "Why," Faela stressed the word, "can't we stay in the forest?"

Looking through the veil of her wild mane, Mireya's nose scrunched in frustration. "I told you. I don't know why. I just know that we can't, okay? Something about it puts my stomach in knots."

"But we traveled through the southern tip of this forest on the way through Dalwend and Jair and Kade and I made it through just fine. Besides, there's no such thing as curses."

"I never said it was cursed," Mireya protested as she hefted a good oval stone with a flat side off the ground.

"This is perfect," Faela observed as Mireya deposited the rock into her hands. Faela turned it over and brushed the dirt off the flat side.

"And they do too," Mireya said heading off in the opposite direction looking for more rocks to ring the fire.

"What?" Faela said as she situated the stones into a rough circle around the depression. "What too?"

"Curses," Mireya said pushing the scrubby grass aside.

"They're just in stories, Mireya. They aren't real."

Mireya waggled a finger at Faela and said, "Just like a Gray is only from the stories."

"Just because that story is true, doesn't mean places are cursed. We were in that abandoned town, Moshurst, and nothing happened. It wasn't cursed."

"A place with no animals, where nothing grows, and if you stay you'll get sick," Mireya recounted. "If that's not a cursed town then what is?"

"But it wasn't a curse. There's a perfectly normal explanation."

"You call what Jair can do normal?" Mireya asked bringing an oddly bulging rock to the diminishing pile as the ring took shape.

"No, but it wasn't a curse," Faela disagreed as she wiggled a rock into the dirt to secure its place.

"I don't know," Mireya said. "There's a place in Vamorines, it's just ruins now. No one goes there. I only found it, because I got lost when I went for a ride by myself. That place is empty of all life, there's just an absence there. I found a stone marker. It said this place is cursed and that any who enter must step into the void where there is no light."

Mireya shivered remembering the crumbled marble and moss growing over the bones of the place, as if trying to bury it. "I turned my horse around and didn't look back until we were leagues away. Curses exist, Faela."

Faela opened her mouth to reply when Sheridan and Jair returned with armfuls of big and little pieces of dry wood. Jair just smiled as Sheridan explained something, but her telling of the story was impaired by her hands holding the firewood.

"So you really used to pop into Kade's room and rearrange his books every night?" Jair asked.

Sheridan nodded with a barely contained smirk. "Oh, yes. It was while we were still training in the Amserian temple. It was a challenge to pop into his room while I knew he was on his way back. Usually right after we'd parted ways for the night, I would go around the corner, pop to his room, rearrange them, then pop directly to my room. It took him three weeks and two days to figure out that I was doing it."

"It took him that long?" Faela asked with surprise as she rocked back onto her heels. She slapped her hands together and began brushing off the earth.

"Well, he didn't know I could pop yet."

"So that's how you decided to tell him," Faela concluded from the snatches of conversation she had heard so far.

Sheridan nodded with a wicked grin. "I knew it was my only chance to get away with something like that. Once he knew, I would be his primary suspect for any pranks like that. It was the only time I had the upper hand and I used his ignorance for my entertainment. Some of my finest work really."

Faela shook her head. In the last few days, she had come to enjoy the tall woman's constant good humor. But more than her enjoyment of Sheridan, she loved watching the side of Kade that Sheridan illuminated. When she was around, a smile was never far from his face. The lines of pain and stress around his eyes never really went away, but they softened considerably in this effervescent woman's presence and Faela appreciated that. That appreciation had quickly turned to affection for Sheridan herself. Even Eve's bristly facade had begun to show cracks here and there revealing a woman Faela could respect and even at times enjoy.

A month ago, Faela traveled alone, which was how she liked it. People meant complications and complications meant trouble. Look at the trouble Kade and Jair had brought her. Though looking back, she couldn't bring herself to regret helping Jair that morning near Ravenscliffe despite all the complications it had brought. So, tonight she set up camp with three other people without any reservations regarding their company. As she focused back on the trio, their conversation melded from noise into words.

"So, Mireya, how does the whole blue thing work?" Sheridan asked as she crouched by the pit. She had the wood stacked by her as she began setting one on top of the others in a pile within the pit.

"What do you mean by 'work'?" Mireya asked as she settled herself next to Faela.

Jair had taken a seat next to the stack of wood and watched Sheridan his hands twitching as she continued placing the wood in the pit.

Unable to contain himself, he snatched her wrist. "Have you ever made a fire before?" he asked her bewildered by the wood strewn about the pit in no pattern he recognized.

Sheridan blinked in surprise. "Um, no, actually," she admitted biting her bottom lip in embarrassment. "I don't really do the whole camping out thing."

"But you do circuits," Jair said.

"I'm a popper, Jair," she explained in exasperation. "Who needs to camp, when I can go back to my quarters in Wistholt whenever I want? Besides, no one would deny a Daniyelan lodging."

"This," Jair pointed to the haphazard pile as if mortally offended, "is a travesty."

Sheridan glared at him for a moment, then swept her arm toward the pit. "Fine, oh-master-of-all-things-incendiary, you do it."

With her arms crossed, she tucked her legs underneath herself and stared at Jair waiting for him to begin.

"You weren't allowing for any air to flow through the fire," he explained as he removed all of the wood from the pit. He picked the sturdiest pieces and stood them on their ends leaning them into each other creating an open pocket in the center. "Without air the fire will die before any of the wood starts to burn."

He started another ring around the initial tent and added smaller sticks around the base for kindling. Pushing a stick with a finger, he reached beside Sheridan to grab some more when the wood burst into flames. With a yelp, he scooted away from the flames. Sheridan sat with an angelic expression on her face, the traces of orange lines vanishing from her forehead.

"What possessed you to do that?" he demanded sucking on his singed finger.

Her dark eyes wide, she said, "I was helping."

"That was not," he emphasized the last word, "helping."

Sheridan nodded emphatically. "Helping."

Jair squinted an eye and glared at her, his finger still in his mouth. At Sheridan's answer, Faela could no longer hold back her laughter at the situation.

"Traitor!" Jair cried. "Don't you encourage her."

Faela clapped her hand over her mouth trying to stop and nodded with mock sobriety.

"Oh, don't worry," Sheridan said trying to sound comforting. "I need no encouragement. My own entertainment is encouragement enough."

"Somehow that doesn't make me feel better," Jair protested.

"You big baby, give me your finger," Sheridan commanded, her hand held out her fingers beckoning him. "Trust me."

Jair hugged his hand to his chest protectively. "Oh no, you don't, you darkness-loving woman. First the river and now this. If I give you my hand, I'll never get it back in one piece."

"It's part of the healing process," she promised and waggled her fingers enticingly again.

"Whatever you have planned, is not," he stressed, "part of the healing process."

Rolling her eyes, Faela grabbed his hand causing him to yelp again. A soft red glow flowed over her hand and covered his. When the light receded, the minor burn had disappeared.

Sheridan stuck out her bottom lip pouting. "Aw, why'd you ruin my fun?"

"This is my life, woman, not your entertainment!" Jair declared cradling his hand again.

Deciding that Jair had provided enough amusement, Sheridan turned her attention back to Mireya. "So, prophetess, now that you've had time to think about it. How does it work?"

"I'm still not sure that I understand what you're asking exactly," Mireya said as she hiked up her skirt to hug her knees to her chest.

"Well, everyone here had to go through training with the

different temples in the Orders to learn how to wield their colors of magic," Sheridan explained, then amended and gestured to Faela and back to herself. "At least Faela and I did. You have to learn to control the colors within and around you. Otherwise, you can accidentally reach out and tap the magic and kill yourself and, well, destroy everything around you.

"I had to spend years in the towers of the Amserian temple at Wistholt to learn to manipulate purple magic. While my ability to wield red is minimal compared to Faela, we both spent years at the Tereskan temple at Kilrood. But no one in the other Orders ever goes to the Nikelan temple beyond the Boundary for training. Why is that?"

"As far as I know, I have no other colors," Mireya said as she considered Sheridan's words. "I never went to any other temples. I've lived almost my whole life at the Nikelan temple. Last year when Dathien and I left searching for Faela that was the first time I've crossed the Boundary since Tobias collected me when I was a toddler."

"Is that how it is for all Nikelans?" Sheridan asked leaning forward both in curiosity and for warmth from the fire. Her hair slipped over her left shoulder like streams of silk.

"Nikelan seekers are either called by the Light at birth through Rivka's visions or they feel the calling when they are old enough to choose. I was the first kind," Mireya explained. "That's why Tobias came for me."

"Is that method typical?" Faela asked. "For your Scion to have a vision of a child when they're born?"

Mireya shook her head, her lips scrunched to the right side of her face. "Most Nikelans feel the call when they're older. That's how it was for Dathien."

"Really? How old was he when he crossed the Boundary?" Sheridan asked.

Mireya's eyes searched the sky as if the stars held the answer. "He was fourteen, I think."

"Were you already at the temple when he arrived? Was it love at first sight?" Sheridan's eyelashes fluttered melodramatically.

"When Dathien was fourteen I was four. That's just gross," Mireya said with an expression of disgust contorting her face. "I was already at the temple, but I didn't met him until I was nine."

"So, that makes it better?" Jair asked his voice cracking. "I mean, I get the whole Grier partnership thing, but that is a little too literally stealing out of swaddling for me."

"Ugh, no," Mireya disagreed waving her hands in front of her face, "I don't think you get it at all."

"Okay, so explain," Sheridan encouraged her.

"Griers don't always marry their oracle. It is common because of the bond they share, but sometimes that bond is merely like the love shared between Faela and her brother, Caleb, or, Sheridan, your love for Kade."

Under her breath, Sheridan corrected her. "I think she means inexplicable toleration."

"So what's this bond then? Did you have it when you met him when you were nine?" Jair asked still looking queasy.

"The bond between a Grier and an oracle grows, it's not instantaneous. Vaughn thought that Dathien would partner with a girl near to his own age years ago. Her name's Anna. They were very close and everyone thought that friendship was the early signs of the bond."

"Can Griers bond with more than one oracle?" Sheridan leaned her chin into her cupped hand shifting her weight toward Jair.

"It's never happened that I know of. The only thing that can sever the bond once it's forged is death." A shadow clouded her clear blue, pupil-less eyes. "We can't survive without the bond. If the bond is cut, the survivor doesn't live for long, not that he'd want to."

"So if something were to happen to you, Dathien would die?" Faela asked, her underlying shock masked by the gentleness of her voice.

Mireya nodded tears forming at the edges of her eyes just at the thought. "It's how the partnership works. It's both ways. I don't think I explained it right earlier. Death doesn't really sever the bond, you see. The bond just pulls the one left in the realm of the living through the veil into the realm of death."

"I don't understand," Sheridan said flatly. "Binding magic doesn't work that way. It dissolves when the person who cast the spell dies or when the person bound dies."

"But binding magic is orange, not blue," Faela pointed out watching the flames lick at the night sky as the stars began to sprinkle across the wide expanse above them like scattered grains of salt.

"Binding magic is," Sheridan acknowledged, "but Mireya said that the bond grows. That's not how any binding spells I know work. They're all immediate. Is there a ceremony of some kind, something that seals the spell?"

Mireya's eyebrows drew together and she looked like she'd go cross-eyed trying to explain when Kade and Dathien emerged from the darkness with small fur-less carcasses in hand.

"Dinner," Sheridan exclaimed with a moan of pleasure.

"And already skinned and gutted," Kade said as he slapped them on the flat stone in front of Faela.

"Someone trained you well," Faela said as she twisted to grab her bag.

"That would be your brother," Sheridan answered pointing to Faela.

"Dathien," Mireya said getting his attention, "I'm not explaining the bonding right."

Dathien settled down beside her and she burrowed into his side both for warmth and out of long habit. Tucking her under his cloak, his fingers stroked her upper arm in small circles to warm her faster.

"That's because your gifts are very different than theirs, love," he said down to her before he raised his head to address his companions. "You were all trained how to use, how to wield magic. You're the ones in control. Simply put, you tell it what to do, what shape to take. But that's not how blue magic operates and our training doesn't involve learning how to control the magic."

"But that's what the Orders do," Sheridan said poking a stick into the fire with the toe of her boot. "They teach you how to use magic."

Dathien shook his head. "That's what all the Orders, save one, do. I was training at the Tereskan temple when I felt the call. I'm from a small fishing village in the southern edges of the Kurinean

Sea."

"I thought you're Deoraghan," Kade interrupted.

"I am," Dathien confirmed. "But my Tribe settled this village after the Cleansings."

"Aren't all the Tribes nomadic?" Jair asked.

"Most still are. It's a small village," Dathien said with a grin. "But as I was saying, in Kilrood, I learned to harness the magic in the blood, to use it. But when I began my training as a Grier, I had to learn that I didn't use the magic. The magic used me. I had to learn to surrender to the magic and to get out of its way. When I first met Mireya, she was still a little girl and I was nineteen."

"That's only a year younger than me," Jair said his jaw slack in shock.

Dathien just smiled. "It's not like that, Jair. She was just another one of the young girls underfoot at the temple to me. I was focused on my training."

"Okay, so how are you two married now and is this story in any way not creepy?" Jair asked frowning in anticipation of the answer.

"Everyone in the temple thought the bond was growing between me and another oracle, Anna," Dathien explained. "I was twenty-six as was she. You have to understand that Anna was very old to be unbonded. You have older Griers sometimes, but an unbonded oracle Anna's age was unprecedented. Then Paul arrived. He had been resisting the call for the past six years. Anna and I found him when I was riding patrol at the Boundary."

"He had been attacked by bandits and had wandered over the Boundary," Mireya explained taking up the tale. "Well, he took one look at Anna and started muttering about the woman in his dreams. It wasn't long into his training as a Grier that they were bonded."

"And I was still unbonded at twenty-seven," Dathien explained. "Vaughn asked me to start accompanying Mireya on her rides after she nearly got herself killed."

"I was fine," Mireya objected with a pouting glare.

"You fell off of a cliff, love," Dathien said trying not to laugh.

"Wait, is this the same falling-off-a-cliff story you told us before?" Jair asked.

Faela chuckled, recalling the mental image of Mireya pitching off a cliff. She flipped one of the small rabbits on the stone and rubbed some herbs into its skin.

Mireya burrowed her face into Dathien's side and said with a muffled voice, "Maybe."

"There's a Mireya-fell-off-a-cliff story?" Sheridan asked her brown eyes flashing with mischief. "Oh, I want details, lots of details."

"Actually, this may help you understand how we don't use blue," Dathien suggested. "Go ahead, Mireya. Tell it."

With an animalistic growl, Mireya sat up and threw her hands above her head in surrender. "Fine. I was collecting plants, herbs and the like, for some ointments and creams I make. I found a really good patch of Klamath weed. It's not as prevalent as you'd think. Well, I needed the roots, not the leaves or the flowers for what I wanted to brew. So, I couldn't just cut what I needed. Instead, I loosened the dirt and was pulling out the roots. There just happened to be one that had a really deep root system."

"This cannot end well," Jair whispered to Sheridan who covered her mouth with her palm to control her laughter.

Unaware of Jair's commentary, Mireya continued. "So I was pulling and it was still stuck. So, I braced my feet and pulled too hard and tumbled off the edge of the cliff."

"How high was it?" Sheridan asked.

Slitting a hole at the base of the neck of the rabbit meat, Faela pushed a stick through and propped the meat over the fire. "One hundred and twenty feet," Faela said as she winnowed the stick into the dirt for stability.

"How're you alive?" Sheridan asked blinking in surprised. "Did you catch yourself?"

"Nope," Mireya said shaking her head. "A protective shield encased me when I fell, I just bounced to the bottom."

"Not even a scrape," Dathien told Sheridan over Mireya's head.

"Wait," Sheridan said with her hands up. "You're telling me you were in a blue protective bubble?"

"Yeah, it was a bit like an unpoppable soap bubble," Mireya said agreeing with the analogy.

Sheridan blinked again, then burst out laughing. Which caused Kade to start laughing, which set off Faela again. Even through her scowl, Mireya smiled. Sheridan fell into Jair's shoulder out of breath.

With tears of laughter streaming down her face, Sheridan managed to say, "You have a protective bubble," before dissolving back into laughter.

After several moments they regained control of themselves and Mireya pouted.

"Do you see what I mean though?" Dathien asked. "Mireya didn't form the field. It just protected her when she needed it. It's the same with all our magic. When we need it, it uses us."

"Okay, but how does that make bonding not creepy?" Jair asked shaking a finger at Dathien.

"There's nothing strange about the bonding itself, Jair," Dathien explained. "How does any relationship grow? As I said, Vaughn asked me to keep an eye on Mireya. Though still young, Mireya's been of marriageable age for almost four years. But that wasn't Vaughn's intent."

"I wouldn't put it pass him though," Mireya said staring into the firelight. "He's a sneaky old man."

Without saying anything, Kade had begun picking out likely sticks and whittling the tops to points then handing them to Faela as she continued spicing the game. They had surrounded the fire with their macabre pikes of cooking meat. Pushing the tip into his thumb, he brushed off the flakes of wood and handed it to Faela. Sheridan watched them pass off the skewer and noticed how Kade made sure that his fingers never brushed hers and she hid her smile behind a hand.

"At least, I don't think it was," Dathien mused. "It just started as me accompanying her on her rides."

"Then I found myself searching for him before anyone else to tell him the latest thing I had learned reading the archives," Mireya continued for him.

The gamey smell of the first rabbit wafted on the smoke as its grease dripped into the fire causing the coals to hiss and spit.

Sheridan inhaled the scent and closed her eyes. "I'm drooling. That smells amazing."

Rotating the skewers to make sure the meat cooked all the way through, Faela said, "This one should be done soon, Sheridan. But I can't guarantee you it'll be much good. Not waiting for embers to cook on makes it tricky to heat evenly."

"I have never doubted your culinary prowess before," Jair said with his fist over his heart in a valiant pose, "and I shan't start now. You could make a rock taste good."

"Taste good?" Faela said with consideration. "Yes. Make sure one side isn't burned with the insides still raw? Not going to stake my life on it."

"Unless I can shove that hare in my mouth now, I need to be distracted," Sheridan declared wiping drool from her mouth in an exaggerated fashion. "Continue regaling us with your tale, my blue comrades."

"Well, Rivka recognized the beginnings of the bond right before I had the prophecy that sent us searching for Faela," Mireya picked up as though there had been no interruption. Though with how Mireya constantly got distracted and seemed incapable of recognizing the passage of time, they were uncertain she did realize there had been an interruption. "Once the bond was acknowledged by the Scion, we were betrothed."

"We weren't going to marry immediately," Dathien said watching Faela poke at the first rabbit with the tip of her dagger. "We were going to wait another year or two for Mireya to finish her training."

"But then I got the smack-in-the-head message from the Light to leave the temple to find Faela. Not that I knew it was Faela I was searching for," she amended unnecessarily. "So we got married and headed out to find her."

Before anyone could express their confusion, Dathien explained, "When a Nikelan oracle gets a calling from the Light, no one knows how long she and her Grier will be gone from the temple. Before Rivka became Scion, she and Vaughn were part of a working for seven, maybe eight, years. Especially with the difference in our ages, it makes things much," Dathien paused looking for the right word, "simpler while traveling for us to be married."

"Oh," Jair said as if Dathien had just told him the most

obvious thing, "well I guess that's not creepy."

Dathien smiled his slow smile. "The bond is magic, but it doesn't make us love each other."

Mireya snorted unattractively. "I'll say."

"The bond exists, because we do," Dathien said with a half shrug, his arm still around Mireya.

"Okay, so there's this magic that binds you even beyond death, or whatever," Jair summed up, "but what's the purpose? That sounds like a big commitment if you ask me."

"For one," Dathien began, "without the bond, a Grier's blue magic is unusable. The power of a Grier comes from his oracle. We are essentially living shields, though it's more than that."

"Much more," said Mireya moving her hands apart in emphasis.

"First one's done," Faela declared handing the impromptu skewer to Kade. She nodded her chin at Sheridan and he passed it to her.

Without even a word, Sheridan had her knife in hand and sliced off a hunk, which she promptly chucked into her mouth. Her eyes started watering with the heat in her mouth, but she chewed and swallowed. "Darkness!" Sheridan cried out sucking the hot grease off of her fingers.

"Careful," Faela warned. "That's really hot still." Then added as an afterthought, "Share it with Jair. There aren't enough for us each to have one."

The night grew deeper as they sat around the fire eating and talking companionably as each piece of game finished cooking until only one remained. Everyone had eaten and the conversation had hit a lull. Faela stared at the fire, but the warmth she felt came from Kade's presence radiating next to her not the fire. Stealing a glance out of the corner of her eye, she saw his gaze slide back to the fire as well.

Sheridan craned her neck around to look across the moor illuminated by the waxing moon that would soon by full. Nothing interrupted her view of the gently rolling waves of the landscape, save for a few scraggly bushes and a scattering of thistle.

"Anyone know where Eve and Haley went?" Sheridan asked after her search yielded nothing but spotting a badger scurrying across the top of a ridge.

"Haven't seen them since we split up searching for game," Kade answered.

"I know game is scarce, but they should have been back by now," Sheridan said her lips thin. "Which direction did they head when you split up, Kade?"

"They headed east along the forest's edge."

Before he could offer to show her, Jair rose and offered her his hand. "You shouldn't go by yourself."

Kade arched an eyebrow at this, but said nothing.

Taking his hand, Sheridan stood and wiped the dirt off of the back of her trousers. "Thanks, farm boy."

"Sure enough, slim," Jair responded.

"I am not skinny," Sheridan protested as they headed toward the forest at an easterly diagonal.

Faela chuckled as she heard their bickering dissolve as they merged with the darkness. Seeing moonlight pooling on the moor, it resembled rippling water. Faela felt a pang in her chest as she realized that the last time she had contacted Sammi was the night the twins and Haley had arrived.

Sensing the shift in her mood, Kade tensed and caught her gaze. Faela averted her eyes immediately to avoid unintentional contact. Despite what Tobias had advised, that was not how she wanted Kade to find out about Sammi or more importantly about Nikolais.

Scrambling to her feet, Faela brushed off her trousers much in the same fashion that Sheridan had. "I need to get some air," she informed them as she began walking toward the forest to the west.

She could hear Mireya calling after her and Kade's voice answering as she started jogging toward the tree line.

CHAPTER TWENTY-ONE

Without even slowing his horse from its canter, Vaughn thundered across the bridge and into the shimmering blue curtain of the Boundary. After leaving Wes in the care of the Phaidrians, he had caught a train heading for Montdell. Late the next morning, he disembarked in the town closest to Vamorines along the railway, Parvaling, and had ridden for two days straight only stopping to change mounts. He had been forced to leave Mesa after the first sixteen hours of the ride. His current mount was number three.

He hated to push any animal this hard, but he needed to reach Rivka yesterday. Not for the first time, Vaughn wished Lior had given him the gift for popping. It would make his job so much easier. Instead, he rode sleep deprived beyond exhaustion less than a few hours ride from Rivka.

The remaining leagues, like the last three days, flew by in a blur for Vaughn and before he knew it, he heard the clattering of the horse's hooves on the marble courtyard of the Nikelan temple's stables. He drew back the reins and the horse stopped gladly, its sides heaving from exertion.

Adolescent seekers assigned to the stables for their chores that day streamed into the courtyard at the commotion. Vaughn saw Jacob, a fifteen year old with curly walnut hair, turn as soon as he saw Vaughn and run back into the stables to get supplies for the overexerted horse. As he turned, Jacob caught the arm of a girl around his age that he spoke a few quick words to. Bobbing her head, she bolted to the side entrance that lead into the temple.

Sliding off his horse's back, he handed the reins to a young girl with two braids and patted her on the back lightly as he passed. "Thank you, sweetling."

"You look awful tired, jha'na," she said with a whistle. She was missing her right front tooth.

Vaughn stopped and crouched in front of her. "That would

be my wife, Lynn," he told her as he recalled her name. "Just Vaughn, all right?"

"All right, jha," she smiled with a slow shyness as she swung her arms back and forth, "Vaughn."

"That's m'girl," he told her with a wink and a pat on the cheek as he stretched to his full height just as Rivka strode into the courtyard.

He could tell from the slight flush on her high cheekbones and the rise of her chest that she had been far from the stables when the girl had found her. Vaughn closed the distance and folded her into his arms. She rested her cheek against his chest and said nothing for a moment, because they both knew that once he spoke the quiet peace of this reunion would have to end. Rivka was the first to pull back with a resigned sigh. Her silver hair had fallen into her face and dark circles bruised the skin under her clear blue eyes.

Tucking her hair behind her ear, Vaughn made a disapproving noise low in his throat. "You haven't been getting enough sleep, m'love."

With an indulgent smile, she laced her fingers through his and pulled him out of the courtyard. "You know why."

"Even after all these years?" He chuckled as they entered the kitchens, which seemed to Vaughn to also never sleep.

She squeezed his hand. "Especially after all these years."

As they walked through the culinary territory of the temple, the head cook, Avery, took the opportunity to have Rivka taste the ginger lemon sauce he had prepared for the braised pork tonight. Vaughn could feel her keeping strict control of the emotions and thoughts roiling in her mind by projecting the poise and calm that seemed to define her. Taking the time to praise Avery for another masterpiece, she rewarded the chef with a smile before moving on. She glided by Vaughn's side never hurrying their pace, though he knew she would have wanted to hear everything he had discovered the moment she knew he had arrived.

When they left the kitchens, Rivka steered them to the archives, not their quarters. Vaughn knew better than to question her, so he followed discussing the trivial matters of his trip as they crossed the temple. Entering the expansive room of the archives, he tasted the salt from the cold breeze blowing through the open doors that led to the balcony overlooking the bay. Rivka shivered as the breeze hit her and Vaughn swung off his thick traveling cloak. Walking up behind her, he draped it over her shoulders. She smiled at him, the worry now plain on her face.

"It's worse than I suspected, isn't it?" she asked without any prelude.

Vaughn nodded and taking her lead, he cut straight to the point. "Tomas is planning to take the Tereskan temple at Kilrood and kidnap Ianos in order to implicate the Nabosian council."

Rivka pulled her fingers in toward her palms slowly as she closed her eyes. "To what end?"

"He's been visiting Lanvirdis regularly since the reconstruction began. The people there love him. They see him as being merciful after the war, helping those most in need. He's shipping weapons for an uprising under the guise of relief for the villages battered by the recent storms along the eastern coast of Mergoria."

"People will accept anything with open arms when desperate," Rivka said as she sank onto a bench pushed against the stone wall. "But why Ianos? If his goal is Nabos, why drag the Tereskans into this?"

"For one, the moment Tomas tried to extend Daniyelan authority Ianos would be at the Boundary to find you," Vaughn said sitting next to her.

Rivka nodded her agreement. "That he would. So before he even begins, he would need to silence Ianos' dissenting voice."

"And at the same time enrage the people against the Nabosian monarchy and council as conspiring to renew their imperial aims."

"Ashalioris preserve us," Rivka breathed out slowly. "The people will demand that Tomas bring them to justice."

"Creating a void in Nabos."

"And as soon as one person suggests in a tavern that Tomas has always been good to them despite their rulers' decisions..."

"It isn't far stretch to someone suggesting that Tomas rule and then the people will demand that he do so."

"Tomas will accept reluctantly and will insist that this is a temporary measure until a new council can be formed and a new monarchy established."

Vaughn laughed humorlessly. "And we know how those kinds of temporary measures have a nasty habit of becoming permanent."

Grabbing Vaughn's hand that rested on her leg, Rivka said, "This is so much worse than Caleb thought. We must leave at once before these plans can be enacted. I will contact Hewitt immediately."

Vaughn leaned in and kissed her hair inhaling the low scent of jasmine. "I'm going to bathe. We can leave once we've eaten. The ships are not scheduled to leave today."

Rivka squeezed his hand and strode out of the room moving in her graceful, unhurried pace.

*   *   *

Shafts of moonlight speared through the canopy of the forest as Faela slowed to a walk. Looking back through the tree line, she could see the fire flickering against the black curtain of the horizon. Unlike the last forest they had encountered in the blighted town of Moshurst, these woods had all the indications of healthy nocturnal life. Moving further and deeper into the forest, Faela heard rustling in the nearby thicket as a small squirrel scampered within its branches trying to evade the hunting owls. The aerial predators called to one another in their low echoing hoots as they stalked their prey. Under the trees, the wind, that had sliced across the moor, here broke against the foliage leaving them trembling in its wake. Other than this underlying noise, the forest remained still and silent.

Wandering down a game trail, she found a small clearing with a felled tree trunk uprooted years ago. Lichen and moss covered it, reclaiming it for the forest. Walking on the balls of her feet to mask the sounds of her passage, she picked her way over to the trunk's dirt covered roots that hung toward the ground in defeat. It looked to her like they were trying to find their way back to the earth when they had given up.

Running her fingers across the springy moss covering the trunk, Faela observed, "Even in death, you're still part of the forest. You can never escape, can you?"

She drew her shoulders up to her ears and sighed. Fishing her vial out from under her shirt, she clasped it in her fingers and closed her eyes. Racing over the leagues between her and Kilrood to the southeast crossing the Higini mountains, her mind approached Mergoria's capital city on the coast of the Kurinean Sea.

Within a few breaths, she felt Sammi's sleepy excitement. She had woken him. Walling away her guilt, tears formed in the corners of her eyes as he smiled and laughed happily. As always, he showed her a series of images and babbled along as if telling her about his day.

Ianos had taken him down to the shores of the Sea. He showed her how the waves had covered his legs, which had surprised him. But his indigence at the shock soon transformed into pure delight. He was very upset when Ianos had taken him home, but he was also hungry, so he was still happy. Faela sent all the appropriate emotional responses to each image and portion of the story. Sammi yawned still sleepy.

The guilt at waking her son hit her again, so she sang him his lullaby to return him to the rest she had stolen him from. *Shine, shine like the sun. Night will end and day will come.*

At the final lines, she caressed his mind and broke the contact. *I'll be home soon. Mama misses you, lamb.*

Like I miss my heart, she thought as she opened her eyes.

When the forest reappeared around her, two men dressed in black stood blocking her view. Before she could even scream, the shorter man backhanded her across the face. The force knocked her backward off the tree trunk and into a juniper bush.

"Oh, you have given us quite the chase, missy," said the man who had struck her. "Lucky for us, master Nikolais was none too specific about what condition you needed to be in when we returned you to him."

"Now why would you run out on your husband like that, girl?" asked the taller, blonde man who shook his head. "And take his only child. That's just cruel, that is. No way to treat a man."

The branches of the voluminous shrub jabbed into her back and neck sharply. Pulling herself out of the juniper, her cheek ached from the force of the blow and her head swam.

With rage clear in her eyes, Faela wiped the blood from her

split lip with a knuckle. "Then I guess it's a good thing that Nikolais isn't a man."

"Oh, ho," said the shorter one with a laugh. "He said you was a feisty one."

"How much did Nikolais promise you?" Faela asked her voice cold and hard trying to keep them talking.

"We might not look respectable to you," the blonde said, "but we don't break contracts, girl. Besides, Nikolais warned us that you'd try to buy us, so he promised us a bonus if you did. Said he would match whatever price you offered on top of our original fee."

Searching for another defense, Faela rose to her feet with her hands away from her body to indicate that she had no weapons. "Do you know who I am?"

"Master Nikolais' wife," said the shorter one uncertainly.

She nodded with a wicked smile. "Did he tell you who I was before we married?"

"What does that matter?" The shorter one snapped his patience wearing thin.

"Oh," Faela said slowly, "it matters if you want to live to spend your fee."

The blonde smirked. "It don't matter who you were or who you are. All that matters is getting you back to Finalaran."

"I'm sure he told you my name," Faela said the smile never leaving her face.

"So you're a rich Merchant brat." The blonde shrugged dismissing its relevance.

"Not untrue," she said nodding, "but that's not what I meant. Because I'm sure that you know my brother, because he knows you two. He knew Nikolais contracted you. He warned me."

She waited for the recognition to dawn on their faces and when it did, she was not disappointed. They fidgeted as they shared an anxious look.

"It don't change nothing," said the shorter man a little too quickly. "We still collect the bounty, yeah? What Murphy does after that ain't got nothing to do with us."

"Do you really think that's how he'll see it?" she said with mock concern.

The blonde yanked Faela by the arm dragging her close to him. "I'm sick of hearing you talk. Let's find another use for that mouth."

The man crushed his mouth onto hers, his breath hot on her tongue. She could taste the sourness of stale ale and onions. She struggled to push herself away from him, but he held her tight as he slammed her hard into a nearby tree. Her heart hammering against her ribs, she felt his hands move from holding her arms to her side. Unable to scream with him covering her mouth, she opened the link between her and Kade.

*　　*　　*

Kade watched Faela disappear into the tree line as he sat back down.

"She'll be fine," Mireya reassured him. "She can take care of herself."

Kade grunted noncommittally. "I don't like anyone going off by themselves." He didn't feel the need to tell her about his promise to Caleb or his own personal discomfort at the idea of her going alone.

"Of course, she can take of herself," Dathien said to Mireya, "but she shouldn't needlessly risk herself either. Besides, you're the one who had a bad feeling about that forest."

Mireya's head snapped up when at Dathien's words. "Ooh, that's right. I change my mind. Kade, can you go find her?"

Sensing Faela's distant feelings of guilt, Kade decided to give her some time to sort herself out before going after her. "Let's let her alone for a bit. She traveled by herself for a long time, I'm sure she misses the quiet solitude." Speaking under his breath, Kade said, "Light knows I do."

Mireya looked skeptical of Kade's proposed explanation. "I'd think after being alone for so long she'd want people around," Mireya argued as she played with the hem of Dathien's cloak.

"Yes, but you, unlike most people, seem to disappear to another place even when in a crowd," Kade pointed out. "Even when in the middle of a conversation at times."

Mireya blushed. "I don't mean to," she said in a quiet voice looking down at the stiff cloth between her fingers.

They sat in silence. The only sound was the popping of the fire and the hissing of the wood as water evaporated in the heat. Staring into the fire, Kade sought Faela again without intending to and found the same affectionate love and masked guilt he had felt the night Eve and Sheridan had arrived. Before he could analyze her emotions further, Mireya spoke banishing the silence and his wandering thoughts.

"I know that I come across as vapid sometimes," she said focusing on the stray threads of the cloak's hem. She wrapped the string around her pinky. "I don't mean to. It's just so hard to stay here, when there's so much distracting me with all the colors and the music. It's just everywhere, never ceasing, always flowing."

As Mireya got that far away glaze to her eyes, Kade rocked forward into his knees watching her closely.

Mireya shook her head. "I'm sorry, I did it again, didn't I?" she asked, her small hands balled into fists in her lap. "Rivka never lets it distract her."

"Rivka also has centuries of practice, love," Dathien reassured her with a squeeze. "You're only nineteen. Give it time."

"Mireya," Kade inquired with an avid fascination, "are you telling me that you can actually see the flows of color magic?"

Mireya nodded her mouth pouting in frustration.

"All the time? You can't shut it out?" he asked his dark amber eyes sparkling.

She shook her head. "It's always there."

"Would you mind if I try something?" he asked as gently as he could.

"What do you want to try?" she asked drawing her eyebrows together in suspicion.

"You don't need to do anything," Kade assured her as his eyes disappeared under a violet haze. As Kade watched the purple pulses that indicated the intersections of the different folds of space and time, he turned his gaze to Mireya who shimmered with a bluish indigo light that radiated from within her skin. Blinking, the purple receded from his tawny eyes.

His mouth, slack for a moment, tugged up at the corners in a grin of understanding. "By the Light, do you two realize what you are, Mireya?"

Looking at little uncomfortable, she looked up at Dathien and then over to Kade. "An oracle?"

"Well, yes," Kade agreed quickly. "But you exist in more planes than, well, everyone else I've ever met."

"What does that mean?" Mireya asked with concern.

Kade organized his thoughts, considering how best to explain what he had deduced. "Not everyone can feel the magic."

Mireya nodded. "Only magic users can."

"Well, where those of us who wield magic can feel it when most people can't, you can not only feel it, but see it and hear it too. It's like you're the only person who can see and hear in a world full of blind and deaf people. To us, life is only tactile, fairly simple and manageable. But for you, you're having to deal with all those sights and sounds all the time."

"Oh," was all Mireya said as she stared at the fire.

"I'm able to understand only a little bit," Kade continued, "because those trained by the Amserian Order can see the flows of purple magic, the flows of time and space. But we have to actively search for the flows and only then can we see them after years of training. It seems though, that you exist in the plane that we only ever enter in order to pop through space or step through time."

Kade looked at the petite, dark girl with a newfound respect. "Darkness, Mireya," Kade said looking at her as though for the first time, "it must be exhausting. Spending only moments there, when transitioning through, feels like an entire day of chopping and hauling firewood. I'm surprised you're capable of carrying on a coherent conversation at all."

Mireya gave Kade a slow, shy smile of appreciation. "Thank you, Kade."

Dathien's deep blue eyes shone with gratitude. "Outside of Vamorines, it's hard for people to understand and harder still to explain. Back home, everyone just understands."

"It gets very lonely out here," Mireya said resting her head against Dathien.

At her words, Kade felt the pull that he had begun to associate with Faela singing. It was her lullaby.

Standing, Kade stretched. "I think it's time I go check up on

Faela." He waved behind him as he jogged toward the trees.

His long strides eating the distance, it didn't take long before he had to weave around tree branches. He tried to slow down his pace. He had meant what he said. He believed that Faela needed this time to herself. It had been days since she had found any real solitude. Though she tried to appear relaxed, being surrounded by so many people all the time kept her constantly vigilant. Kade knew exactly how exhausting that could be.

Taking his time, he paused to listen to the reassuring sounds of the forest. But instead of the sounds of animals scurrying through the brush, he only heard the wind whistling through the leaves. The quiet of the forest was too still. The kind of stillness that indicated a predator crossing a territory, everything staying hidden and quiet in the hope that they would remain unnoticed.

Trusting his instincts, Kade removed the curved, long knife from his waist and let the blade find its balance as he kept his wrist loose. As he scanned between the trunks of the trees, he slowed his breathing searching for anything out of place. It was in this state of relaxed wariness that it enveloped him like an undertow.

The vague sense of Faela's emotions he had felt, the brief whispers of thoughts he had convinced himself he had imagined, tore open inside of his mind like they had that afternoon in Oakdarrow. He felt the pounding of panic, terror, and disgust, as well as waves of shame and guilt.

Only this time the emotions were clear, instead of a tumbling snare. He closed his eyes and saw a cheek with a jagged scar pressed close to his face. He smelled sour beer and felt the rough scrap of facial hair on his own cheek.

He heard Faela's thoughts whisper in his mind, *Kade, can you hear me? Darkness, please hear me.* Then he felt the man's hands and Faela's internal cry that she tried to shield from him, but failed in her panicked state. *Stop, please. Please, not again. Blessed Light, make it stop.*

When Kade opened his eyes, they were veiled with black fire. Without pausing to find any signs to track her, he kept his body low as he sprinted through the trees. He knew exactly where to find Faela. His rage fueled the fire within him and that same fire licked from his hand engulfing the blade of the knife. He was close; he could hear the sounds of struggle and the curses of a coarse male voice.

Without making a sound, he circled around them to get a better view and tested his link to Faela as he removed his matching long knife. *Faela, I'm here. I'm in front of you. Does he have a weapon on you?*

Relief flooded through the link. Trying to push down her panic, her thoughts were scattered. *A knife. At my neck.*

I need you to focus, Faela. Kade told her trying to repress his rage, so he could think clearly, but just as she had failed, so did he. *It'll be over soon. I'm going to move fast and I need to know that you'll hit the ground when I do.*

Faela stifled another cry and tried to pretend that she was somewhere else, that this was not her body. She had done it before, she told herself, she could do it again.

Kade's wrath flared at this thought and repeated more harshly than he meant, *Can you do it?*

She wordlessly indicated her assent. She had to stay connected to what was happening to her or she would fail to respond when she must. Before Kade moved, as she focused her attention back to the physical, to her muscles, to her skin, she shuddered.

I'm right here, Faela. You're not alone. Ready?

Her mind like cold steel, she responded, *Ready.*

As Kade left his cover, neither man saw anything except the movement of the branches as Faela broke the man's grasp and sank to the forest floor. Lifting her face, her eyes glowing red, she sang a low note and the men froze mid-turn paralyzed. Rising out of his low run, Kade brought his blade up and across the chest of the man who had assaulted Faela. The fire of the blade cauterized the wound as it cut. He pivoted and brought the second blazing blade down slicing the second man's throat. But just as with the first, no blood escaped as the wound burned with the black fire.

Letting the note fade, the paralysis released them and their bodies fell to the floor like puppets cut from their strings. Both men had barely had time to see their death's coming.

Faela looked up at Kade who stood with both knives still rippling with the dark fire. His relief at seeing her safe flooded her with a heady rush. The fire receding from his eyes just as the fire flickered and extinguished on the blades and he sheathed them. Then he saw the bruises on her face and the blood dripping from her lip and the anger flared again.

Hugging her knees to her chest, she stared at the floor, the disgust and shame overwhelming her. She could see herself from his perspective, so she buried her face into her arms trying to block the image. She wished he would stop looking at her.

Kade stood unsure of what to do now that the immediate danger was over. All he wanted to do was comfort her and reassure himself that she was all right, but everything about her posture screamed for him to stay away. He took a step toward her.

At that action, her panic returned. "Go away," she said her words muffled by the sleeves of her coat. "Just leave me be."

Kade sat down across from her and said nothing, but his mind kept replaying her thoughts he had heard. Not again, she had said, not again. He reached out a hand, then thought better of it and closed it into a fist bringing it back to his lap.

Aloud she groaned as she began rocking back and forth. "Don't ask me, Kade. Please," she begged, "please, don't ask me."

Uncertain of what to do, confused by the swirling and mixing of her emotions with his, he made a decision. Scooting toward her, until he was parallel to her, he rested his head on his shoulder waiting for her to look up. When she did so, he put a finger under her chin and gazed into her blurry, wet eyes.

"That was not your fault," he told her. "You did nothing to deserve it." He felt the turmoil of her guilt and shame, but she could put none of it into words.

"Nothing gives anyone the right to treat you that way," he repeated.

When she tried to shake her head, he drew her into his arms and she stiffened at the touch. When he did not press her, but neither did he let her go, her resolve melted and she burrowed her face into the collar of his shirt and cried soundlessly. He stroked her hair repeating in soft tones that she was safe and that no one was going to hurt her any more.

After a while, she stopped crying, her throat was dry and the abrasions on her face stung from her tears.

Still resting against Kade, she closed her eyes feeling safe and oddly peaceful. "Thank you for coming," she said in a hoarse voice, but she meant for not leaving and he knew it.

"Faela, when you opened whatever this is. I felt what you felt and saw what you saw." His anger stirred again just thinking about it. "I've felt the righteous anger of justice before, but I've never felt anger like that. When I think about what he did-" Kade broke off not wanting Faela to have to think about it, even through his own thoughts.

Faela felt his smoldering protectiveness toward her and she froze. These emotions were not those of a man keeping his word to a trusted mentor and friend. These emotions differed substantively from the sisterly affection she felt for Jair. Tobias had tried to warn her about ignoring these emotions, these emotions that mirrored her own. How could she have been so blind, so stupid?

Kade watched her as she recognized his feelings and he sensed her reciprocation. With a crooked smile, he ran his thumb against her cheek as he raised her face to his. Faela looked into his warm brown eyes and saw her silver eyes reflected there. For a moment she sat motionless simply staring.

With a start, she shook her head and braced her hands against his chest pushing herself back forcing distance between them. Doubling over, she wrapped her arms around her torso as if in pain chanting a denial.

His hand hanging in the air, Kade stared bewildered. "What is it?"

"No," she repeated. "No, I can't." She just curled further into herself refusing to look at him again. She squeezed her eyes shut, willing the tears to stay away.

Kade waited without pushing any further, his mind piecing together the things that he had observed about Faela. The guilt and shame that shadowed her daily differed in texture from this. That followed her like a cloud, but this, this was more solid. It clung to her, weighing her down. He thought back to the cave where they had spent their recovery and his mind fastened on Caleb's request.

"These were the bounty hunters," he said tapping his index

finger against the opposite wrist, "the ones that Caleb warned me about."

Faela bobbed her head as she attempted to regain control of herself, her chest rising and falling as she tried to slow her tremors.

"Faela," Kade said trying to keep his voice neutral, "I need to know why they were hired. I need to know who sent them and why. I can't protect you if I'm blind to what's going on."

Faela bit down on her split lip without thinking and winced at the stinging pain. Her throat felt raw and gummy as she tried to speak and the words caught. Though she failed to block the thoughts from slipping through. *You'll hate me. It's all my fault. I brought this all on myself. You'll hate me, just like I hate myself.*

Kade knew in his gut that trying to touch her again would only drive her further away, so he forced his hands to stay draped over his legs. "I wish I could promise you that nothing will change," he told her, "but the truth always brings change. Hiding from it will only put yourself in more danger though, Faela."

Still unable to force out the words, she reacted instantly to his. *You don't understand; I don't matter. Only Sammi matters.*

Realizing that he had heard her instinctive, protective reaction, she moaned and her fingers raked back her hair as her forehead rested against her hands. The intensity of her thoughts told Kade more than words ever could. The same protectiveness and love that he had sensed when she sang her lullaby infused her thoughts.

"Is Sammi why you disappear?" he asked, but he already knew the answer.

She peered through the bars of her fingers at Kade, her silver eyes shining with desperation. With an effort, she choked out the words. "He's my son and those men were sent by his father."

Though Kade had suspected this, it did nothing to diminish the tiny flare of anguish he felt at her admission. He didn't reproach or condemn her; he just focused on her eyes and waited.

She maintained his gaze as she continued. "Sent by my husband."

Kade felt the conflict tearing through her as if the words burned her as she spoke them. He just looked at her, numbness insulating him from his own feelings.

"Why?" he asked his voice cold.

"Because," Faela laughed without humor, but finished the sentence internally. *Because I belong to him.*

Though her eyes glinted with moisture, what looked out through those eyes was not Faela. Those eyes were empty as if the memory of this man had stolen her from Kade.

The muscles in Kade's jaw rippled and tensed as he clamped his teeth together. Still detached, just the way he had honed himself to become during the war, he paused sifting through the information he knew. Faela had been running. He had assumed whatever she had done to use and renounce black magic had been the catalyst. Once he had learned of her father's death, he thought he understood why she had a bounty on her. Until Kelso, when she confessed to Tobias that her father had committed suicide because of her gift.

Now, there was this. The way she distanced herself from others, but especially the unspoken boundary she had placed between the two of them, had been more than guilt for her father's death. Though her father's death haunted her still, it had never caused her to run. He had been wrong.

"Where's Sammi now?" he forced himself to ask.

"In Kilrood with Ianos," she answered then swallowed, "for the time being."

"Those bounty hunters were hired to find you, in order to find your son," Kade said, "and you've been leading them away from him. That's why you told that innkeeper in Dalwend what you did."

The ghost of a tortured smile passed over her lips. "Give the boy a prize."

He braced himself for what he had to ask next and Faela tensed. "Faela, did you leave because of your father's death?"

"Yes," she answered deflated, but her mind amended, *no.*

"So which is it?"

"Both?" Faela shoved her fingers into her matted hair, sticky with blood. "Do you remember what I told Tobias about what happened? Well, that was a somewhat censored version. He got the whole truth out of me later that night. Sammi's father was the reason I manipulated my father's impressions and perceptions," her voice dropped with a cynical tone, "because I thought he loved me. All's fair with love, right? It wasn't long before I found out what he really wanted. It was darkness-blighted Merchant politics. That's it."

Faela's shame transformed into animosity and bitterness. "I gave away myself, my vows, and my family. Betrayed them. For what? I was with child, unmarried, and terrified. My family had no idea, not even Caleb knew. In my despair over a situation that I created myself," she pressed her splayed hand against her chest and repeated, "myself, I murdered my father. He's dead, because I deluded myself into believing that man loved me."

Her nostrils flared as her breathing intensified. "Once we were married, his mask of charm and wit revealed the cruel man hidden beneath. He forbade me to return to Kilrood, even to visit Ianos."

Kade's mind immediately went to Faela's earlier thoughts during the assault and through the numbness seeped an icy, calm wrath. His eyes darkened. "He hurt you."

"No more than I deserved," Faela said in a flat, emotionless voice realizing it was pointless to lie about the abuse. "But I wouldn't let him hurt my baby, not ever."

Kade fingers tightened around his wrists leaving the skin white from the pressure. Keeping rigid control of his voice, he said, "So you ran."

She nodded. "I was still pregnant, no one else knew but Sammi's father. I went the only place I knew to go."

"To Ianos."

"I certainly couldn't face Caleb after what I'd done." She stared at the blanket of dry leaves on the floor of the forest. "Where else could I go?"

"So Sammi is still with Ianos," Kade guessed. "Does Caleb know any of this?"

"He knows about Sammi and about," she paused as she almost spoke Nikolais' name, "his father. He knows nothing about the true cause of our father's death though."

"Caleb knows what your husband did and he's still alive?" Kade asked in disbelief.

"He had more pressing promises to keep to you at the time." She poked at a drift of crunchy leaves with the toe of her boot.

"Caleb is heading for Kilrood right now, isn't he?"

Before Faela could answer, they heard voices and the sounds of several people moving through the woods caring more for speed than discretion. Kade offered Faela a hand and they stood to face the noise. One knife back in his hand, he offered the other to Faela.

She shook her head and thought, *I have a more effective means of defending myself,* and her eyes flashed a dark crimson.

Breaking into the hollow first, Jair searched it, panic on his face. When he spotted Faela and Kade, his posture relaxed immediately and he jogged over to them and crushed Faela into a hug.

"Thank the Light," he breathed into her hair, his arms pressing all the air from her lungs.

"Jair?" she said surprised. "What are you doing?"

"I felt. I saw. I heard," he said the words tumbling one after another before he stopped. "You were attacked."

Faela and Kade shared a look of shock.

"How much did you hear?" she asked dumbstruck and anxious.

Jair grimaced with a flush. "Um, everything?"

Before either could respond to this revelation, Eve, only a stride ahead of Sheridan, hurdled a fallen branch.

When she saw Kade sheathing his knife, her eyes sparked and she demanded, "How are you alive?"

"Skill and natural born talent," he answered, but Faela and Jair could hear his unspoken hurt response, *Why would you be so much happier if I weren't, Eve?*

"No," she argued taking a step toward him. "You can't be alive."

"And yet here I stand," he said holding his arms out, "as I live and breathe."

"I felt the binding spell dissolve," she said clearly enunciating each word. "It broke. Only death could have done that."

"I'm just glad you were wrong," Sheridan told her sister as she closed the gap and threw her arms around Kade. After holding him tight, she pulled away and punched him in the arm. "Don't do that again - ever."

"You," Eve accused advancing on Faela menace in her voice.

"What did you do, Gray?"

Faela's shock was dwarfed by the wave of protectiveness rolling off Jair and Kade. Jair, with his arms still around Faela, pivoted her away from Eve, but Faela gently removed his arms and stepped around him revealing the evidence of the attack. Sheridan sucked in her breath at the abrasions and bruises that were beginning to blossom on her face. Faela had not bothered to wipe away the blood streaking her cheek and chin.

"What are you implying?" Faela asked her voice cold as her anger bubbled up inside her with a ferocity that caused Kade and Jair to share a concerned look. Her jaw and back had stared aching terribly.

"Oh, I'm not implying. I'm accusing. That one's just a channel and untrained at that." Eve pointed to Jair. "Other than the Daniyelan council in Finalaran or death, the only thing that can break that particular binding spell is black magic, which leaves you. So, I'll repeat my question. What did you do?"

"What did I," she stressed the word, "do?" Faela jammed her fingers into her tangled hair again as she laughed. The stress of holding her fear at bay, of confronting her feelings for Kade, of reliving her mistakes and the abuse she had suffered, it all came crashing in on her and she laughed.

Eve took an unsure, involuntary step back from the battered woman in front of her who stood illuminated in a shaft of moonlight with her head thrown back laughing. When Faela leveled her gaze at Eve her eyes bathed in the shimmering light glowed with a wildness. She had gone beyond caring. Stretching her arms out to the sides, Faela jerked her chin toward the corpses at her feet.

"Look at them," she demanded capturing Eve's brown eyes, "Do you want to know what they did? Do you want to know why they're dead? You're supposed to be the servant of justice. So, ask me. Ask me why they're dead."

The leaves that carpeted the forest floor partially covered each man's body. Their eyes stared, but they would never see anything again. She and Kade had guaranteed that.

"I am tired, Eve," Faela said softening her voice. "I'm tired of watching what I say and reveal. I'm tired of being hunted and of running. I'm tired of hiding. If you want to drag me back to Finalaran to make some example of me, try it. Just stop making threats and snide remarks, because I'm done watching what I say. So either do something or stay out of my way."

When Eve said nothing, Faela just shook her head and turned toward the moor.

"Why are they dead?" Eve said pushing against the nearer body with a boot. It flopped onto its back revealing the deep trench across its chest. With a wound like that, the ground should have soaked up a lot of blood. But the hollow was clean, like the wound. Sheridan, however, had seen wounds like this before.

Faela smiled, a fact Kade and Jair did not miss, out into the trees before turning back to the clearing. "Ultimately, because I was naïve. But immediately, because he," she said kicking, none too gently, her assailant, "decided he wanted to have some fun before he took me back home. I really didn't want to kill them." Her chest rose with her gusty exhalation.

"You didn't do this," Eve said shaking her head in disagreement. "Kade did."

"True," she acknowledged, "but I still hadn't planned on killing him."

She heard Kade's thoughts as clear as her own. That had always been his plan.

Ignoring him, Faela continued, "I told you I was done hiding." Kade and Jair both questioned the wisdom of this decision, but she told them to hush, because she had to think.

"You're just going to stay suspicious of me until you understand what's going on, am I right?" Faela looked Kade up and down, remembering his intense curiosity about her. "I'm right. Those were bounty hunters hired by my husband to bring me home. More to the point, they were after my son. I will never let my husband get his darkness-blighted hands on my son. End of story."

At her confession of being not only married, but a mother as well, Sheridan sought Kade's gaze. A controlled, impassive mask greeted her. She knew that carefully guarded expression. In the months after the war had ended, he wore that expression even when he thought no one watched him. Under the surface of that outer calm, Sheridan knew the pain that lay buried beneath. While she knew it hurt him, Faela and Jair could each feel the dull ache under the numbness.

Unable to take all the raw emotions, Faela wove her barriers and wrapped them in tight shutting out Kade and Jair. She was alone in her mind. Her breath came easier. It would be easier now.

"Why did you leave?" Eve asked. In a calming gesture, she rubbed the inside of her arm with her thumb.

"Because I married a manipulative, spineless, cruel boy. I would have considered this," she said circling her face with an open hand, "a good day back home."

Sheridan winced at the detached way Faela referred to being abused. As if what she discussed had happened to someone else.

"That man will never lay even his eyes on my son." The quiet vehemence in Faela's voice promised retribution more sincerely than any oath could have. "And it is for my son that I'm heading for the Boundary. I can't say that I'm sorry that these men are dead, but I didn't seek their deaths. You want to know what I did. Honestly, I don't know if I dissolved the binding spell. I'm not even sure how I could. All I know is that I called for help and Kade came.

"You don't know me, Eve. I know you don't trust me. Don't; I certainly wouldn't. I probably don't deserve your trust, but this has been more than I can handle right now. If you want to interrogate me in the morning, fine. But right now, I just want to sleep. So, can we call a cease fire for tonight?"

Her coppery gold hair sparkled as it caught the moonlight, strands of it falling into her face. The bruises were deep blue and purple now along her cheek and jaw. She had dark lines on her neck and collarbones. In the shining light, Faela wavered like a ghastly apparition, an apparition who had been ripped from this world by violence. Taking in each of these details, Eve nodded her consent.

Closing her eyes, Faela's shoulders sagged the weight of everything flowing back over her. With a hand supporting her, Jair ushered her back toward the flames dancing on the horizon. Her hands flexing, Sheridan jogged after them.

"Let's at least clean you up first," she suggested. Her fingertips hovered over Faela's swollen cheek. "May I?"

With an appreciative nod, Faela said, "There's water back at the fire."

CHAPTER TWENTY-TWO

Like many capital cities, Kilrood had expanded over time, due to its location at a natural crossroad. Perched on the northeastern shore of the Kurinean Sea at the mouth of the Nash River, Kilrood had grown from a small fishing village in order to accommodate the influx of trade. Traders moving their wares from the central jungles and plains of Taronpia across the great inland sea to the coasts of Mergoria all passed through Kilrood before heading north to Lanvirdis. As its nearest urban neighbor, Lanvirdian refugees had flooded Kilrood during the war.

Its nearness to Lanvirdis, however, was not the sole, or even the primary, reason for attracting those souls displaced by the war. Those who made the journey down Diarmid Bay and into Mergoria came to Kilrood searching for the sanctuary and hope offered by the Tereskan temple.

As they rode through the gates into its open courtyard, Caleb inadvertently tightened his grip on Chance's flanks. The horse shook his head and whinnied. Caressing the stallion's neck, he spoke reassurances to him.

The absence of the happiness and anticipation he usually felt entering these gates made the familiar action feel empty and foreign. When Faela was little, he had stopped by the temple in Kilrood any time he was near. Even when inconvenient and out of his way, he still made time to visit. She was so young when she was taken for training, maybe too young.

As he reined in his mount and his thoughts, the hairs on the back of his neck prickled. The horses' hooves clattered echoing hollowly off the high walls as they stopped. No one exited the stables at their approach. Already in a guarded mood, Caleb's eyebrows drew down over his eyes as he scanned the deserted courtyard. He caught Talise's equally unsettled gaze. Quieting his breathing, the only sounds he heard either came from the streets behind him or from their horses. No sounds came from the temple grounds.

His knees absorbed the impact as his boots hit the ground silently. He reached a hand behind him. The halls within the temple were too narrow to risk using his revolver. His fingers touched the hilt of one of his long knives. With a fluid flick of his wrist, the knife was out and balanced in defensive readiness. His eyes roaming the courtyard, he stepped forward cautiously. Talise stalked by his side a thin, wickedly hooked blade in her hand. Neither spoke, but they advanced toward the door together.

Caleb stood his back flush to the wall. Directing Talise with hand gestures, she grasped the iron latch on the side door leading into the temple. She opened the door. Its hinges creaked. In a distant part of Caleb's mind, he realized that the squeak still hadn't been fixed after all these years. The familiar recognition felt discordant and caused him to readjust his grip on the hilt. Blade in hand, Caleb ducked through the door gazing to the right and to the left. The kitchen was empty.

The fires in the hearths had burned down to sparkling embers and tendrils of smoke lazily reached up the shafts of the chimneys. A pile of carrots lay half chopped and cook pots hung over the hearths filled with coagulated broth, but nothing else. Feathers blew across the floor from the chickens that were in the process of being butchered.

Straining to hear any sign of movement in the temple, Caleb assessed every corner of the room before moving on. Stepping into the narrow hallway, Talise stood with her back to his as they left the kitchens. Fluttering in the displaced air, the banners lining the hall danced away from the walls. Up ahead, the walkway emptied into the great hall.

As the restricting walls fell away and they stepped into the two-story room, Caleb saw why the kitchens were abandoned. Heaped one on top of the other like a stack of firewood were bodies. Blood liberally streaked the floor. It pooled and ran along the mortar lines of the stone floor, outlining the slabs in dark reddish brown.

Talise sucked in a breath. She resisted the urge to close her eyes. Caleb gestured for her to go left and he went right. They walked the length of the room, checking to see if any of the butchers remained. When they reached the end, Talise nodded that her side was clear.

With only two bottlenecked entrances into the room, Caleb sheathed his knife and met Talise in the middle.

"The Tereskans, why would anyone?" Talise asked, her eyes damp as she took in the carnage. "How could anyone? They're healers, Caleb."

Caleb's eyes were ice, his voice even. "The more crucial question is: Where is our nephew?"

Talise's eyes flew wide and she reached out. Clutching Caleb's hand, she suggested, "Ianos' rooms."

Withdrawing both his knives this time, Caleb held their blades parallel to his forearms as they left the slaughter behind. Passing large windows that overlooked the Kurinean Sea, they found evidence of the struggle now. Blood spattered the floor, the walls and streaks led back the way they had come. Caleb had little hope that they would find any stragglers, but his senses were still heightened and his heart beat steady.

They crossed the formal foyer of the temple, its ceiling soaring four stories above them. Their passage barely sent a ripple of an echo into the vast expanse. They passed through a small vaulted doorway into Ianos' private study, a room that faced the sea with shelves lining the walls. Books slumped on the shelves, at least those books that remained on the shelves. Many had been hurled across the floor. Under the windows, vials and bottles and potted herbs had been smashed on a worktable that ran the length of the wall. Next to the large desk lay an overturned woven, reed bassinet.

Blankets spilled out of the crib onto the cold stone. Checking all the corners of the office, Caleb made his way to investigate the desk. It had been ransacked. The drawers had been removed and upended, their contents mixed with the rest of the room's broken belongings. His knives hissed as he sheathed them and he crouched next to the crib. Rummaging through the blankets, he picked up something. He held it up; his hand shook. It was a stuffed lamb that he had given Faela when she left to train in this place. Drops of blood flecked its spun wool coat.

*   *   *

The swelling had subsided due to Sheridan's ministrations, but the bruises still made Faela's cheeks and neck look like a splotchy watercolor. Two days had passed since the attack and they made good time. Dathien had told them they were within a day's journey from the Boundary now. Soon, they would cross into Vamorines. Since the night in the hollow, Eve had maintained her distance and had left Faela alone. Despite her lack of openly antagonistic behavior, it failed to thaw the tension between her and Faela.

Worrying about Eve, however, did not occupy Faela's thoughts. She intentionally kept her gaze from settling on Kade who chatted with Sheridan a few yards in front of her. She rechecked her barriers for the ninth time in the last thirty minutes and increased her gait to remove the temptation.

Tugging her coat around her more tightly, she heaved a sigh as she shook out her fingers. Tobias had been right about her hand aching for a while. Without any trees to stop it, the autumn wind cut across the moors with bone-chilling frequency. She forced her gaze onto the horizon and the seemingly never-ending dip and rise of the moors darkened by the morphing shapes of the passing clouds.

Mireya broke off from Dathien and scurried over to join Faela. "You have that look," Mireya informed her as she pushed back her wild hair.

"People tend to get looks," Faela responded as she hopped across some rocks.

"No," Mireya disagreed as she scrambled up the small rise instead of venturing, at best, a sprained ankle by following Faela's path. "You have that Faela's-torturing-herself-for-something-she-can't-change look. You get tight lines around the corners of your eyes."

"How much longer till we reach the Boundary do you think?" Faela watched the shadow theater of the clouds, each player endlessly switching roles against the bright afternoon sun.

"At this pace, we'll be there tomorrow late morning," Mireya answered trying to keep up with Faela. "Speaking of which, slow down."

Complying, Faela slowed just enough to keep them in front of Kade and Sheridan. Her back and stomach muscles protested against the pace she set. She knew that s he had torn some muscles during her brush with the bounty hunters, but there was little she could do when they had to hike most of the day and complaining would change nothing. Trying to take her mind off the twinges of ripping pain, she watched the shadow theater in front of them now feature a bunny being chased by a harp.

"Do you the see bunny up ahead?" Faela asked filling the silence.

"Where?" Mireya searched the horizon. "Could we catch him? I love how you cook hare."

"You mean actually cooked?"

"Exactly, no chewy raw bits with you."

"Unfortunately," Faela said with a resigned sigh, "even Dathien couldn't catch that rabbit."

"Why not?" Mireya replied her voice indignant. "He's a really good trapper."

"I would never dream of suggesting he weren't. But tragically, the bunny has collided with the harp and now they've become a ship. So he'll never catch it now."

Mireya stopped, but when Faela didn't even pause, she scampered to keep pace. "I know a lot's happened, Faela, but are you starting to see things that aren't there?"

Faela laughed and snatched Mireya by the chemise drawing her close. With her arm, she directed Mireya to the shape of the shadow cast by the cloud skimming across the short grayish grass of the moor.

"See," Faela said still smiling, "a ship. Well, I guess it's more of a crib now."

Mireya brushed a finger against Faela's temple, just missing the thin scab on her cheek. "That's why you get these lines."

Letting Mireya go, she quickened her gate.

Blowing air into her cheeks, Mireya gathered her heavy skirt and chased after Faela. "Will you stop it?" Mireya complained an edge to her usually sweet voice. "This is exhausting."

"You can always go back with the others," Faela suggested. "I just want to find somewhere with cover from this wind before we stop for the night. I don't like how open this place is."

Browsing the horizon, she spotted the outline of a small grove of trees a few leagues in front of them.

"Stop changing the subject," Mireya accused.

"But I just found it," Faela replied pointing to the jagged lines breaking the vista.

She winked at Mireya and kept walking. Hopping down off a shallow rock ledge, Faela winced at the jabbing ripple of pain.

"Faela, why won't you tell me what's wrong?" Mireya asked after an extended silence. "You don't trust me. Is that it?"

"Is that what you think?" Faela asked her voice a little sad.

"Oh no, you don't. Don't you answer me with a question. Answer me."

"I don't distrust you, Mireya."

"So?"

"It lets me pretend."

"Pretend that none of it happened?" Mireya asked after a few moments of silence.

"No," Faela admitted. "Even when I'm not thinking about it, I can always feel it."

Mireya got quiet and they walked. Neither felt compelled to speak. The stand of trees Faela had spied in the distance grew larger against the sky. Looking to the side, the waning light outlined Faela in its glow as the ground reached for sun. With the pace Faela had set, they would hit the grove before dusk.

"Faela?" Her throat sticky from the dry wind, Mireya coughed to clear it. "I'm sorry, Faela."

"What for?"

"Lots," Mireya answered. "I'm sorry that I get distracted all the time. But I do notice, you know? How much you hurt. Though I know you don't want me to, I see it and it makes me sad."

"Don't let it get you down, Mireya," Faela said her mouth tense with a smile. "I can handle it."

"But that's just it. You shouldn't have to handle it. Those things shouldn't have happened to you."

"Yes, they should have," Faela disagreed. "I made choices and those choices have consequences, Mireya."

"So those men attacking you was your fault?" Mireya put her hands on her hips and stared at Faela.

"In a way and in a way no," Faela answered philosophically.

"And people say I'm confusing," Mireya muttered to no one in particular.

"The fact that they were hunting me is a direct consequence of my choices," Faela explained, "but their individual actions, they chose. And those choices also had consequences."

"No," Mireya objected. "That's not right."

"You think so?"

"You're talking like the choices others made were the only choices someone could make given the choices you made." Mireya paused. "I think."

"That's quite a mouthful."

"But it's what you're thinking. Yes, you made specific choices, bad ones too. But the choices others make, they make them. You don't. Just because you made the wrong choices, doesn't mean you deserved everything bad that happens to you. Don't you see?"

"Not all the consequences are bad, Mireya," Faela said her voice soft. Her fingers went to the leather cord around her neck.

Mireya turned and saw the little smile on Faela's swollen, still healing lips that failed to dispel the lines around her eyes. Something in that smile made Mireya hold her tongue.

That night after diner, Faela walked a good distance from the camp to bury the leftover bones and scraps. Piling the dirt over the hole, tendrils of her hair fell into her face tickling her cheek. On her finger, she felt a different tickle. The glossy black of the spider's back reflected the still bright moon. She didn't move. She didn't brush the spider away. She just crouched watching it slowly picking up its feet and placing them down again in a slow and deliberate crawl.

She also didn't hear the approach of the figure behind her, but the shadow it cut through the light made the spider's back fall back to matte darkness. The spider moved before the figure and it made its way onto to the mound of dirt after its trek across the valley and ridges of her knuckles.

She stood casting an elongated silhouette against the grass. "Do you have something you want to say?"

Kade's arms laced across his chest, only his eyes moved to shadow her. "You're avoiding me."

"And?" Faela asked the hint of a challenge in her tone.

"You've done nothing wrong," he told her.

She kept her eyes on the rustling grass on the next ridge. Each blade of grass cast deep, wavering shadows in the moonlight.

Faela couldn't stop the bitter laughter from bubbling up. "You can honestly say that with a straight face? Well done, ser. You're a much more consummate liar, than I could ever hope to be, which is saying something."

"Don't twist my meaning." He kept his distance watching how rigid she appeared, untouched by the wind that swayed her hair. She was in physical pain. "You know exactly what I meant. Letting yourself trust isn't a crime." Kade prodded her and waited for a reaction, any reaction.

She didn't speak. She didn't turn. So, Kade did. Circling from behind, he faced her.

"Letting yourself love isn't a crime," he said cocking his head to the side as he caught her gaze. Strands of his hair blew across the bridge of his nose.

Her cheeks were damp. "Tell that to my father. Tell that to the men dead in the forest," she spoke in nearly a whisper.

"Loving wasn't your crime," he argued, his amber eyes fierce behind those errant strands. "Abusing your gift was."

"But it's why I did it," she said lacking the energy to argue. "It's tantamount to the same. I lied to myself in the name of love. Those lies led to my father's death."

"So, do you stop loving Caleb? Talise? Ianos?" Kade asked searching for a response in her unreadable mirrored eyes. "Sammi?"

No," she disagreed with vehement shock, "of course not."

"Then why are you now shutting out Mireya? Jair?" he asked, his eyes vulnerable for half a heartbeat.

Faela broke the gaze and walked past him her head tilted back to see the sky. A triad of stars stretched up as if trying to reach beyond the stars around them.

"The people in my life from before," Faela said, her eyes ranging across the heavens, "they're stuck with me. That's just the way it is. But only darkness knows if they'll have anything to do with me once they know the truth - the whole truth."

Kade considered his next words with care. "Do I know?"

"More or less," Faela evaded reflexively.

"That's not an answer," he told her as though she were unaware of the fact.

"People keep telling me that lately," she said, her eyes crinkling in annoyance. "You know the basics, the facts."

"Do I know more than they do?"

"Ianos knows it all," she admitted, shifting her weight onto her right foot. She shivered and wrapped her arms around herself in attempt to consolidate her heat. Her overcoat lay across her pack at the camp and the night air blew through the cotton of her shirt with ruthless efficiency. She hadn't planned on being gone this long. "Other than him, you and Jair know the most."

"Has Jair run from you in horror?"

"You're using him as your example of good sense and sound judgment?" she questioned, her left cheek dimpling.

After a moment of silence, he sought her eyes. "Have I?"

Faela's breath stammered in her chest as she returned his gaze. Shaking her head, her hair came forward hiding her face. She shoved the palms of her hands into her eyes. "Idiot," was all she said.

"Did you just call me an idiot?" Kade asked his lips twitching.

"See, this is exactly the problem," she accused.

"Me being an idiot?" his eyes sparkled catching the moonlight.

"Stop trying to make me laugh," she ordered him.

"I'm just asking simple questions, because I am, in fact, confused," he said with a flawless mask of innocence. "I'm not trying to do anything"

"Kade," her voice pleaded with him to understand, "I'm married."

He nodded and spoke his next words slowly. "I know."

She squinted one eye at him. "What're you playing at?"

"Friendship."

"I don't follow," she admitted suspicious.

He inhaled and gave her a slight smile. "This entire time our acquaintance has been defined by necessity and duty. But it has," he paused, "shifted. What I propose now is that we be friends. I don't have many. Sheridan and your brother are pretty much it actually. Which is shocking, given how truly remarkable I am. So, will you be my friend, Faela Durante?"

"Well, given your supreme humility, how can I refuse?" she answered.   "All my friends vastly overestimate their own self importance. Not sure I could balance another pompous braggart."

"So you'll be my friend, Faela?" he asked holding out his hand to her.

She took it and their stretching shadows shifted and merged into a single, bridged silhouette. "I don't have many myself. Pretty much just Ianos, Caleb, and Talise and Caleb and Talise are family. So you've got me beat there. You sure you want a friend like me, Kade?"

"I'm not sure I can do without," he said, his hand lingering on hers. "You're freezing." He observed, releasing her. "Let's head back to the fire. I think I hear some music."

As they walked back to the camp, the firelight shone in the space between the two.

His back against a fallen log, flakes of bark littered his cloak as Haley strummed his fingers lightly over the strings of his lute. Peering over the fire, he saw Faela and Kade returning from burying any trace of food that might attract any unwanted animal visitors.   Though Faela looked calmer than she had since the attack, they still moved with deliberate care whenever near one another. He smirked.

"How did our noble diggers fair?" he asked as his fingers plucked the strings in a complex pattern changing the song from a haunting dirge to a jumping reel.

Eve's fingers drummed out an intricate rhythm in counterpoint to his playing as she stared unseeing into the flames.

Seeing her sister's fingers and the absent smile playing on her lips, Sheridan hugged her knees in closer. It had been years since she had last seen her sister dance like she used to, smile like she used to.

"I think we'll be safe from any ravenous squirrels tonight," Faela answered as she took a seat next to Jair and Kade sank next to Sheridan who elbowed him in the arm as a way of greeting. "Eve, your rhythm is brilliant."

"You should see her dance," Haley said with a grin. "Now, that is a sight."

Sheridan chin snapped up from her knees. "You've seen Eve dance?"

"Aye, it's how we met," he said, his face lowered over the instrument again.

Sheridan turned to her sister with confusion and suspicion warring in her eyes. "You don't dance anymore. I haven't seen you even notice music since that day."

Her eyes staring at the sea of grass over the moor, Eve seemed to struggle to find words. "Everyone heals, Sheridan. No one can grieve forever."

"No, I suppose no one does," she responded and an uneasy silence fell around them.

Picking up the conversation, Jair asked Dathien a question that Sheridan missed. She didn't look at Eve, instead her eyes drifted to Haley. He sat with an ankle tucked under him and his other leg propped up. In that crook lay his instrument, which his body curled around cradling it as he continued to pick out lively notes. Holding the lute's neck, he tried to brush his hair back over his ear, but it just swung back into his face.

Sheridan's skin tingled. Within a breath, she was on her feet, her eyes glowing with fire. She could hear inquiries of confusion, but the sound was distant and garbled. All she could see was the musician sitting across from her. Cocking her head to the side, her braids slipped into her face. The fire flared in her eyes and she saw the golden shimmer surrounding the man Eve called Haley. She could feel hands on her, shaking her, but she just cocked her head to the other side.

Not even realizing she spoke aloud, Sheridan whispered, "I see you."

Haley kept his face inclined toward the instrument. Sheridan shrugged off the hands and circled the fire. Crouching down, she inclined her head again. Motionless, she stared at Haley.

Without warning, her right hand struck out grabbing his throat. She brought his face within inches of hers and repeated, "I can see you."

At that fire rippled over her hand in a flash that swept through the man. When the wave dissipated, the man before her had pale skin, long auburn hair and squared features, but the silver eyes remained.

"Hello, Lucien," Sheridan said with a guttural growl. She pushed him back using the force to stand.

Eve sat absolutely still barely breathing, but her eyes were wide with horror. Recognizing the new man, the surprise on Kade's face shifted into a quiet disgust. Sheridan turned away from the sprawled man and marched out of the camp, then back in. No one else moved. No one else spoke. On her fourth pass, Sheridan skidded to a halt kicking up dirt and stones.

Her voice simmering with rage and her eyes bright in the firelight, she finally looked at her sister and yelled, "You lied to me!"

Eve just continued starting at the ground offering no explanation, no excuse.

"I held you for hours while you cried for him," she accused throwing a hand in Lucien's direction. "I comforted you. You barely eat for weeks. I thought I was going to lose you to the grief and it was a lie. It was all a lie."

Sheridan started her pacing again, nostrils flaring with her quickened breathing. "You two must've had a great laugh over this one at what a fool I was."

"No," Eve disagreed raising her head. "It wasn't like that. He was as good as dead. I was never supposed to see him again. Sheridan, I never meant—"

Cutting off her explanation with a hand, Sheridan looked at her sister her eyes filled with the pain of betrayal. "You lied to me, Eve. You told me he was dead and he's not." She paused. "How long?"

"While I was hunting Kaedman," Eve dug her fingernails into the soft flesh of her palms. "That's the first time I'd seen him in six years. I give you my word."

Sheridan barked a bitter laugh and covered her mouth with both her hands. Sliding them down from her face, she clapped them together. "Your word?"

"I was never supposed to see him again or," Eve drifted off unable to complete her thought.

"Or?" Sheridan asked her gaze piercing.

"Or she would kill me herself," Lucien answered for her.

Sheridan fixed her eyes on Lucien. "You look pretty bloody good for a man who's apparently died twice." Without looking back at Eve, she held Lucien's unreadable mirror eyes. "He betrayed you, Eve. He betrayed you and you're with him again."

"He never replaced me," Eve blurted out, then slapped her hand over her mouth.

Turning back, Sheridan's eyebrows lowered over her gaze. "What?"

"Oh, please, don't insult her by acting like you don't know what she's talking about, Sheridan," Lucien said with a drawl as his eyes swept to Kade. When their eyes met, the unspoken, but promised retribution in Kade's face caused Lucien's guts to clench.

"You will hold your tongue or I will take it," Sheridan said with a withering glare.

Lucien laughed mastering his anxiety at being exposed to Kade. "You never truly appreciated her. You took her for granted. Then you abandoned her when she needed you the most and made your own family."

Drawing her arms in around herself, Eve looked into the night away from the fire. Sheridan ignored Lucien and went to Eve's side on the ground.

"Evelyn?"

"You were gone," she said to the trees. "You were gone when papa died. I was all alone in Kitrinostow in a new country. I hated Isfaridesh, but you were in Mergoria and you had Kade. I had no one. But then I met Lucien. He was always there."

Sheridan shook her head. "He tried to bind you using yellow - bind you, Eve."

"Which is why he's now Gray," Eve said defensive for the first time. "Just like your two new friends over there who disrupted the Balance and murdered her own father. What makes them any better?"

"That's more than enough, Evelyn," Kade said with a warning in his voice.

"This isn't about them," Sheridan said redirecting Eve back. "This is about you and me, sister dear.   Make me understand. Make me understand how you lying to me for six years is justified. Explain, Eve."

"I couldn't do it," she yelled. "I couldn't kill him. I don't care what the law said. I don't care what he did. I love him."

"So that makes everything all right?" Sheridan asked incredulous. "It's okay to lie to me, because you love him."

"I never said that," Eve retorted. "But I had no choice."

"You always have a choice," Sheridan said leaning in toward her sister. "Everything is a choice."

"Sheridan, I had to."

"No," Sheridan disagreed getting to her feet. "You didn't have to. It's always a decision." Sheridan started walking away from the fire only marginally slower than a run. "It's always been your choice, Eve."

At Sheridan's departure no one moved, except for Kade. Lowering himself until he was eye-to-eye with Lucien, he flicked his wrist releasing one of his throwing knives into his hand.

"I understand why Faela and even why Jair did what they did to turn Gray," Kade said in a voice that only reached Lucien's ears as he twirled the knife.   "But you are a self-serving coward, Lucien."

Allowing his contempt for Kade to finally show itself on his face, Lucien glared.

"It would be wise for you to be gone by the time I return," Kade told him as he stopped the weapon's rotation with his fingers holding its blade. He offered the knife to Lucien hilt first. "If you're still here when I return, you'll need this."

When Lucien failed to reach for the knife, Kade flicked his wrist again. This time the knife quivered in the log, trapping some of the fabric of Lucien's cloak.

"Keep it," Kade said loud enough for the other's to hear as he rose and left the camp in the same direction Sheridan had gone.

After Sheridan's revelation, the evening progressed with awkward and stilted exchanges. No one knew quite how to react to Sheridan's revelation regarding Haley, so instead of trying to think of something to say, most gave up and crawled into their bedrolls. When Faela tried to sleep, Kade and Sheridan still hadn't returned. She could sympathize with Sheridan's desire to be alone right now and Kade's to provide her with a shoulder and an ear. Despite everything she had experienced and done, the one person Faela could always rely on was her brother. She couldn't fathom how Sheridan must feel.

As she lay drifting to sleep, her thighs twitched from overexertion. The pace she had set that day had exhausted her. When she finally did sleep, disturbing dreams plagued her.

A woman with long silver hair hung suspended in a pillar of blue fire, her toes skimming the ground. Red blossomed from her chest soaking her dress. When the fire disappeared, the woman fell, revealing an adolescent girl in chains with a web of tiny scars crisscrossing her young face. The scenes all shifted one into the next in a blur.

After seeing the woman crumple to the ground for the hundredth time, Faela woke with a start dispelling the nightmare. Morning doves called to one another with more cheerfulness than decent given the hour. It was still the gray before dawn.

Squirming her hips to stretch, Faela felt heat running the length of her back. Then she felt warm, moist breath on the nape of her neck and an arm slung over her hips. She froze, her breath stopping. Her heart raced to a staccato. Slowly turning her head, she saw Jair's mussed hair, his head buried between her shoulder blades.

Exhaling in relief, she threw his arm back toward him. He shifted and rolled onto his back. She couldn't help laughing at his sprawled posture and sat up. Running her fingers through her tangled mess of dew-dampened hair, she twisted it and tied it into a knot. She patted Jair on the leg and wiggled her way out of her bedroll. Stretching her arms over her head, she arched her back. Several pops rippled down her spine. Everyone seemed to still be asleep.

As the first hump of the sun began to stain the horizon, Faela decided to make up for not contacting Sammi last night. She picked her away around the lumps of sleeping people and walked through the small grove of trees.

Pulling out her vial, she leaned her back against the smooth, white trunk. Humming Sammi's lullaby, she closed her eyes. She felt the wind chilling her face as the first rays of sun appeared like someone drawing back a shade. The sounds of people's voice hummed just out of range.

Sammi's wide, gurgling smile fixed in her mind, she reached. She reached for his blood. She reached and she fell as if she had put a hand out to grab a ledge that should be there only to find empty air. With no purchase, her consciousness whipped back into her body. It knocked the air out of her like she had hit the ground from a height.

When she opened her eyes, she lay in the dirt. Pebbles and soil dug into her cheek. She exhaled and the dirt billowed around her. She heard voices swimming above her, but it all sounded like buzzing.

"Don't move her," cautioned a voice. "Faela, can you hear me?"

She felt warm, large hands on her. At the contact, she sucked in a breath and pushed off the ground throwing off the hands. Scurrying backwards, she had a dagger in hand and her eyes glowed red. She blinked.

Mireya and Dathien stood back from her, while Jair, Sheridan, and Kade surrounded her. They all wore similar concerned expressions. Closing her eyes, Faela tried to slow the heaving of her chest. The light receded, but the dagger stayed in her hand.

"Faela, are you okay?" Sheridan asked. "Let me check you. Did you hit your head? What happened? Have you seen Eve and Lucien? Did Lucien do this?"

Her knuckles turned white as she gripped the dagger more tightly. She blinked trying to force her vision to focus when the pain exploded behind her eyes. She gritted her teeth attempting to suppress a cry, but the dagger fell from her fingers and she clamped her hands to her temples. Her eyes watered with pain. They were still asking her questions, but she couldn't push the pain back far enough to make any sense of their words.

Then felt hands covering hers, they dwarfed her own. She felt a rush of warmth. While the pain didn't leave her, it did reduce to a manageable level so she could think again. When she opened her eyes, she saw Kade searching them.

"Are you all right?" he asked his voice at a whisper, but even at that volume it caused her to flinch in pain.

Trying to speak, her throat scraped. She coughed. "Yeah, I think I am."

His hands still held her face. "What happened?"

"I can't remember," she said her eyebrows drawing together. "I woke up and came out here to contact Sammi, then nothing."

"Do you remember seeing anyone else out here?" She identified Sheridan's voice.

"No, no one was up except me," Faela said her head still fuzzy. "Can I have my hands back?"

"Sorry," Kade said immediately releasing them and rocking back to sit on his feet. "So were you in contact with Sammi when everything went dark?"

"I reached for him." Faela brought her hand to her vial. "I reached for him and..." Her narrative trailed off as she remembered searching for his blood to anchor her. She remembered being met by nothing, a void were something should have been. Then it all went dark. Her breathing stopped.

She curled her fingers around the vial and hummed. Instead of reaching for him to make contact, she reached to establish a tracer. She had never tried to place one as far away as Kilrood. Her eyes remained open, but lost behind a red shimmer as she searched.

"What is she doing?" Mireya asked in concern as Faela stared through Kade.

"I think she's trying to find Sammi," Kade guessed, his face a stony mask. "I'd guess she's placing a tracer spell, like the one she used to find Tobias."

Faela stared ahead humming, a red light shone through the thin fabric of her shirt. She stared. A drop of blood fell from her nose onto her chin, another drop fell.

"Kade, she's pushing too far," Sheridan said sinking next to him. "We need to bring her back."

Kade shook his head. "Not yet."

A line of red now trickled from her nose to her chin, but Faela showed no response.

"Where is Sammi supposed to be?" Sheridan asked.

"Kilrood," he said, his eyes never straying from Faela.

"Darkness, Kade," Sheridan gripped his arm, "you can't place a tracer from that far away. I don't care if they share blood."

"Don't underestimate her."

"I'm bringing her back," Sheridan told him as she reached out her hand.

Grabbing her wrist, Kade shook his head.

"Do you want her to die?" Sheridan asked wrenching her wrist away from him.

Faela blinked and drew in a gasping gulp of air. She slumped backward against the tree, her head tilted back. Her fingers clawed at the ground as she brought her gaze down. She looked around at them shaking her head back and forth over and over. Her eyes refocused.

"Did you find him?" Kade asked her.

She froze and looked at Kade with a hollow emptiness. "He's gone."

"What do you mean gone?" Sheridan asked.

Shoving her back against the trunk, her feet scrambled against the dirt for purchase to stand. Kade rose and helped her up. She threw his hands off and tangled her fingers into her hair and tapped the sides of her head with her thumbs. She turned in tiny circles.

"Faela, what happened?" Sheridan repeated.

Her eyes feral, Faela was muttering to herself inaudibly. Mireya put her hands on either side of Faela's face, forcing her to stop and look at her.

"He's gone," she repeated trying to make the words not true. She gripped Mireya's hand on her face, mashing her fingers together. "Only void, only nothing. Where there should be, there is nothing."

"What do you mean, Faela?" Mireya asked.

"Kilrood," was all the she said. "Must leave now. Must find

what should be. Must make the nothing, something. Must leave."

"You're not making any sense," Sheridan said her voice a controlled calm.

Crushing Mireya's hand, with terror in her eyes, she pleaded with her. "I can't find him. We have to find him."

"Her son," Kade explained as her panic hit him like a physical blow. "She was trying to contact him right before she blacked out. She failed to establish her anchor."

"What?" Jair demanded feeling helpless as he watched as Faela stood paralyzed. "What does that mean?"

Sheridan couldn't bring herself to say the words for fear of what it would do to Faela.

"It means we're going to Kilrood," Kade said. "Jair, you stay here with Mireya and Dathien. Do not leave this spot. Otherwise, we won't be able to find you. No arguments. Sheridan, take us to the Tereskan temple at Kilrood."

Sheridan threw her hands up in defeat. She walked over to where Faela stood with Mireya. Mireya hugged Faela who barely registered the girl's presence.

"Can you take us both at once?" Kade asked her coming alongside Sheridan.

"Combined the three of us don't weigh as much as Eve's darkness-blighted horse."

Kade's coat strained against his back as he laced his arms across his chest. "Good."

"I don't know how long this is going to take," Sheridan warned the trio staying behind. "Just in case, Mireya, take this." Sheridan removed her silver, knot-work ring and tossed it to Mireya who caught it with both hands. "If something goes wrong, I should be able to find you with this.'"

Sheridan put her palms on Kade and Faela's backs, indigo light surrounded them as the pressure descended.

CHAPTER TWENTY-THREE

The indigo light faded like vapors as Rivka and Vaughn strode out of the receiving chamber of the Phaidrian temple in Lanvirdis.

With a smile and slight inclination of her head, Rivka paused to thank the adolescent boy who had transported them from Vamorines. "Please do give Hewitt my regards, Digory, and tell him that I haven't forgotten that I owe him a scion and king's rematch."

Bowing awkwardly, Digory flushed and with a flash and a pop he, returned to Wistholt across the continent to deliver her message.

With a hand on her back, Vaughn directed Rivka into the hallway. "We need to visit the storehouses first. We need to make sure that cargo hasn't left port yet."

As they strode down the hall, a plump man in green robes carried a flowering potted plant close to his chest as he wandered down the hall as if lost in thought. When he heard their footfall, he raised his head as if confused to find someone else here. Seeing them, he tangled his feet in his robe's hem as he skidded to a stop.

"Scion," he stammered in shock as he pressed himself up against the wall to remain upright, "we had no word of your arrival in Lanvirdis." Some soil now sprinkled his robe and the floor, but he had managed to keep hold of the plant in his flailing.

"The fact that we did not send word might be the culprit," Vaughn suggested offhand.

"Will you be requiring accommodations?" He swallowed repeatedly clearly nervous.

"No, but you have my thanks," Rivka responded with a smile. "We won't be here long." Approaching him, she linked arms with the man and steered him down the hall. He shifted the pot to into the opposite arm clumsily, but successfully. "I have to beg your pardon. It's been some time since I've been to the Phaidrian temple, I'm afraid I don't know your name." Rivka exuded serene competence.

"Maurice, mum." He fumbled over the words.

"My thanks, Maurice. But what you can do for me is let Wieland know that I'm here and wish to speak with him after supper." Rivka gave him a smile, the kind of smile that let him know that he was in on a secret. "Can you do this one thing for me, Maurice?"

Maurice bowed his head nodding his assent. "Immediately, jha'na."

Rivka smiled again. "You are a credit to your Order."

Bowing low at the waist, Maurice hugged the potted flower close and backed away from Rivka around the corner. He bumped into the wall as he turned and disappeared from sight.

"Let's go find this warehouse," Rivka told Vaughn her face transformed. Sober determination replaced the easy peacefulness of her earlier countenance. "I want this finished."

Nodding, Vaughn and Rivka made their way out of the temple and into the city streets, heading for the wharf. It was dark on the streets, but gaslight danced and flickered in the wind whipping off Diarmid Bay that Lanvirdis perched around. Rivka's dress billowed behind her in the wind like those same flames as they walked. Soon they found themselves in the warehouse district of the docks.

The smell of waterlogged wood and decay filled the air as they approached the brick storehouse. Running down the corner of the building were dark streaks where water had overflowed from the building's gutters.

Though Rivka had wanted to deny what Vaughn had reported, she knew that this confrontation had been building for a long time. She interlaced her fingers as she waited on Vaughn. Without him, she had little hope of crossing Daniyelan wardings. His wrists glowing blue for a moment, Vaughn opened the door. He untangled Rivka's hand and led her through the barrier.

Closing the door behind them with a soft click, Vaughn turned and a deserted warehouse met him. Every crate that had been stacked higher than a man's head and had lined the bottom of the floor was gone. In its place sat a single chair. In that chair slumped a small figure. The figure's head fell down so that its chin rested on its chest.

Vaughn swept pass Rivka to the chair. Black hair stuck out in every direction from the figure's head. He increased his stride and halted by the figure and raised the person's head with a hand. It was Wes.

Her face had a spider's web of tiny crisscrossed, half-healed burns. She stirred at the touch. Kneeling, Vaughn untied her hands. Her wrists were raw and covered in blood from the rope. Still holding her chin, Vaughn shook her with his free hand.

"Wes, can you hear me?" he asked his voice gentle.

Wes mumbled something and her eyes fluttered. She lifted her chin out of Vaughn's grasp and looked up at him from slitted eyes.

"You came back," she said, her voice scratchy.

"I told you I would," Vaughn said with quiet conviction.

"Thought you was long gone," she said licking her cracked lips.

Rivka put a hand on Vaughn's shoulder. "Vaughn would never abandon a comrade, my dear."

"I ain't your dear," Wes said rolling her shoulders, which ached horribly. "Ain't no one ever come for me."

"Wes, how did you get here?" Vaughn asked holding her up in the seat now that she was unbound.

"Day after you left, some Daniyelans cornered me. Said I was a traitor working with the Virds. Bunch of sods, they was. They asked me about you, but I told them I ain't know nothing. Then they threw me in here."

Vaughn traced his thumb lightly along one of the burns. "Who did this, Wes?"

"The slick one with the fancy words," Wes said wincing, "Tomas. He said the Virds was conspiring against the Tereskans and that he needed to stop them. He said if we didn't stop them then they would all die. I told him to stuff it."

"Brave, if imprudent, words, Wes," Rivka said her eyes grateful, "Tomas Segar is not a man to be trifled with."

"He made me watch," Wes said her lips twitching. "Said I needed to see the consequences of my choices."

"Made you watch what?" Vaughn asked, his voice wary and

dangerous.

"The tragedy that occurred yesterday in Kilrood," answered a melancholic voice that echoed through the warehouse. "Had she but told me their plans, I could have prevented it."

Rivka and Vaughn turned to see Tomas enter the building with six battle dressed Daniyelans at his back. The aged sorrow of his young face seemed incongruous with his carelessly tousled brown hair as he approached them. His hands hid in the folds of his orange robes of office, its sleeves dipping past his knees. He stopped and brought his hands together. The fabric tumbled back into the crook of his elbow.

"Rivka, my dear, you look radiant as always. Vaughn, I do wish you had come straight to me with this. Then maybe we could have stopped them together."

"What exactly were you trying to stop?" Rivka asked with a graceful arch of an eyebrow.

"Some dissidents, Vird hold outs from the war, attacked the Tereskan temple in Kilrood yesterday. We received word this morning," Tomas said shaking his head as he recalled the events. "I sent some of my men to investigate and they just reported back. I made the girl watch their findings. The only word for what they found is slaughter. It seems that no one survived, such a senseless waste."

Holding her anger in check, Rivka heard the sincerity of Tomas' last statement in his voice. He had meant what he said.

Appearing unruffled, she interlaced her hands. "What of Ianos?"

"They could not find his body in the carnage," Tomas said his forehead creased with concern. "He's unaccounted for, but we've received no demands if he lives."

Refusing to tip her hand, Rivka continued to allow Tomas steer the conversation. "What could they hope to accomplish by attacking the Tereskans?"

"Revenge?" Tomas suggested his voice tinged with disgust. "Who can tell really with these kinds of malcontents? But what is clear, from the intelligence I received mere days ago, is that a shipment of weapons went south and reached their port in time to supply these butchers.

"I only learned of it just after Vaughn left Lanvirdis and from what my sources tell me, we were chasing the same information. I have to say I am hurt that he didn't stop by to see Wieland and me, but I do understand how pressing the demands of the Nikelan Grier can be. It grieves me that we could not work together to prevent this terrible loss."

"Had it been possible, I would have called on you, Tomas. But it is just as you say the demands of my lady surpass all others. Were you able to trace the shipment?" Vaughn asked playing along with Rivka's ploy. "Who was backing them?"

"That's the part that stings the most," Tomas explained with a sigh. "Right here in Lanvirdis, right under my nose. Layton Norris, the harbormaster, let the shipments pass without inspection, because the cargo was sent by the Nabosian council as relief for the flooded towns along the northern coast of Mergoria. We learned too late that the council was smuggling the weapons to their supporters."

"And after all the aid you've given for the reconstruction, Tomas," Rivka told him with a sympathetic smile and met his gaze. "What a betrayal."

"I have yet to arrest the members on the council I believe involved," Tomas told her extending her an arm in invitation to walk with him. "It would strengthen me greatly to have you there when they are questioned. Can you stay for the trial? It would give the people peace of mind to see the Nikelan Scion here during such a dark time."

Rivka looped her arm through his and walked toward the windows. "I am afraid I have pressing business, Tomas. We cannot stay long, but I would speak to the accused. Also, I ask you one small favor in return."

"Anything, Rivka, you have but to name it," Tomas told her patting her hand as they looked out the paned glass to the darkened harbor below.

"Would you put the girl into my custody?" Rivka smiled with the same unearthly stillness that seemed to infuse her very skin. "Vaughn is fond of her and we could always use another girl in the kitchens or the stables perhaps. I seem to recall Vaughn telling me she has an affinity for horses."

"I don't know, Rivka," Tomas said his eyebrows dipping. "She is a thief and a sympathizer with the Vird rebels. I couldn't live with myself if anything were to happen to either of you."

"We would be safe enough with her," Rivka reassured him. "Just as a favor, Tomas."

Tomas sighed and gave her a disapproving glance. "Against my better judgment, you may take her. Hopefully, she's young enough to salvage."

"You are too kind, Tomas." Rivka squeezed his arm and rotated him back toward Vaughn and the chair. "Where will you take the accused once they are in custody?"

"I would question them in Kilrood if I could," Tomas said with a grimace. "Make them see and smell the destruction they've caused, but there is no time. So I will question them at the keep. My men are collecting them now. Would you accompany me?"

"Naturally," Rivka said her voice sobered by the task ahead of them. "Let me speak with Vaughn for but a moment."

Tomas mistook her remorse for a desire to avoid the interrogations and inclined his head with a compassionate smile before he returned to his escorts leaving Rivka alone with Vaughn and Wes.

When he was out of earshot, Rivka said, "I want to see whom he's trying to implicate, but more importantly, I want witnesses from outside the Orders there when I renounce him. Wes, do you need to rest? We can send you to the Phaidrian temple to await us."

Wes shook her head. "I be fine. I want to go with you, yeah?"

Despite the difficulties facing them, Rivka mouth tugged up at the girl's unyielding determination. Vaughn had been right about her. "Very well."

CHAPTER TWENTY-FOUR

Faela felt like her stomach had stayed behind in the grove when the purple light dissipated around them like smoke. They stood in the Amserian receiving chamber of the Tereskan temple. She knew the very stones of this place. She knew their shape, their touch, their smell. It took her only a moment to realize that something was wrong.

Removing herself from Sheridan, she listened. An awful silence greeted her - no hum of activity, no buzzing of far away voices, but it was more than that. The silence went deeper to a cold and still place. That was when she smelled it.

The metallic tang of blood hit the back of her throat. It wasn't the faint hint of blood. The smell clung to the stones, tainting the foundations of building.

Without a word, she raced out of the receiving chamber. Ianos' private chambers were close. As soon as any news arrived to the temple, he had always wanted immediate access, a habit he had developed during his years with the Amserian Order.

Behind her, she heard Kade and Sheridan calling, but she kept running. Nothing could compel her to stop. Her hair streamed back as she ran past splattered walls with bloody streaks smeared across the floor. The echo of her boots as she ran filled her ears pushing out any other sounds. She saw nothing, but the hall weaving in front of her until she reached the double doors. She stopped. The doors stood shut.

She had pushed these doors open so many times. She remembered when she was so small that she had to stretch on her toes just to reach the handle. Now those same handles rested just above her waist. All she had to do was move her fingers mere inches to open the door, but something held her back.

For some reason, now that she had made it, she wanted the door to remain shut. So she stood, her arms dangling at her sides. She heard the reverberation of footsteps echoing off the foyer ceiling as Kade and Sheridan finally caught her.

She had felt possessed by the need to find Sammi in the grove, to know that he was all right, to know that something was wrong with her, that he was fine, that she would find him safe, but now, dread seized her limbs, paralyzing her. She could not open the door.

She heard Kade's voice and she blinked. Inclining her face, she stared at him blankly having no idea what he had just said to her.

"It's the temple," Faela told him matter-of-factly, "but it's a shell. Nothing's inside. Everything got ripped out."

"I don't think she's sailing with all hands on deck any more," Sheridan said to Kade in a low voice. Using every trick she had learned while training in these halls, Sheridan suppressed her conscious awareness of the devastation and distanced herself from it as best she could.

"No," Faela responded, "I'm here. They've gone away, not me. They left me."

"See," Sheridan hissed under her breath with genuine concern. "You know that any severe emotional distress can push a mind healer into madness."

"Sheridan," Kade said in a monotone, "go see if anyone's left."

Sheridan nodded and trotted back across the entryway her lips beginning to turn white.

"And be careful," he called after her as she disappeared from sight. "Faela, where should we start looking?"

At the question, understanding passed over her face before the fear took over. She wrenched the handles open and pushed the doors aside. Papers, books, broken glass, and dirt from overturned planters littered the floor of the room, but Faela registered none of the destruction. One thing captured her attention, a woven, reed bassinet standing next to the desk.

She didn't remember crossing the room, but within the next breath she stood over it, looking into its shadows. She pushed back the soft, tickling folds of the green blanket, a part of the same blanket that she carried with her. The cradle was empty.

When her fingers grazed the bottom of the blanket, it felt stiff. She pulled it out and it unfurled to her knees. Clutching it in her hands, she saw dried blood caked the fabric. Soundlessly, her legs buckled unable to hold up her own weight and she stumbled to her knees.

She stared down at the fabric, remembering the last time she had held Sammi. He had been wrapped in this blanket. Now it was empty, just like the bassinet. There was a patch on the end that where the fabric had been worn down. Sammi used to cling to that edge of the blanket when he slept.

She ran her thumb over the frayed fabric. She jumped when she felt a hand touch her shoulder. She looked up. Kade knelt across from her.

"Sheridan is trying to find someone. We'll discover what happened here, I promise. Is there anywhere else we can look?"

"Gone," Faela told him as she lifted the blanket toward him. Her thumbs glided over the stains of blood as scarlet light covered her eyes, but nothing appeared. It had been too long since the blood had been spilled. She would discover nothing this way.

Sheridan strode into the room her eyes dry, but rimmed with red. Inclining his head to her, Sheridan came and crouched down next to them.

She shook her head. "No one's left. The bodies," she said glancing sidelong at Faela, "they were taken to the great hall and dumped there. I didn't see..." Sheridan cleared her throat. "I couldn't find anything. Who could have done this, Kade? For there to be as many as I saw in there would have required strong magic and a good deal of training. Tereskans are far from helpless."

"I can't see," Faela interrupted holding up the blanket to Kade again. "I can't see anything. It's been too long. The life is gone now."

"That actually made sense," Sheridan said leaning forward.

Kade ignored her. "Faela, I hate to ask," he said as gently as he could, "but do you know whose blood it is?"

Faela swallowed, letting her hand fall into her lap. "Samuel's. It's Sammi's."

"He could still be all right, Faela," Sheridan suggested though her tone revealed that she couldn't even convince herself that her words were true, not after what she had seen in the great hall.

"Whoever did this may have taken him."

Faela swiveled her deadened gaze to Sheridan. "Don't lie to me. Don't try to make this all right. Nothing about this is all right." Faela stood without warning. "Look around you. Look at it. My home has been destroyed. My brothers and sisters murdered. Even if Sammi is," her voice caught as the numbness gradually wore off, "even if he's alive, he's gone. But you mark my words, I will find him. Just don't try to make this all right."

Her hand clenched around the fabric as she avoided Sheridan and left the room.

"At least she sounds lucid now," Sheridan said in a weak voice as Kade stood and ran after Faela. Alone in the room, Sheridan said to herself, "Brilliant, way to be comforting, Sheridan."

Kade caught Faela easily in the hallway as she headed toward the strongest source of the bloodshed, the great hall. "Faela, wait. Where are you going?"

She stopped with an echoing slid. "He's not here. I can look in every corner, but from the moment we arrived I knew. I knew before we even came. He's not here. I need to know what happened here. I need to know who did this."

"So we can find Sammi," Kade concluded stepping next to her.

Faela said nothing and started to tremble. It felt like the void in her chest had ripped open and would swallow her.

"Please stop," she said in a choked whisper.

"Stop?" Kade asked confused.

"Stop saying his name," her voice shook, "just please stop. If you keep saying it, I won't be able to keep my hold here. I'll go away again. I can't help if I go back there."

"Go where?" Kade asked trying to understand.

"The place where nothing can reach me. No other voices, no other emotions, no other thoughts, just me," she said with a small voice and slumped shoulders as she stared at another brownish smear of blood leading away from them. "I shouldn't even think about it or I risk getting pulled back there again and I have to be here. Don't let me go back. Please, Kade. Without Ianos, I'll get trapped if I stay there too long."

"I'll stop," he assured her. "What do you need?"

"I need to find him."

Kade nodded as he looked at the cascade of strawberry blonde waves obscuring her face. "Then I'll go."

"Go?" Faela gripped the edges of her sleeves and pulled at them. "Go where?"

"Not where, when," Kade corrected her with a half-smile.

"But it will take days to search each room of the temple trying to find the right time and place," Faela argued finally raising her eyes.

Kade shook his head. "No, it won't. Not with your help and with my abilities."

"Anything," Faela agreed without thinking. "Anything you need."

"You need to let me in," he told her looking into her eyes. "I need to see him the way you do. I need your blood connection to him as his mother. You need to take down your barriers."

Faela looked at him from under her eyebrows as if weighing her options. He could see the slight tremors rippling across her frame.

Doing this would require her to sacrifice what little privacy and autonomy she had left. That possibility scared her almost as much as the prospect of losing Sammi. That fear for her son, however, overcame any fears she had of losing herself. Without him, she would have nothing left.

Only one thing caused her to hesitate. Her skin crawled at the thought of using Kade this way, but he had suggested it, not her.

"I know I'm asking much of you," Kade began.

"You don't know what you're asking," she said her usually steady voice wavering. "You couldn't understand what you're asking."

"It's the only way I know how to help," he said closing the gap between them as he looped a strand of her hair behind an ear. "Let me help."

Faela let out a shaky breath and nodded her head once. "Are you willing to accept the consequences?"

"I wouldn't have suggested it if I weren't."

"Understand that once I do this," Faela said searching his eyes for a glimmer of hesitation, "I may never be able to sever the connection again. It will always be there for the rest of our lives.

Do you still want to do this?"

Resolutely, he returned her gaze and nodded. "Of course."

Faela stepped toward him and slid her hands against his. Their palms flush against one another, she twined her fingers through his. Scarlet light sparked from her hands and enveloped both of them. She looked deeply into his warm amber eyes and pulled a single thread in the weaving of her barriers. They unraveled around her mind and waiting just the other side of the link was Kade's.

Focusing her thoughts on Sammi, she remembered the first time she had seen his squished and wrinkled, red face when Ianos had placed him in her arms. She remembered his thoughts brushing hers the moment he looked into her mirrored silver eyes, how he had captured her finger with surprising strength. She remembered how boneless he felt in her arms when he slept and how he would always kick his left leg when he dreamed.

She felt Kade's wonder as he experienced each of these memories as though they were his own. Halting the tide of shared recollection, she focused instead on the unique signature contained in Sammi's blood, like a bouncing harmony to her smooth melody, similar in key but with decidedly different arrangements.

Finished, she opened her eyes. Kade's eyes shone bright and his cheeks were wet. Faela shoved the thoughts away again for fear of being overwhelmed by them. Kade winced at the abruptness with which the wall appeared.

Faela apologized and began to ask him if he had what he needed, but he interrupted before the words left her mouth. "Yeah, it was." Kade had heard the thought a half second before she had spoken it. "Well, that's new."

Faela forced herself to think about what Kade had to do now instead of the consequences of what she had just done. "So what happens now?"

"Now, I step back," Kade said letting go of her hands as he physically took a step backward and disappeared in a flash of violet light.

When the light vanished, Kade surveyed the hall. The blood was gone from the floor and the walls. It was before the massacre had occurred. Now he just needed to find Sammi.

Kade jogged down the hall back toward Ianos' study where they had found the bassinet. He passed Tereskans going about their business, but none stopped or even acknowledged him. As he turned the corner, a girl with curly blonde hair in a seeker's sickroom apron looked back over her shoulder. She thought she had seen something moving out of the corner of her eye, but when she turned to look, she saw nothing. Despite the fact that Kade stood directly in her field of vision, she looked right past him.

Crossing the entryway, he opened the doors to Ianos' study and shut them behind him. As he turned to examine the room, he heard a voice.

"Can I help you?" the man's pleasant baritone inquired.

Kade froze. No one should be able to see someone who had stepped back. He turned assuming the person had directed their question to someone who had entered moments before him. But when he looked, Ianos stood behind his desk staring directly at Kade.

Clearing his throat, Kade walked further into the room. As he approached Ianos, he saw behind his desk. A green blanket spread out on the floor and lying on his stomach Sammi pushed himself up on his arms babbling to himself. He continued pushing until he managed to awkwardly shift into a sitting position. Quite pleased with himself, he looked up at Ianos with a wide smile that revealed a few tiny white teeth. Seeing Sammi alive and happy halted Kade in his tracks rendering him speechless.

When he offered no explanation or reason for his intrusion, Ianos looked from Sammi to Kade. "I know my office isn't the most likely location for a nursery, but I trust you've seen a baby before."

Kade tore his gaze from Sammi who had just managed to wrap his hands around a stuffed lamb and happily gnawed on one of its legs. Trying to keep Faela's emotions and memories surging within his mind restrained, he said his voice tight, "Not this one."

"Do I know you?" Ianos asked him watching him even more closely now.

"Kaedman Hawthorn, jha'na." As he resisted the urge to try to grab Sammi and run, he added lamely, "I studied here during the war."

Still assessing Kade, Ianos watched his eyes and saw the edges around Kade's face shimmer as though transparent. "Ah, yes, I thought you looked familiar. You're taller than I remembered. But what brings you back here that requires you to barge into my offices?"

Kade was unsure how to explain or what to even say. As a stepper he should appear as little more than a shadow to any who caught sight of him, yet Ianos Wilkerson stood conversing with him.

"Sir, I wish I could tell you, but I can't," Kade answered him truthfully, but his eyes kept searching out Sammi. Drool covered his chin as well as the lamb that he now bounced off of his legs. Kade couldn't stop the smile it evoked.

"Can't or won't?" Ianos said folding his hands together.

"Can't, sir. I wish I could, you have no idea how much I wish that I could." Kade's eyes held a tortured glint as they slid back to Sammi. The slight shift in his posture caused Ianos to see right through him as though he vanished.

"You're a stepper," Ianos told him point blank with a penetrating gaze.

"Yes," Kade admitted shocked by Ianos' bluntness.

"And you're not here for me, are you?" Ianos said already knowing the truth of the matter.

"Not entirely, no."

"I won't ask you what's happened, I wouldn't put you into such a compromising position. But please at least tell me how she is?" Ianos asked the lines around his eyes deepening with concern.

Startled again by his perceptiveness, Kade answered without really thinking. "You really don't want me to answer that." When he saw the pain shadowed in Ianos' eyes, he drew in a breath and exhaled. "She misses you, but she never says so. But being separated from Sammi is like a part of her is missing and she's trying to overcompensate for the absence. She tries to hide it, but the sadness never really leaves. It's the same with the guilt."

"She never was one to let the past go," Ianos said with an

affectionate smile. "But I'm glad to see that she's no longer alone. But if you've come back here, then I have a feeling she's going to need that bond more than ever."

"Bond?" Kade was surprised by the stress he had given the word.

"Brother Hawthorn, I trained her," Ianos said with a quirk of his mouth. "Her work is distinctive and unique both in ability and execution. I can't say I'm entirely pleased by this, but I know that young woman. She would not have forged a permanent link without compelling reasons. Reasons that I trust have to do with the young man drooling all over himself on the floor."

"I can't say," Kade evaded. He hated tiptoeing around what awaited them. He wanted to yell at Ianos to evacuate the temple before it was too late, but he knew that he could not. What was done was already done. It was then that Kade heard the first shriek.

Ianos shot a glance at Kade whose eyes fixed on Sammi. Kade did not know who was coming, but what.

"So it comes at last," Ianos said under his breath as he opened his bottom desk drawer.

The sounds of shouted orders and boots came muffled through the heavy doors.

Ianos grabbed a thin-bladed knife from the worktable behind him and pulled it across his palm. "You knew what you were coming to find, Brother Hawthorn, yet you still came. That tells me much about the kind of man you are. If they've made it this far into the temple, then we're already lost."

He dribbled the blood running from his cut palm into the vial he had removed from the desk. With his thumb, he pushed the stopper back into place.

He placed the vial deep into a crack in the mortar where the window met the wall. "You must make sure she finds this."

"I can't change anything," Kade told him his eyes desperate as the noises came closer. "You shouldn't even be able to see me."

"You aren't the only one with a room at Wistholt," Ianos said in explanation. "How else do you think I kept her sane all these years? Though my ability works slightly different from yours as I'm sure you've noticed."

Ianos knelt down and scooped an agitated Sammi into his arms who promptly grabbed the sleeve of his robes.

Hugging him close, Ianos placed Sammi in the bassinet with his blanket. "They will be here soon. I can feel the lives of my Order being snuffed out one by one as they move toward this room. Do you think me callus for not having fought back to protect them?"

Kade did not know how to answer such a question. "I don't know what to think."

"There are only a handful of ways these butchers could have survived their initial assault and none of them bode well for our chances. Whoever has done this will try to hide their involvement. Don't let them. Bring them into the light of the truth. This is the tragedy of a stepper, you must watch atrocities that have already occurred and can do nothing. I am sorry, but you must witness this. Someone must give the dead a voice."

Kade could hear them just outside the door now. His voice was clear. "This is why I came."

"Because the men coming through that door are Daniyelans, Kaedman Hawthorn. They won't be dressed like them, but they alone possess the knowledge necessary to set any of the spells that could neutralize my people."

The door began to give way as Ianos picked up a staff resting in the corner and twirled it in his right hand. Two men spattered with blood burst through the door. At the noise, Sammi's whimpering turned into bawling. It distracted the invaders and the first did not see Ianos as the staff caught him under the chin shattering his jaw. The second fared little better as Ianos brought the back end of the staff around to crush his skull, but they were only the first wave. Ianos backed into the study to give himself more room to maneuver.

"Don't harm him," came the bark of a command behind the men. "We need him alive and intact. Any mark he receives, I'll give you its twin myself."

A man with bronzed hair tied back into a high ponytail swept into the room. He flashed Ianos a grim smile and bowed low. "It's been too long, jha'na."

"Eli Westington," Ianos said lowering his weapon, but not

dropping his defensive guard. "I wouldn't have thought even Tomas would have the gall to send you."

Kade felt like the man writhing on the floor. He had trained with this man, served with this man. Eli Westington was the Daniyelan liaison to the militias of every nation. He always was a little too interested in the politics behind the militias, but that was what made him good at his job. He was a man of conviction, conviction that Kade had always respected.

"You misunderstand, jha'na," Eli told him with an appalled stare. "We're here to save you. We caught wind of this uprising of the Virds and were dispatched at once, but I fear we were too late. You mistook two of my men for the invaders. I wanted to ensure my men did not retaliate without identifying the target. Thank the Light we made it to you in time."

Ianos planted the butt of his staff on the stone floor with a resounding thunk, his eyes like granite. "Stop insulting me, Eli. I may be old, but I'm not senile quite yet. I know why you've come."

Eli's face maintained a concerned look. "Tomas did say you had kept in contact with that Nikelan nomad witch. It's a pity really, but my orders remain the same. Darkness, where is that horrible racket coming from?"

Sammi still cried out, confused by the noises and yelling. Taking off his gloves, Eli walked over to the bassinet where Sammi lay. He pushed back the blankets to reveal the little boy within. His face was red and wet and his tiny fists thrust into the air.

Kade circled the desk and gripped its edge staring down Eli, but the man saw nothing. His knuckles were white.

"Darkness, why is there a baby here?" Eli asked with a genuinely confused expression. "We were told nothing of this."

Ianos made to move to the bassinet only to be met by one of the Daniyelans' swords. "Hurt that child and I will run myself onto this man's blade. Do you understand me, Eli? If you hurt him, you will have to explain why you failed to Tomas. Do you really want to do that?"

"I have no wish to harm a child, jha'na," Eli told him sincerely. "But what is the life of one child when compared to the lives of all the children in the world? After today, the people will be united for the first time since the Shattering. We will have peace, true and lasting peace." Eli reached his hand into the bassinet.

Kade made to grab for him, but Ianos reacted first. He brought his staff around and knocked the man in front of him out of the way and spun it to catch Eli in the shoulder. He staggered away from the bassinet and fell near where Kade stood breathing raggedly.

"Jha'na," Eli growled, "that was a very big mistake."

Ianos stood between Eli and Sammi. "No life is more important than another. You have no right to decide that this child's death is justified, because it will achieve some illusion of the greater good. Who are you to decide who lives and dies, Eli?"

"Who am I?" Eli said smoothing back his burnished hair that had fallen into his face. His eyes were hidden in flickering darkness though the light of the lamps shone on them. His hands glowed with an oily, black fire. "I am the divine hand of justice and justice is terrible."

Flicking his wrist, the black fire coiled around Ianos like snakes writhing around him tightly before they sunk into him leaving only a momentary ash. The staff clattered to the ground with a resonating echo of finality.

"With my shielding, your cowardly Tereskans tricks won't on me, but you already knew that. Otherwise, you wouldn't have been waiting with this." Eli bent and balanced the staff in his palm. "But I can't have you hurting yourself. Sometimes justice demands a hard price from us, jha'na. One from which we cannot turn or look away."

Holding Ianos' gaze, he walked past him to the bassinet. All Kade could hear was the blood pounding in his ears and the clicking of Eli's boots on the stones and the low whimpering of Sammi who had cried his throat raw.

Kade swung his gaze from Ianos back to Eli. He could see the seams of Eli's protection spell and the weakest point in the binding spell that held Ianos. Eli reached his hand into the crib. Sammi's whimpering returned to a distressed bawling. Kade's chest felt like it was being crushed by a vice.

He knew he could do nothing that he watched little better than a shadow puppet reenactment. These events had already occurred, but that didn't matter. His rational understanding of his helplessness didn't matter. Sammi's cries grew louder, then muffled as fingers wrapped around his fragile neck. A sound like the snapping of a wishbone hit Kade like a kick to the gut.

"No!" Kade bellowed and released his orange magic like a knocked arrow aimed between Eli's shoulders. The magic rushed back at him like molten iron. It felt like liquid fire pumped through every vein and muscle. The fire that always smoldered inside every Daniyelan seemed to erupt within him raging out of his control. In his agony, he heard the silence. The cries had stopped.

Though every portion of him felt like it was being scorched away, he suddenly felt an icy cold grip him as though it dragged him to the bottom of a glacial lake. In an explosion of light and pain, he was hurled back against the wall. He hit with a crunch and fell crumpled on the floor of the hallway where he had left Faela.

"Kade, can you hear me?"

He felt the fire melting away leaving behind the cold alone. His body shuddered at the sudden perceived drop in temperature. His lips looked like purple bruises.

"Can you feel your fingers and toes? Kade, you need to answer me."

He wiggled his fingers and twitched his foot. "Yes," he eventually managed to stammer through chattering teeth.

He felt soft hands roll him onto his side and warm fingers at his temples.

"Wait here. I don't think I have to tell you not to move, because I don't you could if you wanted to, but don't."

He heard footsteps moving away from him and his mind floated in the silence. Silence had never felt so empty to him before. He had always liked silence, but not today, not now. Before he realized any time had passed, the footsteps returned and he felt something heavy being tucked around him. Its rough weave scratched against his exposed skin.

He heard the voice saying, "This is no good, you're too heavy, but you can't stay on the stone or we'll never raise your body temperature fast enough. Kade, I need you to help me, okay?"

He nodded his head. He couldn't even manage a monosyllabic response with how steadily he shook. He felt hands slip under his shoulders, raising him up off the floor. He tried to lean his weight forward to help. He felt the warmth of another body against his back. It was soft, comfortable. Arms wrapped around his chest, adding more warmth. He rested his head back against the body's shoulder. He smelled dirt and dew and blood.

He didn't know how long he sat there, but gradually the tremors finally stopped. Two voices drifted above him as he tried to break through the surface of the haze enclosing him. Both voices sounded tired. He finally opened his eyes and saw Sheridan sitting directly across the hallway from him.

"So you decided to grace us with your consciousness," Sheridan said with a forced smile. She rocked forward, her eyebrows love over her troubled expression. "Um, Faela. I think you need to see this."

"This?" came the voice from directly above his ear.

He shifted and an arm uncoiled from around his abdomen. He felt the back of her hand on his neck and cheek.

"I think he's returned to a safe internal temperature."

He felt the warmth running along the length of his back move away as Faela adjusted him so that he slouched propped against the wall. Faela's face came into his vision and she checked his body for any other signs of trauma, but it took only a moment for her to see what Sheridan had meant. Her breath caught in a gasp.

"That hideous?" he asked as he resettled himself causing a ripple of pain in his muscles.

"Kade, what did you do?" Faela inquired in a low breath. "You've turned."

He remembered what Faela and Jair had said to Tobias. It felt like being consumed by fire, that's what they had both said. Kade turned his eyes to Faela's and moved toward her. Seeing his face reflected in those silver pools, his brown eyes were gone replaced by his own moonlit mirrors.

"Huh," he said resting back against the wall, "well, that's new."

Chapter Twenty-Five

Marion Lowe's townhouse sat on the corner between Ivycrest Lane and Lamp Wright Street in the market district of Lanvirdis. It was a modest, but comfortable golden brick row house ringed by a wrought iron fence and over the slate walkway arched a trellis covered with wisteria vines. Marion Lowe had moved into these apartments after she had taken control of Irondawn House thirty years ago.

Securing her position as Irondawn's next leader within the Merchant Houses had come at a cost, but then again she had never considered mercy as a virtue. She had lacked the advantages of the old families. As a daughter of a sailor, who went down in a gale off the eastern cost of Isfaridesh when she was only nine, life had hardened her to its injustice at a young age. But what she wanted for in pedigree, she more than compensated for in cunning. If her reputation were to be believed, the last upstart to challenge her claim now enjoyed an early retirement at the bottom of Diarmid Bay.

It was well past supper when the hurried banging at the door roused Marion's household staff. The damp, cold night air drifted in through the hall and down into her study. She shivered as she reached on her tiptoes to pull a volume off the top shelf, when her steward, Irwin, cleared his throat from the office's open double doors.

"Mum, there's a Daniyelan messenger waiting in the parlor," he informed her while she cracked the book open in her palm.

Flipping through the pages, Marion sneezed at the musty smell of the parchment. "What in the bloody name of Darkness could Segar want at this hour, blast the man? Ah, never mind me, Irwin. I just hate the cold."

She tucked the book under her arm as she walked down the green wool runner that lined the hall, her bare toes sinking into its pile. Like Marion herself, it was simple and unadorned.

When she entered the parlor, she spotted a black-haired Daniyelan in battle dress waiting by the hearth. He was admiring the painting, lit by gas lamps that hung over the fireplace. It was a rendering of the destruction of Gialdanis. The painter had taken some creative liberties with the large gouts of flame that cracked open its streets, but Marion still liked the painting. It reminded her that no matter how immutable a power might seem, everything falls eventually.

"What do you want, lawman?" Marion said in her gruff and blunt way. While she had lost the thick accent of the fishing village in which she had spent her childhood, she had never managed to lose their direct manner of address.

"Mum," the man said bowing his head in respect, but he did not flinch from maintaining eye contact, "your presence is requested at the keep for an emergency council meeting."

"Why is one of Segar's pups calling me for such a gathering?" she asked, her natural suspicion raising the hairs on the back of her neck.

No emotions flickered across the Daniyelan's face at her jibe; he merely answered her question. "Scion Segar has not called the meeting, Scion Rivka Peacemaker has."

Marion grunted in surprise. "The Nikelan woman has peeked her nose outside the Boundary, has she? Well, I wouldn't miss this for all the silk of Kitrinostow." She turned her back on the Daniyelan to leave the room. "Run back to your master and tell him I'll be along directly."

It didn't take Marion long to dress in a manner befitting the Merchant House's representative in Nabos. One of her maids had arranged her graying black hair into a cascade of curls at the crown of her head with two silver sticks, while the other had cinched her into a cream colored corset with boned seams. Her emerald green shirt slipped just off her broad shoulders and while it gave a nod to her femininity, she still wore brown trousers that tucked into knee high boots. Though Marion's features were lined with age, the hard strength of their foundation gave her an air of tempered elegance.

When she descended the stairs to the foyer, Irwin waited with her deep chestnut waistcoat. Helping her into the jacket, he said,

"The coach is waiting outside, mum. Would you like me to have tea waiting when you return?"

"Don't trouble yourself, Irwin," she said with a slap on his arm. "I'm meeting a legend tonight. Who knows when I'll return?"

When Marion Lowe entered the council chambers in Lanvirdis keep, many of the council members had already taken their seats in the chamber, but several were still spread throughout the room talking. Even called out in the middle of the night, the council members were well dressed, if a little winkled from their haste, but more than just council members filled the vaulted marble chamber. In the light of the gas lamps that lined the walls, Marion could see Daniyelans dressed in a similar manner to the one who had summoned her.

On the recessed floor of the chamber, surrounded by a horseshoe table, stood several knots of people. A man who look around her own age of fifty-two stood next to a column with a young girl who had spiky black hair and a quiet, but alert expression that captured Marion's attention. This was a girl who had a disposition Marion could use. She tucked the observation away and considered how to approach the girl. Several yards from the girl stood an ageless woman with long silver hair accompanied by a man Marion did know, Tomas Segar. His brown hair tumbled over his forehead ruffled as though he had just gotten out of bed. While his hair looked a mess, the rest of his appearance was impeccable and an easy smile was never far from his thin lips.

Marion took her seat next to Layton Norris the harbormaster of Lanvirdis. The leathery-faced old man gave her a nod before returning to scowling at the room. She didn't bother to hide the amused smile his reaction gave her as she thought about how the council was filled with the finest group of cranky old buggers and shrews as ever governed Nabos. Fishing her watch out of her waistcoat, she clicked it open to check the time. It was nearly midnight.

Wes could feel her fingers itch when a handsome woman with refined features clicked closed a silver fob watch with the floral detailing. Though it was late at night, the woman's salt and pepper hair was piled onto the crown of her head and held in place with two thin, long silver sticks that matched the scrollwork of her watch. In attempt to resist the temptation, she shoved her hands under her arms. She felt Vaughn giving her a knowing look out of the corner of his eyes as he watched Marion return the watch to her pocket.

Wes had to fight to keep from showing her anxiety at being surrounded in an enclosed space by so much finery and so many lawmen. Through necessity she had acquired that skill even before she found herself on the streets, so she waited beside Vaughn hidden in the shadows of a column. Out on the marble mosaic floor of the council chamber Rivka stood with Tomas who surveyed the gathering seeming completely at ease as he chatted with her.

Wes was glad that Vaughn shielded her from Tomas. She had always known which people you didn't dare lift a purse from and in all her years on the streets, she had yet to meet someone who made he blood run cold quite like Tomas did. He seemed so pleasant talking with Rivka, even kind, but Wes knew better. Though she kept herself from shifting too much or too quickly, she couldn't keep her fingers from grazing over the burns running along her jaw for just a moment before shoving them back under her arms.

Though he assessed the crowd, Vaughn spoke in a low voice that only reached her. "When this is finished, Wes, how would you like to return to Vamorines with Rivka and me?"

"I ain't want none of your charity," she said in a knee-jerk reaction to the offer. "I don't like owing no one."

"Who said anything about charity?" Vaughn said in surprise. "If you want to live at the temple, you earn you keep like everyone else."

Wes eyed him skeptically. "Doing what?"

"We're spread a little thin in the stables. The young ones tend to spook the horses more than do any actual good." He watched her reaction out of the corner of his eyes. "You have a steady hand."

Wes recalled how well taken care of Mesa had been. "You can

tell a lot about a man by looking at how he treats his beasts. Yours was happy and healthy. You'd trust a street kid like me with him?"

"You wouldn't let me down," Vaughn told her matter-of-factly. "It looks like everyone is here. Make sure you stick close. Things are going to become very unpleasant soon. So, your decision? Want the job?"

Wes shrugged her shoulders noncommittally, but her eyes snapped with excitement. "Why not? It's not like Lanvirdis has done right by me, yeah?"

Vaughn smiled with genuine warmth for the first time since he had returned with his lady. "Good."

Tomas clapped his hands together to gain the attention of the gathered assembly. Raising his melodic voice, he projected to every corner of the room. "My lords and ladies, masters and mistresses, we thank you for your gracious acceptance of our invitation despite the rather unconventional hour. But of course, tonight we host a rather unconventional guest in my fellow Scion, Rivka Peacemaker."

He swept his hand toward Rivka with an elegant flourish before turning back to the council members. "I wish that good tidings brought us together this evening, but the Light is hidden from us on this darkened night. I received word only a few hours ago that our Tereskan siblings in Kilrood have been attacked."

He paused awaiting the expected uproar that exploded around the room at his announcement.

Layton Norris, dressed in some of the more simple, but still well made, clothing of those assembled, rose to his feet and with a booming voice that could cut across a crowded wharf or a storm-tossed deck demanded, "Were there any casualties? Where are they holding the attackers?"

Tomas inclined his head to the man acknowledging his question. "Harbormaster Norris, tragically we have discovered no survivors."

Marion had remained in her chair while many of her fellows had jumped to their feet earlier demanding explanations, but the jangled mix of voice all ceased at Tomas' words to the harbormaster. The silence hung in the air like their disbelief. Many of the council members who had stood, sank back into their seats wordlessly. Most simply looked around the room as if hoping to find an explanation there.

"Darkness take the bastards," Marion cursed leaning forward onto her elbows. "Any news of Ianos?"

After taking a regretful sigh, Tomas said, "Missing, Merchant Lowe. My people have not yet recovered his body. We will hold onto hope until they do. If anyone could find a way to survive, it's Ianos."

"What can we do to help?" Layton asked. He was a practical man who looked for practical solutions to any problem placed in front of him. "What do you require of us, Scion Segar?"

"Your willingness to aid in this crisis is exactly why I called you all here tonight," Tomas said with an appreciative smile.

Rivka stepped forward and placed a hand gently on Tomas' arm. "Tomas, might I address the assembly?"

Nodding, Tomas patted her hand and stepped back yielding her the floor. "We covet your wisdom and experience at a time of such great loss, Rivka."

As he retreated back, his eyes scanned the room. By each exit stood one of his Daniyelans, his personal guard. He shifted his eyes to the man nearest to Rivka. The man's hand slid along the grip of his curved, long knife, but otherwise made no other indication that he noticed Tomas.

"Council members of Nabos," Rivka said in a quiet yet strong voice, "I wish I knew you all, but it has been many generations since I have visited your lovely city. But what brings me here tonight is of the highest import and cannot be done in secret." Rivka's eyes carried a deep pain, which she allowed the gathered men and women to see before the backs of her hands began to flicker with sapphire light. "Tonight, you all bear witness, because I have come to bring a traitor to justice."

The murmuring rose again at her words. Tomas merely raised an eyebrow at this revelation, but gave no other reaction.

"As the Scion of the Nikelan Order, I have been given the sacred responsibility of guarding the Orders purity and peace. The Orders have been violated and perverted by the taint of the Brethren."

The faces around her nodded as they agreed with her

assessment given what they had just learned about the Tereskan attack. For a reason Marion could not name, her gaze settled on Tomas, not on Rivka as she continued her speech.

"I have also been entrusted with the burden of a particular and unique authority in order to execute my duties. It is the right to revoke the office of another Scion." She paused as she made eye contact with each council member in turn. "Tonight, I have come to Lanvirdis to nullify Tomas Segar's claim to the seat of the Scion of the Daniyelan Order."

The general calm that had descended upon the room under Rivka's steady influence shattered like glass as the assembly broke out in the clamor of dissenting voices. Though the council members were taken off guard, none of Tomas' men even twitched a single muscle at her pronouncement, but even their calm seemed thin and stretched when compared to the placid expression on Tomas' face.

Beneath that expression, however, his mind worked to transform this development to an advantage. He had suspected this outcome when his men had reported that Vaughn had been seen in the city and Tomas had prepared.

While everyone shouted questions at Rivka, Tomas flicked his wrist and locked gazes with Marion. Shadows covered his eyes for a heartbeat before clearing. Marion pushed back her seat at the council table and descended to the floor as if to speak with Rivka. For a woman her age, she presented an impressive and striking figure as she approached Nikela's Oracle.

"Scion, what proof do you have of this treason?" Marion asked folding her arms across her chest. "Why bring this to us?"

"This treason is against the Orders, not the Nabosian council," Rivka answered with unquestionable authority. "You are merely here to bear witness to the action. You have no voice in this decision. I have chosen you as witnesses merely for the sake of expediency. This matter must be closed before any more treachery is turned against our brothers and sisters."

Marion pushed back a stray lock of hair behind her ear and nodded, unhappy and not entirely appeased, but she did not press the matter further. Rivka turned to finally look at Tomas. She held her hands out, the intricate lines of blue on the backs of her hands shone bright.

Her lips pressed together. "Tomas, you stand as a usurper to the seat of Scion." Her gaze was hard as she compartmentalized the pain of the slaughter she had failed to stop. "You have perverted justice to serve your own ends. Do you have anything to say for yourself?"

"You must be mistaken, Rivka," he said in a slow voice. He looked over her shoulder and gave a nearly imperceptible smile. "I could never betray the Orders. I am but a servant for the good of all."

Rivka brought her arms up and out to her sides until they were parallel with the ground. Blue light began to flow from her hands and eyes until her entire body was bathed in the sapphire glow. She looked down at Tomas.

Her voice taking on several ranges at once spoke with a single resonant unity that echoed to the ceiling of the marble chamber. "Tomas Segar, you have betrayed the children entrusted to your care. You are the guardian of justice, yet you would destroy innocent lives to achieve your aims, to destroy those you have sworn to protect."

She opened her mouth to continue, but before she could, Marion was at her back. Her black, curly hair flowed unbound around her shoulders and the needles that had held her hair in place flashed in her hand.

Before anyone could even speak, Marion thrust one between Rivka's ribs piercing her heart. The blue light surrounding Rivka flickered and flared. Marion screamed only once as the fire touched her and the woman who had stood her ground against the intrigues of the Merchant Houses for thirty years fell to ash in a matter of moments.

Rivka stood frozen, suspended within the column of light as the blood spreading down her chest. Vaughn ran toward Rivka, but the shaft of light engulfing her repelled him. He reached a hand slowly toward her, pressing it against the resistance of the column. Feeling his touch, Rivka lowered her head and her pained eyes locked with Vaughn's. The blue lines cuffing his wrists glowed. Reaching out her fingertips, she touched them to his palm and the light suddenly vanished. They both fell to the floor, limp and lifeless with a cracking thud. They were gone. They were dead.

Wes blinked staring at the pile of dust on the marble that had been Marion. Near the pile, one of the silver needles that Wes had admired rolled along the floor. It stopped when it hit Rivka's bent wrist that had broken when she fell. It had all taken only a few heartbeats. One moment Vaughn stood next to her watching Tomas as Rivka made her accusations. Now their bodies sprawled across the mosaic, smearing the stone with their blood. There had been no warning. They were gone. Vaughn was gone.

"No," Wes said under her breath staring at Vaughn's body.

He lay with his hand nearly brushing his lady's. Where the blood stained the back of her dress, an identical stain seeped through the thick fabric of his riding cloak. The blood just kept spreading.

Wes shook her head. "No, he ain't dead. He can't be."

She stumbled over to his side. Skidding to her knees with a shocking jar as she hit the slick marble, she rolled him over and slapped his cheek. Sightless blue eyes looked up at her.

"Vaughn, wake up. You need to get up." She shook his shoulders gently at first, but when he didn't stir, she shook harder. "Vaughn!" His name came out in a choked cry.

Letting his shoulders go, she snapped her head up at Tomas with hatred burning in her eyes. "You," she hissed. "You done this."

"Child, you must be delirious with grief," Tomas told her with sympathy. "To think Marion Lowe was part of the cabal that planned the attack in Kilrood. I know she has a rather ruthless reputation, but I never would have suspected her capable of this."

"Aw, no you don't, I seen you," Wes said clambering to her feet. Her eyes were wild, past caring. "Right before she stabbed mistress Rivka. You made her do it. You pointed at her, yeah? I seen you. I seen people do magic before."

Layton stood clearing his throat. "I saw it too, miss. You did something to Marion, Segar. She was a crafty old bat. She wouldn't've ever done something like that. No profit in it. Scion Rivka was right. You're with the Brethren."

There were murmurs of agreement throughout the council

chamber. Though the Nikelan Scion had not visited Lanvirdis in living memory, the trustworthiness of the Nikelans stood above reproach. Despite the fact that Rivka lay dead, her body getting colder every moment, her words continued to sear themselves into each of the council member's minds.

Tomas sighed. "I had hoped it wouldn't go this way. It truly grieves me that this is your decision. But I can't have Rivka and Vaughn's sacrifice be in vain."

He raised his hand and snapped his fingers and the sounds of crossbows releasing echoed across the room. Wes flattened against the ground at the twang of the first release. A bolt buried into his neck, Layton Norris pitched forward over the council table and onto the floor. Screams rose and faded throughout the room as each council member met their death.

Her cheek pressed into the icy marble, Wes kept her eyes shut as she heard the thunk of bolts hitting their marks and the silence that inevitably followed. When the last gurgled cry ended, she opened her eyes. Shoes waited directly in front of her. When she looked up, she saw Tomas looking down at her, his hands behind his back.

"I know just what to do with you, my dear," Tomas said tapping this thumb against his chin. "I would hate for any more blood to be spilled today. But I can't have you running around telling tales."

Tomas turned to the Daniyelan who stood at his back. The man had jet-black hair and equally dark eyes. It was the same man who had led Marion to her death.

"She looks enough like Deoraghan stock for Victor to take her."

Without further consideration, Tomas walked away from Wes who still lay on the floor just inches from Rivka and Vaughn's bodies.

He looked around the room at the carnage of bodies hideously slumped across the table, the seats, the stairs. "Such a waste," he said shaking his head as he exited the room.

The black-haired man hooked the crossbow back onto his belt. "Get up," he commanded her.

Wes instincts had kept her alive this long. She knew when to fight, when to run, and when to shut her mouth and do as she was told. Scrambling to her feet, she wiped her nose with the back of her hand and met the man's gaze. His dark eyes focused on her, but seemed to look through, causing a shiver to run down her spine.

He took Wes' upper arm and led her out of the room. As they passed Rivka and Vaughn, their bodies looked like broken dolls sprawled on the ground as if abandoned by a bored child. Wes had seen death before, but this room was choked with it now. It had all happened so fast.

Wes' feet shuffled as the Daniyelan man pulled her through the streets away from the keep. He had to yank her up to keep her from falling several times, but she barely noticed. Every time she closed her eyes all she could see was the look of shocked pain on Vaughn's face when the woman had stabbed Rivka. Even when she kept them open the image of his empty face staring past her floated in her mind.

Wes didn't remember how they left the keep, but soon the black-haired man had taken her to the western gate of the city. The smell of spoiled milk, dust, and sweat mixed together in the alley they past. Near the gate sat an inn, an inn with a reputation that made Wes avoid this part of town and with good reason.

When she recognized the inn, the dream-like state, that had engulfed her since that woman had plunged her knife-like silver stick into Rivka's back, vanished like she had fallen into Diarmid Bay in winter. She stopped walking and the man tugged her arm.

"Come now, girl. Don't give me any troubles now," the man warned in a pleasant voice that promised very unpleasant things should she prove uncooperative. "Be a good girl."

Wes shook her head, the panic and fear from the ambush finally set in as she realized her own peril. "No, I ain't going in there. I ain't for sale."

"Don't make this any more difficult for yourself," he said with gentle regret as he wrenched her arm forcing her to walk or be dragged. He didn't seem to care which it would be.

Wes braced her stance and pulled against his grip. The man

sighed and reached to pick her up, which was exactly what she had hoped he would do. As he turned to face her, she brought her knee up between his legs as hard as she could manage. It loosened his grip enough for her to rip her arm out of his grasp.

She pushed against his chest hard and ran for the gate. Sticking to the shadows, she ran as fast as she could in the dim light coming from the western gatehouse. She was close. If she could make it to the gate, she might be able to escape.

Slowing her run, she stole a look behind her and prepared to make her dash for the gate. She turned back and standing directly in her path was the black-haired man. She cursed colorfully and none too quietly and ran. But as she ran, she felt her legs lock as though bound with ropes. Before she could cry out, she fell and hit the ground. She tried to move, but her limbs didn't respond. She was paralyzed.

She heard the slow deliberate clicking of the man's boots on the cobblestones as he made his way toward her. Her heart pounded in her ears.

He knelt down and sighed again. "Why did you have to make this difficult?"

He scooped her up and threw her over his shoulder. He entered the smoke filled inn and asked a question of the barkeep that motioned him upstairs. Wes whimpered as the man climbed the creaking and warped stairs. He walked down the hall and pounded on a door. A growling bark of curses answered him telling him to leave. The man sighed and kicked in the door. There were high-pitched shrieks from the inside, but slung over his shoulder, Wes couldn't see the source of the screams.

"Who in the bleeding name of darkness do you think you are bursting in here?" a deep male voice demanded and stopped. "Oh, I didn't realize it was you, ser."

"We need you to make a problem go away," the black-haired man said with a sneer of contempt as he sat Wes in a chair. The invisible force binding her was released. The man didn't look at her, but referred to her. "This little hellcat will try to run. See that she does not. You are not to sell her anywhere near Lanvirdis. Is that clear?"

"Aye, ser," the man Wes assumed was Victor said.

He was bald, though not from age. He had a compact build with a set of matching scars on his shoulders and stood beside the occupied bed that had clearly been in use only moments ago. A red-headed woman and a blonde woman hid under the blankets.

"She should fetch a good price in Finalaran. They like them young there."

The black-haired man gave Victor a look of disgust before slamming the door behind him as he left Wes there without a final look. Her eyes searching the room, Wes tried to figure out how long she would have to wait before the Daniyelan would be gone.

There was a window on the other side of the room with gaudy red lace curtains blowing in the slight night breeze. Thinking back to the stairs, she figured they couldn't be any higher than the second story. She had jumped from higher before and still managed to run several blocks after the impact.

Victor sauntered over to Wes to inspect his new merchandise. To get a better look at her, he reached a scarred and callused hand to lift her chin. Wes kept her mouth shut. He lifted her wrist to get a look at her body. She could feel blood in her mouth from biting down on the inside of her cheek.

Victor grunted. "Too skinny and them Daniyelans did a number on the face. That'll drive the price down." He reached a hand to feel her ribs and she threw her free fist into his jaw. He absorbed the punch and looked down at her seething face. He laughed. "But the spunk might appeal to certain customers. Right then."

He went to a heavy canvas bag lying on the table. Throwing open the top, he removed a set of interconnected wrist and leg shackles. They clattered as he walked back to her. Grabbing Wes' wrists, he looked at her eyes for the first time. She felt a tingle run across the surface of her skin.

"Don't think you can run just because the Daniyelan is gone. Either we use these or I break your legs now. Make no mistake, you belong to me and no one steals what's mine, especially not you."

CHAPTER TWENTY-SIX

"Blast it, Kade," Sheridan said staring at him from across the hallway. "What am I supposed to think?"

Kade laid his head back against the wall. He still felt stretched like a wrung out dishrag. "They didn't recruit me, Sheridan. I told you already."

"Then how," she demanded waving her hand at his now silver eyes, "how is this possible?"

"It's not that hard to understand," he answered. "I used black magic."

Sheridan put her head in her hands and screamed into them before pushing her fingers into her hair. "I cannot do this again. I just can't. First, Evelyn lies to me every day for the last how-ever-many years, then she abandons me without a word to save that manipulative blighter – again. Now this. Don't you do this to me too." Sheridan's eyes pleaded with him. She was close to cracking. "Not you too, Kaedman."

"A week ago, yesterday even," Kade began unapologetic, "I would have told you that I would do what I did again in a heartbeat."

He stopped the edges of his voice shaking. Then the hardness returned to his eyes, hardness that held back something else. Sheridan was unsure what he hid, but on top of everything else this withholding of information stung like a slap, but Faela, she dreaded what waited behind that barrier.

"So what's so different about today?" Sheridan demanded her patience utterly destroyed.

"I am," he said with a quiet certainty. "Sheridan, you know that I killed Gareth. You just don't know how." He splayed his fingers against the tops of his thighs as he felt the tingle of his nerves reawakening in his legs.

Sheridan folded her hands around her shins and waited for him to continue. She feared that if she spoke he would redirect her back into his hall of rhetorical smoke and mirrors.

Looking at the inconsistent thickness of the glass at the bottom of the high window, he steeled his nerves. "When I realized Nessa was gone, I tracked Gareth and when I caught him I trapped him within a locking spell. He didn't even have a chance to fight back or run. He deserved to die for what he had done to Nessa. So, I turned his own magic against him. I let him know what it felt like to be trapped and helpless."

He lowered his eyes to Sheridan. "But I knew that a normal locking wouldn't work on him. I didn't know how far he had gone into the darkness, but I couldn't take any chances. So I had to cut off his magic the only way I knew would guarantee the locking would hold. There was no other choice. I had to."

"By casting it with black," Sheridan concluded with a despondent sigh.

They sat in silence not looking at each other. Faela curled into herself next to Kade, watching and waiting.

Finally, Sheridan levered herself to her feet without a word and aimed a swift kick at his outstretched left shin. "You bloody idiot!" she yelled and kicked him again. "You and Evelyn sure make a pretty pair, you know that? Why do I keep hearing everyone around me saying that they had to do anything? Why?"

In full rant, she threw her hands in the air. "I swear the next time I hear someone say 'I had to,' I'm popping them into the nearest river and I am not fishing them out."

Kade opened his mouth, but no one heard what he was going to say, because Sheridan interrupted him. "No, I don't want to hear it. I don't want to hear your wonderfully convincing rationale for why you had to make that decision. You didn't have to do anything, Kade. You chose to. You chose. So, don't waste my time and your breath."

She turned back around and kicked him in the opposite shin. "Idiot!"

"You're right, Sheridan," he said with a crooked, sad smile. "It was a choice and it was mine and I was wrong."

"Blah, blah, blah, you just take those excuses and shove–" Sheridan stopped with her finger pointing up and looked back at him. "Wait. Did you just admit that you're wrong and that I'm right? I mean of course I am, but did you just admit it?"

Kade nodded. "Don't get too used to it."

Sheridan narrowed her eyes suspiciously. "Why?"

Rubbing his palms on the tops of his trousers, he turned to face Faela. "Because I saw what happens when someone believes that anything can be done as long as the desired result is achieved."

Faela's face drained of all color, even her lips. For a moment Kade feared she may faint, but she didn't. She just drew her arms into her chest. He leaned over and took hold of one of her hands. He licked his lips and looked into her eyes. It was easy now, like breathing her in like air. He didn't have to speak the words aloud, but he did so for Sheridan's benefit.

"Even justify taking the life of a child," he said as he replayed the images from Ianos' offices.

When she saw Eli reach his hand into the bassinet and the snap that preceded that awful silence, Faela screamed and tore her hand out of Kade's. Crimson light rippled out from her hands that clutched her head as her cries of denial devolved into a shriek and deep scarlet light pulsed out from her like a wave, which flung Sheridan hard into the wall, but Kade remained unmoved and untouched.

He crawled closer to her and put his arms around her as she rocked back and forth howling in pain. She threw off his arms and struck out at him. He caught her wrist and she glared at him her eyes wild and filled with burning hatred and raw grief. Snarling, she struggled in his grip, but he would not let her go, though his cheek bled where she had struck him.

He locked eyes with her and pushed her arm back down to her side. His eyes glistened with tears as well. He reached into the tempest of her mind, his own grief plain for her to see.

He put a hand to her cheek forcing her to see him. "I tried," he whispered. "I tried to stop it. Even though I knew I could do nothing. Even though I was only watching shadows, I tried. Rafaela, it wasn't enough. I'm so sorry; it wasn't enough."

"He can't be," Faela said in a fierce voice. "I would have known. He can't be." Shaking, she just kept repeating those words to herself in a chant.

Kade pulled her in toward him by her wrist that he still held.

This time, she collapsed into him without a fight. Burying her face into his neck, she laced her arms under his, gripping the back of his shoulders. An arm encircling her waist, he held her close and brushed her hair back from her face.

"I should have known," she demanded in a muffled voice. "I should have known that something was wrong, that he was in danger. I should have known."

Stroking her hair, he rested his cheek on the top of her head. "I know," he said in a soft voice. "I thought the same thing once. You see, I had a little brother named Liam. Everything was a competition with us, because we were only a year apart in age, I guess. Who could run faster and further, even who could eat more.

"Typically I won, except when it came to tinkering. He was always taking things apart to see how they worked. I could take them apart well enough, but when I put them back together they never worked right. Until Liam fixed them, then they worked better than before. He had a gift.

"When we were tested for the Orders, he had no discernible gift for magic. So, I was sent away from home to train. During my eighth year, he was apprenticing, doing a job at the mines in Tillywhel. Their steam pump had broken, but it was winter and the shaft was frigid and damp - nasty place. He caught a fever. It went to his lungs fast. Fast enough that by the time my parents called for a Tereskan it was too late. He died."

Kade looked straight ahead, but still ran his fingers through the waves of her hair. "The war had been going on for years by then. People were losing family every day. But I didn't lose Liam to the war; I lost him to a fever. He was only fourteen. He was my own brother and I didn't know for weeks until the post came from my father. I had no idea. Before I learned of his death, nothing had felt different in those weeks after he had died. I had no idea that anything had happened to my little brother and he had been gone for weeks.

"I questioned whether I had loved him enough for a long time, because if I really loved him I should have been there. I should have just known somehow. I could have done something. That's what I kept telling myself. I should have known."

He slid his face down to her ear and whispered, "But I did love him, just as you love Sammi and you always will."

"He shouldn't have been alone," she managed to say around the sobs. "I never should have left him. I never should have gone to find Tobias and the blasted Shrine. I never should have left."

Feeling her guilt wash over him, Kade knew better than to argue with her. He just continued to hold her as the sobs shook her body making further conversation impossible. While she cried, her eyes made their way to the bloodstains on the wall, the floor. Her home, this was her home. Death was a fact of daily life at any Tereskan temple, but this was different. Ghosts now filled this place.

"They're all gone," Faela managed to whisper, "just taken away."

"Who's gone?" Kade asked his voice still quiet.

"Everyone," she whispered back. "I don't have a home. It's gone. They're gone. Ianos is gone. Sammi is gone. They all left me behind. Now it's just me."

Kade didn't have to feel her emotions to read the boundless despair in her voice. Everything she had to live for had just been taken. Though she had never admitted it aloud to him, Kade knew she had left to find the Shrine for Sammi's sake. It was clear from the first days that Kade had met her that she had little regard for her own welfare. She had tended to his wounds leaving no energy to heal herself. When she had fought, it was with a fierceness of necessity not the survival instinct he typically saw. She had left chasing Lusican legends for the chance to give Sammi a life untainted by his mother's mistakes, but now he was gone.

Kade tightened his grip on her instinctually as if she would slip from his hands that very moment. Lifting his cheek from her head, he looked down at her small body clinging to him. She had nothing left to hold on to. She had nowhere to go and if he let her, he knew she would just fade away and never return. But he had no intention of letting her go, not without a fight.

Looking at the light smattering of freckles along her forehead, he combed her hair back. Faela looked like a wet ragdoll in his arms. She had stopped crying. She had no tears left. She just stared ahead sightlessly sniffling. Untangling her arms from his back, he drew her into his lap. She burrowed in close and rested her cheek on his chest.

Sheridan pushed herself up off of the floor, shaking her head. Blinking, she rotated and met Kade's eyes over Faela's head. She limped toward them and sank to the ground across from Kade with a wince. Sheridan's raised an eyebrow significantly at Kade and Faela as she held her hand to her ribs on the side where she had landed. She had never seen Kade look so openly hurt, not even after Liam had died.

Kade gave Sheridan a grim smile and returned his gaze to Faela. This caustic and lethal man had few acquaintances that he could tolerate and fewer friends. His life was a life of duty and sacrifice. It was a hard life that left little room for anything else and he had believed he wanted nothing else, until that day, more than a month ago, when this woman had stood in his way.

Though he knew this strong, yet tragically fragile woman could never be his, not the way he wanted, though he knew he could ask nothing of her, he also knew he could not change what had happened to him. He had willingly given himself to her knowing the consequences, knowing that they could have no future together, but he had decided. Regardless of how much pain it would cause him, he would stand by her. He would help her find a reason to keep going.

Reaching for her hand, he knit his fingers with her own as he rested his face against her hair. It tickled his nose as he breathed in. It still smelled of dew. "You've haven't been left behind," he whispered, "you're not alone."

CHAPTER TWENTY-SEVEN

Jair paced. He had paced in the same five-yard patch of scrubby grass since Faela, Kade, and Sheridan had left hours ago. They should have returned. If everything were fine, they should have returned by now, but they hadn't. With Eve and Haley, well Lucien now, leaving during the night and Faela's frenzied departure, Jair felt like a swarm of butterflies had decided to take up permanent residence in his stomach. Mireya had tried to persuade him to eat, but he had refused. Instead, he just paced.

"Jair, will you please stand still?" Mireya asked looking up at him from the grass. She sat cross-legged with her chin in her hand. "Pacing constantly won't bring them back faster."

"Something went wrong," Jair said rubbing the back of his neck. Letting his hand slip down to his side, he kicked a rock with his toe sending it flying out of sight down the rise of the small hill. "I can feel it. Something went wrong."

Though it was faint, like the resonant echo of a voice, not a voice itself, he felt the fading vibrations of pain in his chest. The emotions felt like the vestiges of a nightmare dissolving away as consciousness returned to his mind, always just out of reach.

Mireya bit her lip. She couldn't bring herself to tell Jair that everything was fine. Watching Faela who had always appeared so steady and guarded, completely lose control like that had scared Mireya. They had seen her lose control only once before, but it had not compared to this. Oakdarrow had paralyzed her defenses; this time whatever it had happened had nearly shattered them. What those defenses restrained frightened Mireya, though she would never admit that to Faela.

"They left because something was wrong, Jair. Faela wouldn't have-" Mireya cut off before reminding Jair of Faela's frantic state when they had departed. "It was serious. They wouldn't have gone otherwise. We just have to be patient."

"Patient?" Jair asked his voice cracking with stress. "They're thousands of leagues away and I can't do anything to help and you want me to be patient?"

Trying to steer the conversation away from the obvious strain Jair felt at the separation, Dathien asked, "With Haley, I mean Lucien, gone what's our next move, Mireya?"

Mireya shrugged her shoulders in an exaggerated fashion. "I'm not feeling a nudge to go after him, so besides sit here and wait for those three to return, I couldn't say."

Thumbing through a book, Dathien leaned against the cracked and fallen log where Lucien had done the same the night before. When he reached the page he sought, his index finger ran across it as he read.

He grunted as he found the passage he had been searching for. "Here it is. When the twins and Lucien showed up you gave the same prophecy again. I'm not sure we interpreted it correctly."

"Well prophecy doesn't exactly come with step-by-step instructions," Mireya pointed out. "There's a lot of room for error and misinterpretation."

Dathien nodded. "Right, listen to these lines: *Twin branches extend, a choice here resolved, / Either shall end betrayed or absolved.* We just assumed that Lucien was the catalyst after we saw he was a Gray. I think it may have been Sheridan and Eve. You prophesied when Sheridan showed up, not when Lucien did."

"What?" Jair asked stopping in his latest round of pacing. He sounded particularly testy.

"Call it a gut reaction," Dathien suggested as he continued reading. "I've read a lot of the Nikelan chronicles, which give not only the prophecies, but their possible interpretations and the historical events tied to each. Trying to interpret the prophecies too literally can be as dangerous as ignoring them. Prophecy is a slippery thing and our choices make it even trickier. A choice was made last night and I don't know how it will effect what is coming."

Mireya twirled the silver ring Sheridan had given her on her thumb. It was too big on her small fingers. It fell loose even on her thumb, but something about this ring entranced her. She kept following the liquid lines of the metal weaving over and under each other. In the firelight, the metal sparkled and danced, as though it were alive.

"That's the problem with prophecy," Mireya said with a sigh. "It doesn't provide any answers, not really. All it does it provide questions to wrestle with."

"I'll say," Jair snorted finally sitting for the first time in hours. His eyes were ringed with dark circles and though he sat, his fingers drummed in agitation. He was too tired to keep up the pacing. "I question any prophecy that has the bad taste to include me."

"Don't sell yourself short, Jair," Dathien said with his slow smile. "We all have roles to play in life. This is just another you'll have to shoulder, but like Mireya said prophecy doesn't give us the answers, it just prods us into searching for them. You're not a puppet, Jair. You're a person with the ability to choose and your choices matter. Sitting here with us proves that."

"Yeah, sitting here doing nothing," Jair said throwing some grass he had torn up into the fire. Each blade curled in on itself in lines of flame.

Mireya breathed out gustily. "Try not to think about, okay?"

Jair began to protest when sapphire light began swirling in the clouds above them. Standing up, Mireya lifted her head to the sky to get a better look. "What is-"

She never got a chance to finish her question before the blue light struck the ground like lightning. Mireya screamed, but the cry cut off abruptly. The blue fire engulfed Mireya, suspending her in its light. Her arms fell behind her as her chest pulled up toward the sky. The light seemed to be coming from within her, glowing beneath her skin.

An intense force seemed to press down on Jair and Dathien keeping them flat against the ground. The pressure seemed to resonate with a low rumble that could have been words, but Jair couldn't make out anything that resembled any spoken language he had ever heard. Then Mireya shrieked in pain as the column of fire evaporated like steam in a single instant.

Collapsed like a discarded marionette in the dirt, Mireya lay unmoving. Dathien found his feet before Jair did and twisted Mireya onto her side. Brushing back her dark mass of hair, Dathien saw her breath pushing the dirt away from her face. She was alive.

Blinking, Mireya looked up at Dathien everything a watery blur. He put her head in his lap. Her head felt like it was stuffed with straw. She knew Dathien asked her something, but the words refused to make sense. There was too much inside of her. She felt like she would burst out of her skin. Then she heard the voices, too many voices inside of her head each demanding she listen to them.

Sitting upright, Mireya held her head between her hands and screamed. The roaring vortex inside her mind quieted, each voice dropping away until a single voice remained.

It was firm, yet gentle, a voice that Mireya knew well. *Two alone will fail, but three will stand strong. To pierce darkness' veil, they must learn the light's song.* As the voice faded away, she heard. *Fare well, Mireya. We are sorry.*

When she opened her eyes, her sight no longer blurred from the trauma. Fat tears fell onto her collarbones in wet splotches. She turned her head to Dathien and threw her arms around his neck.

"Rivka's gone," she said as she hiccupped from crying. "She's dead."

The lines around Dathien's eye deepened as he rocked Mireya as she cried. Jair sat with a blank look on his face unsure of what he had just witnessed or what to do next. The fire still crackled as the logs broke in half as the ash ate through the wood. The wind still whistled through the small grove of trees rustling the leaves in counterpoint to the sounds of the flames. The thick cover of clouds dissolved as they dissipated to reveal the pinpricks of winking stars against the black sea of the sky. The moor had returned to the night as though nothing had happened.

"They're inside me now," Mireya told Dathien pulling back from him. "I can hear them all."

Dathien let go of her and knelt on one knee in front of her laying his closed fist over his heart. He bowed his head; the fire threw dancing shadows across his cheek as its light glinted off his dark hair.

Lines of blue light cuffed his wrists and ran up his arms encircling his neck before they covered his face. "To you I pledge my service and my life, Mireya Rosemary Pascal, the 33rd Scion of Nikela."

Made in the USA
Lexington, KY
21 May 2010